WINDS OF DARKNESS

"No, Mom, go back!" Ronnie called. "Go back!"

Wind and thunder combined in shell bursts that shook the tree. The hurt hawk shrieked and flapped the floor with its one good wing.

In the middle of the yard, the boy's mother, panic coursing through her body, collapsed to her knees.

"Where are you!" she screamed.

Confused and frightened, she pushed herself to her feet and ran back to the house.

Ronnie twisted around to the entrance of the tree house, but the rush of a thousand wings and a nerve-shattering screech stopped him. The hawk, terrified and prompted by something beyond instinct, sank its talons deeply into the boy's bare arm, then jerked free and clambered through the tarpaulin flap covering the tree house entrance.

Ronnie screamed; warm blood streaked down his arm and soaked into his shirt and jeans.

Above Half Moon, a black funnel was emerging from a cloud-cauldron of boiling darkness. Morning had become night, and the night was about to claim its victims. . . .

HALF MOON DOWN

by Stephen Gresham

ZEBRA BOOKS
KENSINGTON PUBLISHING CORP.

In memory of Chester J. Gresham
(1920–1968)

ZEBRA BOOKS

are published by

Kensington Publishing Corp.
475 Park Avenue South
New York, NY 10016

Second printing: May 1987

Printed in the United States of America

PROLOGUE

It was known as Christmas Oak.

With an imposing size over a hundred-feet tall and a spread of nearly two hundred feet, it held observers spellbound. The trunk itself was as big around as a farmer's silo, though the ravages of time had split and torn its bark and inner core. Its primary branches, larger than the main trunk of any other tree in the area, were rough-barked and serpentine, and they had grown so heavy that they loomed but a few inches off the ground at their far reaches. Spanish moss and mistletoe graced the ghostly darkness of its upper branches.

No one had ever known the precise age of Christmas Oak. But in early historic times, the Creeks, Cherokees, Choctaws, and Chickasaws, who had lived near it, cultivating crops of corn, beans, squash, and tobacco, had venerated it. The Cherokees had referred to it as *usunhiyi*, "the darkening or twilight place." And it was already a mature tree when Hernando de Soto explored that region of Alabama in the mid-1500s.

When white men settled the surrounding area in the 1830s, the tree was the focal point around which they built the town of Half Moon. After the War Between the States, it had gradually acquired the name "Christmas Oak," for in those gray, depressing years, the townspeople were eager to bring a flicker of joy into their lives, and saw the tree as a symbol of hope. Thus, in the Christmas season, many in the community would decorate it and send boys high in its branches to gather sprigs of mistletoe. The men would build small fires, completely encircling the tree with them, and expectant voices would lift rapturously in the singing of carols.

Legend, however, spoke of a dark side to Christmas Oak.

The Indians believed, and passed their beliefs on to the superstitious among the white men, that it was a tree of magic, of power. Further, they believed that an evil spirit inhabited the tree, sometimes nesting high in its shrouded branches, sometimes abiding within the massive trunk.

This spirit, this thing of evil, was old—older than the tree itself, older than the mound builders who had first called what was now the state of Alabama their home several thousand years ago.

No one knew the origin of the dark spirit; no one knew from whence it came. But the Cherokees claimed that it sprang from the great race of *Nunnehi*, "those who live forever."

And though it was considered an evil spirit, the Indians believed it possessed certain benevolent powers, chief among them its capacity to control the weather. Over scores and scores of years, they noted that the area around the great oak had never once experienced the devastating storms or howling winds that threatened other parts of the land not far away.

This, they reasoned, could only be attributed to the oak spirit, and so they shaped names for the nameless entity. Some tribes called it The Storm Ruler; others, The Spirit That Calms the Winds. Out of the many names, one gradually emerged which came to be accepted: Windkiller. It was a name to be chanted reverently by the old, to be whispered in fear by the young.

Windkiller.

As is often the case, when the legend of Windkiller grew and aged, the number of its powers, the range of its evil, increased. Besides its control over the weather, the spirit, it was said, could assume any shape it desired. It could send terribly vivid nightmares; it could speak to the minds of men in the language of men; it could reanimate the dead and make ghosts walk the land; and it was a fire carrier, capable of setting the earth or even the night sky itself on fire.

And what did such a fabulous entity look like? Here legend balked, for it was believed that anyone who stared into the eyes of Windkiller would either go mad or die. Accordingly, the depictions of its form resulted from hearsay compilations, from fantastic mergings of real or imagined features: the face of a beast, horns, black velvet wings, cloven feet, and the cry of a predatory bird.

Naturally, the more educated, the more enlightened among the first white men to hear this description, shook their heads and smiled condescendingly. Windkiller, they agreed among themselves, was the creation of a savage's consciousness. Not surprisingly, they gave little credence to an ominous caveat associated with Windkiller and the great oak.

The caveat was as follows: Windkiller would remain appeased as long as the tree stood, but if it were ever felled, the dark spirit would be driven deep into the earth where it would bide its time until one day it would be released by monstrous winds. Fueled by a desire for revenge, Windkiller would return to spread hours of desolation, seasons of despair—and it would be a time when sentient Evil would hold sway.

But as the years passed and Half Moon prospered modestly, the dark legend of Christmas Oak was no longer alive in the memory of most. And so it was in 1922, when the town elders, led by the Reverend Malcolm Shepherd, declared the tree to be a symbol of false worship, a pagan icon, and cut it down. On the site they built a new school, using most of the solid oak for joists, flooring, and molding to enhance the massive brick structure.

More years passed and the legend dimmed further. In the reasoning light of day, no one believed in darkness. . . .

Part One

THE WINDS OF DARKNESS

CHAPTER 1

Easter morning, 1982

The large oak in which Ronnie Cartwright's tree house nestled could well have claimed to be a distant cousin of the more famous Christmas Oak felled so unceremoniously years ago. Young Ronnie's oak, for he liked to think of it as his very own, rose as tall and with the same eye-catching splendor as a stone monolith. And though Ronnie's oak was smaller than Christmas Oak had been, hardly an elderly resident of Half Moon could pass the Cartwright home and gaze into the backyard without conjuring up memories of that gigantic landmark, the holiday gatherings around it, and the legends generated about it.

But for Ronnie, never having set eyes on Christmas Oak, his oak was like no other. It was his strength and his shelter. Along with his homing pigeons and his pet crow, the massive tree was his friend, his protector. Its limbs provided a firm foundation for his tree house, and, in turn, his tree house spared him from the chill spring rain that tapped at the branches of the oak and the plywood roof.

He was waiting. And the thought of what he was waiting for brought a smile to his lips. He sat against a wall, his knees pitched up so that he could rest his chin, open to a rush of warm feelings as he envisioned his mother inside the Cartwright home, secreting about, performing a yearly ritual of planting slips of paper, clues to the location of an Easter basket. Finding the basket was the fun part, the easy part. The hard part came in waiting until after church and Sunday dinner to plunge into the mouth-watering array of treats.

As he waited, he sighed and yawned. Then he shifted in front of his porthole, his window on the world, to watch the gentle rain and to glance at his pigeon pens below. He was tired and suddenly realized why. It had been an unusually big week for the miniscule city of Half Moon because it had been observing a very special occasion: one hundred fifty years of existence.

Susquicentennial. That's what his teacher, Mrs. Letlow, called it. She had even required her students to learn to spell it. Ronnie was quite certain that he would never be asked to spell a longer word for the rest of his life.

His class at school, in order to play some humble role in the momentous affair, had decided to create theme posters, the most creative of which were to be show-cased in the windows of various downtown merchants. As directed by Mrs. Letlow, the posters were to depict some significant element of Half Moon's history, perhaps an important building, a person, or a historical event. With varying degrees of success, some of his classmates had scratched out drawings of the old cotton warehouse, the Confederate cemetery, and the venerable McCammon mansion and historic homestead, while others had tried to capture the likenesses of the governor (who had once campaigned in Half Moon to everyone's surprise), Indians, Confederate soldiers, and even Mr. Wolff, the principal of the school.

Ronnie had chosen a nontraditional approach. Only a few things had come to mind when he'd considered what in Half Moon was most significant to him: his oak, his tree house, and his birds. So those were what he drew. With his best brown crayon, he had darkened his poster, outlining the oak, charting its branches and filling in its trunk. Next came a black box to depict the tree house, though Mrs. Letlow had routinely questioned why he wanted it that color. In the porthole he'd sketched a stick-figure face, his own. On the roof of the tree house, he'd drawn a solid black miniature of his crow, Joe, and above the oak, a sky splotched with a flurry of white wings, his homing pigeons. Across the bottom of his poster, he'd scrawled a title: *Half Moon is the Home of My Tree House.* It won no prize and failed to be selected for window display; in truth, it was a pretty ragged, though heartfelt effort. But his mother had seemed to treasure it, adding it immediately to a folder of his accumulated school drawings.

The rain was slackening. From his vantage point Ronnie could see that Half Moon was stirring, as now and again a car would hiss past on the rain-glazed street. Most folks must be sleeping late, he concluded. Too much celebration yesterday. He smiled involuntarily at the sights and the sounds that he had experienced. It had been a fun day for every kid in town, and yet Ronnie secretly observed that most of the grownups had seemed to enjoy the festivities every bit as much.

All the men in town, his father included, had grown, or had tried to grow, beards. They sported them self-consciously, laughing and elbowing one another at the relative thinness and grayness of their facial hair. A few were able to produce long, thick, hillbilly beards, but others could barely coax a stage or two beyond peach fuzz. Likewise, the women of Half Moon had captured the spirit of the occasion by donning long dresses, bonnets, and whatever other vestiges of nineteenth-century attire they could lay their hands on; teenage girls had tittered about in antebellum hoop skirts as if they had just stepped off the set of *Gone With the Wind*.

A late-morning parade had launched the celebration. Ronnie had taken part, marching along Main Street with Joe the crow on his shoulder. They had, in fact, drawn considerable attention on the comically short parade route because of a trick that they performed. To the delight of onlookers, Ronnie would toss bits of crackers high into the air, and with uncanny agility and accuracy Joe would explode from Ronnie's shoulder and catch each piece before it hit the street. By the end of the parade, however, Joe had crunched his fill of crackers. Moreover, some of the parade watchers, boys especially, tried to confuse the bird by tossing pennies and pieces of gum for him to retrieve.

The parade had given Ronnie a growling appetite, but it was no match for the feast waiting at the town park. A veritable carnival of edible delights had greeted him there: open-pit barbeque, fried chicken, and cauldrons of Confederate stew, not to mention homemade bread, biscuits, and every kind of cake and pie imaginable. There were vats of hot grease for the deep-fat frying of hush puppies and fresh catfish, and horse tanks of icy water in which watermelons bobbed as they chilled. There were huge drums of iced tea and soft drinks, and one corner of the park had been roped off for a syrup sopping.

Late afternoon was punctuated by indigestion, games, drawings for a whole host of prizes, mule races, and a bluegrass musical duel between two bands, "Kudzu Fever" and "Dusty Roads." But the citizens of Half Moon had appreciated both bands so much that they were unable to pick a clear winner, and thus the prize money was split, and everyone headed home for a brief respite before the evening's special event, "The Pageant of Half Moon," to be presented in the school gymnasium.

To an outsider, the pageant might have provoked little beyond a yawn. But most the town's few hundred citizens packed into the humid gymnasium where they heard three overly long speeches, concluding with a rousing chorus or two of "God Bless America" and a solo trumpet rendition of "The Battle Hymn of the Republic," which trailed off into several notes of "Dixie" and exhortations that the South would rise again.

Molly Harvester, self-proclaimed historian of Half Moon, droned on about the founding of the town in 1832 on a tract of land obtained by the Creek cession. The frail elderly woman then reminded the audience of the town's participation in the War Between the States, the Spanish-American War, World Wars I and II, Korea and Vietnam. The V.F.W., in honor of the occasion, had created a long and ornately lettered scroll listing every Half Moon resident who had served in these conflicts. Two local Cub Scouts proudly but nervously displayed the unrolled document for all to see.

Ronnie had tried his best to listen intently to Molly Harvester's history lesson, her anecdotes about Reconstruction, Prohibition, and the era of desegregation, but nothing caught his attention except her brief foray into the legends of Christmas Oak and the evil spirit known as Windkiller.

Could such a creature have existed? It sounded suspiciously like a fairy tale, albeit a dark one. But there was one aspect of Molly Harvester's review of the legends that crystallized all of the boy's unease. On the gymnasium stage a marvelous painting was unveiled, the work of a half-black, half-Indian woman by the name of Zephra Firethorn. Although no explanation was necessary, Harvester had pointed out that the painting was of Christmas Oak and that the winged beast, depicted where the roots of the tree would naturally form, was the artist's conception of Windkiller.

The painting brought a curious hush upon the audience. Through the remainder of the program, Ronnie could barely keep his eyes off the haunting massiveness of the tree and the unsettling countenance of the legendary creature. It was, indeed, as if the creature whispered into the boy's mind every time he made eye contact with it.

The Reverend Jack Shepherd followed Molly Harvester, and Ronnie had felt instant relief in having something other than the painting to hold his attention hostage. Shepherd, a giant of a man who earlier in the day had successfully challenged every other man in

16

town to an arm-wrestling bout, talked of Half Moon's first church, a primitive log-cabin structure where the religious needs of the area had been met by various circuit riders. Despite its reputation as a rough town, breeding small corruptions of one sort or another, Half Moon, according to Reverend Shepherd, had been smiled upon by God. And with pride he alluded to the generally recognized fact that his grandfather, Reverend Malcolm Shepherd, the man most responsible for the removal of Christmas Oak, had seen to it years ago that the town would maintain its spiritual health, that, with God's help, it would meet any crisis and prevail.

The final speaker was Dale Taylor, city manager and owner/operator of Taylor's Grocery, who spoke in glowing terms of Half Moon's potential for growth. Well-liked by everyone in town, Taylor had been an eager promoter of the celebration and had personally handed out a sack of candy and peanuts to each of Half Moon's youngsters. So popular were he and his wife, Carol Mae, that no one had raised an eyebrow when their daughter, Jennifer, was crowned Little Miss Half Moon and rode in the parade perched high on the backseat of a shiny convertible from which she timidly waved her white-gloved hand to onlookers.

Finally it had ended. Taylor had concluded his spiel by saying, "I love Half Moon, its woods, its rocks, its streets, its stores, its people. I'm proud of this little town, and you should be too. I hope it lasts another hundred and fifty years."

As the audience joined in the singing of "God Bless America," Ronnie had stared at Zephra Firethorn's painting. He felt suddenly afraid.

*　　*　　*

His mother's voice bridged memory and reality. She was calling him into the house, and with breakneck speed he scrambled down from the tree house and galloped her way.

His mother was an exorcist. That is, she made a special effort to be there when he needed her, to play the dual roles of mother *and* father and beat away the demons of growing up, particularly during those times when his father was in no shape to assume a role of any kind.

He viewed her in an angelic light even though she failed to give him that matrix of strength that only a father could provide a son. But she tried. Dear God, she tried. She was a master at planning memorable moments. Such was this Easter, a steel-gray rainy morning, coated thickly with bleakness.

"Slow down," she chuckled as he raced past her, vaulting up the stairs to his room.

Propped against his lamp was a square of white notebook paper with writing on it. He read it and warmth stirred in the pit of his stomach. His mother's handwriting blinked at him; the letters were shaky and childlike.

> Happy Easter, my Ronnie,
> A hunt I've planned
> for you.
> There's something waiting
> ahead,
> So please look under your bed.

He flopped to his stomach, a smile expanding until

his face grew hot and tight. He dug into the shadows
under the bed and pulled out another slip of paper.

> This note will lead you closer,
> If you'll just carefully read.
> To get what you want,
> Check behind our old TV.

Trailing giggles, he raced to the front room and all
but tackled the television set. Another note. It read:

> I bet you're
>   getting eager,
> A prize you will
>   have,
> If you'll go now
>   and look
> Where you take
>   your bath.

His laugh became a happy whinny. By this time his
mother had caught up with him and was standing at her
bedroom door with her hands in the pockets of her
robe. Her sleepy green eyes were smiling.

The note on the bathtub fixtures sent him reeling off
a final turn.

> You're growing
>   more impatient.
> At least, that's
>   what I think.
> Let's get this

over with.

Look under the

kitchen sink.

—Love, Mom.

It was a ragged shoebox filled with pine straw, three hardboiled eggs, each dyed blue, a half-dozen rocklike candy eggs, and a foot-tall solid chocolate bunny like last year's which he'd carefully savored for over a month before he finally ate it all.

It was a good Easter.

No, it was a great one.

As usual, Ronnie and his mother attended church and ate Sunday dinner alone while Bert Cartwright secluded himself in his den. After dinner, Ronnie helped his mother with the dishes and became, ironically, her confessor.

"Your father . . . now, some days he has to be alone in there. He says he has to crawl into that black box and be by himself. But Ronnie, honey, he's going to get help soon. Don't bother him, you know . . . don't knock on the door or anything like that."

The boy listened to his mother; he had her red hair and freckles and even her turned-up nose and her thin lips. He watched her as she busied herself in the kitchen, masking her apprehension as best she could. On "black box" days she cleaned and recleaned the kitchen. Curious and naturally a bit frightened about his father, the boy would linger and sometimes pretend to help her. Mostly he wanted reassurance of some kind.

But always his eye would be drawn to his father's den at the top of the stairs. The door would be closed, shadowed gray by the darkened hallway. No lights were on in there. The boy could see that there was no slit of light under the door.

"You know, Ronnie, that your father loves us," his mother exclaimed, brushing back several strands of frazzled unruly hair. "He loves us . . . and that's why he's going to get some help."

"Mom . . . what is—?"

"Important thing for us," she interrupted, not wanting to field all his questions, ". . . important thing for us is to remember all the fun times the three of us have had."

She searched his face with an intensity bordering upon desperation.

He nodded and their quiet kitchen ritual, performed for no other eyes or ears, began. It was like throwing slides of the past upon the wall of the present with some kind of mental and emotional projector.

"What's the most fun you think we ever had?"

And as she waited for his answer, she poured him a glass of Gatorade, his favorite drink.

"Camping in the Smokies. The night Dad fought that momma bear . . . only he really didn't . . . he just pretended to. 'Member that?"

She remembered, but she liked to have him recount it anyway. It was as if there were some unnamed strategy at work: counterbalance all the negative feelings by parading all the good times.

"Yes, I do. I was afraid . . . weren't you?"

"No, I wasn't . . . well, maybe a little . . . but when

Dad got back behind those bushes and made all that growlin' and crashed around, well, I knew he weren't really fightin' with no big momma bear."

She smothered a laugh at the thought of how the feigned bear fight had ended.

"Your father was brave to take that cub away from its momma and bring it to you . . . don't you think?"

Her eyes twinkled.

"Oh-h-h-h Mom!"

They laughed heartily, and the boy's Gatorade moustache glistened.

"He . . . he had my ole Ted bear in his jacket all the time, didn't he? He thought I'd b'lieve it was a real bear, but I didn't. He couldn't have brang back a real bear."

The image of his blond-haired father emerging from the pine woods with the stuffed bear zipped within his jacket, the bear's button eyes peering out as if actually frightened, was clear and distinct.

"We had a lot of fun, camping and hiking and seeing the mountains. Almost caught a fish, too, didn't we?" his mother added.

"Dad said we used the wrong bait. I caught a dead one . . . 'member? It was floatin' along and Dad held my hand and I reached down and got it. It was pretty dead. Dad said it was a trout, a spotted trout."

"You mean a speckled trout?"

"Yeah, that's what it was. A speckled trout, real cold and slimy. Dad said if we left it on a rock a bear might come and get it. He said bears could just reach down in the water and catch a fish. A live fish. It was fun fishin' in the Smokies and sleepin' in a sleepin' bag."

"Hey, I know what would be fun for us, now," his mother followed, a mock kind of excitement in her

22

voice as they got ready to complete their ritual of "good times" with a trip down memory lane through the pages of their well-worn photo album.

"Do you remember being that small?"

Here were the usual baby poses: father cradling newborn son, followed by a series of candid shots trailing off in number after the first nine months. Ronnie's first Christmas. Ronnie's first birthday. Instamatically captured moments. Emblems of a long childhood.

"Look at this one, Mom. Disney World. Look at Dad's funny hat."

"Oh, my goodness. Where did he get that hat, anyway? But look at this one. Goofy's got his arm around you. You look a little scared."

"No . . . I wasn't really. 'Member, Mom, when Pluto put his arm around *you*?"

"Uh huh, I do." She rolled her eyes. "Pluto got a little fresh."

"I wish we had a picture of that," Ronnie laughed.

And there was more.

School pictures—the grade-by-grade evolution of Ronnie Cartwright—highlighted by his Little League championship baseball team and the building of the tree house. For the latter, there was the juxtaposition of before and after: the massive oak seemingly barren, then holding the tiny tree house as if it were a precious jewel. Serious-faced father and son were captured on the same page, carrying boards, hammering, and sawing. The final shot framed father and son with heads poking through the tarpaulin tree-house door, grinning like neighborhood pranksters.

"You guys made a real nice tree house. The nicest I've ever seen."

He nodded.

And then, as always at about this juncture in the ritual, his eyes followed the carpeted stairway to the closed door, behind which his father battled to win oblivion with a bottle as his sword.

Black box.

The boy's voice, squeaky and strained, faded as if he were drifting away in a balloon.

"Can't we help him, Mom?"

She closed the photo album, propped it under her chin, and shut her eyes tightly. For an instant it appeared to the boy that her lips were fumbling with some silent prayer, or maybe an incantation. He was afraid she might somehow disappear into her own black box, a magician's box where grown-ups hide themselves when they are afraid.

"No . . . ," she said, but an explanation pushed so close behind the single word that she hesitated only a moment before giving in to it.

"Ronnie, honey . . . we can't help him. I've tried . . . I've tried to help him."

Tensing, the boy chewed at one side of his lip.

"I could pray for him and be a better boy," he half-whispered.

She squeezed his hand and blinked back tears.

"Oh, honey . . . I've tried praying . . . and you're a fine boy, a good boy. Ronnie, that . . . what we do doesn't really make a difference. He needs a doctor's help, a special kind of doctoring."

The boy's fingers tightened into baseball-sized knots under her touch. He was trying not to cry.

"Ashley at school said his dad said our dad is drinkin' so much his brains are goin' to be slush," the

24

boy sputtered.

His face flamed with embarrassment and hurt and his mother pulled him to her shoulder and rocked him as he began to cry. She wondered what might siphon off his fears. She held him and talked; drained of adult pretension, she relaxed and let the truth come forth.

"Your daddy has a disease. A bad disease. Worse than a cold or the flu or the measles."

"Does he have the cancer or a heart attacker?" the boy interjected softly.

"No, but it can be as bad as those things. It's called 'alcoholism' and it makes his mind sick. It's something that makes him have to drink alcohol . . . a lot of alcohol."

"Mom . . . how? . . . where did he catch it? Is it contagerous?"

"It's hard to say how he got this way, honey. Stress in his job . . . he works so hard . . . and does the best he can . . . I don't know."

Images of his father in suit and tie, folders of paper under his arm, flickered in the boy's mind. He knew that his dad was in real estate, that he was in on a project to build a nursing home for the elderly in Soldier, and that once policemen had come to their house and asked him questions in the living room. But they hadn't taken him, and, oh dear God, the boy was still afraid they would.

His mother's voice ghosted through.

"It's not really your father in there . . . he drinks and it kills little pieces of himself, inside. What's left is like . . . it's like his ghost."

The boy pulled away, shaking his head slowly in confusion.

"Honey, I know this is hard to understand. It's like a masquerade person. Your father up there now has on a mask. Some people in Soldier, some special doctors, are going to help him take off that mask and be himself again. And there'll be other men there, and women too, who will be wearing the same kind of masks. Lots of people need this kind of help."

A lunatic rush of images filled his thoughts. A room of adults with ghastly masks: devils, witches, Frankenstein monsters, and hairy visages with protruding fangs mingled aimlessly in an empty white box of a room. Men in white coats moved methodically through the room tearing at the masks. But even the men in white coats had masks, and when they removed the monster masks of the sick people there were other masks beneath.

"Mom?"

"Yes, hon."

"Why does there got to be masks and black boxes?" Ronnie asked weakly.

She rocked him in her arms, rocked him a dozen heartbeats before her exhausted mind could jump-start to think of something more.

"I think it's because . . . because there's just a kind of meanness in the world."

And he accepted those words as if they had formed a chain that he could wear around his neck and touch every once in a while when the world seemed to make no sense.

Through the change of seasons, Ronnie sought out his tree house. His emotions on tiptoe, he tended to his pet crow and his pigeons, and wondered about black boxes and the meanness of the world. His mother threw her heart and soul into giving his life some semblance of hopefulness, and Grandma Cartwright, though often cranky and broken in spirit, tried to contribute as well.

"The way you love those birds, Ronnie," his mother would muse, "I think you're going to be another Audubon. Maybe loving birds will bring peace to your heart."

And sometimes it did.

But at other times he sat in his tree house and listened to the uninhibited restlessness of the wind, and in those moments he thought again of Zephra Firethorn's haunting portrait of Christmas Oak and its resident creature. He would imagine a voice stealing upon his solitude. A tiny chill would worm its way down his spine.

From time to time he would tell his mother—never his father—of this far voice calling out of mystery.

"Is more meanness coming?" he would ask her.

And she would wrap herself around his fears.

"Don't worry, Ronnie. Don't be all the time worrying. You're just a little boy."

CHAPTER 2

April, 1983

It's coming!

Darkness gathered in the late-morning sky over Half Moon, Alabama. An eerie, breathless calm held sway. The oppressive spring air was heavy with humidity.

Inside his tree house, Ronnie Cartwright brushed his fingers through his sweaty, long red hair and listened. The acerbic taste of fear filled his mouth; saliva pooled beneath his tongue. But all he could hear was the nervous clatter of his laboring heart.

It's coming!

He knew it was. A storm. A tremendous storm was coming, building its fury moment by moment. He had known for days, perhaps a week or more, that it was coming.

The voice. The voice had warned him. No, the voice had *promised* him. He didn't know the source of the voice. But it spoke to him, sprang to life in his head like a remote-controlled radio whenever he sought the refuge of his tree house. Sometimes it was a human voice—the harsh yet resonant voice of a wizened old man. Sometimes it was his father's voice, alcohol-slurred, wildly demanding obedience and respect when none were called for—or possible.

And sometimes it was not a voice at all but a piercing cry—the shrill, insistent call of a predatory bird. The penetrating cry, as well as the voices, seemed to rise from within the large oak which cradled the boy's tree house in its branches, or from deep within the earth below the tree. Then they would lodge in his mind and steal upon his ear. It was as if something old, something that had always been a part of the terrain of Half Moon, was struggling to tear itself free, to give tongue to its demands.

On these possibilities, the boy could only speculate; but on certain realities, he could harbor no doubts. The voice, however it manifested itself, always generated within him panic, confusion, and fear.

It's coming! the voice suddenly challenged.

Cupping his hands over his ears, the boy folded his knees up against his chest and rocked to and fro.

"Stop it!" he whispered. "Please stop it!"

Hot, stinging tears tracked his cheeks.

At his side, the mound of feathers shuffled. Talons rattled against the plywood floor. The eye of the hawk dilated to a hammered black dot of fear.

The boy dropped his hands and began absently to stroke the hawk's soft, feminine feathers; they were silky to the touch, and the bird seemed not to mind, for it did not respond with the steel of its beak or talons.

The boy snuffled once, bringing his tears under control.

"It's okay, fella. We'll be okay if we stay here in the tree house. I know we will. The storm can't hurt us here."

His fingers traced the smooth slope of the hawk's neck, then hesitated at the bloody, clotted shoulder of the broken wing that trailed off to one side pathetically like a tattered banner. The dried blood held the sharp stench of a fresh wound.

"I won't let anything hurt you again. Somebody shot you. A farmer probably. You can't fly yet, but maybe . . . I have to keep you here. My dad won't let me keep you on the back porch. He doesn't know you're here. Says I got enough birds already with Joe the crow and all my pigeons."

The hawk shifted its awkward position and raised its head with precise alertness as the wind gusted, scraping limbs across the top of the tree house.

"My dad . . . he . . . my mom says he didn't really mean to hit me last night when I brought you home. She says he's sick. Got a bad disease. Lot worse than a cold or flu. It makes his mind sick, you know . . . and then he drinks too much and gets real mean."

The boy's tears flowed freely. Tears that kept his real fear at bay, just as talking to the crippled hawk kept his mind off the approaching storm.

It's coming!

And the rabble of voices clamored in his head.

The hawk spun away from his hold, wheeling in a painful, flightless circle on the floor of the tree house.

Then, in the distance, another voice.

"Ronnie! *R-a-h-w-n-e-e!* Come in now. It looks like rain."

Scooting on his knees, the boy squared himself in

front of his foot-square porthole in time to see a red-haired woman step through the back-porch door.

"That's my mom. She knows I'm out here . . . but she doesn't understand. Grandma Cartwright's here. Baked me a birthday cake . . . ten candles . . . today . . . and they got me a new BB gun I think . . . to keep stray cats away from my pigeons. But. . . ."

It's coming!

He saw the dark clouds thicken overhead, heard advancing rumbles of thunder, and felt the air lose some of its tortuous humidity with cooling gusts of wind.

He turned to the hawk. Its beak was open wide, and it panted, not from the heat or lack of air, but from some primal fear it had never experienced before.

"We'll be okay here," the boy explained tonelessly. "I know we'll be safe here."

The wind gusted again and the plywood walls of the tree house groaned. Confused, the boy framed his face within the porthole and looked down to his right where a few feet away his pigeons cooed nervously in their wood-and-wire-mesh pens.

"My homers," he whispered. "What's going to happen to my homers?"

A rush of black feathers landed atop one of the pens, cawed once, and tiptoed a few inches to steady itself.

"Joe!" the boy cried. "Come here, Joe. You'll be safe here."

Its head cocked as if hearing something beyond the voice of the boy and the voice of the wind, the crow ruffled its feathers and tightened its grip on the top of the pen.

"What is it, Joe? What's wrong? Come here like I've

31

taught you."

The boy felt his heart sink. The storm was redoubling its mass of clouds; the eerie calm, broken by the occasional gusts of dust-scattering wind, was now almost palpable.

And there was desperation in the boy's tone.

"Joe, please! Please come here!"

The mounting panic and terror then seemed to focus in the eyes of the crow; mesmerized, the boy witnessed their ghostly yellow sheen, an opaque blankness like the approach of car lights on a dark road.

With the unexpected suddenness of a door slamming, the wind boomed high in the surrounding trees, then dipped savagely to the ground and tottered the flimsy pigeon pens. The crow took flight, but as it winged past the tree house, it cried out. And what the boy heard was a raspy caw that pitched to a penetrating scream born of an all-consuming fear.

The echo of the scream drifted through the air like a cold fog.

Another blast of the wind followed.

"No! *No-o-o!*" the boy shouted as the spindly legs of the pigeon pens rocked, lost contact with the ground, and crashed over backwards. And the resulting *whop* was the sound of a guillotine blade performing its task.

Tears glazed the boy's eyes, and yet what he saw, he saw clearly. With a crash, the pens splintered and broke apart, and in a white, dazzling flash, the captive pigeons exploded to freedom. But as they ascended, they trailed a brief shower of blood that flecked the dust in front of the fallen pens.

The boy rested his head against the porthole opening and wept. A dark transformation—one he could not completely understand—was in process.

It's coming!

Something more than the storm. Something was being released from the unseen corners of Half Moon.

Stay in the tree house. Stay here and you'll be safe, his intuition advised.

His fear-tinged moment of resolution dissolved with the sound of his mother's voice.

"Ronnie! Where are you?"

Dazed and confused, the woman held her head and staggered through the backyard. Behind her, standing at the screen door of the porch, was his grandmother, her outline gray and indistinct like an old and fading photograph.

"No, Mom, go back!" the boy called. "Go back! Go back!"

Wind and thunder combined in shell bursts that shook the tree. The hurt hawk shrieked and flapped the floor with its one good wing.

In the middle of the yard, the boy's mother, panic coursing through her body, collapsed to her knees.

"Where are you!" she screamed.

"I've got to save her. Got to save all of them," the boy murmured as he twisted around to the entrance of the tree house.

Outside, his mother, confused and deeply frightened, pushed herself to her feet and ran back to the house.

The boy steadied himself to leave the tree house, but his movement was stayed by what seemed the rush of a thousand wings and a nerve-shattering screech. The hawk, terrified and prompted by something beyond instinct, sank its talons deeply into the boy's bare arm, then jerked free and clambered through the tarpaulin

33

flap covering the entrance to the tree house.

In shock more than pain, the boy screamed; blood streaked down his arm and soaked into his shirt and jeans.

It's coming!

The blood felt warm, almost steamy to the touch and smelled faintly bitter like sweat.

Above Half Moon, a black funnel was emerging from a cloud-cauldron of boiling darkness. Morning had become night, and the night was about to roar.

CHAPTER 3

Two blocks away, Molly Harvester rose from her overstuffed chair, drawn by the blanket of darkness and the shrill blasts of wind beyond her living-room window. Slowly negotiating the distance to the window, she listened to the wind toy with a shutter. A hard frown creased her forehead.

She was afraid.

In her arthritic hands, she clutched a book: a history of Half Moon that she had written years ago, its pages dog-eared, yellowed, and crumbling. Its staleness mingled with another odor, one intensified by the sudden change in the air pressure—the musty odor of old buildings, of long-closed rooms—of Death itself.

Her terriers smelled it. Two of them clattered about her feet, twirling apprehensively, yapping sharply, seeking reassurance from her.

"Tiny, Fritzie, for goodness sakes, lit-tul men, hush now."

Whining softly, they nudged one another and hugged close behind her.

At the window, she raised one hand reflexively to her throat when she saw, before a flash of lightning destroyed it, her own image—the blue eyes now twitching with fear, the Bette Davis look-alike face.

She stared into the expanding darkness.

"The darkness is like my dream, lit-tul men. Last night, I dreamed . . . and out back I saw . . . and Mister Carl's ole cap . . . I found Mister Carl's ole cap."

Hesitating, she glanced down at the jittery dogs, and then around the memory-filled walls of the small antique shop that she and her husband Carl operated.

"I saw darkness, heard awful screams and cries . . . and our lit-tul town . . . it was down . . . houses and trees, don'cha see. Winds of darkness had destroyed Half Moon . . . and Mister Carl, I-I couldn't see Mister Carl."

She patted her fingertips to her lips to stay them from quivering.

"I told Mister Carl about my dream, lit-tul men, but you know, my bad dreams, they upset him sometimes. I've had so many bad dreams this past year . . . and, oh, it was such a vivid dream."

Outside, the wind screeched with renewed intensity.

She turned to survey a nearby bookshelf crammed with glass figurines. Resounding claps of thunder shook the antique shop and, in turn, vibrated the figurines so that they issued a muted tinkling like a wind chime responding to a breeze.

"My owls," she murmured. "Oh, heaven's love, don't let anything happen to my owls."

Again the wind droned, and again the old woman caught the ever-stronger odor of decay, the insinuating odor of Death. The terriers renewed their barking, eyes dilating in reaction to a threat they couldn't recognize.

"We must tell Mister Carl a storm's coming, lit-tul men."

She smiled down at them and gestured with her hand for them to cease their barking.

The smile faded.

"Where's . . . where's Freddie?" she gasped. "Oh, my Lord."

Trembling, she tried to hurry her steps to the dimly lit kitchen. The terriers trailed at her heels.

Her voice quavered as she sat down at the table.

"Carl? It's Freddie, Carl. That lit-tul rascal is out there somewhere?"

"What say, Moll? Yer mutterin' agin, babe."

Carl Harvester put down the morning paper, his Lincolnesque face straining under a baseball cap sodden over the years with sweat. He cocked his right ear her way.

"Storm's coming, Carl. Bad storm . . . don'cha see? And Freddie's out there."

Her hand fluttered vaguely toward the kitchen window.

"See those clouds? Hear that wind?" she added, placing her book on the table so that she could pick nervously at the veins on the back of her hand.

"Didja call 'em? He usually comes right back when ya call 'em. Alwis does fer me, babe."

A dark pall suddenly closed like a fist around the antique shop. The calm was dense, a tingling, reverberating quiet. Nature's fuse was burning down. Tornado weather.

The old woman and the old man experienced the

blinding fear at the same instant.

"Freddie's out there," Molly cried.

"Lord love us, you sure 'bout that?"

"Yes!" she screamed, and Carl scrambled from his chair and threw open the screen door.

He was but a shadow against the matrix of blackness formed by the approaching clouds. Wind and big drops of rain kicked ahead of the low-hanging, churning darkness.

"Freddie! Freddie! You dang potlicker, where you be?" he bellowed.

"Oh, please get him, Carl. He's out there scared somewhere. I know he is. I'll help look."

"No, babe," he swatted at her playfully to stay inside. "I'll find 'em. You jist wait right here fer me."

He leaned into the wind and pushed his way past their dilapidated utility shed thirty or forty yards behind the shop. She saw the storm swallow him. That was the only way Molly could describe it. Then darkness pressed close to the ground and tore at the shed until it collapsed like a toy house built of popsicle sticks.

"Come back, Carl! *Car-r-r-r-ul!*"

She ventured a few steps beyond the door and the wind rose in an ear-splitting shriek, a rage that redoubled itself, passing but not directly centering the shop in its path. It was like the thrumming rush of gigantic preternatural birds of prey swooping down for the kill.

Then, in the blue-black whirlwind of darkness, she thought she saw him. She thought she saw him being lifted, thought she saw his feet leave the ground. And the air rang out with the piercing cry of the wind—or something within the wind, for Molly Harvester believed she saw a winged creature grasp her beloved Carl in its rapacious talons. Screeching like a hawk, it merged with the clouds.

And disappeared.

Time stopped as Molly's mind struggled to accept or reject the scene.

Rain splattered into her face, mixing with tears. She stepped back inside, and closed the screen and the inside door, but kept looking outside for any sign of her husband and the wayward terrier. *It can't be! I've imagined this!* Her anguish brought the excited barking of her little dogs. They jumped against her for attention, for words of comfort in the face of the thunderous *whoosh* of wind.

It was then that she noticed Freddie, barking and leaping about with Fritzie and Tiny as if determined not to be overlooked.

Molly stared at the dog in horror.

But not for long.

You jist wait right here fer me.

As the ghostly echo of Carl's final words penetrated her shocked senses, Molly heard the discordant screams of another blast of wind, a fresh approach of darkness. But before the storm lowered its fury for a second time, she peered out at the spot where Carl had disappeared.

And she feared her heart would stop.

Within a crystalline shield of rain, a figure materialized. It stood erect like a man, but its feet were cloven hooves; it appeared to have a dark, hairy face and small horns. The rest of its body was hidden from view by glistening black wings.

As Molly looked on in disbelief, the creature spread its wings and took flight. In that instant, it seemed to Molly that a page of Half Moon's history had leapt to life.

And the vibration of the creature's wings drove terror deep into the old woman's frail body.

CHAPTER 4

Oh, dear God, the sky is falling, Jack Shepherd thought as he guided his red Volkswagen over the pine-clad hills east of Half Moon. On its last leg, the car chugged and coughed to the top of each slope of the highway, then sped downhill as if it had been dropped from the sky.

Shepherd switched on his lights and wipers.

Darkness seemed to have collapsed upon his destination several miles away, the small town where Shepherd served as minister of the First Methodist Church. Gusts of wind slammed against the side of the car, threatening to toss it into the opposite ditch. The rain drifted over the pines in diaphanous sheets; Shepherd had to strain to see the road as only the wiper on the passenger side was working properly.

The sky is falling.

Bearlike, Shepherd hunched over the steering wheel, his six-four, two-hundred-and-forty-pound frame pinched by the bucket seat. His palms were sweating so profusely that he couldn't tighten his grip on the

41

wheel. Nervously, he scratched at his reddish-blond hair and bushy beard.

It had been unseasonably warm for early April. Getting gas at Ben Davis's Amoco, Shepherd had joked about the dramatic change in the weather before driving across the state line hours ago to Columbus, Georgia. Coming back, he hadn't really noticed the clouds until now. Hadn't heard a weather report.

He drove on, accelerating as much as visibility would allow, hoping he could reach Half Moon ahead of the heart of the storm. Tensing with anxiety, he rubbed his forehead as if soothing a colossal headache.

Moments later, the rain suddenly stopped. The wind died away. A dark, rain-glistened lull held the countryside. And Shepherd crested Fletcher's Hill, a granite-bordered, treeless vantage point from which all of Half Moon, a mile ahead, could be viewed.

And there Shepherd braked and swerved onto the shoulder.

"Oh, dear God," he whispered.

The sky is falling.

And it was.

To Shepherd, it was like something out of the Old Testament: a thick bank of clouds, black, majestic, and ominous, swarming from the southwest toward Half Moon.

Hell from the heavens.

With the roar of a freight train, the tornado funnel slipped from the low-hanging cloud mass, reaching its tail toward the ground like a long black finger. But when it touched down, Shepherd heard a different sound: a cacophony of screams and shrieks pitching into one continuous note—a demonic howl that pricked Shepherd's chest with hot needles of fear.

It was an ugly sound, and as the twister skipped through Half Moon's downtown, Shepherd heard the deafening booms of stores and houses imploding from the tremendous generation of pressure. Dust and debris seemed to swell the spinning cloud pillar, and the path of destruction seemed to widen as the air vibrated with dissonant blasts.

Side winds, given extra velocity by the funnel, whipped at the Volkswagen, rocking it, screaming through it so intensely that Shepherd could imagine the winds as angry demons torturing the landscape and all its inhabitants with the maddening clamor of their voices.

In less than a minute, the single black column of cloud passed on. Driving sheets of rain swept down upon the town in the wake of the powerful winds.

Drained of emotion, his mouth as dry as cotton, Shepherd almost welcomed the thrashing sound of the rain, a natural sound in contrast to the hellish shriek of the tornadic winds. And when the aftermath shower relented, Half Moon's spiritual leader lowered his head onto the steering wheel and shuddered.

"Dear God," he whispered, his eyes closed as if the omnipotence of thought could magically wish away the vista of ruin and horror that would present itself to him.

A fresh gust of wind awakened echoes of the demonic voices.

Shepherd opened his eyes, and at that moment the realm of Christian hope within him died.

From another rapidly developing cloud mass, a second funnel dropped and began hurtling toward Half

Moon, the volume of its approach surpassing that of the first storm. As Shepherd watched, it rumbled through on a parallel path, and trees, telephone poles, buildings, and homes unscathed by the other twister went down like dominoes standing in a row.

And again, the tumultuous voice of the wind struck his ears as a demonic howl, the amplified rabble of non-human entities—the denizens of Hell in full cry. Shepherd covered his ears and buried his chin in his chest, but it helped little.

"Dear God," he whispered again.

Vicious blue-white streaks of lightning etched the horizon as the storm clouds finished rolling over the town, dumping heavy rain and marble-sized hail. The hail angrily pattered the road and Shepherd's car before losing its punch.

Then came the worst part.

For a period of time, the Reverend Jack Shepherd, a man of great physical strength, a man who believed he possessed a complementary measure of spiritual strength, sat in his car and felt empty. Hollow. His large hands fell into his lap, and he stared at them.

He made no effort to judge how much time passed; the blaring sirens of a sheriff's patrol car and one or more ambulances roared by, and as they did, his body stiffened, for the sirens seemed but echoes of the menacing winds. Confused, and yet racked by guilt for not immediately driving into town to help, he sat and he wept. And then he folded his hands as if in prayer.

"Our Heavenly Father . . . we . . . we ask . . . help me to. . . ."

But it was no use. His normally deep, resonant "pulpit voice" pitched high, then broke, snapping like a rubber band.

He sobbed once, pinched the bridge of his nose, and as he listened to the humming notes of the cool aftermath winds, he thought of the people he knew in Half Moon—people like Francis Hayman, a tiny bird of a woman who had asked him last night to pray for her because she felt her end was near—people like those in his congregation, friends—people like his mother. Had they survived?

And he thought about the town itself. Often he had preached about its little evils, its corruption, its acts of passion, its distorted minds. Was this God's punishment? Had demons and all manner of pagan evils selected Half Moon as a perfect site in which to settle?

"Dear God, what has happened?" he muttered, averting his eyes from the horrific scene beyond his windshield.

Another ambulance screamed by, causing him to look up.

Someone was standing in front of his car.

At first no more than a filmy outline, the figure gradually became more distinct. It was an elderly woman wearing a light-blue robe with a band of white ruffles around the collar. Her hair was silvery gray and wind tousled; her face was hard and drawn, and yet she managed a tight smile. One gnarled hand rested atop a gold-crowned, black cane.

She looked directly into the car at Shepherd and began to gesture, to beckon him.

He couldn't believe his eyes. Warmth coursed through him. He blinked several times to convince himself that he wasn't hallucinating.

"Mom?" he whispered.

He could imagine the lilac scent of her perfume.

The woman continued to beckon. He couldn't hear her voice, but he could read her lips.

"Come home now," she was saying. "Come home now. Come home now."

He shouldered the door open and pried himself out. The air was cool and moist. Sprinkles of rain whipped across his face, and the din of emergency vehicles drawing down on Half Moon echoed in the distance.

"Mom, are you all right? Thank God you're—"

But the figure was then twenty or thirty yards beyond, inching toward Half Moon with the aid of the cane.

Shepherd chuckled with relief and amazement that the woman was strong and steady enough to move at such a clip after what she must have experienced in the storm.

"Mom, wait up! Let me walk with you!"

She turned and again beckoned.

"Wait!" he called and began jogging through the wet grass and red clay mud at the edge of the county blacktop leading to town.

Then he felt an icy net drop over his heart.

Regardless of the speed of his advance, he closed only a few feet of the distance between himself and his mother. Fear turned his saliva into hard balls that threatened to choke him when he tried to swallow.

He ran on. Confused, frightened, desperate.

And every few minutes the figure would slow, turn, and beckon him.

"Mom!" he called at the top of his voice. But to no avail.

Come home now. Come home now. Come home now.

The ghostly mimic of his mother's voice played on monotonously in his mind.

At the edge of town he stopped running and bent down on one knee to catch his breath. Ahead, he could hear the dissonant sounds of people in pain, people shouting and crying, and sirens wailing. Then his eyes traced the shape of something in the red clay mud where the figure of his mother had walked.

There were no footprints.

Instead, what he saw touched him with terror: clear and distinct, the indentations were small split-prints, the unmistakable marks of cloven hooves.

By the time he looked up, the figure had disappeared, its outline having blended into the gray horror and confusion of Half Moon's darkest hour.

His senses dazed, Shepherd stumbled into a nightmarish collage. He saw power lines down and knotted together like backlashed fishing line, and tin siding laced around a broken telephone pole, resembling a child's fumbling attempt to wrap a Christmas present. Most houses had been ripped from their foundations, lumber scattered like toothpicks. Gashed and splintered trees crushed car hoods with maniacal, almost comical precision.

Upholstery stuffing clung to trees like a preternatural snowstorm. Newspaper and other litter blew around the streets like aimless wild birds in flight.,

He staggered on and saw Archie Harris, pastor of the Half Moon Deliverance Tabernacle, the town's all-black church, groping through the rubble of bricks that was once the post office. Harris carried a shiny, rain-glistened black umbrella, and was babbling crazily.

Shepherd grabbed him by a shoulder. Harris wheeled, eyes bulging with terror, and shouted into Shepherd's face.

"God's will! . . . God's will!"

Shepherd, saying nothing, released the man only to face a more horrid image, a gray and opaque image: people, his friends, some of them members of his congregation, crawling across the street or through their yards like worms, deep in pain and agony and bleeding.

Stung by guilt, he turned away from the scene to seek out his mother. Running down Cherry Street, he met a wet and muddy dog searching for its master. Shocked cries and moans chorused from both sides of the street. Behind him, there was renewed siren activity.

Then suddenly the blank, slate-gray face of Doris Fincher loomed in front of him, spitting out words in a frightened tone.

"Where's Mrs. Shepherd at? Her trailer house is gone clear down. Where's she at?" she stammered, apparently not recognizing to whom she was speaking.

Shepherd pushed by her, slowing only when he had reached the frame of the mobile home he shared with his mother while his congregation made plans to build a parsonage.

The frame was twisted like strands of licorice. But the mobile home itself was nowhere in sight. Nearly a block away, he found it, crushed at its middle like an aluminum can. Two men, John Howard and Darwin Cook, were to one side of the wreckage, standing over a body covered with a white sheet.

"Oh, God, no!" Shepherd exclaimed.

John Howard, little more than half Shepherd's size, rushed to meet him.

"Jack, no, . . . no, it's better that you don't look. Not the way she is, Jack. There's nothing . . . there was nothing anyone could do. Darwin and I are going on to see where help's needed."

Shepherd kneeled.

"Mom? Dear Lord in Heaven . . . why?"

Too stunned to cry, too confused and saddened to know what else to do, Shepherd lifted the sheeted body in his arms and began walking to the Methodist Church. His church.

The sky fell on it, he thought to himself when he saw that only one wall was erect. But out front the church marquee, miraculously untouched by the storm, announced in white plastic letters that the sermon for Sunday would be entitled, "Testing the Spirit."

Shepherd stood and swayed with the body of his mother in his arms. He scanned the surrounding scene, and in Sam Fenton's yard, next to the badly damaged church, he noticed a pillow. It was a decorative, over-stuffed pillow, baroque borders of flowers, a sunrise with birds flying about as if ushering in a bright new day. Against the black background, stitched in painstakingly done gold letters, was the timeworn prayer:

God grant me the
Serenity to accept
   the things I cannot change,
Courage to change the things I can
   and Wisdom to know the difference.

Shepherd began to weep.

Still carrying his mother's body, he sat on the front steps of his church amidst its rubble, and he wept. He continued until a hand grasped his shoulder, and Willard Kemper, a small, dark weasel of a man with a deep gash above one eye, began shouting into his face.

"God damn you! Damn you, preacher! Why'd you let God do this to us? Why? My little children . . . damn you . . . three little children! Damn you! Damn you!" he screamed, and then ran on, hunched low to the ground, running wildly like a rabid dog.

Shepherd winced at Kemper's words and the bitter odor of the blood streaked and caked on one side of the man's face. Then, while panic and confusion reigned in the tiny town, Shepherd began to sense another sort of presence. Behind broken trees, in the wreckage of houses and buildings, he sensed something demonic, something old: lurking, waiting, watching, biding its time—preparing to take over.

"Reverend Shepherd? Mr. Shepherd, let me help you with this."

Two black hands reached toward the body of Shepherd's mother.

"We have a place set up over by the school," said the deputy county sheriff, Herman Jackson.

Shepherd stared up at him and shook his head.

Jackson pulled back his hands.

"Do you need something, Reverend Shepherd? The Red Cross is here, and a few paramedics, too."

Again, Shepherd shook his head.

"What . . . what are you going to do?" Jackson asked, perplexed by the situation.

The cold flinty look in Shepherd's eyes unnerved him.

"Do?" Shepherd whispered. "Why . . . why I'm going to fight it. That's what I'm going to do. Fight this demon. It has returned. My grandfather knew. The storm released it. I'll fight it. If I have to labor unto madness . . . I'll fight it."

CHAPTER 5

The garbled radio transmission changed Dale Taylor's life forever.

Standing at the counter of Brooker's Hardware in nearby Soldier, he had just closed a deal on a new freezer and glass-top display for the fresh meat section of his grocery, and with another ten minutes of wrangling, Clarence Brooker would have tossed in two used hive units for Taylor's fledgling honey operation.

Brooker, his tanned face a mass of wrinkles, had knuckle-rubbed his graying crewcut, heaving his ridiculously bloated belly against the counter. "Dale, them hives cost me forty bucks a throw new. Can't jist give 'em away you know."

Taylor had smiled. Tough nut that he was, Brooker would have backed off on charging much for the two hives. Taylor had known it and so had Brooker.

"Clarence, I've seen those hives. If I take them, I'm gonna have to practically rebuild them. You know I'm just getting my honey operation going. Struggling with it right now. You get all my hardware business. No reason for that to change. But I need those hives, and you and I both know they're not worth more than a few dollars."

He had studied Brooker's crosshatched face, then added, "What do you say, Clarence? I need to get back to Half Moon. Left Carol Mae and Jenny running the store. They'll be wondering where I am."

"That Jenny's sure a pretty little thing, Dale. You got a real sweet little girl there," Brooker had mused, his face animated with an uncharacteristic smile.

"Favors her mother," Taylor had exclaimed. "Now how about those hives, Clarence?"

Brooker had squinted out the front window at Soldier's main drag, a stretch of buildings and a brick-top street that had been polished to a steely gray by a heavy rainstorm not fifteen minutes earlier. "Crazy damn weather, ain't it? Guess we was lucky not to get some high winds, you know."

Taylor had nodded, but he had been thinking about how everything in his life had been going so well lately. His grocery, the only one in Half Moon since Velmer Short had closed his and retired to Florida, was thriving—witness the need for the new meat display. The honey operation, though it needed seed money and more planning, promised to turn a profit after a couple of years. Besides that, the rows of hives took advantage of the vacant lot behind his store, keeping it from being an eyesore.

Behind *our* store, Taylor had mentally corrected himself.

Without Carol Mae's help and encouragement, Taylor's Grocery wouldn't exist, he often admitted. And Jenny, *she's as precious to me as Carol Mae.*

53

"Crazy damn weather," Brooker had muttered again, stalling so that when he gave in to Taylor's terms, it wouldn't look as if he were a pushover.

At that moment, Brooker's CB had cracked to life.

"God in heaven, no," a static-filled voice broke in over the emergency channel. "No, . . . power's down, everything's down . . . the storm . . . oh, God . . . never seen anything like this . . . get all the help you can . . . Half Moon's down . . . we need help . . . town's down . . . nothin's left but its name."

Taylor's chest ballooned with an icy gust of air.

He was in his pickup and on his way to Half Moon before Clarence Brooker could get any further information from the anonymous caller. Face glazed with the sheen of cold white marble, Taylor slammed the accelerator to the floor and roared along the rain-slickened county road between Soldier and Half Moon oblivious to the act of driving.

The radio message repeated itself in his mind like some dark, apocalyptic voice from the heavens.

. . . *oh, God* . . . *never seen anything like this* . . . *get all the help you can* . . . *Half Moon's down* . . . *we need help* . . . *town's down* . . . *nothin's left but its name.*

He felt cold. The cab of the pickup seemed to surround him with an icy fog. He couldn't feel his fingers on the steering wheel. The chill of anticipation, of not knowing, but expecting the worst, had a paralyzing effect.

It was like being buried alive.

He tried to imagine the town—*Half Moon's down*—how bad would it be? A few broken trees? A few power lines down? Or worse? Houses? Buildings? People?

Good God, people hurt? Maybe—?

The rainswept landscape rushed past. Low gray clouds scudded overhead wildly.

And Taylor felt the freezing touch of his darkest thoughts.

Jesus, no . . . I've lost them.

An involuntary shudder passed through his chest, lodging in his groin.

"Jesus, no . . . I've lost them."

A nauseating instant of vertigo caused him nearly to swerve off the road into the ditch. He chocked back tears and tried to remember the last thing he had said to his six-year-old daughter and his wife.

Jenny, a black-eyed, black-haired, dark-complex-ioned doll—a miniature of her mother, had wanted to ride with him.

"No, sugar lamb, you be a big girl and stay and help your momma."

They had shared an extra-firm good-bye hug.

"You have one of those for me?" Carol Mae had smiled and pressed close to him.

"Won't be more than an hour or so," he had said and then kissed her.

"Be careful on the road. It looks like rain," she had followed.

Like a hundred other good-byes. Except maybe this one. . . .

Jesus, no . . . I've lost them.

He raced on, covering the dozen or so miles between Soldier and Half Moon in a dreamlike, meager span of time. He slowed on the edge of town. The ringing echo of gunshots brought him out of his dark reverie. Harold Masterson was stalking through his feed lot, shotgun at his shoulder, methodically killing his milk cows to spare their suffering. Masterson's house and barn had been leveled; later, Taylor learned that the farmer's wife and two children had perished. That evening, still mired in panic, confusion, and dread, Masterson would turn the weapon upon himself.

Taylor drove on.

Half Moon's one-block downtown swarmed with rescue workers and law enforcement officials; ambulances blared discordantly under the funeral gray skies. At the south end of Main Street, Taylor saw that only two walls of his home remained standing; the house looked as if it had been cracked open and its contents spilled into the yard to lay jumbled amongst uprooted pecan trees, power lines, and mud.

He parked the pickup and ran into the front yard, vaguely waving his arms as if shooing away pests, though in reality it was a futile and pathetic gesture of helplessness.

Carol Mae. Jenny.

There was no time and no excess of emotion to mourn the destruction of the house.

Jesus, no . . . I've lost them.

Forgetting about his pickup, he picked his way hurriedly toward his store, scrambling over fallen trees, avoiding power lines and a scattering of stunned townfolk, many of them injured, many in tears. He saw the hulking shape of his friend, Jack Shepherd, sitting on the steps of the Methodist Church, seeming larger than life against the desolation of the building. He couldn't make out what Shepherd was holding in his arms.

As Taylor hesitated, the ghostly, quaking figure of Mildred Cartwright appeared. She wailed and clutched

56

at him with quivering, gnarled fingers. Her head was bleeding.

"Ronnie—the boy, my grandson, he saved me! He-he pulled me out and saved me! Brave as can be . . . he saved me. But his folks—they're under a wall. I can't even see them."

Young Ronnie Cartwright, blood on his arm, his shirt, and his jeans, huddled next to his fear-crazed grandmother and peeked around her skirt, not with dread and terror but with innocent confusion. Shyly and sadly he whispered,

"Today is my birthday."

Then he disappeared behind her.

Taylor frowned and started to say something, but chose to unlock himself from the woman's grasp and continue his way through the surrealistic destruction until he reached the site of his store.

The aluminum storefront had been torn loose; it was coiled like a giant serpent and writhed in the chilly, aftermath breeze. The store had been completely leveled. Its heavy concrete blocks had caved in, but in the middle of the rubble one shelf somehow still held its place with canned goods and jars of mayonnaise, jelly, and peanut butter stacked neatly in order. And the checkout counter had hardly received a scratch; all the change was in the proper slots in the cash register. But broken glass, mostly from the long, rectangular storefront window, coated the floor. During the storm, each piece must have been a potentially deadly missile.

Taylor staggered to the back of the store where two men, paramedics he assumed, stood over a small body covered with a dark green blanket. Taylor suddenly felt cold again. His tongue was a numb and sluggish worm.

And he felt trapped. Out of nowhere it seemed, he found himself thinking about the day a sparrow had flown into his walk-in meat locker, volleying itself futilely between the cold walls. He had tried to shoo it toward the door, but the panicking bird had never righted the course of its desperate fluttering.

He never told Jenny and Carol Mae about the sparrow. They would have been saddened.

Eyes fixed upon the blanketed body, Taylor stumbled through the wreckage of his store.

"Jenny? Is that my Jenny?"

One of the white-coated men, a young one with a smooth face and short brown hair, caught his arm. The young man's voice was cold, measured, and distant.

"I wouldn't advise you to look. There was a lot of flying glass. One of your neighbors identified her for us."

Over a choking rise of tears, Taylor muttered, "Carol Mae? Where's my wife?"

"We're . . . we haven't found her yet," said the young man reluctantly.

Taylor glanced down at his daughter's body, saw the outline of her face ghosting through the blanket, and turned away.

Minutes later, he and one of the paramedics discovered Carol Mae. Her stockinged foot, twisted grotesquely, could be seen jutting freely from a large heap of concrete blocks that had once formed the store's back room. Block by block, they dug until her body was completely visible.

Her clothes had been torn off.

Taylor touched her foot, and suddenly his knees buckled weakly and he sat down hard. The paramedics covered Carol Mae's naked body, lifted it from the

58

rubble onto a stretcher, and carried it away.

Belief suspended above him like a sword, Taylor stared off into the vacant lot behind the store. His head filled with a rising hum. Tears ran down his cheeks, but he was too numb, perhaps too exhausted, to sob and let the full hammer of his grief fall. That would come later.

He stiffly gathered himself up and dimly realized that all of his hives had been blown away. And then he knew the source of the hum—not the sound of his grief struggling within to be vented, but rather the buzzing of several hundred of his bees, swarming in confusion, vibrating the air with their monotonous and somehow ghostly noise.

In front of the store, one of the paramedics directed him to a flatbed truck lined with blanketed corpses, those of Carol Mae and Jennifer among them. A Red Cross worker helped him aboard, though Taylor had no idea where the truck was headed or why he had gotten on it.

One word, one cold, irrevocable word, repeated itself in his thoughts.

Lost. Lost. Lost.

"I've lost them," he exclaimed.

The Red Cross worker, a man in his fifties who looked like an ex-Marine, leaned toward him to hear over the rattle and whomp of the truck.

"Didn't catch what you said."

Taylor shook his head.

"God-awful thing, isn't it?" the worker half-shouted. "I count better than fifty bodies so far. Number's goin' higher. I'd bet on that. This truck's headed for the dead zone over behind the school. These bodies all have to be properly identified and tagged."

Taylor lowered his chin and whispered to himself, "I've lost them."

The truck chugged and sputtered, lurching to a halt behind Half Moon High School, an aging, three-story red brick building, one of the few edifices still virtually intact. The baseball diamond behind the school had been converted into a field hospital of sorts. Along the third-base line were rows of plastic body bags—a scene infinitely more appropriate to some massacre scene in Vietnam or Lebanon than to Half Moon, Alabama.

A unit of the Alabama National Guard patrolled the area.

Taylor sat on the edge of the truck bed as several men jostled around him to unload bodies. Below him, a hefty Red Cross nurse, her heavy thighs spilling across an aluminum chair, held a clipboard in her pudgy fingers. On it she kept a tally of the dead, a macabre honor roll.

Disoriented, Taylor jumped down and approached the nurse, who, in turn, smiled sadly up at him.

"I've lost my wife. Carol Mae Taylor, my wife."

The nurse glanced down at her clipboard and her smile faded.

"Yes, I see that. I'm very sorry."

"It's all right," Taylor muttered softly. "I'm going on back to my store to find her."

Twilight, the hour between dog and wolf, descended early on Half Moon that day.

Mildred Cartwright, whose car had escaped major storm damage, found strength enough to attempt to drive back to her home in Soldier after receiving medical attention. Her grandson Ronnie rode with her, his face wet with a fresh round of tears over the loss of his parents, his home, and his beloved birds. As they drove out of town, Ronnie allowed himself a final look at the destruction. But what he saw was the whispy white blur of his pigeons wheeling through the darkening skies over the town. And he heard the voice, the panic-inducing voice that seemed to be trapped in his head.

Come back! it said. Not a warning, but an invitation. One the boy somehow knew he would eventually accept.

Come back! the voice insisted.

Elsewhere in the town, Molly Harvester, with her three terriers trailing closely behind, searched the perimeter of her backyard, pausing every few feet to call out her husband's name. In one limp hand, she carried his cap, the only trace of him she had come upon.

On the steps of the Methodist Church, Jack Shepherd preached a nonsensical sermon to the rubble, while Dale Taylor methodically looked beneath the concrete blocks that had once formed the walls of his store, certain that he would find his wife and daughter.

Emergency crews continued working; there was muted conversation, the occasional whirring of a car or a chainsaw, and the lonesome barking of a dog. There were also flappings and rustlings, and the eerie buzzing of Taylor's bees seeking a new colony.

The men and women who stayed to start the massive cleanup required moved about like shadows. Some of them noticed that in and around the edges of town, small sentrylike fires sprouted—fires that burned but gave off little light, fires that smelled putrid with foul decay.

Twilight slipped into darkness.

Over the devastation of Half Moon, a thrumming of wings stole upon the night.

The dark spirit of Christmas Oak had returned.

Part Two

THE AFTERMATH OF
HALF MOON DOWN

CHAPTER 6

One year later . . .

"We had big plans."

Dale Taylor hitched back in the driver's seat of the county's Chevy van; a weak smile born of nostalgia lifted the corners of his mouth.

"Carol Mae and I thought we could do anything we put our minds to, you know. Together, we were gonna put Half Moon on the map. Try to do something about the town's poor reputation. Remember listening to all our plans, Shep?"

Swiping an unruly shock of reddish-blond hair out of his eyes, Jack Shepherd grunted, "Yeah, I remember, Dale."

Shepherd's short-sleeved khaki shirt was open at the throat and the sleeves were turned up a couple of times, revealing rippling weightlifter's biceps. Taylor looked small and frail compared with his muscular companion.

The van clicked along the little-used asphalt county road toward Half Moon, rolling past scrub pasture and dense but scattered gatherings of pine; here and there the soft greenish-white glow of blooming dogwoods stood out. Farmhouses intermittently blended with dilapidated shanties to complete the countryside. It was rural Alabama—poor, undeveloped, and dispossessed.

Conscious of his friend's subdued mood, Taylor tightened his grip on the wheel and burrowed deeper into his memories.

"Remember when Carol Mae and I opened the grocery, Shep? God as my witness, I was scared. I mean, I had worked in Stanley Knox's grocery while I was in high school, but, man—running one myself—I really half-expected the thing to fold in a year. And it would have if Carol Mae hadn't been there to encourage me at every step. Can't believe how hard that woman worked to see our dreams come true."

Taylor paused and glanced toward the slump-shouldered, bearded figure of Shepherd, whose massive frame appeared pinched and uncomfortable. His knees were tucked up against the dashboard. It seemed that if he were to stretch or shift his position, the front section of the van would crumple under the force.

"She was a good woman, Dale. Carol Mae was as supportive to her husband as any wife I've ever been around. You and she deserved all the success in the world . . . good people, but not enough of your fellow citizens were like that. Half Moon wasn't worthy of you," Shepherd confessed quietly. His brow furrowed as he engaged in Taylor's reminiscences.

Taylor blinked his eyes rapidly, set them hard against the road ahead as if that would help him digest Shepherd's words.

"We wanted a large family," Taylor exclaimed. "You know, lots of kids—six, seven maybe. Like the Walton's on TV. An old-fashioned, big family."

Aware that he was shifting away from Shepherd's more serious tone, he added, "I don't know whether Carol Mae and I ever told you, Shep, but we . . . we sort of had this idea of someday buying the old Mc-Cammon place north of Half Moon. You know the one—Victorian style. That monster had five bedrooms upstairs. Course, it was in real bad shape." Taylor shrugged his shoulders, then surrendered to another memory-induced smile.

"On Sunday afternoons, we'd get in the pickup and drive out there. No one had lived in the place for three or four years, you know. Well, we'd sort of pretend—just pretend, you understand—pretend like we'd just bought it. We'd walk through it, you see, and plan how we were gonna fix it up. The place had great possibilities—big ole stone fireplace, solid oak molding throughout, double walls—Carol Mae would have turned the inside of that house into a showplace. It was something to look forward to . . . something to work for."

Shepherd's giant hands cupped his knees. He was silent, almost meditative as Taylor looked for signs of a shared reverie in the future he and his wife had mapped out. Getting no response, he rolled his window down, propped his elbow onto it in the time-honored manner, and studied the gray-black widening of road. Through the April waves of heat, he watched it disappear into a vanishing point.

Lost . . . no, Jesus, I've lost them!

The shadow of thought dissolved, and other memories surged forward. "We were gonna expand the grocery. Make it the kind of store that folks from Soldier and as far away as Goldsmith would drive to. Not some little piss-ant crossroads place where folks stop when they have a sinking spell—I mean a real supermarket. And the honey operation—I was gonna build an apiary and have more bees than anybody in east Alabama."

He hesitated and shook his head. "We had big plans, Shep. Before the storm—"

"Stop it, Dale!"

The suddenness and intensity of Shepherd's remark took Taylor by surprise.

There was silence except for the drone of the van moving through the warm spring air, a drone steady and expressionless like background static from a radio, or the muffled metallic hum of a swarm of bees.

Morning was slipping unnoticed into afternoon.

In the shotgun seat, the muscular physique that had once helped Shepherd become the state's best high school heavyweight wrestler shifted in search of more room.

Taylor swallowed hard. His voice began to trail off, jerking awkwardly like an exhausted runner having finished a race. "I can't . . . I can't stop it, Shep. I'm sorry. I just can't . . . can't forget . . . all our plans. Carol Mae . . . Jenny . . . all our plans."

Shepherd nervously clenched and unclenched his fists. It seemed to him as if Taylor were some kind of bizarre magnet drawing sorrow and pity.

"I know it hurts you to remember those things, Dale," Shepherd whispered. "It's a wound that'll take a long time healing. No proud flesh I know of can scar it

over completely. I know . . . I know about wounds."
He cut off his comments abruptly, amazed at how easily he had fallen into his counseling pose—the curse of being an ex-preacher, if only for a handful of months.

Taylor felt a rush of embarrassment. He sighed. A dry, hollow whistle of regret could be heard. Then he blinked away his momentary softening, bracing himself to speak.

"Carol Mae and Jenny . . . they were all I ever wanted. The store, all the hard work—it was for them, for *us*—a family, a real honest-to-God family. And Half Moon was our home. I know the town had its drawbacks. Just a rough little southern town, and I know that few of the folks in it gave a damn much about whether anything good ever happened to it. But Shep, Half Moon was our *home*. Now it has a chance to start over . . . to be a decent town and forget about its past."

"Dale, that's going to take a lot of doing," Shepherd countered. "Half Moon over the years invited in about every form of corruption possible—political, business, social, moral—you name it. Racial hatred was still as strong there just before the storm as ever. It was a town guided by distorted minds. We both know that."

He glanced down at his hands, kneaded the knuckles of one hand into the palm of the other, and began speaking more slowly. Each word appeared to give pain. "What I regret most . . . is when Half Moon really needed strength . . . it didn't have it. It had no spiritual backbone . . . and it had no spiritual leader."

Taylor watched out of the corner of his eye as Shepherd fumbled with something in his shirt pocket, finally withdrawing a tiny black Bible, the kind that the V.F.W. and D.A.R. used to give to every Half Moon graduating senior. Red italics for the words of Jesus.

"Shep," Taylor muttered. "Shep, don't. Don't start this. Don't go blaming yourself for things that couldn't be changed."

Shepherd squinted out into a stand of pines, then bowed his head. "You know what I wish sometimes, Dale? I wish . . . I wish I'd gone down with Half Moon . . . that God had taken me along with the others." His words broke off with a curious tone of finality, like the sound of a door closing.

Taylor's jaw tightened. "I'm not going to relive it, Shep. I'm just plain not going to. That's not what we're coming back for."

Confusion in his eyes, Shepherd cocked his head toward Taylor.

"What we're coming back for?—Dale, you're not fooling me. You might fool yourself, but you won't fool me. Listen, the Lord knows I owe you a lot. You got me this job with the county when I didn't know what in the world to do. It wasn't in my heart to go back to the pulpit, and I really wasn't trained to do much else except use my muscles. I appreciate what you've done for me. I'll be forever indebted to you, but Dale, *I know* why we're returning to Half Moon . . . and so do you."

"No, Shep. No, you're wrong. Look, Catlin County had a soft-money government grant to build a mental-health facility, and state funds to encourage new industry, and our job in the County Development Office is to find suitable sites. If we don't find something feasible in the next month, the grant is void . . . and I don't expect the Reagan administration to support this kind of thing in the future—not with all the budget cuts."

Taylor paused to circle his point more precisely before continuing.

"We'll go in this afternoon and stake off a couple of sites before we call in some contractors for estimates. Our job will be easy enough. We'll be back in Soldier tonight. My point is, Shep, why shouldn't Half Moon be a possible site? The county, or at least the state, owns most of the property now. There's just no earthly good reason for not considering it. That town can live again."

Shepherd pulled out a black wallet, polished smooth with wear, and fished through the inside slots until he found what appeared to be newspaper clippings.

"You're forgetting what happened, aren't you, Dale? You seem to think we can go back to Half Moon and wave a magic wand—dump some government money on the place and everything will change. God in Heaven, Dale, my mother's gone . . . my church . . . Carol Mae . . . Jenny . . . they're gone. The McCammon place is a heap of boards and bricks. Half Moon is down and it won't ever get back up. Ever."

He handed the clippings to Taylor, who groaned and took them reluctantly.

The headline and double column of story unfolded into something like a giant *L* on its side; Taylor's mouth went dry as a microcosm of dark memories emerged. His chest prickled with ice points and he felt nauseous. Just above the crease the date read April 4, 1983, and below it, in bold, two-inch type, was the headline: TWISTERS LEVEL HALF MOON. The other clipping was dated March 1984; juxtaposed against a tally of the nation's unemployed, it was a feature story with the enigmatic title:

AUTHORITIES PUZZLED OVER
AFTERMATH AT HALF MOON

"I don't need to see these, Shep," Taylor said thickly. "It's all in the past, now."

But he could feel something rumbling inside, like a tiny buried life about to erupt in the pit of his stomach.

Shepherd's face, despite the reddish-blond beard, became chalky white and luminous; the disconcerting smile of one who had battled horror and, by slow degrees, had lost, shadowed forth, and he snatched the clippings from Taylor's limp grasp.

"Here, Dale, you have a short memory," he said bitterly. "Let me read these to you. Don't you remember? Half Moon even made the national news that day. Here's the first one:

Two mammoth tornadoes ripped through the Catlin County town of Half Moon yesterday morning, leveling everything in their paths, killing at least 89 of the 212 residents and seriously injuring scores of others. The incredible death toll makes it the worst disaster of its kind in Alabama history, and officials fear that the number may rise as workers continue to dig through the rubble.

"But Dale, we all know the story doesn't stop there. Dear God, it doesn't stop there."

His voice was quaking. The eruption inside Taylor

was closer now. Much closer. Shepherd pressed on.

"Something evil got into our town. A demon. Something pagan and bestial. Maybe God put it there—maybe it was there in Half Moon all the time waiting to be released. But it's there. I've seen its marks. I've felt its presence. I've seen it spread panic and confusion among all who've tried to rebuild their homes, their businesses. No one had the courage to fight what's there, and I didn't—"

"God damn it, Shep, shut up! Shut up! That's crazy talk. Roaring crazy talk, do you hear me!"

Even as he denied it, though, cold, sticky fear filled Taylor's stomach.

The explosion of words slammed Shepherd back into the seat as if the van had accelerated. Then he slumped into his former position. He fingered the second clipping as if it were a rare medieval manuscript. He read softly, reverently, in the monotone of a ghostly litany that might have been repeated an untold number of times.

Is Half Moon haunted? Puzzled authorities are beginning to wonder as they seek to understand why this small town which had nearly one-half of its residents wiped out by killer tornadoes last year has not started to rebuild. Personal belongings have been removed, and some lumber and bricks salvaged, but otherwise the town lies in ruin much as it did in April of 1983. Authorities grimly admit that the aftermath of Half Moon down reveals an inordinate number of cases of serious depression, insanity, and suicide. Rumors of bizarre occurrences have—

73

As the van thudded to a stop on the shoulder, Taylor tore the clippings away from Shepherd and began to shred them into bits and toss them out his window. The spring breeze caught the bits and fluttered them across the asphalt as if they were confetti from a celebration.

"I don't believe all that nonsense. I don't believe in spirits or demons, and I don't believe God sent the storm or that something evil took over the town. I mean, I just don't believe it, Shep."

But the buried life, reborn, twitched and squirmed deep within him.

Puffs of spring pollen and dust swirled about the parked van. Beads of sweat flecked out on the faces of both men. Suddenly Taylor was thinking about the aftermath, about little things like not wanting to talk with a *National Enquirer* reporter who had been eager to pursue the town's story.

"Look, I'm sorry, Shep. I didn't need to do that."

In the ensuing silence, Taylor pulled the van back onto the road. He felt guilty. There was something about the way Shepherd made a point—his "preacher ways," Taylor called it—that set off fires of guilt. He found himself wishing that Shepherd would say something, anything. But they were two miles closer to Half Moon before he spoke.

"Dale, you and I have always been able to talk," he began.

Shepherd was spell-casting. Preacher ways. Taylor grimaced.

"We used to talk about everything," he continued. "Like, for instance, the night I decided I would become a minister. We talked about it half the night, didn't we? Or the day you decided to ask Carol Mae to marry you.

And we talked about the tragic things, too. When we were both ten and you were staying all night on my birthday . . . and your folks were driving back from Montgomery . . . the bridge outside of Soldier . . . and Jimmy Braddock had been drinking and tried to pass. Mostly we cried, but we talked after their funeral."

The faces of Taylor's parents ghosted momentarily on the sun-splashed windshield and then phantomed ahead as mirages before dissolving.

Preacher ways.

"Dale, I almost didn't come with you today, but I felt obligated because of this job and what you've done for me. All along, though, I was thinking you'd finally own up to the real reason you're going back to Half Moon."

Through the palpable silence Taylor's countenance tightened; he struggled to avoid revealing that Shepherd was touching pressure points with every sentence.

Shepherd continued. "Something's very wrong with Half Moon. I know. Call it 'preacher's intuition' or whatever. What scares me most is that the town is pulling us back to it, and it has nothing to do with the job assignment we're on. Whether you admit it or not, Dale, you're letting it pull you for one reason: you think you can find your lost wife and daughter. And I'm going back because I think I can fight whatever has taken over the town. It's like we're both on some dark quest. . . ."

Taylor gazed uneasily toward Shepherd. He met the eyes of that gentle giant, eyes desperate and wild, like those of a haggard sorcerer.

"Remember that old empty cistern on your grandpa's farm?" Shepherd followed. "We were scared of it until one day we talked about it and went over and pried up the rotted planks and looked down into it. Going back to Half Moon is like looking down into that cistern. Only this time we're going to have to climb down into it. I don't know what we'll find. Maybe you'll find one thing and I'll find another. But let's at least admit to ourselves why Half Moon still has such a hold on us."

For a moment Taylor was a child again, creeping to the edge of that cistern, flashlight in hand, every muscle tensed with fear. Through the slot where a plank had been, consummate darkness rushed up to meet him. His flashlight was ineffectual.

Omyjesusgod, whatamigoingtosee?

Then relief.

"The only thing we saw was our reflections, Shep," said Taylor, forcing a smile and a strained laugh. "Just our reflections deep down there in that stagnant water. That's all. Now, I don't think your talk about cisterns makes sense."

But something was tugging at Taylor, clambering its way into his thoughts until finally it made its small voice heard.

Don't go down into that cistern alone, it said.

The town lay drabbled and defeated like a dying old woman. Here was a thing leprous to the faithful—those who had called Half Moon "home." A deep and awesome silence held sway during the day now that few people ever entered. But at night the ghostly ruins came alive with the sounds of something winging, the hollow clatter of cloven hooves, and a lonesome wind that bore aloft an eerie, triumphant cry.

They crested Fletcher's Hill and soon the van was pulling onto the quarter-mile side road leading into Half Moon. Yellow and black-striped sawhorses, placed there several months ago, blocked the way. Taylor got out and deftly lifted them aside. The rubble of Half Moon loomed ahead.

The two men stared at the lifeless scene.

Shepherd's eyes seemed to be asking Taylor to reconsider. Taylor returned the look, managing a note of resolution as he spoke. "We have to, Shep. It's our job. We have to do it. That's the whole thing."

For Shepherd, the moment was like a bizarre transfusion of something radically foreign to his system. It was as if all the nerves in his body had turned to live ants and all of them were biting him at once.

For Taylor, it was the sensation of muscles tensing as he peered over the rim of a bottomless cistern.

Maybe you'll find one thing, and I'll find another . . . Shepherd's words echoed from deep within that cistern.

Taylor drove slowly on. To their left stood a diminutive clapboard building surrounded by weeds. On the porch roof a rusting sign with the word "Antiques" threatened to fall.

"Carl and Molly Harvester's shop," Taylor mused. "They never found Carl's body . . . that's what I heard. Just never found it."

Shepherd glanced at the small building but said nothing.

Taylor continued. Talking gave him the illusion of control. "I suppose that ole gal's the only one still living around here. That's her ole yellow Pinto, I believe. She must have a pretty strong feeling about this town, or she wouldn't have stayed."

He shifted in his seat. Shepherd's silence was disconcerting.

"You know, Shep, it's strange, isn't it, that a few places in town were left standing . . . like the Harvester's antique shop and the high school . . . makes you wonder, doesn't it?"

Shepherd nodded, his attention drawn for a moment to a tree house resting in the bowl of a huge oak.

The site inspection, despite the penetrating unease they felt, went smoothly, with surprising alacrity. Yet they worked with a degree of caution. Taylor, in fact, mentioned to Shepherd that he kept a small caliber revolver in the glove compartment, hoping it might allay surface fears. When Shepherd questioned the need for the gun, Taylor replied, jokingly, "Rats. There may be scads of rats. It's my Boy Scout habit. I came prepared. I even have all my camping supplies in the back of the van. Never can tell when you might need something."

By late afternoon they had staked off three sites: the town's park area, the site of the old American Legion building, and the high school baseball field. The latter transported Taylor back to the day of the storm. But while Taylor lingered, letting his thoughts convert the silent, vacant field to the horror-filled dead zone, Shepherd walked to where the van was parked near the rubble of the Methodist Church. After a few minutes, Taylor joined him. They sat on the foundation blocks of the church and shared a thermos of iced tea as twilight began to descend. The humidity was oppressive.

"We'd better be heading out, Shep," said Taylor.

But Shepherd was lost in his own forest of thought, thumbing carefully through his tiny Bible. Finally he spoke. His voice quaked.

"A small town is a fragile, ghostly thing. People create small towns in their own images and give a town a soul. But this one has none, has no sense of place. It's just one big dark spirit, filled with the projections of distorted minds."

Taylor tried to humor him.

"Wasn't it Faulkner who said, 'Years ago we in the South made our women into ladies, then the war came and made the ladies into ghosts'? It's funny, but that's the only line from Faulkner I can ever remember. Maybe he would have said that the storm made us all into ghosts."

Shepherd seemed not to be listening. His gaze drifted toward a partial moon rising in the east. Then he began to speak, not wildly or incoherently, but with a subdued intensity that conveyed a departure of the senses.

"The Bible tells us what happened to Half Moon. I found what the scripture says about Half Moon. In Isaiah 13:20-22 we hear of the desolation of Babylon, but it's Half Moon, not Babylon."

In the ever-dimming light, he read aloud.

"'It shall never be inhabited, neither shall it be dwelt in from generation to generation; neither shall the Arabian pitch tent there; neither shall the shepherds make their fold there. But wild beasts of the desert shall lie there; and their houses shall be full of doleful crea-

79

tures; and owls shall dwell there, and satyrs shall dance there. And the wild beasts of the islands shall cry in their desolate houses, and dragons in their pleasant palaces; and her time is near to come, and her days shall not be prolonged.'"

Shepherd closed his miniscule book.

"Satyrs and doleful creatures and ghosts and dark spirits right here in the ruins of Half Moon," he exclaimed, gesturing at the shadows.

"I saw hoofprints in the park. Grandpa Shepherd told me . . . the creature would come . . . and Half Moon would be desolate."

Taylor cringed at the sight of his distraught friend, and then led him to the nearby van, helping him into the front seat. Shepherd slumped limply against the dash.

Time to leave Half Moon, Taylor thought to himself. *It doesn't look the same, half in shadow.* But something caught his eye as he started to climb into the van. Something flickered, seemed to flare out with a subtle luminence across the way, downtown where Taylor's grocery once stood. The curious light had a hypnotic effect. And with it came a rising hum, a ghostly buzzing.

Something twitched and squirmed in the pit of his stomach. "I'll be right back, Shep," he mumbled, and then was gone.

In the van, Shepherd's head lolled from side to side.

"Shadows and ghosts and the hoofprints," he whispered despairingly into the darkness of the front seat.

"Windkiller . . . the creature . . . the town belongs to the creature and it knows what we fear. Got to fight it. Oh, dear God."

Then he realized he was alone. He reeled about looking for Taylor. Night insects droned. Taylor was nowhere in sight. But Shepherd saw something that took his mind off his friend. Nervously he rolled down his side window to see more clearly.

"Dear God, what . . . ?"

He could feel it as he had never felt it before: a kind of primal terror.

The flickers of light came from the rubble of the church. A tight circle of flames, like an arrangement of newly kindled campfires, burst forth there. He could feel their heat, and he could smell them—a rotting, decaying, dead animal smell seemed to drift from the center of each fire.

Deeply frightened, he worked his tongue against the roof of his mouth. His saliva tasted bitter and oily. Swallowing seemed impossible. He watched the flames evolve, and, reflexively, he clenched one of his massive fists. With his other hand, he slipped his Bible from his shirt pocket.

Shadowy figures seemed to flow from within the rubble, and soon they were dancing around the circle of flames. The soughing of wind filtered through from the thickening darkness beyond the flames.

The figures, menacing satyric figures, cast grotesque shadows.

A dance of shadows, he thought. Stifling a shriek, he gripped his tiny Bible and rubbed it with his thumb the way a child rubs a security blanket.

One impulse was to run, run wildly and find Taylor. The other was to stay and fight. But as some of the figures linked in a snakelike, writhing dance and closed

81

the circumference of their circle, others materialized and spanned out in a larger circle—one that surrounded the van.

Shepherd froze. He looked away from the figures and stared at the glove compartment. Resolution was at hand.

I'll fight them. If I have to labor unto madness, . . . I'll fight them.

The small gun felt cool, and it was loaded.

The figures in the outer circle danced on tiptoed cloven feet, wafting out of the blackness, stealing closer to the van, howling low and demonically, enraptured by the eerie gusts of wind.

The inner circle of figures tightened around something, blocking Shepherd's view. They howled and cried, then fell silent. A new sound emerged, one that tapped at every nerve in his body.

Krk, krk, krk.

Still holding the gun in one hand, Shepherd let the tiny Bible drop from his grasp.

Krk, krk, krk.

Ringing from out of the past with a tinge of laughter, his grandfather's voice seemed to fill the van. *Don't let Ole Muskie make you afraid, Jackie! Stand up and face your fears, Jackie boy!*

Shepherd cried out and wrapped his arms around himself. He gasped for his breath in the humid night air.

Krk, krk, krk.

The shadowy figures parted. The circle of flames suddenly flickered low.

In their midst stood a nightmare from Shepherd's childhood, a nightmare sent by Windkiller: Ole Muskie, a vicious, white Muscovy duck, seemingly twice as large as Shepherd recalled it, flapping its wings. For an instant, it looked like a huge, preternatural bat.

The bird rose on its webbed feet and kept rising until . . . until it became something else. Cautiously Shepherd released the protective self-embrace. Sweat found rivulets down his face and chest and back.

"Oh, please . . . no, God, no. Please make this stop."

Where the duck had materialized, there now appeared the figure of his mother dressed in a white robe, one gnarled hand resting atop a gold-crowned ebony cane. Even at a distance of twenty-five feet or so, he could see that the ornamental gold had been carved into the winged semblance of Windkiller.

The vision of his mother faded, leaving the ebony cane standing by itself against the backdrop of flames. Then the cane began to move. To writhe. To twist. To coil. And then, in a final dark metamorphosis, it dropped to the ground as a golden-headed serpent.

And slithered away.

The flames extinguished themselves. A palpable darkness beat its way across the rubble. The wind stopped. The shadowy figures were no longer visible, but Shepherd sensed another presence, larger, more commanding. He rolled up his window, and with the back of his hand wiped sweat from the corners of his mouth, sweat that tasted as bitter as gall.

He waited.

Dale, for God's sake, where are you?

Something seemed to be toying with the handle on the outside of his door. Terrified, he pressed his weight against the door and heaved his upper body to find air to breathe. He trembled from the loud gasps.

"Dear Heavenly Father . . . give me . . . dear God . . . it wants me!" He squeezed the handle of the gun and muttered helplessly, not hearing the other door being opened.

He waited, and began to feel more secure braced against the door, gun in hand. He breathed a long sigh of relief.

And then he glanced over his shoulder into black eyes set deep within a hairy visage, a visage that hovered a few inches from his own as if watching to see what terror could do to a man's face.

Despite the oppressively humid warmth of the evening, Dale Taylor felt cold.

As he walked toward the shards of light, he rubbed his arms, hugging himself to stave off a numbing chill. He shivered and his teeth chattered, and the unnerving sound was like a death rattle.

I shouldn't have left Shep alone, he chided himself. But he continued on, straining to see the source of the flickering light. It drew him as did the purling, eering buzzing, which reminded him of the distant hum of saws at a pulpwood mill.

The bees have returned. Looking for their hives. Looking for their queen.

And he thought of Carol Mae.

I've lost her.

Up ahead a light flared. Part of him wanted to believe there was a small, mysterious fire burning, a home fire, beckoning him to reestablish the bond of family. But another part of him reasoned that it could be will-o'-the-wisp leaping up from pools of stagnant water.

Suddenly it felt good to be walking toward the grocery, to be walking down the deserted main street despite a lingering residue of fear. It felt good because Half Moon was the only place he had experienced love: Carol Mae, Jennifer, his parents, the grocery, and the friendship of Jack Shepherd.

Yet the rubble, except for the buzzing, now lay silent, waiting like a beast ready to pounce; the shell of the town, in its acquired sentience, donned darkness like a mask, creating a sense of terror within him, the kind of terror that couldn't exist without the hope for love and the dream that one day the town would be rebuilt and its dark past forgotten.

The light, bouncing off twisted layers of aluminum roofing, flashed out like shaken foil. And then, amidst the shadows, a shape emerged. At first, it seemed to be the outline of a child. But then he heard buzzing, and he saw the bees rise in a great black cloud.

And he smelled ripe bananas. It was as if the sickeningly sweet odor were being exuded from his skin and clothing. He stretched his arms out away from him, and the fatal attraction of the ripe bananas' odor began to draw the bees.

"Oh, God, no."

Swarming as they were, angry, hungry, the bees would be extremely dangerous.

Two landed on the back of his wrist. Then six more, a dozen more.

I'm going to die. Right now . . . I'm going to die.

Helplessly, he watched his arms coat with bees. Like

fur. And he knew that it would do no good to run. No good at all.

He closed his eyes tightly. His body quaked. He felt naked, and he imagined a block of ice forming in his chest.

But the bees did not sting.

They amassed upon his arms and hands, crawling over them and . . . and *through* them . . . as if his arms and hands weren't there.

Oh, Jesus, what is this?

Suddenly, in response to a shrill cry from somewhere out of sight, the bees exploded into flight, and they reamassed, slowly, like a pooling of black velvet. Their movement gave off a soft murmur, a whisper. Curiously, it reminded him of nights years ago, when he and Carol Mae would lean over Jennifer's crib and listen to her breathing.

The metamorphosis of the bees completed itself.

The young girl stood with her back to him, engrossed in some childlike diversion. He thought he recognized her.

Regret and fear mingled; he couldn't hold back the words.

"Jenny, sweetheart, I could have taken you along, but your mother needed help in the store. You understand that, don't you?"

The figure responded only by turning slowly his way; bathed in the shadows, her form was as sweet and innocent as ever, but her face was a dark void, a blackened caul. And the blackness seemed to squirm with a subtle animation.

The cry from afar drifted closer.

The ghostly buzzing returned, and before his unbelieving eyes the shadowy outline that he imagined to be Jennifer began to shred and dissolve as the swarm of bees took flight into the darkness of Half Moon.

Taylor felt numb. He felt like a man hopelessly lost in a blizzard who knows that if he dares surrender to sleep, it will be his final sleep, his letting go.

By degrees, the sounds of bare feet scuffing over broken chunks of concrete blocks ushered him back to the realm of sensation. The scuffing of bare feet and the voice that seemed part human, part something else—a soft siren of a voice, as if half woman and half bird.

He turned toward the sounds. Another shadowy figure loomed before him. A woman, naked, her body wrapped in a silvery sheen of moisture. A desirable woman. She had the face and body of Carol Mae. And then he noticed her feet, twisted grotesquely as they'd been the moment he'd discovered her that morning a year ago.

"Dale? Dale, honey?"

And the voice was almost Carol Mae's.

"Here. Over here. I'm here," she called.

Taylor stumbled forward. He wanted desperately to touch her.

"You're the heart of all I ever loved, Carol Mae," he said. "I'm afraid that sounds corny, but I mean it . . . oh God, I mean it."

But the figure seemed not to hear. Behind her, a shrill cry drifted upon the air, and the figure scurried back amongst the rubble like a frightened child. She issued a sound, perhaps a whimper. It was the inarticulate sound of a woman trapped by fear.

Taylor felt his chest tighten and prickle with needles of ice.

Something loomed beyond Carol Mae, and she scrambled toward it. Even in the half-light, Taylor could see that its lower body was shaggy with hair, that it pranced upon cloven feet. But its upper body, unclothed, resembled a man's, save for a pair of small, sharp horns protruding from its coarse dark hair.

Carol Mae stood before the creature, suppliant to its control over her. Whisper soft, the creature's wings of pure shadow lifted, stirring the night air and driving pungent waves of decay toward Taylor. The enormous wings vibrated, gently lilting like the wings of a preening bird.

Carol Mae cried out.

And then the creature's wings enfolded her.

Taylor's vision began to fog; he felt as if his head were filling with a sac of cold blood.

A shot rang out.

Darkness and silence immediately settled again on the site of the grocery. To Taylor, the shot penetrated to the bottom of his fear.

One thought dominated as he raced in the direction of the gunshot: *he's done it, he's done it, and I left him alone!*

He found an empty van.

There was no response to his calls at first. Then, somewhere beyond, he heard groaning. With his powerbeam flashlight, he began searching. A block away he found Shepherd's body in a shadowy heap in front of the high school, silent and unmoving. One hand loosely gripped Taylor's gun.

Taylor reached him and began looking for a wound.

"God in heaven, Shep, what have you done? I shouldn't have left you, I shouldn't have."

But there was no wound. No blood.

Shepherd, having been jostled roughly, began to moan and then to speak.

"They trampled on me, trampled me down... shadows... Windkiller's shadows... trampled on my soul."

"Shep, damn it, what are you talking about?" Taylor's voice rose in agitation, but it masked tremendous relief at finding Shepherd still alive. "What were you shooting at for God's sake?"

"Hoofprints," Shepherd groaned.

"I'm going to get the van. Stay right here. I'll be right back," Taylor exclaimed, but then hesitated.

The outer circle of light radiated across Shepherd's face. His eyes were intense marble-green specks of fire, the eyes of a frightened animal.

A catspaw of wind brought the haunting, birdlike cry from somewhere in the darkness.

"It-it's real," Shepherd stuttered. "You saw something too, didn't you? It's real. Dear God, it's real. Trampled me."

"There's not a cut or a single bruise on you," Taylor responded. "But Shep, I did see something... or thought I saw something where the store used to be. It wasn't real. Something deep inside me *wanted* to see something. I can't explain it. Like a reflection maybe."

Trancelike, Shepherd stared into the night sky. "I can't leave now. Ever. Been marked. Trampled on my soul. I've got to fight them." Strings of saliva threaded down from his twisted mouth. His hulking frame seemed to have shriveled.

"No, Shep. Whatever it is, we're leaving it, we're burying it... like the way we put planks back over

Grandpa's cistern. I'm going to go get the van. You won't ever have to come back to Half Moon."

Shepherd sighed and shook his head.

"No use. I've seen the darkness . . . I have to fight this demon. My duty. And you have to stay and find Carol Mae."

But Taylor was already running toward the van, his flashlight beam patchworking the night with an amber brightness.

Reaching the van, he jumped in, starting it with a roar. Taylor threw the van into gear, and sped back to the high school, back to the echoes of groans trapped in his memory, back to the spot where he had found Shepherd hardly a minute ago—back to a snatch of barren schoolyard now showing no trace of his friend.

CHAPTER 7

The boy was awakened by the voice.

It seemed to reach his ears from a vast distance, or from the bottom of some deep chasm. He not only heard the voice, but he also *felt* it, as if it were coarse and shaggy, as if it possessed rough hands that were shaking him.

The womblike darkness of the tree house surrounded him. Earlier, the darkness had lulled him into sleep before the voice announced its presence with an imperious necessity.

Terrified, the boy scooted along the floor of the tree house and pressed his back into a corner. A breeze tugged at the flat, square tree-house roof, and the giant oak spread its protective limbs around the tiny fortress much as it had the day of the storm a year ago—the day Half Moon went down.

The voice suddenly closed upon itself so that it sounded tenuous, evanescent. The voice had called Ronnie Cartwright back to Half Moon, back for a confrontation the nature of which Ronnie could only dimly perceive. But he would learn. He was determined to understand what dark quest awaited him.

He clenched his fists and gritted his teeth.

I'm not going to cry! I'm not!

Through the twilight sky it came: a muted cry, shuttled along by the wind; it bounced off scattered rubble and broken trees, masking its location with echoes. A gunshot crackled in the distance, and beyond the porthole of the tree house, the boy heard the soft rustle of wings.

And he recalled running away from his Grandma Cartwright's and the mysterious manner in which he had been led back to Half Moon. Leaving the night before had been the easy part. Grandma Cartwright had fallen asleep in her rocker-recliner at about nine o'clock as she did nearly every evening. The boy had slipped out of the house, but it had taken him all night to get to Half Moon from Soldier. Fortunately, the weather had been clear. He had traveled light: the BB gun (last year's birthday present) and a backpack bulging with another shirt, a thermos of cola, a flashlight, and a box of snack crackers.

Outside of Soldier, something very curious had occurred. The voice, which had exhorted him—*come back*, it had whispered, *come back*—suddenly broke off. In the pasture where he was walking, a dark corridor materialized. At a vanishing point ahead of him, small blue flames burned, dimly illuminating what appeared to be an altar. Caught by its magnetic pull, the boy started down the corridor, its darkness smelling of decay, mold, and mildew—the smell of a long-closed room.

But the corridor rapidly dissolved. The boy panicked.

He reached for his flashlight.

Lost. Where am I?

The birds seemed to come from nowhere.

"Joe?"

The crow, its eyes a ghostly yellow sheen, hopped and fluttered beyond him. There, too, was the broken-winged hawk, a soft, pathetic ball of feathers, hobbling, flopping over the terrain, still unable to fly. Beyond the crow and the hawk, white pigeons flocked, shifting rhythmically in the air, never close enough for the boy to see them clearly. But he knew that they must be his pigeons, his homers.

He followed the birds, smiling at first, then laughing with the sheer joy of such a mysterious happening. And the realization hit him like a starburst.

Leading me to Half Moon! They're leading me home!

And they did.

Yet they stayed out of his reach. It was as if they were no longer his. They were no longer pets; he no longer controlled them. Something else, some wild god of the world, did. Even their voices seemed not to be their own; the caw of Joe the crow and the call of the wounded hawk were grotesque—like ghostly parodies of themselves. And not once did he hear the comforting cooing of his pigeons.

But he let them direct his way.

On the edge of Half Moon, the birds led him across what had been Harold Masterson's farm, and it was there that he found a belt of cowbells twisted around a barbed wire fence. He took it with him for good luck. Dawn was a pinkish-gold promise by the time he climbed into his tree house and collapsed. But it felt good. It felt like home. It had been his private kingdom since the day he and his dad built it back when the boy was in the second grade.

He had good reason to believe that nothing could harm him while he was within its protective walls. After all, somehow it had sheltered him from the storm—the one that had flattened the town and swept away his parents, his home, and his birds—the one that had howled through on, of all days, his birthday, scattering his dreams, leaving him in the care of a sickly, bitchy woman who lacked the patience to cope with old age, let alone a young boy.

The memory of the journey to Half Moon faded.

Suddenly the mysterious cry redoubled its sound.

Stifling a whimper, the boy searched the shadows for his weapons: the plastic-stocked BB gun and the belt of cowbells. But the gun was useless, its trigger mechanism having broken months ago. Now it was only a pretend gun in a world unkind to pretenders.

The boy slid his fingers away from his ears, his eyes away from the gun. Coiled near his foot, the cowbells, he reasoned, offered possible protection. He wanted to believe they had power. Magic. He reached for them, and they softly jingled as he lifted them into his lap where they lay across his legs like a listless snake.

"Make it stop. Please make it go away," he whispered over the bells.

A shrill cry swirled through the warm spring air and perched in the stumps of branches and clumps of foliage at the top of the massive oak. The boy imagined that the sound was stalking him. He *knew* it was.

Scrambling to his knees, he swallowed back a rising clutch of fear.

"Scare it away," he stammered, and shook the belt of chrome-plated, golf-ball-sized bells with both hands. The harsh jangle exploded, filling the tree house with a discordant rabble of tinny echoes. The echoes escaped, and a breeze whisked them upon skitterings of dust through the empty streets. They were empty because curiosity seekers came rarely now, most having convinced themselves, despite the stories, that the town was dead. All the signs indicated death. But the town lived on; it beat on, with a feeble and haunting pulse, and bided its time, and when twilight sought to set its design upon the rubble, eternity was reminded that Half Moon had shadows.

The town was the locus of a dark summons.

The boy cried harder and screamed at the thin roof. He joggled the bells until his shoulders ached and the immediacy of fear was replaced by exhaustion. Then he slumped back against a wall and let the bells slip from his hands. His crying gradually softened.

But the sound beyond continued. Now it came from below, calling up from the foot of the tree: knowingly, persistently, impatiently. The boy calmed himself and listened. He swiped at his tears and his runny nose with the back of his hand.

The cowbells possessed no magic. Disappointed, he shivered and hugged himself. I'll be all right, he told himself . . . I'll be okay when Mom and Dad come home. I'll just wait right here . . . wait right here till they get back.

And in this he found momentary comfort as twilight slowly thickened into early darkness.

Soon he needed light. Mechanically, he fumbled for his backpack, grasped the flashlight, and clicked on its feeble beam. It revealed a poster of "The Incredible Hulk," a modern Hercules, on the opposite wall. On his knees, he cautiously crawled to a square porthole in the plywood wall, his window on the memory of a world he used to know.

Only the haunting gray foundation of the home he loved remained. The family car was gone. There was no longer a fence around the backyard; the row of wire-mesh pens in which he kept his prized pigeons was also gone, though earlier he had thought he heard some of them circling above the tree house, their rhythmic winging, but not their familiar cooing. Even so, he had felt a surge of hope.

My birds will help me. They led me home.

But hope threatened to die. He remembered that his parents were gone. Forever.

Sadness tore at his chest. The shrill cry returned, and he pulled himself away from the porthole, turned off the flashlight, and pressed his forehead against his knees. No more crying, he chided himself. No more.

Anger welled up within him: if only I had a gun or a knife, a real gun, a sharp knife, he reasoned . . . I could fight it. Worthless BB gun. Worthless bells. Better just wait right here. Maybe it won't come in the tree house . . . maybe it won't. Maybe it'll just get tired of waiting for me to come out . . . and just go.

Just go. But a cold fog of recognition was gathering around him, seemingly drifting up from the insistent piping. It was like accepting punishment. Only in this case he couldn't imagine or recall any wrongdoing.

Something out there won't let me leave Half Moon.

And suddenly, below him, the cry ceased.

The silence was deep and rich. Curiosity drew the

boy back to the porthole. He remembered that earlier that afternoon a white van had pulled into town. He wondered who it could be. Someone sent to find him? To help him? Why else would anyone come around Half Moon now? The town is dead. Everyone knows that.

If he yelled for help, maybe someone. . . .

The rush of wings spread fanlike above him, a star-fall of sound. Were they the beatings of his wayward pigeons or circling birds of prey? They descended and hovered close to the porthole, close enough in the darkness that he could reach out and touch one. But he didn't. He clutched the flashlight; it cut ineffectually into the night, sufficient only to capture a glimpse of something, and he cowered back.

A grim, owl-like head, rapacious beak . . . or a product of his fear-inspired imagination. He dropped the flashlight and it pooled a dim oval on the floor.

"Hide me," he whispered to the tree house walls. "Hide me here."

Tears, despite his efforts to hold them back, flowed freely. He leaned his head against a wall and sobbed. His cheek rested next to a knothole in the plywood, a rough circle of darkness the size of a quarter. Through a gauzy curtain of tears, he noticed the knothole and reflexively peeped out into the night. More strangeness greeted his eye: small sentrylike fires, stinking of decay, dotted the surrounding rubble, former houses of neighbors and friends. Shadows hunkered near those fires, which burned but gave off meager light.

The boy's lower lip quivered. "Dad. Mom," he whispered. "Come home now. Right now . . . please!"

Something waited at the foot of the tree.

A swath of tarpaulin serving as a door hung down over the entrance to the tree house. It was not designed to keep out things threatening, things of darkness. he retrieved the flashlight and shined it upon the tarpaulin.

He scrunched into the far corner; his cries and pleadings rose dramatically.

"Dad! Mom! Help me, please! Help me! Help me-e-e!"

There was the muffled thud of hooves at the foot of the tree. There was an excited, animal-like breathing and snuffing. The flashlight dropped to one side, and the boy cupped his hands over his ears.

Something jostled the tarpaulin.

The boy waited, holding his breath, his mouth filled with the bittersweet taste of fear. And as mysteriously as they had started, the clatter of hooves and the predatory breathing ceased.

The aftermath silence calmed him, but he dared not sleep or allow himself to drowse. Whatever was out there could return. He imagined himself a raccoon treed by a hound, yet he sensed that something much more dangerous than a dog lurked out in the darkness.

But what?

He shivered involuntarily. His fingers fumbled over the stock of the broken BB gun that he clasped against his thighs. The gun gave him some comfort, because he reasoned that he could at least wield it as a club, smash at the face of the unknown menaces that stalked him. Get in one good hit . . . he wouldn't give in without a fight.

What's out there?

No, he cautioned himself, don't think about it. Don't try to imagine. That will only make it worse. Pray.

Maybe that's the right thing to do. On the bulletin board in his Sunday school class, he recalled a slogan composed of red construction paper letters that read, "Prayer Is Power." It was worth a try.

In the darkness, he bowed his head and closed his eyes.

"Dear Lord Jesus," he muttered reverently.

He paused. Words that he expected would flow freely seemed damned up. "I don't exactly . . . know how to pray, you see. . . ."

He hesitated, waiting for inspiration.

"Dear Lord Jesus," he began again, ". . . I . . . you see . . . I'm real scared . . . real afraid . . . please . . . could you help me?"

His nose began to run and two reluctant tears squeezed out of the corner of one eye. He snuffled and his voice quavered.

"Jesus . . . and God . . . you see . . . I'm . . . I'm just a boy . . . all by myself . . . need help . . . Amen."

He opened his eyes and shook his head. That was a dumb prayer, he scolded himself. Jesus wouldn't listen to a stumbly fumbly prayer like that one. Maybe it didn't make any difference anyway. Maybe Jesus couldn't help. It seemed to the boy that he needed someone who was big and mean and a good fighter . . . maybe someone with a gun, too. A real gun.

The boy hoped he wouldn't be sent to Hell for thinking that . . . but he wasn't sure that he needed a man who walked around carrying baby lambs in his arms, advising people to turn their other cheek to their enemies. The Incredible Hulk or Mr. T seemed better suited to help. Or even Reverend Shepherd, Half Moon's own strong man.

99

"I'm sorry for thinking this way, Jesus," he murmured.

A slip of wind moaned high in the oak. Something scraped across the roof of the tree house mimicking fingernails raking down a blackboard. The boy cringed, but then realized it was probably a branch.

Well, maybe the tree house is the safest place to be tonight, he told himself. Better than being . . . *out there*. The tree house is a good place. A secret place. A place to parade your secret thoughts.

His stomach growled. How long had it been since he had eaten? He couldn't remember. And he needed to relieve himself, but that meant going *out there*. He could hold it.

"Think about something else," he exclaimed.

Secret things. Pleasant things. Like Megan Whitlock. The only bright spot about having lived with Grandma Cartwright in Soldier during the past year was meeting Megan Whitlock, the prettiest girl in the fifth grade, the prettiest girl he had ever seen: dark hair and big brown eyes, eyes that could gobble up a boy the way Pac-Man gobbles up ghosts.

Before Christmas they'd traded school pictures.

He reached into his back pocket and retrieved her photo. The palm in which he cupped it sweated freely. When he looked down at his hand, he saw that the back of the photo was stuck to his sweaty skin. He peeled the treasure away only to discover that the blue ink in which she had printed her name was so smeared that no single letter was decipherable.

But then, of course, that didn't matter. He knew her name.

"Oh, man," he whispered as he turned the photo face

up and looked into brown eyes that bounced him off the walls of the tree house like a ping pong ball.

Then he remembered one thing more.

With his flashlight he searched the far corner, a secret place where the floor met the right angle of the walls. There it was: his secret thoughts ritualized into markings meaningful only to himself. In pencil, he had scribbled "R.C. + M.W." within the borders of a heart. It was one of the first things he had done when he returned to the tree house after running away from Grandma Cartwright's.

That was yesterday, and now yesterday seemed but an illusion.

Through the high angle of the porthole he could see faint flashes of lightning in the distance. And that brought new fears. How dry would the tree house be during a hard rain? Where else could he go? What if there were a storm . . . another tornado?

"Dear Lord Jesus, no," he murmured.

And if the storm doesn't drive you out, he thought, what if whatever is waiting in the darkness does? Or what if he were trapped forever in the tree house?

His stomach growled again, louder this time.

How had he gotten into such a mess, he wondered.

The voice.

Why had life turned out to be one long, continuous night journey?

The voice.

Why had he become a runaway?

Runaway.

The word had a hollow frightening sound, a little like some incurable disease, some condition that was irreversible. A kind of damnation.

101

His thoughts grew colder, ice-tinged.

What would Megan think? Would she miss him at school? Would anyone? He could imagine his empty desk, his classmates whispering about him in the hall. His grandmother would have notified the school, of course, that he was missing. Would the police be looking for him? And what . . . what would his mother have thought about him? Disappointment. Yes, that was the worst part.

"We're very disappointed in you," the ghostly words echoed from some dark chamber in his memory. He was glad she would never know.

He wished now that absolutely no one knew where he was. But one person knew. He couldn't keep from telling someone. He and his friend, Bobby Lee Hollins, had been walking home from school two days ago . . .

Bobby Lee was jammering obliviously about playing baseball that summer and the prospects for his separated parents to get back together. Somehow the two topics were connected. Ronnie waited for a pause in Bobby Lee's ramblings to dart in with his decision.

"I'm going back to Half Moon, but don't you dare tell anyone."

Bobby Lee Hollins was a short, thin, hapless boy with an old face, made older and more pathetic because of a harelip and a glass eye. He was the kind of boy who needed a friend so desperately that Ronnie couldn't resist befriending him. When Bobby Lee, more than slightly incredulous, soaked in the full import of Ronnie's comment, he seemed to shrivel like a wintering kudzu vine. His one good eye flitted, and he spoke with a nervous bleating intonation, a voice that sounded remarkably like a terrified sheep.

"Whatcha want do that for?"

Ronnie stared into the less-wretched side of Bobby Lee's face.

"Because it's . . . because it's . . . *my home*," he stammered, and then cleared his throat. He said nothing about the voice.

"Ronnie?"

"Yeah, what?"

"Well . . . listen, thanks for telling me whatcher gone do. And I promise I won't tell nobody, no way, never. I really won't."

Silence.

Bobby Lee screwed up his face. "Geez, you're really gone do it, ain'tcha? Man, . . . juss running away . . . juss like that."

Ronnie nodded. Then, goaded by some impulse he didn't understand, he frowned at Bobby Lee and reached out to touch his shoulder.

"Maybe I'll see you someday. I'm going tonight . . . after dark."

Bobby Lee's crooked mouth gaped as he watched his friend sprint ahead, as if to signal that the running away had officially started.

The growl of his empty stomach suddenly brought the present back in full force. He needed to find food. He had emptied his box of snack crackers long ago. But was he hungry enough to face the darkness? And where would he find food? Scouting around earlier in the day, he had discovered one possibility. He had promised himself to try it after dark . . . if he could muster the courage.

Wings whispered above him.

For a moment he forgot about his stomach. Had some of his racing homers returned, searching for their lofts? The boy pressed his face through the porthole, hoping, scanning the branches above him for a glimpse of them. He wanted to believe in his pigeons, in the power of that supernatural sense which directed them back to Half Moon no matter where he might release them. They apparently believed in him, for they, along with Joe the crow and the wounded hawk, had guided him home.

Mostly, he wanted to identify with the beauty and strength of these birds, especially their delicate, yet proud heads and their sensitive eyes. He knew that you could judge a good racer by its eyes: if it had distinct color in both the inner and outer circles of the iris, if the colors didn't blur.

He longed to see one of those magnificent heads again and the artistry of his homers in flight. But there were immediate needs to attend to first. It was time to take a chance on leaving the security of the tree house.

Flashlight in one hand, broken BB gun in the other, the boy edged his way through the tarpaulin door and placed a foot on the highest of the slats nailed into the tree trunk. He sprayed the darkness with light. And saw nothing threatening . . . no stalking creature . . . no waiting menaces.

Cautiously he waded through his backyard, now

strangely unfamiliar, into the narrow weed-choked alley, nursing a certain pride in the fact that he was taking care of himself. Surviving. And that pride buoyed him for another thirty feet. Then his heart folded upon itself as if responding to the touch of something extremely cold.

He was being followed.

CHAPTER 8

"For heaven's sake, lit-tul men . . . let's us calm down. Y'all gone have to be calming down, don'cha see. Be good lit-tul men."

Pressing the large Tupperware bowl of popcorn against her stomach, Molly Harvester lifted her chin high, reaching within herself to maintain control over her voice. She trembled, arched her eyebrows, and spoke again in her soothing yet firm drawl.

"Sit, now. Sit. Y'all must stop this racket. My land's."

She forced a smile, but behind the smile fear crowded threateningly.

"I have popcorn for my lit-tul men . . . and now we will sit and listen to the Philco . . . and wait for Mr. Carl, don'cha know. But we must calm down."

The three small terriers danced at her feet, barking excitedly; their eyes were fixed expectantly upon the old woman as she shook a bony arthritic finger at them. The dogs sensed what was outside and instinct set them spinning like tops. Moments earlier their barking had subsided, but then a distant jangling of bells had filtered through the back screen door, reanimating them.

"Stop it, now. For heaven's sake. Mercy, now, let's stop this. Fritzie. Tiny. Freddie. No popcorn for y'all. No Philco, if y'all gone be bad lit-tul men."

Two of the dogs danced into one another, causing the older one, the one with gray peppered on his black snout, to growl and snap.

"Goodness, no!" the old woman shrieked. "What is going on?"

Her tone was indignant, the chosen stuff of reprimand. "Fritzie, Tiny . . . what would Mr. Carl think of y'all? Good heavens! Oh, for shame! Be good lit-tul men. No more crossness, now . . . do y'all hear me?"

The older dog sat and whined softly as if embarrassed and contrite. But the other dog kept his distance. The third dog pirouetted on his hind legs, suddenly more interested in the promise of popcorn than anything else.

"This is better. Be gentlemen. That's right."

She sat down in an overstuffed chair bunkered with small square pillows. One at a time, each dog eagerly reached for a piece of popcorn, carefully placing his paws on her knees as if praying before an idol. As her dogs crunched their popcorn, she listened. Half Moon was stirring. She was confused and frightened. A gunshot, the jangling of bells earlier, and the appearance of a white van that afternoon—what could they mean?

She masked her apprehension with a pleasant tone.

"I'll turn on the Philco now, and we can eat our popcorn and enjoy some music. How does that sound, lit-tul men?"

The monolithic old radio, almost as large as a juke-box, responded slowly to her touch. The dogs turned and sat as if in human anticipation.

"Let's us let it warm up, now. It's old like your ole Miss Molly."

She forced another smile, but it was laced with hurt. In the radio's tuning shield, she saw her reflection, a face on the edge of panic.

"Mr. Carl will be coming back soon," she chortled. "He is so-o-o forgetful anymore."

The radio hummed and popped. Static muffled the signals.

"Mr. Carl thought one of y'all lit-tul men was out in the dark lost, and so he's gone out there looking and probably calling. I hope he doesn't stray too far. Doesn't hear well anymore, don'cha know."

The radio crackled and whistled sharply, sending the small dogs into another round of excited barking. The old woman eventually hushed them, but her nerves were growing brittle. Having broken her glasses a week ago, she struggled to read the number on the dial.

"Here. Here we are, now. Nice, pretty music."

Easy listening filled the room as the dogs resumed their begging posture at the old woman's knees and she continued to feed them. Her hand, however, stopped in mid-motion after a few seconds. She heard someone calling.

"Carl?"

Her hand trembled.

No, it sounds more like the voice of a child.

Then the music scrambled; static rasped, and a different signal emerged: a shrill, birdlike cry, a sound

108

that penetrated, a sound seemingly beyond the reach of the radio to produce. A sound that Molly Harvester recognized.

Windkiller! Took my Carl!

Frightened, the dogs leaped into her lap. The bowl of popcorn spilled out onto the seat cushion.

"No, lit-tul men," she cried. "My goodness. Oh, my goodness."

She pushed to her feet, scattering the dogs and the popcorn. Hurriedly she reached for the dial to switch off the macabre cry, but she turned it the wrong way at first, greatly intensifying the sound. The dogs whirled in a frenzy of barking, fur rising almost comically on their hackles.

"Oh my, no!" the old woman bleated before she managed to arrest the sound. She collapsed back into the chair and clutched her chest. Her face twitched uncontrollably. She closed her eyes and clasped the armrests for support. Her eyelids fluttered and tears began to slide down her cheeks.

Still whimpering, the dogs gathered at her feet, and one by one, timidly, they jumped back into her lap and nested in a circle, nosing one another for comfort. Their keen black eyes flickered with fear.

The old woman awakened as if from a swoon, dabbed at the corners of her eyes, and weakly smiled down at the quivering trio of dogs.

"Here, now. We gone be just fine. We are all jumpy because Mr. Carl isn't back yet."

Lovingly, she stroked the dogs and they responded by licking her frail fingers.

"Don't know what's gotten into the Philco," she murmured distractedly, tossing a bewildered glance

109

its way.

Windkiller. Something is going to happen. The creature is feeding on my fears.

The dogs watched her lips and jostled one another for more of her lap.

"Lit-tul men, we have spilled our popcorn and need to clean it up. What will Mr. Carl say when he sees the mess we have made? Oh, I know . . . y'all want some nice music, don'cha? Well, y'all see the Philco's not working right. So. So, y'all want me to sing . . . I suppose that's it."

She smiled faintly, arched her brows, and puppeted her head lightly from side to side. The song was couched in the rhythm of a lullaby.

"Oh-h-h lit-tul men, oh-h-h lit-tul men, you're my joy and com-fort . . . oh-h-h lit-tul men, oh-h-h lit-tul men, you're my fi-nest lit-tul men."

The words faded into tender humming. But as she hummed, she became aware of a curious and deep silence in the room and beyond.

"Lit-tul men . . . I best be looking out for Mr. Carl, now. He's been gone now much too long. Y'all get in your beds. Go on."

She slowly rose to her feet, brushing the dogs from her lap. Obediently they scampered to one corner of the room where there were gatherings of rags and brightly colored food and water dishes.

"Good. Fine lit-tul men," she called after them.

Stray kernels of popcorn crunched beneath her feet as she made her way to a window. The journey was not easy, for her living room was a labyrinth of clutter: boxes of books and magazines stacked and overflowing; pieces of antique furniture, some of which had

110

become makeshift shelving for old ashtrays; jars of buttons and marbles; a collection of thimbles; chipped cups; and an assortment of cheap ceramic figurines. One wall was dominated by a foursome of whatnot shelves brimming with an array of perfume bottles and decanters, few of them possessing monetary worth, but each filled with a priceless memory. Another wall was occupied by her pride and joy—a collection of owl figurines (two hundred forty-seven at last count), roosting on fine oak shelving purchased years ago by her husband, Carl. Lined along this miniature aviary were owls of every shape, color, and size. Most were made of glass; all were special to her.

The centerpiece of the collection was a large specimen, nearly two-feet tall, made of fine crystal—an anniversary gift. The old woman thought of it as her favorite and often gazed in admiration at its perfect feathers and its wise yet placid eyes.

Her attention fixed momentarily on the stunning figurine before she groped her way to a window.

"Carl . . . now, best be coming on in," she exclaimed.

Sprinkled in the darkness out beyond her window were small fires tended by shadows. She could smell their decay, and so could her dogs. She stared at the fires and patted her fingers nervously against her lips. Loneliness had taught her that if you look into the darkness long enough, it will look back at you.

Then it began.

The window rattled. It was the sound of a trapped bird.

A vibration, as if generated by an unseen wind or a sonic boom, shook one wall. And then another. It redoubled itself and the shelving of empty perfume

111

bottles caught its rhythm and the glass started to chatter gently. Then more intensely.

The old woman stroked her throat with one finger and her head began to jerk spasmodically. The vibration of the wall spread.

"Oh, merciful heaven," she whispered. "Oh, Carl."

Like frightened children, the three dogs bolted from their corner and raced to the old woman's feet, barking, spinning, and jumping excitedly. But she took little notice of them. The hand that had been stroking her throat was extended in a gesture of helplessness. It was pointed toward her owls. The vibration had seized that wall; the oak shelving rippled ever so slightly.

The owls began to dance.

The undulation heightened, and on the center shelf the crystal owl, as if on a revolving pedestal, was turning, edging forward.

"No, please no!" she cried.

She moved toward it, but in slow motion, weighted down by fear.

The owl spun and tottered.

Elsewhere in the room other bottles and figurines plunged to the floor and shattered. The old woman saw only the crystal owl . . . and its eyes . . . no longer the wise and placid expression . . . now it bore a sinister and malevolent countenance.

It was about to fall. She reached frantically to save it.

With her fingers clasped around the owl, she stood perfectly still. Something like an electrical charge seemed to pass from the owl to her fingers and then to the rest of her body.

A frozen brightness streamed into the room, but the

old woman's eyes darkened. Grew cold and distant.

There was thick tension in the air as her hand locked onto the owl with the strength of predatory talons. Time spiraled and the vision began to unfold.

She and her little dogs were in a cavernous, shadowy room. But they were not alone. Surrounding them were others—two men and a boy, familiar looking, yet she could not quite identify them.

There was a long-faced, grief-stricken man; the other man was bearded and heavily muscled, but madness dulled his eyes. And there was a boy, blanched with fear and confused. The three of them joined the old woman around a light. A bond of purpose seemed clearly to have fused the foursome so that their shadows were one.

Then the vision momentarily blurred; its angle widened, allowing the old woman to see that below the four figures there appeared a great auditorium of mottled darkness, peopled with shadows and ghosts. In their midst, dominating the scene, was Windkiller, the creature of Christmas Oak, controlling the preternatural denizens.

Windkiller began its cry. And the men and the boy and the old woman nodded toward sleep. For each, this creature of the unseen world was preparing a dream, a Windkiller-begotten hallucination. The creature would feed upon their fears. Each would experience a nightmare given life.

Abruptly the cry ceased.

The old woman blinked awake. Her lips moved, but there was no articulation of words.

The frozen brightness streamed away, and with

agonizing slowness, she removed her fingers from the crystal owl.

Molly Harvester held onto the broom as if it were the only thread of reality available. The vision, the ESP flash, had faded. The vibration had stopped. The dogs had settled, but even as they curled chins over one another's bodies, each kept a tense gleaming eye on her. She was sweeping up broken glass, taxing her memory to identify which perfume decanters had shattered and which owls, if any, had met a similar fate.

And, most of all, she was thinking hard about what the vision might mean.

Through one window, she noticed a filigree of lightning on a distant horizon—or was it the flickering of one of the sentry fires? Demon fires tended by shadows. Windkiller's torches. Tonight there seemed to be more than she had ever seen before.

The broken glass sparkled with its own mixture of fire points that tinkled as she swept the glass from the badly worn rug onto the hardwood floor, where a dustpan waited. She swept the entire room, and yet there was more glass, always more glass, crunching beneath her house slippers, skittering away from the advance of the broom. It seemed to sprout from the rug, reproducing itself geometrically like some bizarre crystal.

She swept faster, her fingers tightening on the broom handle until she felt that she would not be able to release it. The multiplication of glass began to merge in the center of the rug and then to pool into an oval mirror. Her reflection, popeyed with fear, stared back at her. And that was enough. The sound that escaped from her trembling mouth was a throaty gurgle, something on the edge of terror.

With half-stumbling steps, she managed to lean the broom against a wall and sink into a chair next to the card table where she often worked puzzles. The terriers pricked up their ears, relaxing them only after she buried her face in her hands and seemed, at least to them, to nod off.

"Oh, Molly . . . get a hold of yourself," she mumbled.

She glanced at the shelves of owls.

"Grandma," she muttered to herself. The owls always reminded her of her Grandma Rice, who'd once told her: "Molly dearest, in our beautiful South when old folks die, well, don'cha know, they don't die at all . . . they become owls."

Apprehension stabbed at her.

Life's taking something away from me again.

It had started early in her life, when her older sister, Rose Ann, bullied her, stole hair ribbons and jewelry from her, and once, even her boyfriend.

Later, cancer took her mother; heart disease, her father. In return, life gave her Carl, the best husband a woman could possibly have—a man who for forty years served as Half Moon's postmaster and rural mail carrier. The war borrowed him for two years and sent him home hard of hearing, compliments of a shell exploding too near his foxhole. Half Moon welcomed him back as a hero. So did Molly.

She loved Half Moon because Carl loved it. He wanted nothing more than to live in this east Alabama

115

hamlet and raise a family and love his Molly and tolerate her eccentricities. Molly, his "weird little princess," as he was fond of calling her.

"Carl, I tried so hard to give you children."

She'd carried two full-term babies. Oh Lord, she reflected, life took them for no reason. Through everything, Carl stood by her, a calm and infinitely patient man, who was totally devoted to her. Such was the steadfastness of his fidelity that friends would often joke with her about trading husbands.

"What's your secret, Molly dear? Share it with your friends, won'cha?"

The companionship she enjoyed with Carl aged like fine wine. And their "little men," the three terriers, filled the void of life without children.

Then the storm.

In the ensuing months, neighbors, distant friends, and even the county sheriff, tried to talk Molly into leaving Half Moon.

"Molly Harvester, why there's nothing left here for you. Everybody else's leaving. Not even the banker is staying around. Half Moon's down. You'll be here all by yourself," they said.

But Molly stayed.

And once every morning and once every evening, she ritualized her grief with an unsteady pilgrimage to that spot beyond the former site of the utility shed . . . the spot where the storm and a winged creature had devoured her Carl. Her little men would trail along, a kind of sadness in their eyes as if some glimmer of understanding penetrated their animal oblivion.

These sojourns, however, failed to satisfy Molly, and thus occasionally she would fire up her worse-for-wear

116

Pinto, shuttle her little men into the back seat, and slowly cruise the town and the area roads. It was a pathetic sight. Still in all she kept her vigil, waiting out the hot summer months, the melancholy of fall, and the chill of winter, while everyone else abandoned hope in the future of Half Moon.

Release from the apprehension came slowly.

Get a hold of yourself, Molly.

Some hot tea and a few saltines would help, she decided. So she fixed herself an evening snack, stopping once to let Freddie, the most adventuresome of the terriers, out the back screen door. But the normally high-spirited dog returned quickly, growling, obviously frightened.

"See your shadow out there, lit-tul man?" she smiled down at the jittery dog. She reminded herself that she should latch the screen before returning to the living room.

Minutes later, she felt much better. Sitting in her overstuffed chair, she cautiously sipped at her tea, blinking her eyes rapidly as wisps of steam rose from the cup. The terriers, like small children, reassembled at her feet, hoping for a snatch of cracker.

But at first she paid them no heed. Her moments of relaxation were passing; her thoughts kaleidoscoping to darker matters: the vision, for example, and her decision months ago to stay in Half Moon when everyone else had left.

Suddenly she glanced at the expectant terriers and smiled.

"We stayed, lit-tul men, because Mister Carl told us

117

to. He said . . . he said for us to wait right here . . . and that's what we've done, don'cha see."

She fought a welling of tears, tears of recognition—for weeks earlier she had finally admitted to herself that her Carl would never return. Still, she maintained the pretense. It was, she reasoned, a strange and sad, and yet somehow hopeful, world. And what could it hurt to pretend?

"Mister Carl . . . he loved Half Moon, lit-tul men."

From beneath the chair cushion she fished out a ragged handkerchief and patted at the corners of her mouth.

"I love it, too."

She paused and composed herself, punctuating the gesture with a brave smile.

"Let us look at our favorite book, lit-tul men," she exclaimed, and rose to retrieve her well-thumbed copy of *Southern Memories: The History of Half Moon, Alabama.*

The terriers stirred; one softly whined.

Fingers trembling, the old woman opened the book. It was her Bible. Since a teenager, she had been interested in the past. Over the years, in fact, she and some of her closest friends, fellow lovers of local history, had formed the Half Moon Historical Society and had gathered every so often to share their particular devotion.

But the storm and the ravages of old age had dissolved the group. And now only Molly's best friend, Carmilla Carfax, survived, and she had chosen to live out her days at Elderness, a retirement center in the nearby town of Goldsmith. And that left Molly alone with her book of history and her increasingly dark thoughts about the haunted remains of Half Moon and the legend of Windkiller—and how she'd obtained her knowledge of it.

Carmilla Carfax, knowing of Molly's fascination with various versions of the legend, had acquainted her years ago with a local woman, Zephra Firethorn, who claimed that her mother, a full-blooded Creek, was well-versed on the subject of Windkiller.

One Saturday Carl had driven Molly and the Firethorn woman to the northern part of Catlin County, to a tangle of red-clay, pulpwood roads near a rather large body of water known as Moon Lake. According to Zephra, the lake itself was a locus of magic for her elderly mother, who believed that its water had restorative powers.

That Saturday long ago, as they'd approached a pinewood and tarpaper hovel, the abode of Zephra's mother, Zephra had told of her black father, of his death, and of a ritual that her mother performed almost daily. From hyacinth-choked Moon Lake, the old woman would draw a small pitcher of water and pour it onto her husband's crude grave, certain that it would free the man's spirit and allow it to reside with her in her hovel, thus staving off the lonely nights. And just as the old woman believed in the ghostly powers of Moon Lake, so too did she believe in the malevolence of Windkiller.

"The Windkiller creature, before it was driven from Christmas Oak, drank only from the waters of Moon Lake," Zephra had said. "That is what my mother believes."

119

Into the dark and squalid hovel Zephra had led Carl and Molly that day.

"Momma Nanwha?" Zephra whispered.

The shadows had stirred and a face, small and monkeyish, had leaned forward.

"Momma Nanwha, these people come to learn about the Windkiller creature. Will you teach them?"

Molly had stared at the diminutive old woman whose high cheekbones and long, silver-gray hair carried the sheen of wisdom—or perhaps madness—Molly could not be certain which. For the next hour, Molly had listened as Momma Nanwha had talked and her daughter had translated a fantastic interweaving of myth and visions and beliefs about the powers of Windkiller.

"But will the creature ever return?" Molly had pressed.

"My mother says, 'Yes. Dark winds will bring it back to Half Moon one day to destroy and to spread despair,'" Zephra had answered.

"Can anything oppose it?" Molly had queried.

And the response, through Momma Nanwha, that Zephra delivered had sealed itself forever in Molly's consciousness.

Courage and love will blind Windkiller. But only the bravest warrior, aided by friendly spirits, can defeat the creature.

Suddenly Molly closed the book. The terriers tensed; each eyed her with a precise expectancy.

She shook her head; it seemed a kind of hopeless gesture.

120

"Where is our courage and love, lit-tul men? Where is Half Moon's bravest warrior?"

The room began to chill, not because of the approaching storm, but because of the inner dread she felt. She wished that she had a friend close-by to talk with . . . someone to tell her that she was thinking foolish thoughts.

Carmilla; wonderful, brash, and crazy Carmilla would be perfect. If only. . . .

With paper and pen, she did the next best thing.

Dearest Carmilla,

So lonely tonight I thought I'd cheer myself up with note to you. Yes, I know. How long has it been since I've written? Too long, for such a precious friend! I don't deserve you!

How is Elderness? Great, I'm sure. And your presence there makes it even better as the other residents have found out by now. Do they know you're really a witch yet? Queen of the Night! Ha! Guard your secrets, dearie!

Any elderly gentlemen there you plan to weave a spell on? A little behind-the-scenes witchcraft? Ha! Ha!

You know, just getting these few lines down on paper has already done wonders for me. I don't feel nearly as—

She hesitated as one of the terriers growled. Faint, scratchy, shuffling noises carried through the pre-storm calm.

There was someone in the kitchen.

Before fear blocked out reason, she chided herself

121

for not latching the screen.

Forgetful old woman. Deserve whatever happens to you.

She listened, too frightened to swallow or take a breath. The terriers shifted apprehensively. Who could it be? Who would be roaming about in her backyard? Who would . . . ?

The upsurge of warmth lifted her from her chair.

"Oh, Carl . . . Carl . . . oh, he promised me he would," she cried eagerly as she reached the shadowy doorway to the kitchen.

"I waited right here . . . right here."

A cupboard door slammed and there was a blunted exclamation of surprise.

Molly's words broke off in a scream.

"Who's there?"

And the silhouette of a boy rushed out and quickly blended into the night.

CHAPTER 9

Taylor scoured the spot where he had left Shepherd. By day the grassless patch of clay was red orange, the color of a new basketball, but the cover of night shaded it to gray.

The spot transfixed him. At that moment he could easily believe that some trapdoor in the earth had slid open and disposed of his friend. Then he began to reason: he couldn't have gotten far. Not far. What's happened? The strain of the return to Half Moon must have been too much for him.

Taylor widened his search.

God in Heaven, what's happened to Shep? Gone mad? Coming back broke his mind?

Confused and frightened, Taylor calmed himself with an emphatic vow: *I'm not leaving Half Moon without him.*

Thunder murmured low to the south. Lightning flickered intermittently, and ground-level gusts of wind touched off swirls of dust around him. The school itself seemed the obvious place to start looking, yet he walked the boundaries of the schoolyard first, just to satisfy himself that Shepherd hadn't crawled to one side or the other of the building. Finding nothing, he was on the sidewalk facing the entrance to the school, its black outline more intimidating than it had ever seemed before.

Built in 1922, the three-story, red brick monolith had passed the tests of time, standing solid, fulfilling the educational needs of Half Moon's youth. Until the early 70s, the building had housed not only the high-school grades but all of the elementary grades as well. It had been like one big happy family of Half Moon children converging on the edifice each school morning, learning, maturing, struggling with all the little atrocities youth must face. Rites of passage and all that.

The school had always been a bastion of optimism. And despite its disrepair, Taylor saw it that way now. Of course, the beautiful oaks standing to the left of the front side were denuded, and most of the school's windows were broken or missing completely. The school gymnasium, which jutted out as a rectangle to the rear of the building, had roof damage, but otherwise the building had weathered the destruction of Half Moon. Even the school bell and the small belfry housing it remained atop the central building, fiercely holding their positions.

The oval of his powerbeam played across the wide brick front, dotting into black squares when it passed over a window. He was surprised by the brick, for it had the look of patina, a faint green coating, as if bronze had oxidized there. It was the rough sheen of old leather. Like everything else in town, the building needed refurbishing. It could function again, though,

124

Taylor believed. As before, it could be the heart of the community . . . the real spirit of the town.

The thought buoyed him as he stepped to the front door.

Something glimmered on the first step. He reached down and picked up his revolver. Shep must have dropped it here . . . must be inside, he thought to himself as he tucked the revolver in his belt. He swung open one of the double doors; the heavy chain that had kept them closed fell to the steps. It had been snapped cleanly at one of the links. Not sawed but snapped. He examined the break, concluding that vandals must have had a heyday in the abandoned school.

Once inside, he hunkered down, and with the power-beam traced a double line of footprints across the dusty foyer toward one of the main stairwells to the left. The smell of mildew and disuse permeated the air. Plaster dust from the flaking and cracking walls filled the stair-well with a thin white fog that blunted his powerbeam somewhat. The high ceiling and dark wood finish of the foyer trapped the silence and dank, dusty air.

He walked cautiously to the stairs and rested his left hand on the dust-covered newel post while he shined his light up the shrouded spiral of steps reaching to the third floor. Cobwebs were etched into the corners of many steps and some hung from the high corners of the stairwell like Spanish moss.

"Damn," he muttered involuntarily. A bead of sweat trickled down his rib cage.

The footprints, bordered by other indistinguishable marks, followed a consistent path up the first flight of steps. Obviously Shepherd had more physical strength than it had appeared earlier. But why in the world had he climbed the stairs?

Taylor put his hand to the side of his mouth to funnel a call, but before he could holler, the bell atop the school began to ring. Its resonant clang echoed down the stairwell, seeming to swirl motes of plaster dust into gauzy patches.

"Jesus, what's he up to?"

Taylor's throat felt tight and dry.

The dull repetition of sound drummed on as he began to take the steps two at a time. He swallowed some of the dust and stopped twice to cough it out of his lungs. At the foot of the last flight, he leaned against the rail, his breathing labored, his legs aching as much from fear-generated anticipation as from fatigue. The blackness above him seemed impenetrable; the harsh clanging was now louder and more discordant, echoing and reechoing, expanding and filling the dark cavity ahead.

Then suddenly the ringing stopped, died away, its fading afterechoes pulsating in his ears.

"Shep? It's Dale. Where you at?"

There was no response except for a shuffling, skittering noise from the roof. It was most likely the wind in advance of the storm front, tearing at a loose flap of tarpaper. As silence recaptured the stairwell, he noticed a change in the air. Cooler. More dank. He shivered once, arching his shoulders against the back of his neck. Though he told himself it was only his imagination, he took one step and his foot slipped as if coming into contact with a thin coating of moisture. Like a cave floor.

His sense of direction tilted. The dark labyrinth of the stairwell turned upside down. The cave walls narrowed, the plaster dust became pinpricks of ice, and the ceiling dripped muddy lime-colored drops of moisture. He could hear the voice of his grandfather warning him, warning him and Shepherd about something. But it was not about a cave. The stone walls of his grandfather's cistern encircled him like a sleeve; the railing was stone, etched with moss. He clung to it desperately. Either way he flashed the powerbeam, above or below, blackness blunted the light. He fought the dizzying sensation that he was about to fall.

God in Heaven, Shep is at the bottom! Grandpa warned us!

"Shep! Shep, are you down there?"

His call bounced from ceiling to floor at the top of the stairs. He pulled himself to the final step and the cistern memory instantly faded. Bracing himself against a wall, he rubbed his eyes and steadied himself.

Got to get out of here.

"Shep . . . I know you're up here. Come on. We're going home now."

He reached the first classroom, sliding past metal lockers, several of which were open and layered with dust and cobwebs. As he entered the room, he instinctively fanned the light across the door leading to a narrow stairway which, in turn, angled up to the belfry.

"Shep?" he whispered.

The door to the belfry was ajar. He felt foolish being so cautious, but he inched the door open, half holding his breath.

"Shep? Shep, are you up there?"

His question seemed to hang in the air. What his light discovered nailed him to the doorframe with a stroke of revulsion: thick layers of dust, *undisturbed* layers of dust, blanketed each step, and, halfway up, whorls of cobwebs and spiderwebs matted into a curtain which closed off the belfry.

"There's nobody up there, Dale."

Taylor juggled the light as he whirled around.

"Shep! Damn, you scared me!"

The powerbeam found him, hunched in the far corner of the empty room, his long hands resting atop his knees. His tiny Bible dangled between a thumb and forefinger. His eyes, tossing back the light as amber dots, were somehow too bright, too much like the eyes of a madman.

Taylor slowly released his breath.

"I've been looking all over for you, Shep. Why didn't you let me know where you were? I mean, my God, I didn't know what had happened . . . you should've waited until I brought the van back, you know." He felt like he was scolding a young child.

"I told you I can't leave, Dale." Shepherd's voice was so calm it was frightening. "Please shine the light out of my eyes, Dale," he added.

"Oh . . . oh, sorry."

Self-consciously, Taylor dropped the angle of the powerbeam. Then, after hesitating, he stepped closer to his friend, his mind racing to decide what to say next.

"The bell . . . I heard you ringing the bell and—"

"It wasn't me, Dale."

Taylor chuckled nervously.

"Well, Shep, I heard it . . . who the hell was it then, if it wasn't you? I mean—"

"The wind, Dale. Maybe it was the wind. The wind calling the darkness. Maybe it was the wind."

Taylor hunkered down in front of him, close enough

that he could have reached out and touched his foot. The powerbeam sprayed off to one side.

"Shep . . . now listen to me," he replied softly. "I know that something . . . that you thought you saw something earlier . . . gave you a bad scare. And hell, I mean, the town kinda gives me the creeps, too . . . the way it is now, I mean. But everything's going to be all right now, you see. We're going to get in the van and go on home."

Shepherd's head lolled to one side. "Half Moon *is* our home, Dale," he intoned.

Taylor put one knee to the floor and shifted his position. "I know that . . . I know that, Shep. Half Moon used to be our home. We grew up here . . . and . . . and one of these days soon, when the town is going again, why, you and I will come back and live here again. But right now—"

"I explained before, Dale. I read the passage to you. I explained about the hoofprints . . . how I'm marked. I've got to stay and fight. The Windkiller has returned."

He turned at the pages of his Bible with his forefinger.

"No, damn it all, Shep," Taylor hissed. "Don't give me that—it's just a legend, a story. You can't believe that."

His hands were trembling from the welling of anger. "Shep, I'm through listening to all this nonsense. Now I'm going to take you by the arm and we're going to walk back down those stairs and leave. Do you understand that? I'm not leaving you here, now, that's all there is to it."

He clamped one hand on Shepherd's forearm, but the other man firmly removed it.

129

"Windkiller, Dale. My grandfather told me. Shadows and ghosts and doleful creatures . . . from Christmas Oak. The creature's making me one of them. Marked. I can't let you be touching me. You need to leave here while you can. The bell . . . they'll be coming here soon . . . Windkiller and his dark forces. Half Moon . . . we cut down the tree . . . the sacred oak. Windkiller's going to make us suffer."

Taylor stood up and backed away a few feet. Out the row of windows he could see an occasional flash of lightning, hear an accompanying rumble of thunder. He calculated another hour before the thunderstorm would arrive.

Then his hand slipped over the handle of the revolver.

No, for Christ's sake, that'll be a last resort. Calm yourself down and talk sense, and he'll go without force.

"Okay, Shep, let's . . . let's talk things over," he replied, but his words sounded empty. Hollow. He had the unnerving feeling that he was speaking to a total stranger. Then Shepherd responded.

"It's not safe for you to stay, Dale. But the choice is yours. Me . . . like I told you . . . I have to stay and fight . . . I can't leave now. Ever."

Preacher ways. It was that spell-casting tone. But the voice of this gentle giant was laced with dread and regret. A funereal tone.

Taylor was unsure what to say next.

"But maybe . . . I mean, I'm thinking . . . well, maybe you're wrong, Shep. About having to stay and fight, I mean." Confidence began to return to his voice.

"We've both had a long day, Shep. Maybe we should

just relax awhile and then decide what we ought to do."

Shepherd neither moved nor spoke.

"Listen, I've got an idea. I know what will fix us up," Taylor exclaimed as the illusion of control held sway. "I've got my backpacking stuff in the van. I can bring up my little two-burner campstove and brew us some coffee. There's water in that other Thermos I brought. Course, all I've got is instant, but it sounds good to me. How about you?"

"You don't have to stay with me, Dale," Shepherd muttered. "It's not safe."

"We'll talk about it, Shep. I'll fix us some coffee and we'll talk."

Handling the equipment gave him a chance to consider the situation. The obvious choice seemed the best: stay and talk, humor him, let the shock pass, and he will agree to leave. Shepherd was normally a calm, rational man. Whatever had disturbed him couldn't overcome his cool reason for long. He'll see it my way before much longer, Taylor concluded.

Down at the van, he decided to load all of the portable equipment into one carrying unit so that he wouldn't have to make a second trip. The stairwell played tricks on his imagination. No use giving it any extra opportunities.

The storm continued to advance; a hard spring rain seemed likely.

Returning to the third floor, Taylor lifted free the heavy pack and began spreading equipment and other materials in the center of the room. Shepherd hadn't moved, and said nothing as he watched Taylor unpack methodically: two Dacron sleeping bags, a lightweight cotton blanket, a nesting set of cooking utensils, a portable two-burner stove, a hatchet, a gasoline lantern, and a pouch of dry goods including packets of instant coffee, chocolate, and soup.

"Here we are. All the comforts of home," Taylor exclaimed.

The lantern circumscribed them with a rough circle of light, filling the rest of the room with shadows that danced weirdly as Taylor set about boiling water for coffee. The third-floor light could be seen from nearly any vantage point in Half Moon.

"My Boy Scout habits are going to pay off for us, Shep. Plenty of light and hot coffee will make us both feel better."

Shepherd stared blankly at him, mumbled something inaudible, and then surveyed, with a childlike fascination, the play of shadows on the wall near the door. Taylor raised his head, searched his friend's face for some sign of the old Jack Shepherd . . . the sensitive and sane man he had known for years.

In a matter of minutes they were drinking the coffee in silence, a silence that lasted until Shepherd set his cup to one side and rested his forehead against his knees.

"Want some more coffee, Shep?"

There was no response. Shepherd seemed to have fallen asleep.

Poor guy's exhausted, that's all. Let him sleep awhile and maybe he'll return to his senses. And so Taylor waited as his head buzzed with nervous exhaustion. He drank another cup of coffee and stared at his watch as it marked off the next five minutes.

He felt drowsy. The disparate noises of the old

school settling within itself lulled him. The wind moaned low as it swept now and again through the paneless windows. On the edge of sleep, at the entrance to a dream perhaps, he noticed a light in the hall, a light like the muted oval from a dim flashlight.

It was moving very slowly, but it was moving toward the doorway of the room that he and Shepherd occupied. The hardwood floors creaked as the light advanced. A rhythmic, high-pitched mewing seemed to be following the light, a stray vacant sound like that of a lost kitten.

Or, if he listened very closely, it was a single word repeated with childlike simplicity.

"Daddy? Daddy?"

Then another sound—another voice—an adult voice: warm, feminine, and yet ghostly.

"Dale? Dale, honey? Here. I'm here."

CHAPTER 10

Flecks of blood darkened the ragged scrape on his left palm. Knives of pain stabbed his wrist, and further up his arm fire points pricked and burned. And perhaps worst of all, he had crushed the box of saltines when he fell. He rolled onto his side and with his flashlight continued to examine his bloody palm. Bits of sand and dirt were embedded in the oozing blood. He dabbed the palm against his jeans, then licked at the wound and flexed his fingers. The blood and scraped flesh tasted bitter.

The saltine box was flattened, with one seam torn, revealing broken pieces of crackers through the cellophane package. Punishment. That's what it was.

God punishing me for stealing from an old woman who had nothing to protect her but tomcat-sized dogs. Why did I have to steal the crackers anyway? If I had told the old woman I was hungry, she would probably have given me something to eat. She wouldn't have turned away a boy, would she?

It's done, he scolded himself. Besides, you can't

"unsteal" something . . . you can't sneak back and put the saltines where you found them. Life doesn't work that way.

I've never stolen anything before.

He stood up and brushed himself off. Over his shoulder he could see a dim, lonesome light break up the shadow box that was Miss Molly Harvester's antique shop. Everybody called her "Miss Molly." Her scream had stayed with him. Suddenly he felt sorry for her. A poor old woman living alone except for her pets. Not very Christian to scare her like that. She didn't deserve it. Just like Granny Cartwright didn't deserve. . . .

Several blocks away the school bell began to toll. Thoughts of Miss Molly and Granny Cartwright dissolved. The boy felt the hair on the nape of his neck stir.

"Oh, man," he whispered. Who in the world could that be? The only sign of anyone else in town except Miss Molly was that white van. It might be someone sent to look for him. Part of him hoped it was. Part of him was confessing that running away was not such a good idea. He was hungry and lonesome and scared, and he sensed that something very strange was happening to Half Moon. All that he had imagined in his tree house, for example, and then the feeling of being followed as he made his way to Miss Molly's. Something or someone had been watching, waiting for him to leave the tree house. It had stopped following him a block from Miss Molly's.

Bobby Lee Hollins. That explained it. Maybe Bobby Lee had broken down and told someone where he was.

The tolling stopped.

Part of him was already racing toward the school,

racing toward whoever had been sent. Maybe somebody cared what happened to him. Tears threatened.

But what if it's somebody bad?

He angled the flashlight to either side of him, a mild
desperation rising within. He had lost track of the BB
gun. Must have dropped it around the antique shop, he
decided. No point in going after it.

Fear rekindled, he traced his way along the alley
until his tree house was in view, a black box lodged in
the oak as if last year's tornadoes had tossed it there.

Black box.

He slowed his approach and forgot about the school-
bell, and thought instead of his father.

Out of that stuff of memory, the shadows found sub-
stance to animate. Shadow magic. The face of his
father materialized. Blond hair and blue eyes . . . these
were clear to the boy even in the darkness. So was his
father's ready smile that always waited impatiently at
the corners of his mouth. A hair-trigger smile. One that
complemented an eager handshake. "Glad-hander."
That's how one of their neighbors, Glen Barlow, had
referred to his father.

Glad-hander in a black box. Grownups sure talk
funny, the boy thought to himself, momentarily distracted from his fears.

But the first image of his father had dissolved, melted
like a thin sheet of ice struck by a mid-morning sun.
Another image of his father's face replaced the first
one, a bedraggled, stubble-bearded face, red-rimmed
eyes. It was the countenance of a man whose life, weakened by the force of alcohol, had collapsed upon itself.
A black box face.

And the face of Death came next, bringing with it a

flash flood of new memories. Dark ones.

At the funeral of his parents, he had witnessed that face. His mother's casket, at the insistence of the funeral director, Wilson McFarland, had sensibly been left shut during the services at the Soldier Methodist Church. The storm had apparently transformed her soft, loving face into something . . . well, "unrestorable" was the word whispered around by relatives and others who had come to Granny Cartwright's home bearing casseroles and baked goods. *Unrestorable.* Such an ugly word.

They'd opened his father's casket. People filed by it, took one look, and then dropped their eyes. Kept their funeral masks on until they reached the safety of the sun-splashed morning air outside the church. The boy had sat in a second-row pew determined not to join the line of those paying his father their final respects. Only Granny Cartwright's tugging words of advice had changed his mind.

"Aren't you gone to give your daddy one last look?" she'd whispered to him, her eyes filmy with tears.

"No, Grandma. I don't want to."

He had squirmed on the hard slick surface of the pew, hoping she would let it go at that.

"Now, Ronnie, you'll regret this the rest of your life. Don'cha know if you don't see him this last time you'll never have made your peace with him. You'll never accept his death, don'cha see?"

Her whisper had cracked and splayed with emotion as she dabbed at her lips with a handkerchief.

Never accept his death.

It had that adult ring of wisdom despite the surface absurdity of the statement. So he joined the line. He shuffled along in it reluctantly, his eyes fixed on the stained-glass window on the far side of the church. A crucifixion scene. Christ's blood was a sickly purple, a shade darker than the lips of the man in the casket.

This is not my father, he thought at the time, a thought that bordered on a hope that some phenomenal mistake had been made. The man in the casket was dressed in a shiny, cheap-looking suit. The boy knew that his father owned no such suit, but when he'd mentioned it back at Granny Cartwright's that afternoon, someone had explained that it was a fake suit with only a front side. It saddened the boy to think that his father was not even buried in a whole suit.

It had saddened him even more to look at his father's peaceful, yet hard, cold face propped slightly on a silken blue pillow. It was an expression beyond sleep. When the boy managed to unlock his eyes from the death mask of his father, he'd done something that he would always regret. Reflexively, giving into a need to make some final contact, he'd reached toward his father's hands which were folded atop one another at his waist.

"Good-bye, Dad," the boy had whispered.

And touched the icy mound of marblelike flesh. And, in turn, it had sparked a chill that ran up his arm and plunged through his chest into the pit of his stomach. That chilled spot had radiated its cold once again the moment his father's death countenance had ghosted into view amid the shadows of the night.

*   *   *

Soft flutterings filled the darkness surrounding the monolithic oak and the square nest of the tree house. He speared the tree house with light. From thirty yards it seemed curiously unreal, in one piece, as so little else was in Half Moon. He released the "black box" memory and it floated away like a bubble. Wings battered the air with a feathery purr. Ghostly white reflections circled the tree, diving awkwardly as if something were pulling them with an invisible string. They bobbed in the air like tiny flaming kites with no tails, or like the white gloves of a magician in the middle of a trick.

The homers.

Warmth showered his throat. He tucked the box of saltines under his arm and stepped up his pace to the tree house. He'd known they would return. The only thing in his life he could count on. His beautiful homers.

He smiled broadly as the homers, now a dozen or more in number, cartwheeled and spun threads of the flashlight beam into quickly dissolving webs. Some looped and plunged close to the ground, seemingly confused. Had being on their own, in the wild so to speak, damaged their flight senses? He hoped they would roost in the oak. Somehow they knew that Half Moon was their home.

Within twenty feet of the tree house, he could see them more clearly. Most raced high above the oak, thrumming the air frantically as if being pursued. They sliced through the beam of light like flying torches, and when lightning flashed along the horizon they were momentarily extinguished. Several were clumsily perched above the tree house but didn't coo. The boy thought that was strange.

One thudded to the ground behind him, a soft ball of rags that spun around like a dying top.

"Come here, fella," said the boy as he turned.

He fished a saltine from the box and switched off the flashlight so as not to blind the bird. Then he squatted and held out the cracker.

"Come see what I have for you."

He chuckled as the bird strutted through the darkness, disregarded the cracker, and stumbled onto his wrist. There it fluttered, reeling back and forth to gain balance. The boy searched for the reflection of its golden eye, but it twisted its body and groped up his arm, continually flapping and lurching to maintain a hold on his jacket. He stood and extended his arm straight out from his body. Other pigeons joined the first one.

"Hey," he giggled. "You think I'm some kind of scarecrow?"

He extended his other arm so that he stood in proper scarecrow stance while three pigeons tottered back and forth from his wrist to his shoulder.

"I knew you guys would stay around," he exclaimed. "You're just like me. Half Moon is your home. You brought me back to my home."

One brushed against his cheek and ear before climbing onto his head. Its feathers were wet and smelled like overheated copper wire. He didn't like that smell.

"Hey, don't you guys coo any more? You used to." The bird on the boy's head crouched as if it were going to nest down in his hair. The other two huddled against his neck.

Then the boy touched moisture on his cheek. Even

before he switched on his flashlight, he knew the moisture wasn't water.

"You're hurt. You've been cut or shot," he stammered as he reached for one of the birds. "Let me take a look at you."

One from his shoulder settled on the back of his wrist as he carefully swung it around into the light. Calmly, it remained perched there in the spray of light.

It had no head.

Only a bloody stock of bone, pencil-thin, protruded from the white ball of feathers.

"Oh-h-h!" he shrieked and shook his wrist.

The headless birds struggled to get airborne. Once in flight they gradually descended until they hovered above him like huge hummingbirds. Another eight or ten homing pigeons, each headless, joined the others, steadying their flight so that they were only a few feet above him.

He felt as if a hot spear had been thrust into his chest. Too frightened even to scream, he grunted and thrashed at the air with his flashlight. He swung and swung, hitting nothing but darkness with the frantic beam. Finally his knees buckled and he fell, and the grunting turned to sobbing.

The feverish rhythm of the wings sounded like drums. Then, through the drumming, he heard another sound: a cry, tenuous and distant, and yet close—just as before. The birds rapidly gathered in a tight cloud and disappeared.

He scanned the sky, the oak, and the tree house. They were gone. Eyes blurred with tears, he doubted whether they had been real. No, it was impossible. He stayed on his knees, dazed, listening to his pulse hammer in his forehead. He wiped his nose on his jacket sleeve. A few involuntary sobs shook his chest. He switched off the flashlight.

In the shadow-strewn oak a black box was perched.

But, of course, it's the tree house, he reminded himself.

The tree house: the last remnant of home. He checked again for signs of the pigeons and thought about the strange birdlike cry. It was foolish to stay in Half Moon, but he needed to think. The tree house was the best place for that. Hugging the box of saltines and the flashlight against his heart, he grasped a rung of the ladder and took a deep breath. The pigeons, real or imagined, had shaken him, as had the cry. A patch of blood on his cheek, dried and crusted, was itching, but he forced himself not to stop and scratch it.

Run to the highway. Run somewhere for help. Miss Molly's. Anywhere.

You just imagined those pigeons, he told himself. They couldn't be . . . they couldn't fly around . . . like that. The tree house is the best place to be. At least until morning. In the morning things will seem different. If you run now, you're just running from yourself.

He was exhausted. Wearily he climbed another rung and paused again.

No heads!

Another step and he reached to push the tarpaulin flap aside.

But his hand stopped. He swallowed and it sounded like a bomb going off in his head.

Something inside the tree house began to jangle the cowbells.

He ran, ran wildly, blindly, clutching the box of

142

saltines and the flashlight to his stomach, fullback style. He ran a block into the darkness before something stopped him.

It descended into his path like a shimmering white cloud.

"Oh, man!" he whispered, his breath coming in vaulting gasps. Each lung burned like a torch.

His pigeons hovered, then swooped to one side, wheeling, seeming to maneuver him around as if they wanted him to follow.

"Okay," he exclaimed. "Okay, fellas, I'm coming."

They ghosted ahead.

Riveted with wonder, the boy smiled, then laughed in pure joy at the intricate movements of the headless birds.

Can they be real?

And then to his right he noticed something hopping along, keeping pace with his walking. He speared the object with his flashlight beam.

"Joe the crow!"

The bird's eyes shone with a marble-bright, maniacal yellow sheen.

And then to the boy's left, another movement.

The flashlight beam showered the wounded hawk as it thrashed the ground, moving straight ahead with the same degree of purpose as the crow and the flock of pigeons.

Where are they taking me?

One more block and he knew.

Dead in his path was the school, and a light burned in one of the third-floor rooms. The light seemed to reach out to him like the guiding light from a lighthouse.

But who was up there? he wondered.

A white van was parked in front of the school. He didn't recognize it except that it was the one he had seen that afternoon. Under nearly any other circumstance, he would have been relieved to see it.

But here, now—did it represent help?

His birds drew him on until he stood within thirty yards of the front door of the school. And there the voice—his persistent companion—seized his attention.

Come into my darkness, it said. *Come into my darkness forever.*

It felt as if something powerful, like a huge generator or a textile loom, had been switched on in his head. He could imagine that deep within the school there was a dark corridor, at the end of which small blue flames burned, eerily illuminating an altar. The corridor of darkness smelled of decay and death, yet it pulled him toward a black-curtained box in front of the altar.

Black box.

In his mind, the boy approached the mysterious box. And the curtain parted.

His face, his eyes . . .

In the black box . . .

Little pieces of himself . . .

Dad's face and oh God . . .

Like a ghost . . .

Just a mask . . .

Another mask mirrored forth from behind the mask of his father: malevolent sort of glee, hooded eyes, grim, owl-like head, rapacious beak . . . ready to take flight. A strong animal smell gradually fronted the smell of decay and death.

Behind the owl face was another face. He couldn't

see it, but somehow he knew there was another face. Something asleep.

Look-at-it-don't-look-at-it . . .

Look at it . . .

And you'll die . . .

Inside . . .

And become a ghost . . .

Even as he stepped toward the school and the dark vision faded, an evanescent cry filled his ears.

Above him, a feathery white cloudfall. The headless pigeons hovered, haloed him like tiny guardian angels with their heavenly voices forever stilled.

CHAPTER 11

At the doors to the school, the boy paused to watch the white blur of the hovering pigeons, to listen to the whisper-soft beating of their wings. They had led him to safety. Real or imagined, they had led him to the school, led him out of the swing of the storm and a menacing darkness.

He pulled open one of the doors and caught his breath reflexively. The foyer of the abandoned school, dust-laden and dispossessed, ticked with the fall of secret footsteps. It was as if someone had been waiting his arrival only to creep into hiding the moment he entered the building.

There was something more, and he sensed it there in the hollow darkness. Magically, it seemed, he had stepped into another world, an indefinite world, a world somehow without boundaries, a world listening to the ragged pattern of his heartbeat.

No, it's only the school!

Yet it carried the *feel* of something else. A depot of mystery and fear, with powerful forces moving through like midnight trains with no destination.

Locked into that uncomfortable sensation, the boy was barely aware of something stirring by his feet until the something shrieked as if deep in pain. And then the boy matched the shriek and stumbled to one side.

The wounded hawk shuffled past him, followed closely by the crow. In a matter of moments they had blended into the darkness of the foyer and disappeared. As if taking their cues from the hawk and the crow, the headless pigeons then poured through the door with a rhythmical whoosh, animating the blackness and the plaster dust before disappearing as suddenly as the other two birds.

The boy coughed and spit away the bitter taste of the dust. Like the motes of dust, his thoughts swirled, piecing out a confusing collage of reflections: the scrape on his palm, Miss Molly, the bell tolling, his father, *black box,* masks, and the birds. The birds. What seemed to possess them? Who controlled them?

Afraid to move, the boy stood and experienced the chilling sensation of ghostly hands reaching into his memory, groping around excitedly, searching for something he feared.

Welcome, the familiar voice in his head intoned. *I have a place for you here.*

As always, the voice was at once frightening and reassuring. A parental voice.

You know the place, it teased.

And he did. But until that moment he hadn't thought of it, for it was a place that never failed to evoke a penetrating fear in him. Now memory, coerced by the source of the voice, had surrendered what had been safely closeted for at least a year.

The fallout shelter.

"Oh, man," the boy whispered. A shudder gripped his shoulders and shook him like parent reprimanding child.

The fallout shelter.

In that instant, he realized that whatever had pulled him back to Half Moon, whatever dark quest was yet to unfold itself or whatever dreadful confrontation awaited him, the fallout shelter would play an integral role.

He also knew this: it was the last place on earth he would ever voluntarily seek out.

The fallout shelter.

To the boy, it was no shelter at all.

In the school's gymnasium, behind the stage, was a door that led down a half-dozen concrete steps to the fallout shelter. In his memory, the cavelike shelter was always dimly lit. Its low-watt bulbs transformed into primitive torches, suffusing the darkness with light, but an ineffectual light at best. It seemed, in his mind's eye at least, that the light would beat back the darkness there only to have it first retreat and then, by terrifying degrees, recover its former boundaries.

There could never be enough light in such a realm of predatory darkness.

Yet the shelter had its purpose. Its long, low, narrow corridor led to a massive, stomach-shaped inner area which could hold nearly one hundred fifty students and teachers—the entire populace of the Half Moon elementary, junior high, and high school. To this inner sanctuary, students, giggling, excited, and anxious, would be herded during civil-defense exercises.

The boy recalled the shelter's nests of cobwebs, its

moisture-laden concrete walls, and its stacks of boxes of "survival crackers," each box grimly labeled with the number of days that its contents would allow someone to exist "in the event of a natural or manmade disaster."

The entire shelter smelled of mildew, and, at times, one caught whiffs of something sour, as if someone had opened a refrigerator in which a container of milk was going bad. When filled to capacity, the shelter trapped a layering of additional smells from the crush of sweaty bodies and scores of pungent perfumes; the mixture produced a stifling, cloying atmosphere.

And the boy believed that the shelter even harbored an array of real or imagined tastes: the mealy, bland taste of soggy crackers and, worst of all, the slimy, sodden taste of moss and fungus. Leaning against one of the shelter's chill walls, walls as cold as the touch of the marble flesh of a corpse, those tastes would insinuate themselves when you covered your head as the teachers directed.

And you would hear your heart beat a message to your brain—perhaps a warning. Of course, there were other sounds. An occasional drip of water. The echo of the school settling above. The discordant conversation, laughter, and squeals of the kids.

Beyond all of these sensations, however, one impression dominated the boy's response to the shelter—one image wholly characterized his fear of the place—the belly of a beast. *Swallowed. I've been swallowed*, his mind would protest. For being in the shelter was like having been swallowed alive by some brick-and-concrete monster. And there, in the belly of a beast, you braced for the moment the beast's digestive fluids began to seep into and over you, signaling the first stage of a long, horrible, and inexorable process.

"No!" the boy exclaimed.

The present reasserted itself, and he hugged his flashlight and the box of saltines to his chest. The fallout shelter. Yes. Down there, down there is the darksome abode of the voice.

What must the place be like now, after a year of disuse? For a year no one had frequented that dark realm, that stifling underworld, that tapped so menacingly at the boy's imagination.

No one except the voice.

Lightning flashed. A shimmering blue curtain of light rose before him, and with its presence he felt a pull toward the hallway leading to the gymnasium and the fallout shelter.

No! I won't go there. I won't. Can't make me.

Resisting the pull, he switched on his flashlight and turned to the stairwell. Dust, cobwebs, plaster fog, and the roar of silence greeted him instead. He fought a strong urge to call out.

What if they're not friendly? a small voice asked. As he stepped toward the stairwell, he thought as hard as he could to recognize the white van outside, but it wasn't familiar to him.

Keeping the flashlight beam angled directly in front of him, he began creeping up the stairs, holding his mouth closed part of the time to keep from breathing in the plaster dust. He carried the box of saltines under his arm like a security blanket. Lightning sheeted across the high vacant windows at the top of the first landing, coloring the dustlike fog a crystal blue. Thunder rumbled in the southwest, close enough to vibrate the derelict building and give the boy cause to stop before negotiating the next step.

Confused, uncertain whether to go on, the boy rested on the first-floor landing. The old school settled around him, and the tortured creaking of the steps echoed in his ears. His lip quivered and he frowned. He hunkered down and nursed his sore palm with his tongue and lips. In the spray of the flashlight, the palm was patched with a bruised and blood-flecked purple. It needed a band-aid. The boy flexed his hand to ward off the growing stiffness. His throat was sore and exhaustion was beginning to tug harder at him.

He needed a grownup.

The admission kept him going, cautiously, one step at a time. He would pray and cross his fingers that whoever was on the third floor would help him.

The light drew Taylor as it would a moth. He thought of the hallucination earlier that evening.

Can't be Jennifer and Carol Mae. Can't be. But who is it?

Vandals. Crazy kids sneaking around in an abandoned school for kicks, he reasoned. They probably drove in from Soldier and parked their car on the edge of town. Probably brought girls with them, daring them to go into the school, playing up Half Moon's haunted reputation.

Oh, what the hell; I'd have done the same thing at seventeen, he admitted to himself. Ringing the school-bell, scaring adults . . . scaring themselves. Yeah, to be a kid again. To do a few things differently.

Near the door he glanced over his shoulder at Shep-

151

herd, who was still sitting with his back against a wall, head resting on his knees. The lantern light cast him half in shadow, a massive man casting an even more massive shadow.

Turning as if to say something to him, Taylor stared at his friend, now a stranger, swallowed back a few pointless words, and braced one hand against the door-jamb.

The faint semicircle of light in the hall was receding, drawing away tentatively. If there were footfalls, they were soft, ever so soft.

Shunning the use of the flashlight, Taylor licked his bottom lip and inched himself into the middle of the doorway. He glanced immediately to his right. But, at first, the swath of light upon the floor seemed to have no source.

"Who's there? Who is it? Come on out," said Taylor, with not quite the authoritative tone he had hoped to muster.

Behind the ribbon of light, a shadow materialized out of the wooden flooring, gradually taking shape, forming a small, but definably human countenance. Taylor squinted at it. His entire body felt numb.

"Jenny? Is . . . is that you?"

The shadow was like stone.

"What is it, Jenny?"

On the second-floor landing, the boy, flushed with curiosity and fear, listened intently to Taylor's ghostly questioning.

The man's bittersweet play of shadows continued.

"What is it, Jenny?"

Suddenly the shadow drifted toward him, insubstantial darkness and the suggestion of a face.

"What is it, babe?" He hunkered down to the level of the shadow.

Balancing first on one foot and then the other, the shadow whispered near his ear.

"I think I might need to cry a little."

Taylor smiled and reached for the shadow hands. "OK, hon. It's going to be all right, sugar babe."

Softly at first, a buzzing so faint it might have been trapped within a bell jar radiated out from the shadow.

And instinctively Taylor pulled back.

"Please, no."

The buzzing escalated. The shadow tottered. For the briefest of moments, he thought he saw the shadow face smile. But then the smile tore open and out of the Jennifer-shadow's mouth the ghostly bees began to pour, to release themselves from their false image, to swarm, to deflate the shape of the little girl as if it were a balloon.

Taylor staggered to his feet and looked away.

Womanly laughter filled the void left by the bees as they seemed to disappear through the floor. The naked sheen of Carol Mae's body drew his eyes. And the siren's voice, distant, yet seductive and inviting.

"Come for us. We need you. Come and take us away."

He knew it would happen, and with his first step in her direction, it did. The ghostly shape pooled, glimmered diamonds and ice, and was gone.

Taylor cowered back toward the room, convinced that the sensible part of his mind was breaking off, about to take flight like the imaginary bees. He felt cold and horribly lonely. He missed Jennifer and Carol Mae more at that moment than ever before. And maybe that explained everything. All the hallucinations. Grief-inspired hallucinations made all the worse because they were coming alive in the town he still loved.

Down on the second-floor landing, the boy continued listening to Taylor's interrogation of the darkness. He didn't recognize the voice, but it sounded like a grown-up's. Hopeful, he began edging up the next flight of steps.

Meanwhile, Taylor, repressing the effects of his ghostly encounter, found himself at Shepherd's feet.

"You ready to go now Shep? Why don't we get our stuff together and move on out ahead of the rain?" Shepherd didn't respond, so Taylor pressed on.

"We're both kinda tired. Our work here's done. Lotta memories here, but. . . ." He collapsed to his knees, closed his eyes, and jerked his head back in a delayed reaction to the hallway's animated shadows.

"God, Shep . . . what's happening? I don't understand what's happening. Talk to me, Shep. Talk to me, friend." He reached out and steadied himself with a hand upon Shepherd's knee.

"More signs," Shepherd replied evenly.

Taylor rocked back away and shook his head. But said nothing.

"Windkiller's shadows. They're out there . . . that's what you've been hearing and seeing," Shepherd continued, tilting his head first to the row of windows and then to the hallway. "Out there . . . and in the school, too. Half Moon belongs to Windkiller now. And so do I . . . so will you, Dale . . . if you stay and try to fight."

Not looking directly at Taylor, Shepherd added,

very softly, "Go on. Go back to Soldier. Nothing you can do for me now."

Taylor pushed himself to his feet and staggered to the windows. Behind him, Shepherd's haunting monologue reeled on.

"If I could explain all of it, Dale . . . if I knew exactly . . . it's one of those things we can't really know about. Not meant to know about. It's darkness. Windkiller's darkness. And demons. My own demons. They'll be coming and I'll have to fight them."

Something rasped in Shepherd's throat and then he was silent. Taylor leaned his elbows on one of the window ledges. A jagged piece of glass remained in one quarter-pane. He broke it off, and let it drop to the barren schoolyard below where it shattered with a faint tinkling.

Cool rain-driven air gusted into his face. Lightning flashed in irregular patterns; even the thunder sounded unnatural, approaching in scattered bursts as if directed by some cosmic machine. Each roll of thunder vibrated the room. A few pieces of loose plaster thudded to the floor over near the door.

Time to do something. Anything but listen to Shep, Taylor warned himself. Unconscious of the movement, he discovered suddenly that his hand was fingering the butt of the revolver jammed in his belt.

Below, he could see the van, a dull white rectangle, appearing miniscule and useless. But it was their deliverance from Half Moon. Around it, uncomfortably close, small fires seemed to have erupted from the clay. Darkness stirred near them.

"Jesus," he hissed and blinked hard. But the fires were still there, burning darkly. Like the hallucina-

155

tions of his wife and daughter, they persisted.

His thoughts rebounded to Shepherd.

He won't come along any other way. I'm not leaving him here like this. Just hit him hard enough to knock him out. Not enough to seriously hurt him.

As if his senses were hypnotized by the flaring branches of lightning, Taylor imagined the aftermath of the action he planned. He could see himself raising the butt of the revolver over Shepherd's head. Then the dull thud. And he could picture himself struggling with Shepherd's body slung over his shoulder, dumping him into the van, and roaring out of Half Moon, leaving behind the cold touch of the past.

Tomorrow, the Alabama sunshine would usher in the present, with no sign of the nerve-chilling hallucinations except for the scar of memory. And Shepherd would return to his old self. And the site report? Well, that might be a problem.

I can make it work. Forget about this evening. The county doesn't need to know that Half Moon has shadows.

He glanced at his watch. Nine o'clock. They could be home in time for local news.

Clinging to phantomlike hopes, the boy continued his way to the third-floor landing. He had nearly convinced himself that the voices he had heard were those of adults. His palms sweated freely. He had switched off the flashlight minutes ago, but had to keep shifting his grip on its plastic surface—which was what he was doing when it slipped through his fingers and bounced and banged its way to the second-floor landing. To the boy, the sound of the errant flashlight was like a round of machine-gun fire.

At that moment, Taylor was approaching Shepherd, gun in hand but hidden against his thigh. Surprised by the clatter on the stairwell, he wheeled and almost fired. Fear sucked some unintelligible word from his lips, and he grabbed his flashlight and raced into the hallway.

"Little bastards," he muttered, but he detected the fear in his voice.

Someone was scurrying down the stairs. He could hear him before he could see him.

"Stop right there, I've got a gun!" he shouted. The words echoed and stirred the plaster dust.

"No, . . . no, please. Don't shoot!"

It was a boy's voice.

Unsteadily, the beam of light, shifting as Taylor's hand jerked, caught the boy's frightened eyes. He had his hands lifted above his head like someone in an Old West movie.

They looked at each other until relief closed the gap on fear.

"Who are you?" asked Taylor, aware that his voice sounded curiously unreal.

The boy was trembling, fighting back tears.

"Ronnie. I'm Ronnie Cartwright."

"Bert Cartwright's boy?"

"Yes, sir."

Sighing heavily, Taylor aimed the gun at the floor and cleared his throat. He could hear his heart drumming.

"Who else is with you?" he asked.

"No one," said the boy. "Nobody else is with me. Is

that . . . is that you, Mr. Taylor?"

For the first time all evening, the boy felt a degree of security standing in the lantern light of the schoolroom. The presence of the two men, even though one said nothing and remained sitting with his back against a wall, added immeasurably to his sense that everything would be OK now.

As a feathery light rain pattered into the window frames, Dale Taylor fumbled with the revolver, which now bulked awkwardly next to his belt.

"Brought the gun along because I thought we might see a few rats. Good target practice," he muttered self-consciously. He smiled at the boy and wondered why he was feeling so uncomfortable. He caught the boy's lingering glance at Shepherd, and his unease heightened.

"Shep," Taylor began, straining to sound natural. "You remember Bert Cartwright's boy, Ronnie, don't you? He found his way here to get out of the storm," he explained, not really knowing why the boy had been sneaking around on the stairwell of the school.

Then, as an afterthought, he addressed the boy. "Reverend Shepherd is now working with me in the county's Development Office . . . we, uh, . . ." But he hesitated there, struck by the glint of fear in the boy's eyes.

Cocking his head wearily to one side, Shepherd said, "Hello, Ronnie." Then he ducked his eyes.

The two words whistled through the boy's mind like a dry dusty wind. Scarecrow voice. A straw sound. For a fear-tinged instant, the boy could imagine himself in

Oz conversing with the Scarecrow, helping him poke wayward straw stuffing back into his body.

"Reverend Shepherd?" the boy whispered. He glanced back at Taylor as if for confirmation. Taylor, wincing as if in pain, nodded and drew his lips together tightly.

The boy paused, then directed his question at Taylor.

"Why are you here? Did . . . did my grandma send you after me?"

"I was about to ask *you* why *you're* here, but, since you asked first," Taylor replied, "might as well sit down a moment and rest yourself. Reverend Shepherd and I were just getting ready to leave. Maybe we could give you a lift back home if you need one."

Taylor hunkered down and stared at the boy, who chose a sleeping blanket as a seat and edged it another foot or so away from Shepherd. The boy gave no sign that he needed a ride.

He's running away from home and trying to play it cool, Taylor thought to himself.

Then he recounted for the boy the aims of the Catlin County Development Office regarding Half Moon, and explained about staking off possible location sites for business, industry, and medical facilities.

"And when we finished with the site locations, we got to talking about all the good times we had in school and decided we'd just come on over here and explore for some more memories," Taylor lied.

He smiled broadly and half chuckled. "Lots of memories here. And, well, we didn't think we'd get shot for trespassing or anything. We weren't looking for you. Didn't figure anyone else would be around. We

159

got a little tired roaming around in the school, especially Reverend Shepherd who's not in as good a shape as he thought he was, so I got out my camping gear here and we were having us a coffee break before we headed back to Soldier."

It sounded so convincing that Taylor almost believed it himself.

No use mentioning Shep's delusions, and I hope to God Shep doesn't start talking about them on his own. An interior babble raged within Taylor's thoughts.

"I heard the school bell ringing," said the boy.

Taylor detected suspicion in his voice.

"Oh, that was the wind. Yeah, the wind gusted up and caught it just right, I guess," he answered quickly. "Thought it might be vandals, you know, at first, but I guess it was just the wind."

The boy bit nervously at his lip. "Am I going to get into trouble for being here?"

Taylor shrugged and smiled. "You done something to deserve trouble?"

The boy twisted his fingers together. "Ran away from home," he said softly.

"Well . . . why don't you tell us about it?"

Shifting his attention occasionally to the stone figure of Shepherd, the boy told of his inability to get along with his grandmother and of his decision to come back to Half Moon. Then he confessed to being frightened away from his tree house and to being drawn to the light of Taylor's lantern. He was careful not to be specific about what all he'd seen.

"You've had a rough couple of days, I bet," said Taylor. "But don't you suppose your grandma's worried sick about you, not knowing where you are or what's happened to you?"

The wind whined through the row of windows, spraying both of them with a cool mist.

"Yes, sir. But . . . but . . . and then there's something else I did, too."

"Well, what's that?"

The boy patted his fingertips absently over his scraped palm.

"I took something . . . I stole something," he said finally. And he glanced immediately at Shepherd for his reaction, but there was none.

Moved by the boy's sense of guilt, Taylor tried to lighten the matter.

"Not much left in Half Moon to steal, is there? Can't rob the bank," he chuckled.

The boy's voice quavered. "I stole from a helpless old woman. I took this here box of crackers from Mrs. Harvester's kitchen. But I only did it because I was hungry . . . and I haven't even eaten any of them. Only a few of them are broken."

Taylor lifted the crumpled box of saltines in one hand and put his other hand on Ronnie's shoulder. "Listen, I'll tell you what, Ronnie. On the way out of town we'll stop at Miss Molly's and return these crackers. I'll explain what happened. I'm sure she'll understand. I'll talk to her for you."

Head bowed, the boy seemed lost in thought. "No," he replied after a few moments, "I'm the one that stole it. I have to take it back and tell her about it."

Taylor squeezed his shoulder. "You know, Ronnie, I bet your mother and dad would have been real proud of your honesty."

The boy shook his head. "But I scared her, too. Mrs.

161

Harvester screamed and was real scared. I didn't mean to scare her like that." His eyes searched for Taylor's and pleaded for understanding.

"It's dangerous for an old woman to live here alone," the boy added, sounding mature beyond his years. "It's dangerous. I've seen. . . ."

Taylor shifted his weight and studied the boy's tense face.

"What have you seen? I mean, anything . . . unusual? Have you seen or heard anything unusual here in Half Moon?"

The evening's tapestry of hallucinations renewed their haunting effect. Taylor was probing for affirmation and he knew it.

"You mean ghosts?" asked the boy matter-of-factly.

"Well, no . . . no, not really. Just . . . just . . . well, you said something frightened you earlier."

The boy stared off into the shadows blankly; his voice took on the tone of a confessor. "I heard things . . . and saw them. Bad things. I think maybe they're bad and evil. But I don't know what they are. Maybe they're not even real."

Taylor felt a vague sense of relief. "I believe you're right, Ronnie. I believe so. Isn't it funny, though, how a person's mind can start to make him think he's seeing things. I guess that's how people got started saying Half Moon is haunted."

Without acknowledging Taylor's comment, the boy took the box of saltines from him.

"I want to go take this back now. I want to go by myself."

"No reason for that, son. Help me load up things here, and we'll stop and check on Miss Molly and see if

162

she needs anything. And you think . . . isn't it about time you got back to your grandma's?"

"I guess so," he answered quietly.

"We need to get truckin' before the storm hits," Taylor exclaimed. "Looks like it's already started to rain some."

He had forgotten momentarily about Shepherd, who was slumped against the wall like a sandbag. Resolution seeped into Taylor's thoughts like cold damp air.

"Ronnie . . . listen, might could be better if you went ahead on your own and saw Miss Molly. By the time you get back I'll have things ready to go." He rifled through the camping gear and pulled free a roll of yellow plastic.

"Here, you better wear this. Stay as dry as you can and get back as quick as you can." Taylor slipped a poncho over the boy's head. "Take my flashlight . . . and be careful."

He followed the boy out into the hallway, their footfalls echoing faintly. Suddenly the boy stopped and peered back over his shoulder into the room.

"What is it, Ronnie?"

"Reverend Shepherd . . . is he sick? What's wrong with him?"

Hands on his hips, Taylor stared at the floor.

"I believe he's just tired, Ronnie, you know. And maybe . . . and maybe it makes him kinda sad to come back to Half Moon and see it this way. It's hard on him, but he's going to be OK. He's had a long day."

From the third-floor landing, Taylor watched the boy descend the dust-laden angle of the stairway, the darkness punctuated with the feeble beam of the flashlight. Something caught in Taylor's chest as the boy funneled lower and lower. And suddenly the stairway was not a stairway at all, but rather a gaping cistern; Taylor had to stop himself from calling out to the boy. Words threatened to break his silence.

Then they screamed within.

Don't go down there alone!

And the boy dropped out of sight.

CHAPTER 12

Molly Harvester sat in her overstuffed chair listening to her heart wham. Its drumming had gradually slowed since the intruder had raced from her kitchen. In a vertiginous blur of terror, when some survival mechanism within had clicked on, she had managed to lock her screen and bolt the inside door.

"Please Lord, no more visitors," she mumbled.

Was it a boy, or one of Windkiller's shadows?

She had returned to the overstuffed and collapsed as the terriers chorused their barking. They, too, had finally settled down, but would not let their eyes leave Miss Molly.

"Gone have to call the po-lice . . . I am. Call the sheriff about that visitor. Took something from our cupboard, lit-tul men."

Was it real?

An involuntary shudder seized her and shook her like a pile of rags. "I feel awful, don'cha know? Feel old, old as winter's grandmother."

Thunder growled low, then redoubled itself, slamming her roof like a fist. The shop vibrated, walls hummed, and the living room shelving jittered. Two or three glass decanters plunged to the floor, exploding like firecrackers. Molly jolted forward and the terriers whined pathetically.

Streaks of lightning pressed low to the ground and her lamp flickered.

"Oh, my Lord."

Get to that phone, Molly, she chided herself. She was silently thankful that she still had electrical power and a phone. Alabama Power had rigged her up a single line that carried to the county road. The Ma Bell people had been equally amenable in keeping a phone line available to her. But now the approaching storm was threatening both conveniences.

Forcing herself out of the soft chair, Molly raised a warning finger at the excitable terriers.

"Y'all gone have to be quiet. I gone use the phone and call us some help. Mr. Carl, he woulda wanted us to."

Fritzie and Tiny obeyed, but their little eyes teared and their fragile bodies trembled. Freddie, her self-assigned protector, pattered after her into the kitchen, his stub of tail wagging, ears flattened in obeisance against his head.

Nervous and tense, Molly wondered distractedly whatever had happened to good old-fashioned Moxie.

Get a hold of yourself, old woman.

Freddie sat on his haunches and watched as Molly switched on the kitchen light and began rifling through a cupboard next to the phone.

166

"Best get us out some candles and matches. We're fixin' to be left in the dark, I'm supposin'. Now Freddie, darlin', don't get right under my feet. If I have to look down at every step, this ole head a mine gone get dizzy as a spinnin' jenny."

The tiny dog's toenails clicked noisily over the surface of the linoleum floor; Molly glanced down once and then back up quickly to the window above the sink. A trio of small fires blazed through the rain-glistened pane. Molly squinted. A sheet of lightning dropped at the same moment, but it was so bright that the fires seemed to disappear.

"Might need to call the fire department, too . . . if those fires are real . . . oh, Lord, I don't know."

The huskiness of her whisper surprised and frightened her. She cradled the phone to her ear.

"Not supposed to use a phone when it's stormin' like this," she exclaimed, as if she were giving advice to a child. "Lightning can come right down a wire and ram right into your ear, don'cha know."

Talking had a way of exorcizing fears.

Freddie's intelligent little eyes followed the movement of her lips.

"Don't know where I put that phone book, so I'll just dial the operator." Her forefinger danced around the rim of the slot; thunder pounded so near that she had to cup a hand over her other ear. She listened for the connection to be made. Had the operator answered?

"Hello. Hello, this is Mrs. Carl Harvester in Half Moon and . . . and you need be sendin' the sheriff over here because I've had a visitor . . . a prowler, don'cha see. And my electricity might gone be cuttin' off on me

167

here, and . . . and I'm alone here with just my dogs, just lit-tul dogs, not really watchdogs or nuthin' like that."

She paused for the operator's response. The thunder died away, and the kitchen was silent except for Freddie's intermittent whining and Molly's rough breathing.

The old woman frowned. She would have given the world for Carl to have been there, taking care of her, being her protector, her strength against the darkness.

The silence on the phone seemed to deepen.

"Y'all there?" she whispered. "Talk to me. Help me."

It started with a low resonant note, pitched higher as the receiver jostled against Molly's ear, and settled into its familiar, yet bizarre, cry until she slammed the receiver down.

Pressing her fingers over her ears, she cried, "Please . . . please don't do that!"

Freddie jumped against her legs and barked, and his barking set off his companions in the next room.

A fresh round of lightning illuminated the outer darkness with a blue-white haze. The kitchen light flickered once, twice, a third time, and then blackness. Molly held onto the kitchen countertop as if it were a life raft.

Candles. Get a hold of yourself, Molly.

"Hush, Freddie. Hush now," she gasped. Four matches later she succeeded in lighting a candle and anchoring it to a saucer. A couple of years ago a friend had surprised her with a gift of a half-dozen candles molded into the shape of owls with wicks extending from their heads.

The owl-light guided her steps out of the kitchen

back to the overstuffed chair.

A nimbus glow of orange bathed the cluttered room, but in it was a modicum of comfort, a protective circle that quieted the terriers and bonded Molly and her pets and her memories of Carl together as a family. But its effect was fleeting.

"What we gone do, lit-tul men? We can't stay here. Carl . . . don'cha see . . . we can't stay here."

Her thoughts singsonged in despair.

We can't stay here
Can't . . . lit-tul men
Carl . . . can't wait
No more . . . for you
Please forgive me
Can't stay.
Can't.

A vigorous thunderclap started the vibrations anew. Even the candle's flame quivered. Shelving hummed. And like lemming plunging into the sea, glass decanters and figurines toppled to the floor.

Molly stared through the candlelight into the shadowy front room, where glass exploded as if a miniature war were raging. And what she saw then drove her from the only world that had ever given her peace and love.

Light rain soaked into her scalp as she stood at the door of her rundown Pinto and called for Freddie; the other two dogs were restlessly bouncing around in the front seat.

"Freh-deee, come on! Freh-deee!"

Damn his lit-tul hide, she grimaced to herself.

But suddenly he treaded out of the darkness and was at her feet.

"Get in this here car, lit-tul man. For shame. Why do you always run off?"

As Freddie rejoined the other two, they yipped and growled and shivered, but Molly paid no attention. She was digging through her purse to find her keys, digging past a nest of odds and ends, including several pouches of Bacon Bites (the terriers' favorite packaged dog food), which she had somehow managed to grab before stumbling out the door.

But she was not thinking of keys.

The earlier scene suddenly ghosted before her on the rain-spattered windshield: the demon fire, its oily light pooling the floor, flickered shadowy tongues. Then it began to expand before her eyes like some hellish mushroom growth.

Something danced within the flame.

The surrealistic image, its countenance adorned with a red-orange glow, pranced menacingly. She saw its shaggy head and the finger-length horns. And then she heard its hooves clap against the floor, coming, threatening to trample its marks upon her.

Yet it seemed to allow her time to escape. It had taunted her, and now it possessed the shop. It. Windkiller. And the voice of Windkiller rising within her drove her to the edge of terror.

"I'm sorry, Carl . . . I'm just so sorry." Key in hand, she desperately pressed it into the ignition slot.

The rain had dowsed her candle, she reflected helplessly. It was all that she could remember of the frantic dash to get herself and the terriers out of the shop. It was a silly old woman's thought, and she chided herself for it.

She cranked the engine several times with no success, though once it sounded close to catching, as close as worn points and plugs would allow it.

"Just settle down, lit-tul men. We be gone in a minute," she exclaimed. "Come on, my dear Pinto," she whispered affectionately, yet intensely. "Come on jitny. Come on lady. We need you to get us outta here." She pumped the accelerator, but the Pinto only sputtered and coughed.

"We'll go to Carmilla's, lit-tul men. Nice folks there at Elderness will take us in, you'll see. We'll have us a place of our own again, I promise."

She hesitated, then added, "We waited for Mr. Carl as long as we could . . . as long as we could."

Twisting the key with all her strength, she coaxed the engine to start, but the metallic grinding merely repeated itself idiotically.

She sniffed the air. "We've gone and flooded it," she whimpered.

Slumping back in the seat, she closed her eyes; her lips moved as if in silent prayer. Light rain continued to fall and the terriers crowded against one another for warmth. Thunder and lightning filled the darkness with intermittent sound and light.

When Molly opened her eyes, she noticed that the shop glowed a faint orange within. Confused, she studied the otherwise darkened building until the source of the curious glow became evident.

"Oh, dear Lord, no!"

As if in a hypnotic trance, she watched as flames crawled toward the outer walls. Thunder rumbled low, vibrating the small car, but nothing drew her attention from the gathering flames . . . at first, not even the dark face that hovered close to the driver's side window.

CHAPTER 13

"I know what you're planning to do, Dale."

The note of pity in Shepherd's tone angered Taylor. He stood in front of his friend, feeling like a child who had been caught in the midst of some mischievous plot.

Shepherd dovetailed his fingers in front of his face, then released them as a preamble to his next statement. "Dale, take the boy and go on back to Soldier. I know what I'm saying. I know it's hard for you to understand . . . but this is the only way."

Taylor rocked gently on his heels. An empty coffee cup dangled from one hand, and he slowly, painfully shook his head.

Suddenly Shepherd lurched forward from the wall and shouted at him.

"God as my witness! As God is my witness, Dale, I'm telling you to get out of here! Get out of Half Moon!"

Like a marionette with its strings loosened, Shepherd fell back against the wall, bowed his head, and seemed to lapse into a trance.

Heart beating in his throat, Taylor edged away from

him. He crossed to the row of windows where the wind puffed ragged pockets of mist into the room. "Can't do that," he whispered to himself. "I can't leave him."

Below, the small fires circled the van, fire points against a dark void.

No, not real. Can't be real.

Where is the boy? he asked himself, grasping for something other than Shepherd and the mysterious fires to occupy his thoughts. He scanned the night in the direction of Molly Harvester's antique shop, hoping to see the flicker of Ronnie's flashlight. But the only light he saw was from the eager flames spreading through the distant building.

"Miss Molly's! Oh, God, no!"

In seconds he was bounding down the stairs.

Molly's scream, a piercing, animal-like wail, staggered the boy as if he had been slammed by a strong gust of wind. The shrill barking of the terriers seemed to amplify the old woman's anguished cry, and had the boy not focused on the present danger of the burning shop, he might have run, and never have stopped running until the long nightmare of Half Moon down had dissipated.

Though Molly tried stubbornly to hold the door closed, the boy succeeded in jerking it open, yelling at her to get out of the car and away from the burning building. The light rain was proving itself powerless against the flames.

In the next agonizing minutes, he managed to prod her forty yards or more from the steady roar of the fire,

174

and as they turned to look, they saw the building implode, collapse within itself in a tumbling fury of red-orange fireballs.

"What if Mr. Carl comes back?" Molly shrieked.

In the light from the conflagration, the boy watched the old woman's eyelids flutter, and with another step she fainted, pulling him down with her.

And there they remained until Taylor, having run faster than he could ever recall, reached them.

Chilled by the rain, his muscles protesting under the strain of near exhaustion, the boy followed Taylor and Miss Molly and tried to make certain that the three terriers stayed with them on their trek to the school. For a block or so, Taylor had carried Molly, the old woman babbling incoherently all the while. The boy felt deeply sorry for her, and the sight of her being carried to the security of the school forced him to think of Granny Cartwright. How worried she must be.

The journey to the school was tortuous and feverishly enervating. When they finally settled into the third-floor camp, clothes sodden and senses numbed, Taylor fired up the portable gas stove and took much of the dampness out of the air. But the moderate rain continued to fall, and when an occasional gust of wind swirled the droplets, the room was again permeated with darkness.

The boy huddled near the stove. Taylor draped a blanket around Molly's shoulders. Despite the blanket, the old woman shivered and her eyes teared as she absently petted with trembling fingers the three terriers snuggled in her lap.

There had been one surprise development as they awkwardly got to know each other better. Taylor, feeling a special need to maintain civility, had directed Molly's attention to Shepherd, who did not stir from his position against the wall when the others entered the room.

"I'm sure you remember Reverend Shepherd—Jack Shepherd, here, don't you, Miss Molly?"

He looked hopefully at Shepherd; then he traded apprehensive glances with the boy.

Molly smiled at Shepherd and nodded her head. "Oh, yes, of course I remember. It's good to see you again. But oh, my land's," she chortled, her accent becoming suddenly more pronounced. "I must look like a sight—positively a drowned rat. You must excuse me."

The past glinted in Shepherd's eyes. The boy held his breath as Shepherd nimbly pushed himself to his feet. His towering frame seemed to diminish the shadowy room.

"Mrs. Harvester—Miss Molly . . . it is a pleasure to see you again," said Shepherd, bowing slightly. It was his preacher's voice; Taylor and the boy recognized it immediately.

Shepherd, his demeanor gracious, continued. "I'm sorry you had to get out on a night like this. Dale will make you comfortable, though. We've all been driven here out of the darkness, you know."

Shepherd said nothing of the fire, Taylor noted. Perhaps he hadn't gone to the window to look. But at least he seemed more in control, less despondent than earlier. More sane? Yes, probably. Yet the comment about being driven out of the darkness, the shift in his tone as he spoke those words, touched Taylor like an icy finger at the nape of his neck. The boy was affected the same way.

Shepherd resumed his former position moments later.

Curiosity pricked, the boy stole a glance his way, but was disappointed to find Shepherd staring at the falling rain just beyond the window. A cosmic blank had recaptured the man's face. It was as if he wore a mask.

Then Molly pointed at a packet near Taylor's knee. "Oh, is that instant coffee?"

Her sudden question, oddly enough, reminded the boy that he hadn't apologized to her for stealing the crackers.

"Yes, I'll boil some water for us. Got some packets of hot chocolate here, too, Ronnie," said Taylor.

The boy nodded toward Taylor's smile.

"Course, now," Molly began, "coffee'll keep me up all night, don'cha know. One cup and my ole eyes are open wide as a hootie owl's all night."

The boy found himself grinning as Molly imitated the piercing, all-seeing stare of an owl. Then her words seemed to battle one another.

"I . . . I had a big, fine crystal owl . . . probably gone now. All my owls. And Mr. Carl . . . and, can you tell me . . . is the shop gone down, too?"

Taylor lowered his eyes and pursed his lips.

"Well," she exclaimed resolutely, "that's not the worst of it . . . not the worst of it at all."

Silence claimed the room with a death grip.

It was finally broken by Molly's sobbing, a sobbing that blended with the steady thrumming of the rain.

The boy squirmed uneasily. Fear and sadness crawled up inside of him, burrowing into the dark hollow of his stomach like a small, predator-driven animal.

"We'll leave when the rain lets up," Taylor announced.

When the boy heard those words, he waited for Shepherd's reaction, but there was none.

"Ronnie will be going back to Soldier," Taylor added. "Is there any place in particular that we can take you, Miss Molly? I can help you contact your insurance agent about the fire in the morning."

Puppeting her head from side to side in exaggerated fashion, Molly braved a smile. "Y'all are perfect saints . . . perfect saints to help an old woman in her distress like this. There is, I believe, a place where I can go. My dear friend, Carmilla Carfax, resides at Elderness . . . you know, that retirement center in Goldsmith . . . oh, it's a fine place. Nice lit-tul carpeted rooms . . . lots of activities. Kind of expensive, but they let you pay pretty much what and when you can."

In the spray of lantern light, the boy could see the trail of a drying tear on her cheek.

"Does that mean you won't be coming back to Half Moon? Won't be rebuilding the antique shop?" Taylor asked gently.

Molly hesitated. Obviously the issue hadn't yet occurred to her. "Mr. Carl," she began, and reached down to fondle one of the terriers, "you knew my husband, Carl Harvester, I'm sure."

Taylor nodded.

"Well, he . . . he-he asked me to wait for him to come back, don'cha see. But, now . . . he wouldn't expect me to stay, would he? My ole Pinto's probably all that's left."

Taylor began pouring the boiling water into cups. "Carl Harvester was a fine man," he said. "I'm sure he would have wanted you to go where you'd be among friends. I'll help you see about things, Miss Molly. Don't you worry none."

In a tear-strained voice, Molly answered, "Thank you, Mr. Taylor. Y'all are so kind . . . not like some of the folks in Half Moon."

The boy felt warm and secure huddled near the lantern and the portable gas stove. Taylor, Miss Molly, and her terriers were also pressed so close that, to the boy at least, it was like sitting around a campfire. Some distance away, Shepherd's huge frame continued to slump silently against a wall. The boy noticed that Taylor seemed to be pretending Shepherd wasn't even in the room; Molly, on the other hand, let her gaze drift nervously to him every minute or so.

Here it is, she realized. *Here is the vision. Here with two men and a boy. Windkiller sent the vision. The creature is feeding.*

Playing the role of host, Taylor passed a cup of coffee to Molly and a cup of instant cocoa to the boy. Though watery and not very chocolaty, the cocoa warmed and relaxed him. He stifled a yawn. Despite some aches and pains and scrapes and apprehensions, he felt that he could fall asleep in this comforting presence of adults.

"Reverend Shepherd, wouldn't you like a cup of hot coffee?" Molly asked, sporting her finest smile.

Windkiller is feeding upon this poor man.

Shepherd acknowledged her with his eyes, but shook his head in response to the offer.

Frowning, cocking one eye severely, Molly leaned his way. "Are you feeling poorly this evening, Reverend Shepherd?" She lifted one hand in a vaguely solicitous manner.

"Yes ma'am," he said feebly, "I am." Then lowered his head again.

Taylor seized the opportunity to interrupt.

"Miss Molly, Reverend Shepherd and I put in a pretty long and tiring afternoon with our site inspections. I think Jack just got worn out, you know. Good night's rest and he'll be as good as new." Having retrieved Molly's attention, Taylor proceeded to explain more fully what had brought them to Half Moon, careful to splice in positive projections about the regeneration of the town.

"I hope y'all are successful," Molly observed. "Mr. Carl, my Carl, so loved this lit-tul town . . . and Half Moon's had more than its share of dark times now, hasn't it?"

In silent agreement, Taylor considered the whorls of steam rising from his coffee.

Shepherd's somber mood had thrown a blanket of unease over the conversation. It was especially unnerving to the boy to see an adult in such an apparently depressed state. It reminded him of his father and the infamous black box days.

180

What's bothering the Reverend Shepherd? the boy wondered. Does it have to do with all the strangeness? He guessed that it did. Does something evil have control of Half Moon? But, then, couldn't Reverend Shepherd simply pray for help? It would be easy for him, wouldn't it?

As they nursed their hot drinks and listened to the rain and to the subtle sounds of the building settling, Freddie wiggled loose from Molly's lap and trotted toward Shepherd. A yard away from his shoes the dog halted, stretched his neck, and sniffed. Then he inched closer until his nose touched Shepherd's shoe. Suddenly the dog's hackles rose and he growled deep in his throat.

Shepherd took no notice, but Molly, seemingly horrified by the dog's behavior, sternly reprimanded him.

"Freddie, stop that! You come right back here this instant, lit-tul man. For heaven's sake, what got into you, growling like that at Reverend Shepherd? What a thing! Oh!" She scooped the dog back into her lap and swatted his rear.

"I'm so, so sorry, Reverend Shepherd. Do forgive my Freddie. I assure you he's normally better behaved than this."

As she cupped her hand over the dog's mouth, the room shouted with light. The vision locked into place, shunting her other thoughts and sensations. She saw a darkened hall and a monstrous projection of Shepherd stalking that darkness, clutching a hatchet in his two strong hands. But before she could determine his quarry, the vision clattered to a halt as if it were a clip of film.

Molly shuddered and a tremor of sound vibrated in her throat.

Shepherd lolled his head toward the rain. His jaw stiffened and relented, then stiffened again. His fists clenched and unclenched like a boxer priming himself for a bout.

Lost. That was the only word that came to the boy's mind in assessing Shepherd's expression. It was a lost look. Not a desperate, searching, panic-ridden lost, but rather a resigned lost. A condition that had been thought through and accepted.

A condition that frightened the boy.

Turning to Taylor as if for support, Molly, eyes wide and etched with lantern glints of fear, rambled on, tightening her hold on the dogs. Her voice pitched comically high. "But, you know, they've been tense all evening, don'cha know . . . and the shop, before it caught fire—I don't know how I could have been so careless as to let that fire get started—well, and so my lit-tul men had been jumpy, don'cha see. The ole Philco bleating out funny noises and the ole shop got to shaking so hard it pure knocked some of my glass knickknacks off the shelves. I could barely keep the lit-tul men quiet. Yes, that's so." Her eyes searched Taylor and the boy for understanding.

"Storms seem to make animals more nervous, too," Taylor offered in support.

"Oh, and yes, that's a fact," said Molly, and took a sip of her coffee. She forced herself not to look at Shepherd. "My, that's scalding . . . but fine. Really warms my ole insides, it does." She smiled at the boy. "You know, Ronnie, . . . that's your name, isn't it? Ronnie?"

"Yes, ma'am."

"Well, Ronnie, did you know these lit-tul dogs, why they each one have them a particular personality . . . just like people." ▪

The boy shifted, warming happily to the topic of the terriers.

"You take ole Fritzie here," she replied, petting the dog's head with a motherly kind of resolve. Somewhat lethargically the dog responded, licking twice gently at her arthritic fingers. "He's kinda grumpy and cranky sometimes, you know."

Recalling something from the past she arched her eyebrows and smiled. "Mr. Carl used to call him 'Gramps' . . . used to tell him he was gone sign him up for Medicare, don'cha know." She laughed, and the laughter was like the distant jingle of bells. Taylor and the boy chuckled with her.

"And ole Fritzie gets cold so easy. Gets it in his lit-tul ole bones, I suppose. Look at him right now—he's shivering like he's got snowflakes for a collar, isn't he?" Jealous of the attention Fritzie was receiving, another of the terriers, the smallest one, nosed its way under her arm. "Oh, and look at Mr. Green Eyes . . . the Green-Eyed Monster's got you, hasn't he, sir?" she chattered in baby-talk fashion.

"This one is Tiny," she explained. "Quiet as a church mouse most of the time. Kind of sickly. A few years ago we thought we were gone lose Tiny to the heartworm. But we pumped him full of pills, and the vet over in Soldier got those nasty things out of him . . . yes, he did, didn't he lit-tul man?" she cooed, bugging out her eyes toward the dog.

"I think I like Freddie the best," the boy volunteered,

183

delighted by Molly's fantasizing about the humanlike characters of her dogs. "I don't have any dogs, but I have some pigeons and a crow, and I found a hawk that'd got shot. They just stayed here in town after the storm . . . and . . . and I really like birds."

Molly smiled. "Oh, that's wonderful. It shows you have a kind heart." And for a span of seconds that disconcerted the boy, she stared at him. "My favorite birds are owls," she added. "But some people, don'cha know, why they think owls are omens of death."

To one side Freddie sat on his haunches, seemingly taking in the conversation, but casting a wary eye every so often toward Shepherd. A thin ridge of fur on the dog's back remained erect.

Molly fell silent. Her admiring smile shifted to Freddie. Her eyes sparkled as if to signal that her reverie had been fueled.

"Though a mother should never, I'm told, admit to favoring one of her sons over another, well, I'm gone have to say that Freddie's the one I tend to like the best, too. But oh, now, let me tell you," her voice comically hardened, "he can get into ten times his weight in trouble." Some dark thought appeared to cross her mind before she continued.

"Mr. Carl . . . he favored this lit-tul rascal, too. Caused him grief, though. Would have been a good companion for Huck Finn or Tom Sawyer. Always stealing off on some lit-tul adventure. I don't know how many times Mr. Carl and I have had to go looking for him when he took a notion to go off exploring. He's a free spirit, I'm telling you. Always on the verge of trouble. Right up on the edge." She shook her head in light-hearted exasperation.

Taylor reached toward Freddie and scratched behind his ears. "Seems like a real nice little dog," he said wistfully. "My wife, Carol Mae, you know, she likes dogs. All animals, in fact. Can't stand to see them suffer. Puts out scraps for all the strays in town and. . . ."

Jesus, . . . no, I've lost her.

Molly eyed him sadly. "Mr. Taylor, you know I-I never got around to telling you how sorry I was about the tragedy of your wife and daughter . . . and, of course, your store, too. Words can't, just can't touch the depth of your sorrow, I know. Mr. Carl, now, he was . . . lost during the storm." Her hand fluttered near her mouth like a disoriented bird. "Who knows when he'll . . . come back, you know . . . find his way back. If that's meant to be."

Taylor cringed, glanced apprehensively at the boy, and then turned back to Molly. "But every town has had tragedies," he said, "and Half Moon can rebuild. One of these days we won't even recognize this town. It'll be alive again."

"Oh, I hope that you're right, Mr. Taylor, I honestly do. Yet the town lost so much. Like your family and Ronnie's parents." Hesitating, she tilted her head sympathetically toward the boy, and he felt something coil in his stomach.

"And we lost Mrs. Shepherd, too," she said.

The three of them almost simultaneously tensed, anticipating some response from Shepherd.

"Reverend Shepherd, she was a dear, dear woman and—"

But there a curtain fell on Molly's words.

Hatchet in his hands. Stalking the darkness.

Shepherd blanched. His lips moved and made a hollow sound, painful to hear. He cleared his throat, but if he had in mind to say something, he never gave voice to it.

Uncomfortable with the silence that had descended, Taylor followed a crooked bolt of lightning beyond the film of rain.

"Storm's coming. Sure glad we have the school for a shelter," he exclaimed.

Wistfully, Molly surveyed the shadow-strewn walls.

"This ole school, well, it's had its dark moments, don'cha know."

Puzzled, Taylor shrugged his shoulders and then recalled something from his past. "When I was a freshman in high school, I believe it was, I remember that the boiler blew up. School closed for two days. And there was a bomb scare my senior year, but I don't remember much else in the way of dark moments for this school."

Molly shook her head. "Oh, your memory doesn't reach back far enough then. I graduated from Half Moon High in nineteen hundred and thirty, don'cha see. There used to be—don't know if they still have it—a revolving mechanism or thingamawhich of some type down by the gymnasium that had all the graduates pictures going back to, oh, land's, I think nineteen hundred and three. There I'll be, looking like some young Hollywood starlet."

Cocking her head to one side, she laughed and batted her eyelashes. "Well, and . . . school was fun and my

186

folks were quite well to do, and so I had nice clothes and thought of myself as a free-spirited woman who could take on whatever challenges the world presented. Three things occurred, though, in my final year of school that changed my life forever."

She paused again, examining the shadows as a matrix for her memories. Both Taylor and the boy felt drawn to her tale. The rain continued to fall, and Jack Shepherd lapsed more deeply into an untrammeled oblivion.

"First, in the fall of nineteen hundred and twenty-nine, there was the stock market crash. My father, a genuine Horatio Alger story if there ever was one, suddenly found himself in a totally different financial situation. It was as if one day he awakened and the sun failed to rise. He was a speculator in cotton and other farm commodities, and he simply never recovered from his losses. You might say our family went from riches to rags on Black Thursday." She smiled weakly before continuing.

"Equally disturbing to me was a most tragic situation that developed at the beginning of the new year. This school was blessed with a most efficient and eminently likeable custodian in those years. A man by the name of Norbert Day, a large, rather heavy man who when he moved through the hallways resembled a circus bear toddling on its hind legs. But . . . oh my, he was such a gentle man, an angel of a man. He had served as custodian here for, oh, I suppose since the end of World War I . . . was custodian in the building that was formerly the school, too. He had received a head wound in the war . . . Spanish-American, I believe. Well, and one ear was virtually gone, useless to him in terms of his hearing.

"Well, as it happened, a couple of my classmates, Wilma Singleton and Ophelia Peacock, out of pure maliciousness, boldly declared that Mr. Day had made unseemly advances to them. A horrid, horrid lie it was. But in the end school officials were forced to terminate him.

"Mr. Day, understandably, was devastated. For several days after he was let go, no one in town saw him. Then one evening our drama class was rehearsing for the school play—*The Importance of Being Earnest*, I seem to recall—when someone pulled up the backdrop curtain, and as it slowly ascended, the body of Mr. Day, a thick rope looped around his neck, descended like a bale of cotton. I shall never, I pray to God, see a more horrible sight or hear more penetrating screams. And the poor man had apparently cut off his good ear, for there was a bloody hole where it should have been. It was like he didn't want to hear the screams that he knew his suicide would provoke."

The boy's eyes followed Taylor as he began heating more water from a tall Thermos.

"When I was very young, I believe I did hear my parents mention Mr. Day," said Taylor.

It was evident from his perfunctory manner that he hoped Miss Molly would shift to a less horrific subject. But he didn't want to be rude.

Hesitantly, the boy joined the conversation. "My dad told me once that for a long time you could see bloodstains on the stage. He told me about what you're saying."

"I couldn't believe," Molly explained, gazing past the

boy's shoulder, "I couldn't believe that something like that might happen to such a good man. My life, my way of seeing things, took a decidedly cynical turn then, don'cha know. The crowning blow, however, was the . . . the demise of my favorite teacher, Miss Whitby. Miss Cassandra Ayrans Whitby." Something like a whimper escaped Molly's lips before she pressed her fingers to them and wrestled for control of her voice.

Taylor frowned. "Maybe it's best not to dig up these memories, Miss Molly," he cautioned.

"Oh, but you see, Miss Whitby fostered my love of history. She was such a marvelous teacher, don'cha know."

The wind suddenly whined through the windows, jetting droplets of rain into the room. The terriers burrowed deeper within each other on Molly's lap.

"We never knew what caused it," she whispered.

"Caused what?" blurted the boy before he could check himself.

Molly seemed to be meditating on the ceiling, and when she spoke again it was in a kind of distracted monologue. She seemed to be talking to herself.

"Such a bright and talented woman. But no one really knew her background. Her folks lived in Georgia as I recall. Maybe . . . I suppose it's quite possible . . . she had a lover. But I think some thoughtless, vicious people in our own lit-tul town caused it. They thought she was strange. Talked about her behind her back."

Molly rolled her eyes along the shadowy walls. "It may have been in this very room that they found her one Monday morning. You see, they kept all of the students away from the third floor that morning. But we heard her, nevertheless. Shrieking like a hag from hell, and the most hideous laughter. They put her in a white belted jacket, a straightjacket, I suppose. I saw her face when they carried her out the front door. Three grown men carried her. Three. Her face was a mask of agony."

Mask.

For a split second the boy could see Miss Whitby, a snarling demoness, her head filled with every shade of darkness.

"Oh my, I've talked on like a ninny," Molly replied. "I'm sorry." She bobbed her head as if deep in regret.

The boy scooted closer to the lantern.

"Miss Molly, ma'am," he stammered, unsure of how to couch his question, "do you believe in . . . in ghosts?"

Her eyes slipped to the ceiling, and she clasped her hands lightly in front of her as if she were about to pray to the heavens.

"Well," her voice lilted, "I've lived in a haunted house this past year." Then, more seriously, "I feel the presence of Mr. Carl in the shop, but now . . . oh, I'm not answering your question, am I? OK, then, my answer is 'yes and no.' Yes, because life is kind of a ghostly thing . . . and that makes each of us ghosts. But no, I've never seen one of those pale or sheeted kind, if you know what I mean."

The boy nodded, though he was concentrating on his next question. "Are there really evil things, you know, like evil spirits, bogeymen, or vampires?"

He was slightly embarrassed to find that he was holding his breath while he awaited her reply.

Molly looked to one side thoughtfully. "I read a very strange lit-tul book once. I don't remember who wrote it. Don't remember its title either. But I remember one line from it, and maybe it will answer your question. The line went like this: 'There are creatures born of the nefarious passions that arise in distorted minds.'"

"What's 'nefarious'?"

"Means wicked or evil. Most evil creatures come right out of here." She tapped the side of her head knowingly.

"My mom told me there's just a kind of meanness in the world. Just all around us kinda like the wind," said the boy.

Molly thought a second, then responded. "Sounds like she was a pretty wise mom to me."

At that point Taylor began rifling through his camping supplies.

"There's a kind of meanness in my stomach right now because it's empty," he mused. "Anybody interested in some hot soup? This rain ought to let up before much longer, but we might as well head out with our stomachs full."

The soup suggestion met with everyone's approval, though Shepherd remained in his glassy-eyed stupor, mumbling to himself, ever more drawn to the penetrating darkness and the patter of rain beyond the windows.

Taylor served up the soup, chicken noodle laced with green bits of something the identity of which no one could be sure, in aluminum bowls. They ate with plastic spoons, but there were no complaints. While Molly spooned her soup, she took time to offer the terriers dog-food nuggets from a cellophane bag in her purse.

"They love these here lit-tul bacon bits," she said.

As he watched the terriers sit up, pirouette, and beg

for each morsel, the boy suddenly realized that he hadn't actually apologized to Molly for filching the box of saltines. Somewhere in the night's hectic panoply of events, he had lost track of the box. Still, he knew that she deserved some explanation from him.

"See if Reverend Shepherd wants some of this soup."

Before the boy could settle on some appropriately apologetic words for Molly, Taylor handed the bowl to him. Something in Taylor's manner was cautious yet hopeful that Shepherd would be more receptive to the boy than to him or Molly.

"Okay," said the boy, and, balancing his own bowl with Shepherd's, he slid to the outer rim of the lantern light. In the meantime, Taylor and Molly began engaging in small talk, their attention focused casually on the terriers the way adults nonchalantly observe children at play.

With a measure of trepidation, the boy nestled down a few feet from Shepherd, close enough to hear his uneven breathing and to smell his strong body odor, an animal odor, like that of wet fur.

"Here's some hot soup."

Eyes filming, Shepherd ignored the soup. Through the whole of a deliberate pause, he studied the boy's face.

"It's going to be up to you," said Shepherd.

In part, it was a recognizable tone. The boy equated it with the "invitation" segment of sermons. "Jesus wants to come into your life. He's knocking, knocking at your door. He can't come in unless you invite Him. It's going to be up to you."

But that wasn't what Shepherd was saying. There was fear in his tone. And the immediacy there had nothing to do with Jesus.

"Don't you want the soup?" the boy asked nervously.

"Drawing evil to it. This building's drawing evil to it. I've been given to know. Fire and storm."

Shepherd's glazed eyes were hypnotic; the boy felt nailed to the floor. "What do you mean? You're . . . you're scarin' me," whispered the boy breathlessly.

"It's going to be up to you. You will know what will make it stop."

The boy wanted to slide away, but couldn't. "I don't know. I don't understand . . . what you're sayin'."

Shepherd jerked his head toward the windows, then back to the boy. "Dark clouds seeded with evil. Rain. Fire. A rainbow of fire. Dreams. No morning light."

The boy swallowed. "Has God—"

But Shepherd interrupted. "The Bible tells of satyrs and doleful creatures . . . pagan . . . things that can't be looked upon. Dark forces in a godless town. Hoof-prints." A gust of wind drew Shepherd's eyes to the row of windows.

"My grandfather knew," he whispered. "Wind-killer . . . the creature. He heard the voice of the creature. He knew the creature would return. I have to fight it. And so will you."

Their conversation having waned, Molly and Taylor strained to hear what the boy and Shepherd were talking about. The boy guestured to them helplessly.

The rain suddenly stopped. The wind died away. The terriers stirred, whining and cowering, searching for a passage under the blanket wrapped around Molly.

The faces of Taylor and Molly, bathed in the lantern light, seemed frozen against the darkness like gaudy masks painted onto the shadows.

193

Lilting through the windows, a shrill, birdlike cry set their teeth on edge. The night pitched to a bottomless blackness.

And then a preternatural rain came crashing down.

"Oh, God!" someone cried, barely audible over the rain.

The boy knew that it was Shepherd.

CHAPTER 14

The thunderous rain muffled Taylor's shout. Recovering from the initial shock of the sudden cloudburst, Molly and the boy scurried about helping Taylor move the camping equipment to the wall opposite the windows. The terriers spun around crazily like tops out of control, lurching blindly for the comfort of Molly's voice. Although the boy could see their tiny mouths jerking as if they were barking hysterically, the rain cascaded with such a roar that, absurdly, the dogs appeared to have had their vocal cords removed.

The clamor of the rain redoubled itself, slamming Molly, Taylor, and the boy against the wall where they reflexively cupped their ears, huddling together like three monkeys who hear no evil. Knotting themselves beneath Molly's blanket, the terriers quaked and trembled.

Shepherd had not moved from his spot; spray from the torrential rain sifted through the window and nimbused around his head. His body writhed gently and his lips moved. He must be praying, thought the boy. But that was his only thought, for the steady hammer of the rain obliterated thought and reduced the range of his senses.

Beyond the windows tumbled a waterfall. And it was as if they were directly under it, and at any moment the roof would cave in and the pounding water would crush them and then sweep them away.

For a solid half-hour the waterfall cataracted upon the abandoned school, thrumming above their heads like a jumbo jet flying low over a housing development. Nature's darkest sounds chorused, and the night exploded in a mysterious chain reaction.

Dark clouds seeded with evil.

Shepherd, now crumpled in a heap on his side, apparently had passed out. Scanning the outline of Shepherd's body, the boy tried to recall the man's upsetting jibberish. He felt deeply sorry for him, wanted to help him. But how? Survival was the immediate task.

The unnatural, drenching rain continued.

Finally, having poured unceasingly for the better part of an hour, the fury of the rain relented, its thunderous energy spent. But a postlude was already under way. Penetrating the encroaching calm, the harsh clang of the bell atop the school pitched rhythmically; then, as its peals softened, deep rich laughter and a rush of wings filled the hall, echoing discordantly for a matter of seconds. Silence returned for ten quick beats of the boy's heart. There would be something more. He knew that.

It began in the window frames. The wood strained and creaked. The vibration took hold, and the walls began to shake. And then the ceiling and then the floor.

196

Thirty seconds later it ceased with mechanical suddenness.

The boy saw that Molly's eyes were closed; she was moaning to herself. Taylor scrambled to his feet, gave Molly and the boy a cursory glance, then fell to his knees by Shepherd.

"Shep?" he whispered. "Shep?"

The boy joined him.

"Is he OK?"

"I think . . . I think he's just exhausted," Taylor responded. "Let's leave him alone."

Unnerved by the trancelike silence of his hulking friend, Taylor rose and went to the windows. The boy followed.

"Where did it come from?" Taylor murmured distractedly.

It was an odd comment, but at that moment, after what they had experienced, it seemed appropriate. It was like no other rain, and they both knew it. No other rain ever.

Still huddled with her terriers, Molly whispered, "Windkiller. The creature of Christmas Oak sent it."

But neither Taylor nor the boy heard her words.

The air circulating through the windows, air which should have gathered coolness from the rain, brushed warmly at their faces. Below them, the schoolyard was pocked with pools of water, but the clay did not appear to be muddy.

Near the van, lights flickered. Will-o'-the-wisp or demon fires? His jaw set firmly, Taylor stared at them. But the boy's eye was drawn to the faint trails of steam and smoke lifting from the remains of Molly's shop and

197

then gradually to the night sky beyond Half Moon.

"Look at that!" the boy suddenly exclaimed.

Taylor's expression told the boy that he also saw it. If it were a hallucination, then it was working on both of them.

"My God," said Taylor.

A rainbow of fire burned eerily against the distant backdrop of a milky cluster of stars.

Something the Reverend Shepherd had intimated ghosted into the boy's mind.

It's going to be up to you.

Part Three

AND GROW BLOODLESS
WITH DREAMING

CHAPTER 15

Her voice feeble, nothing more than a thin croak, Molly looked up at Taylor and the boy.

"I believe I'll just sit here a spell longer and get a hold of myself," she said. "That storm punked me out. Never in my seventy years have I seen such. . . ." But she pulled up short, as if completing the observation would force her to relive the incredible downpour.

The boy recognized that Taylor was reaching within himself to cover his fear. That's what being a man is, the boy thought to himself. You can be afraid, but don't let it show. Least of all not to a terrified old woman and a little kid.

"Well, all right, Miss Molly. Sure, that would be fine," said Taylor. He placed one hand gently on her shoulder and hunted her eyes for danger signs of an impending blackout . . . or, worse yet, heart failure. "You can just wait right here. But I really think we should be getting on here directly. I'm going to go start up the van and let it run a minute, and then I'll come back and we'll load up."

"Can I go down with you?" the boy asked.

Hands on his hips, Taylor considered the request, his head dizzied from tinnitus generated by the rain. "Ronnie, I think maybe you should stay here with Miss Molly."

Molly lifted her hand weakly in protest. "My land's, don't nobody need stay with me. I'll be fine, shortly. The boy's needin' your company more than mine, don'cha see."

And she was right. He needed a man's company at that moment. He needed to be near Taylor, to be near his strength. Nagging the boy . . . haunting him . . . was the fear, however unfounded it might be, that something would happen to Taylor.

It's going to be up to you. You will know what will make it stop.

"OK, then. We'll come right back up," Taylor acquiesced.

"What about . . . ," Molly began, concern in her eyes as they ranged to the outline of Shepherd. "What about the Reverend Shepherd? Does he need tending to?"

"He's asleep. I checked on him and he's asleep. I'll help him down to the van when we get back. No need to worry about him, Miss Molly," Taylor assured her.

But the boy sensed Taylor repressing another round of fears.

Molly shrugged her shoulders and shook her head. "Don't see how a soul could fall asleep with the awful, awful noise of that rain. I've just never. . . ."

Windkiller sent the storm. The creature's in control. It won't let us leave.

And then the terriers, as if they had just been released from a pen, clambered eagerly around her for words

202

and touches of comfort.

Blank-faced, Taylor considered the scene: the old woman; the dogs; the silent shape of his friend, Shepherd; the boy; the shadowy-room—the boy could sense his growing bewilderment. Here was a man whose mind was struggling to put things in some rational context, searching for some understanding of a process not wholly evident to him.

Steps were missing, and the boy could tell that frightened Taylor deeply.

After more seconds of awkward lingering, Taylor, with flashlight in hand, motioned for the boy to follow. "Let's get the van warmed up."

There was a suggestion of doubt in his tone.

As they started down the stairs, the boy crossed his fingers that the van would roar into life. What if it didn't he questioned himself. Then we'll walk. Get out on the county road and hitchhike. Not much traffic this time of night, but *someone* would eventually pass by. Yes, it'll be all right. He could imagine Taylor, Miss Molly, her dogs, Reverend Shepherd, and himself trekking along the side of the road. Half Moon's outcasts. But it would be OK. Whatever held Half Moon would no longer hold them.

"Watch your footing on these stairs. Rain's blown in on them. Might be slippery," Taylor advised.

The boy shadowed him cautiously down the first flight. The unnaturally humid air funneled up into their faces, but the moisture had fortunately settled the plaster dust. The sky beyond the windows was black, yet clear.

Eyes searching each approaching step, Taylor coughed nervously. "You know, Miss Molly will be all right. Something like this is hard on her, I can imagine. But she'll be OK."

His comment was as much for his own benefit as it was to reassure the boy, and the boy knew that. What Taylor couldn't have known, though, was that the manner in which he talked about all they had experienced frightened the boy. For example, what did he mean when he said, *something like this* . . . "Something like this is hard on her. . . ." What is *this*? The vagueness of the expression increased the boy's uneasiness.

"It's bad that her house . . . her shop burned down like that," said the boy. "All those antiques and things." He hoped that the sound of his own voice would calm his fears.

It didn't.

On the next landing, Taylor slowed. "Ronnie, what happened at Miss Molly's shop? I mean, I know it burned, but what I mean is, what did you see? Anything peculiar?"

"Peculiar?" the boy echoed. "Nothing. I didn't see nothing. It just caught on fire, I guess."

Taylor nodded. Apparently it was what he had wanted to hear.

As they continued their descent, the topic was dropped. By degrees their attention was drawn to the lowest flight of the stairs, drawn to muffled noises: an intermittent vibration, soft creakings. Taken together, recast by their imaginations, the noises emerged as something like a growl. The threat of a mean dog on a weak leash. Or no leash at all.

Hot chocolate and soup warred in the boy's stomach, churning and gurgling. Final flight. The boy half expected something to meet them at the bottom. Something. Taylor was uncomfortably quiet. But the dark foyer was all that greeted them after the last step.

Walking out into the night relieved them. The white van, its right side facing them, looked small, insignificant.

"Glad to see it didn't wash away," Taylor exclaimed.

And more to their relief, the lights—will-o'-the-wisp, demon fires?—had disappeared. In fact, by all appearances, the ruins of Half Moon had returned to normal.

Taylor and the boy climbed eagerly into the van; it was as if a wave of security swept over them.

"OK, sweetheart, let me hear you turn over now," Taylor whispered as he patted the dashboard affectionately. The jingle of his keys was the best sound the boy had heard all evening; it cancelled out his notion of recounting to Taylor the Reverend Shepherd's nonsensical, yet frightening ravings.

It's going to be up to you. Rainbow of fire. You will know what will make it stop.

No. The situation dictated silence. Time to ride out of Half Moon. And never return. Not even to the tree house.

With the concentration of a safe-cracker, Taylor hunched over the steering wheel, maneuvered the floorshift, and inserted the key.

"Don't worry," he said, as much to himself as to the boy, "the taxpayers of Catlin County put a new battery in this baby just last week."

Twice the metallic grind held as if in one long, choking syllable. But it wouldn't catch.

"This time, sweetheart," he purred.

Again, nothing.

"Once more."

The boy held his breath and crossed his fingers.

The engine suddenly roared. The headlights shattered the darkness.

"A-l-l-l right!" Taylor exclaimed and offered his open palm to the boy, who, in turn, giggled and slapped it.

Taylor winked at him. "Let's go get the rest of our crew."

The boy slid to the door and pushed it open. "Yeah, I'm ready," he said happily.

"Like a kitten," Taylor beamed, and then joined the boy.

"Hope Miss Molly feels strong enough to make it down the stairs," Taylor mumbled as they walked back to the school.

"I can help her," volunteered the boy, and then, feeling a surge of energy, ran ahead to open one of the double doors.

A smile stretching across his face, the boy held the door open as the spray of Taylor's flashlight spilled past him. But the smile disappeared when he glanced beyond Taylor and saw the van . . . and what surrounded it.

"No," the boy muttered. "No, look! Where did . . . ?"

He felt as if invisible hands were strangling him.

The small fires sprang to life like a covey of quail bursting into flight. They encircled the van; near each fire a shadow danced.

"What is it, Ronnie?" But even as he asked, Taylor could see points of fire reflected in the boy's eyes. He wheeled angrily. One of the fires burned in the front seat of the van. Taylor began running toward it.

"Damn you! Damn you!" he shouted, and flailed his arms, dropping the flashlight to one side.

For an absurd, almost comical moment, it seemed to the boy that Taylor was merely shooing crows out of a patch of sweet corn. Then reality locked into place; the press of terror returned in full force.

"Come back! Please come back!" the boy screamed.

There was a sudden *whoosh*, the ugly sound of a mammoth suction, and the van was engulfed in flames. Shadows seemed to snuff out the surrounding fires so that the burning van stood alone as the focus of the animated darkness.

Helplessly, the boy watched Taylor run to within twenty feet of the flames before he stopped and began scrambling away, stumbling, the clay slippery beneath his feet. He fell once, pushed himself up, struggled another five feet, and then fell again. The boy started to run to help him, but the explosion parted the curtain of shadows separating them before his first step was firmly planted.

What followed was a surrealistic collage of war movie clips: the deafening roar of a mortar shell clearing out a bunker; the fire shower of light; the furnace blast of heat; and the macabre sight of Taylor's dark silhouette tumbling once, twisting once in the air, landing, bouncing at the boy's feet like someone's misshapen duffle bag being tossed from a troop truck.

The fist of fire had smashed into Taylor, literally knocking him out of his shoes, before his body slammed down to the clay several yards later. A ridge of fire ran up his back, but when he hit the ground the force rolled him, snuffing out his flaming clothes.

Pain jabbed into the boy's shoulder. He grabbed at it

as he hunkered near Taylor's body. Orange flames and greasy black smoke poured out of the gutted van. Even twenty-five yards away from it the heat mounted an ovenlike intensity.

Face down, Taylor at first was silent. Fighting back tears, the boy rolled him onto his back, and then Taylor groaned; prolonged, sickening groans. The boy reached down and touched his face and felt something warm.

"Oh, man . . . no!"

He hustled after the flashlight so that he could see Taylor's wounds more clearly. The pain in his own shoulder stitched like fire. Then his fingers discovered the jagged shard of glass that had penetrated his skin. It had stuck in his shoulder like a dart. He pulled it loose; fortunately, it was not a deep wound. Not deep enough to matter in the scheme of things.

Writhing and gasping for breath, Taylor was trying desperately to crawl away. Having found the flashlight, the boy returned, knelt by his side, and attempted to comfort him. Trails of blood and clay and perspiration cut through Taylor's face. One ear appeared to be bleeding heavily, sliced or punctured by flying glass or metal.

"No. Stop trying to move. Don't move. Please don't move," the boy whispered hoarsely, his throat dry-racked with fear.

But Taylor continued to pull himself toward the door of the school, his groans and cries of agony filling the shadows. Seeing Taylor's almost maniacal determination to drag his body into the school, the boy began to help.

In the distance, he could hear a woman's voice barely rising above Taylor's groans and the muffled roar of the burning van. A woman's voice. The boy felt a surge of hope.

"Down here! Come quick!" he yelled.

The explosion had drawn Molly to the third-floor windows; she looked down with horror at the conflagration and the injured body of Dale Taylor. She called out something incoherent, a rabble of words with no meaning. But when she heard the boy's panic-ridden voice reaching out, she headed for the dark stairway clutching the gas lantern.

In the meantime, the boy had grasped Taylor under his arms to help him slide himself into the foyer and through the doorway of the first room on the right, the room which for so many years had served as the principal's office.

"Carol Mae . . . Carol Mae," Taylor moaned, flattening out on his back, stretching a clawed hand into the air. "Jesus . . . no, I've lost her."

The boy stared at Taylor's face and then at his leg. Even in the shadowy light it was like looking at an optical illusion. Some familiar sight that just couldn't be: like looking at a brand-new Louisville Slugger bat bowed out at its trademark.

At the knee, Taylor's pant leg was torn and already soaked with blood. The boy directed the flashlight onto it; the knee itself resembled a shattered pane of glass. Above the knee, the ripped pant leg revealed a swollen, bluish thigh.

The boy felt empty, boneless.

Then Taylor suddenly raised himself on his elbows, his face calm except that his cheeks were pouched out. There was a loud gurgle. Taylor's upper body pitched forward and he vomited to one side. Again and again.

The floor pooled with a hot, steamy, putrid mixture of coffee, chicken-noodle soup, and blood. His body shook from the dry-retching that seized him once his stomach had been emptied; then the delayed response to the pain in his leg held sway, and he screamed until he collapsed. His face glistened with sweat, and threads of vomit covered his chin. But the bleeding around his ear had all but stopped. The boy glanced at the ear; it was a soft, oozing red mound. He thought grimly of Norbert Day.

Taylor's breathing was shallow, irregular. His right arm lay obliviously in his own vomit.

He's going to die.

The boy leaned close to Taylor's face as if he were about to kiss him.

He's going to die . . . Just like mom and dad . . . And the people of Half Moon.

Suddenly he grabbed Taylor's shoulders and began shaking him violently.

"Don't die! Don't die! Damn it, don't die! Don't you die, too!"

Sobs wracked him; his forehead lowered upon Taylor's chest. And that's how Molly and her terriers found him when they reached the bottom of the stairs.

When the boy finally lifted his head, it felt as if it were inside a clear plastic beach ball. Nothing was real. Not even his own heartbeat.

Caught on fire by itself, an inner voice intoned rhetorically.

Filtering through, louder as her concern heightened, he could hear Molly. "We gone have to get help! Get Reverend Shepherd, right now, don'cha see!"

Her head bobbed in front of him, blurring like poor

reception on a TV screen. "Caught on fire by itself," the boy whispered.

One of the terriers licked at his hand.

"Never you mind that, Ronnie. Don'cha see Mr. Taylor needs help?" the old woman shrieked, incredulous that the boy was not responding properly.

Taylor groaned. Half-conscious, he once again raised himself up on his elbows. He muttered something, but it was unintelligible.

The boy, frightened and bewildered, shot a glance at Molly. "I don't know what to do," he cried.

Molly tightened talonlike fingers on his wrist.

"Fetch down Reverend Shepherd, I'm tellin' you," she exclaimed, repeating each word slowly, carefully, as if she were addressing a very small child.

Taylor's lips moved dryly. "Kit," he hissed. "Kit . . . first-aid kit." His head fell back and his eyes closed tightly.

Molly looked at the boy. "Go on, Ronnie. It must be with the camping equipment. Bring Reverend Shepherd and the first-aid kit back with you. Go on."

The boy stood on rubbery legs; the small wound on his shoulder burned, and the sour stench of Taylor's vomit made his stomach roil. And nothing, nothing whatsoever, seemed real except the possibility of Taylor's death.

"Don't let him die, Miss Molly," he stammered, and then charged at the stairs, taking the steps as quickly as his fear-weakened legs could manage.

The van's fireball explosion reeled through his memory repeatedly before the third-floor landing was under his feet, and with each replay Taylor's body disintegrated a bit more. Limb from limb.

211

Tears coursed down the boy's cheeks as he entered the third-floor redoubt and fumbled through the camping equipment in search of the first-aid kit. So preoccupied was he that for nearly a minute he didn't notice what was different about the room.

Shepherd was gone.

That detail registered nebulously. He found the kit and raced back downstairs.

"Where's the Reverend Shepherd?" Molly asked, taking the kit from him.

Propped up with his back against a wall, Taylor seemed reasonably alert. He had scooted himself several yards from the pool of vomit.

"He's gone," said the boy. "He wasn't in the room."

Molly looked dazed.

Hatchet in his hands. Stalking in the darkness.

"Well, we're gone have to find him," she replied, not bothering to soften the immediacy and fear in her voice. She seemed to be assuming control of things, but the boy sensed that it was a tenuous control at best.

Taylor lolled his head to one side and asked for water.

"The Thermos is up with the rest of the stuff. I'll get some water for him."

But before the boy got to the stairs, Taylor moaned and his body slumped over to one side.

"Oh, dear God," Molly whispered.

The boy hesitated, considered staying next to Taylor to somehow make certain that he wouldn't get worse.

Water. He wants water.

And then the boy ran for the steps again, unaware that the nightmare had only just begun.

*   *   *

212

Poised on the third-floor landing, the boy rubbed at his lightly bloodstained shoulder as he prepared to move the remainder of the camping equipment to the first floor. On the landing, the thought hit him; it was like an ugly black smear on a canvas filled with a pastoral scene.

It's going to be up to you. You will know what will make it stop.

Shepherd's chilling prophecy dizzied him. His throat constricted to the bore of a pencil. And when he eventually stepped off the bottom stair he could not recall negotiating the three flights. He could have easily believed, in fact, that the stairs had transformed into a dark escalator which had conveyed him all the way down.

I can't do this. I'm just a boy. I need Mr. Taylor and I need Reverend Shepherd.

He plopped the equipment to the floor inside the doorway of the principal's office. Molly was offering a cup of water to Taylor, who was now lying down, his feet slightly elevated, because she believed he was partially in shock. A wool blanket covered most of his body.

One of the terriers growled as the boy approached Molly's back; she shushed it and smiled at the boy weakly.

"Poor Mr. Taylor," she murmured, "he goes from sweating like he's about to melt to shivering like it was January. I cleaned and bandaged his cuts, but his leg . . . his poor ole knee . . . it's bad, Ronnie, real bad, don'cha see." Then she frowned.

"Still no sign of the Reverend Shepherd? You suppose he just took off on his own to look for help? Seems like he would have told us he was going."

213

"No," the boy answered. "I think he's still in the school. Maybe he's off somewhere . . . praying."

Molly nodded absently, her face etched with doubt and confusion.

The boy noticed that she had found something to clean up the pool of vomit with and, although the tight square room was small, with no windows, somehow it exuded a more comfortable air than the third-floor room.

Molly gestured vaguely toward Taylor's body. "I rubbed some salve on his back. Has some burns. Not bad ones. Might not have got all of them. He's too heavy to roll over very easy. We're gone need some help with him because we can't lift him, I don't b'lieve."

The boy heard only part of what she was saying. His thoughts gravitated to fires.

Fires don't start by themselves, do they?

"Miss Molly . . . those fires? Did you see those fires?" He couldn't recognize his own voice. It was a false voice. Somehow that was the right word—false.

She stood up and idly scratched her cheek. "I saw them. Been seeing them off an' on lately. Thought I was seeing things."

"But what are they? Where did they come from?"

"Windkiller's torches," she answered matter-of-factly. "They could be the creature's fires, don'cha know."

"Windkiller? But there's no such thing, is there?"

Molly winced at his expression of fear and waved a hand in front of her face. "Oh, Ronnie, I'm sorry. I don't mean to be scarin' you. But, oh, don'cha see . . . I think I know where those fires come from . . . and . . .

214

and we need to get out of Half Moon."

"I'm real afraid, ma'am. I'm going to find Reverend Shepherd so he can help us," the boy declared.

She hugged him, and he realized how frail she was.

"Please be careful. I'm frightened too, Ronnie. So are my lit-tul men. Reverend Shepherd . . . *Stalking in the darkness . . . oh, my Lord, is it true? . . .* he's not himself . . . please be careful . . . he's not himself."

The boy's heart was a hot rock of fear in his throat. He believed the old woman was right.

The boy had been gone ten minutes, had disappeared up the stairs with flashlight in hand, when Taylor roused himself. His leg struck lightning bolts of pain. He looked about groggily. "Where's Ronnie?"

"Gone after Reverend Shepherd."

Taylor closed his eyes and rolled his shoulders as if to summon strength from some secret area. "Miss Molly . . . fetch me that backpack there by the lantern." He spoke slowly, painfully. She handed it toward him.

He shook his head. "Look in it. There should be a gun and a hatchet . . . get them out so we can have them handy."

Feeling a fresh surge of fear, Molly pawed through the backpack, pulled the gun free, and then searched some more.

"Oh, my Lord, no! No hatchet here!" She searched the rest of the equipment to no avail.

"Did the boy take it with him, maybe?" Taylor asked hopefully.

Molly's face jerked; her mouth quivered. "No. No, he just took a flashlight. Oh, we need to call him back. I'm frightened he—"

Taylor deflected her fear. "No, wait. I may have left it in the van," he lied, hoping to calm the badly shaken old woman.

Lord God, he thought to himself, *why am I so afraid?*

CHAPTER 16

The glow from the fireball awakened something within him. It was a signal.

The old woman had taken the lantern and shuttled out of the room, her tiny dogs trailing her like chicks behind a mother hen.

You belong to me, now, the darkness whispered to Jack Shepherd.

"God forgive me!" he exclaimed, but it was a hollow sentiment, and he knew it.

Lost. Marked. Deliverance. Hoofprints.

The aftermath of Half Moon down.

Jack Shepherd wanted to cry.

Instead, he began to think, to remember. In the darkness of the empty room, he realized his dilemma. The Windkiller creature was now in total control—it was drawing upon his memories and his fears, forcing him back to childhood, back to seemingly innocent days in which he'd spent the entire summer on the farm of Grandma and Grandpa Shepherd while his mother worked at the cotton warehouse. . . .

She worked so that he would have clothes on his back and food in his stomach, her husband, Jack's father, having been killed in some far-off place called Korea fighting communism. The Red Horde. And years later, when Jack Shepherd became an adult, he would watch "M*A*S*H," and imagine that his father, wounded severely, had been brought to the 4063rd to be operated on by "Hawkeye" or "Trapper John." But it would have been an episode without a happy ending, and perhaps "Radar" and "Colonel Blake" and "Hot Lips" and the surgeons would have mourned the death of Jack's father—at least, Jack chose to believe they would have.

On the farm there was freedom and some compensation to a boy who was growing up without a father. There were pleasantries only a boy could fully appreciate. He recalled, for example, the kitchen wizardry of Grandma Shepherd, "Miss Edna," as her husband affectionately referred to her. The things she could conjure up in the kitchen: the wonders of fresh, hot molasses cookies and the cosmic delight of her Confederate stew. Besides the good food, there was space and fresh air and a myriad of places to explore. But such a mecca for boys harbored a few sources of fear as well. There was old Muskie, the truculent, ill-tempered barnyard duck, its blood seemingly warmed by the stimulating prospect of scaring young Jack Shepherd at every possible opportunity.

There was also The Singer.

Remembering it was like remembering the cold sweat chill of a nightmare, one that periodically leaps the boundaries of a dream and haunts you throughout the day.

Grandma Shepherd would roll the fear-evoking machine into the shadowy corner of the living room, and young Jack would give it a wide berth. Grandma didn't call it a sewing machine; she called it "The Singer." And Jack remembered her control of it.

Even now he could easily call up the memory of her darkened figure hunched over the body of the menacing entity, concentrating with the intensity of a medieval alchemist seeking to extract gold from baser metals. Seated among the shadows, she was a sorceress demanding magic from a spinning, thrumming Caliban. She spoke its language and it obeyed.

Grandpa Shepherd knew it in a different way, in a mechanically intimate way. He knew it part by part and kept it well-oiled so that Grandma could weave her magic on it. And every so often when Jack grew bored, Grandpa would collar him and say, "Let's go break down The Singer," which always overjoyed Jack, because the terrifying machine seemed helpless when it was no more than puzzle pieces scattered on the hardwood floor. In that state it couldn't possibly sneak around and grab him, or run him down or spit needles at him or catch his bare feet in its treadle board.

To Jack, The Singer was like a vicious dog that senses you are afraid of it. When he approached it in that dark corner, a sign would neon-flash in his mind, but instead of "Beware of Dog," it read "Beware of The Singer." Thus, Jack felt safe when Grandpa methodically dismantled it to maintenance it.

His grandpa, the Reverend Malcolm Shepherd, a large, grizzly bear of a man who farmed to supplement his meager income as minister of the Half Moon Methodist Church, loomed as a stone monolith, as a surrogate father, in Jack's eyes. Jack cherished those moments when his grandpa would talk to him as they polished and examined each piece of The Singer.

"You know, Jackie," his grandpa would muse, "some machines have a soul—just like people."

Young Jack would bristle and counter. "This one got's a *mean* soul, Grandpa."

The old man would laugh heartily. "Maybe so, Jackie. Maybe so."

Putting The Singer back together would rekindle Jack's apprehension, though it was fascinating to watch his grandpa slip the pieces together with medical precision. In fact, to have overheard the pair working might have sounded like a surgeon calling out instruments for his assisting nurse to hand him: "Bed slide, feed dog, throat plate, presser foot, face plate. . . ."

And slowly, the black-metal menace of the machine head would rematerialize, intact once again to blanket Jack with thick dread.

But now as he sat in the stillness of the abandoned school, oblivious to the turmoil on the ground floor, Jack tried to recall what exactly frightened him about that infernal machine. He couldn't truthfully label the machine *ugly*, for it was a striking model of the Singer treadle machine equipped with BA3 motor and foot control. The cabinet had a dark wood stain and ornately carved drawers, two on each side.

The machine head gleamed a deep ebony which matched the treadle board and belt housing, and the fancifully inviting word "SINGER", all in caps, had been outlined not only on the treadle board and the parallel bars running just under the cabinet, but also on the machine head itself. The lettering on the latter reflected a soft, golden fluorescence, and up close one could note a touch of the baroque in each letter. *Handsome* was the only word for it. An added feature of its appearance was the sewing light on the machine's neck. It was encased in a blue glass lens; to most who saw it, it resembled a Christmas bulb.

But not to Jack.

That eerie blue light would cast a spell over him, rendering the visage of the otherwise attractive old machine sinister and threatening. With its blue light shining steadfastly through the shadows, the machine head, which to Jack looked like a gigantic black wasp without wings, seemed poised to pounce upon anyone who feared or hated it.

And the sound it made! It was like the tumult of cacodemons racing from the confines of one of Breughel's hellish canvases. In his dreams Jack sometimes heard that sound: a macabre thrumming with machine-gun rapidity—a hideous beast growling long and low, or a swarm of mutant black locusts.

He could hear the sound . . . even now.

Is that The Singer coming up the stairs, Jack?

He listened, but heard only the dull background hum of memory.

The machine could be dangerous, he used to caution himself: the treadle board, the belt, and, of course, this beast had something worse than teeth—it had *needles*! Even the machine's accessories held violent possibilities, or at least their names veiled haunting threats. Grandma kept the accessory pieces in one of the top drawers; Jack liked to play with them, but there was something about them that gave him a quiet *frisson* of terror.

He remembered the names of the pieces, each of which sounded like a gangster's nickname: the gatherer, the ruffler, the quilter, the tucker, and, finally, the insidious combination threader and seam ripper. Together they formed a zoo of treacherous wild metal animals, and they were at The Singer's disposal, ready to do its bidding.

But one part of The Singer was his friend; one part gave *him* power—the electric cord. He used to fondle it like a pet black snake, and he would be ecstatic when Grandma would finish sewing and ask him to "pull the plug." With pleasure! And the thrumming, growling Singer, which he sensed yearned to attack him, would strangle to inaction, powerless, its grotesque blue light extinguished.

The black cord was his sword against the electricity-breathing, much-hated Singer. Then, as his final gesture of triumph, young Jack would kick the machine's belt housing and sidle away with the pride of a knight having slain his first dragon.

Yet the residue of fear would linger, and he would seek solace in his grandpa's protective presence. Here was a man who would scoff at fear, or so Jack believed, until one day, sitting next to his grandpa on the front-porch steps, he asked, "Grandpa, are you ever scared of anything?"

"I have a fear of the Lord," his grandpa boomed, but then slipped out of his pulpit tone when he recognized that the boy wanted a more down-to-earth answer.

The rough-hewn man of God stroked his chin and jaw, measuring the impact of his personal secrets on the relative innocence of a small boy. But here was a boy who seemed to understand fear and to expect the truth.

And so it was that the Reverend Malcolm Shepherd held the consummate attention of his grandson for the next score of minutes as he chronicled the legend of Windkiller and the cutting down of Christmas Oak.

"Grandpa? It's just a fairy story, ain't it? Like Mother Goose and Jack and the Beanstalk?"

The old man fell silent; his jaw stiffened and his brow registered pain.

"Jackie," he began cautiously, "I've never shared what I'm about to say with anyone except the Lord, you see. But I'm getting old . . . I'm not a well man. The Lord will be calling for me soon, just as He calls for each of us one day. Maybe . . . oh, it might could be that the Lord's testing me, but . . . that Windkiller . . . that demon . . . I hear its voice . . . in here." He tapped a finger at the side of his head. The boy felt a shiver dance across his shoulder blades and his mouth go dry.

"That demon's voice, Jackie, . . . I hear it speaking blasphemous things, things leprous to the faithful. It wakes me in the middle of the night . . . in the middle of the night and says it's coming back."

And the man of God paused to gesture boldly in the air with his large hands. "Says it's gone send clouds of fury, winds of vengeance, for cutting down Christmas Oak."

"You don't believe it, do you, Grandpa? God won't let it happen, will He?"

His grandpa suddenly smiled broadly. "Course He won't, Jackie. We must have faith in the Lord in our dark hours. But . . . I've weakened . . . and, oh, I have dreams, nightmares to be exact." The smile disappeared. A shadow from nowhere crossed his face.

"Same dream lately . . . of being in my church and seeing that demon Windkiller at the pulpit . . . and the demon raises its great ugly black wings and my church begins to crumble and shake . . . until . . . until it falls in on top of me. And it's like Half Moon gave that demon strength because our people worshipped that tree more than they loved the Lord."

He shook his head and clasped the boy on his shoulder. "I told ole Doc Culpepper about the dreams, and he just said I'm gettin' old and worn out. Well, sir, I knew that. Like I said, soon enough the Lord will take me."

Jack reached for his neck and climbed the man's chest for a reassuring hug. "No, Grandpa, tell the Lord to wait. Who'd protect me from The Singer and old Muskie?"

And Jack remembered one more thing. At the precise moment that Malcolm Shepherd died of heart failure, Doc Culpepper laid aside his stethoscope and muttered, "His church finally collapsed upon him."

Memory faded.

Jack Shepherd stared into the darkness and realized that Windkiller had gained a measure of revenge in the death of Malcolm Shepherd. But the demon wanted more. It wanted the haunted remains of Half Moon. Slowly, inexorably, through its own darkly inscrutable ways, it would come to rule this realm of ghosts and shadows.

I've got to fight it!

Shepherd's resolution flamed briefly, then a fresh surge of darkness filled the room. The doorway assumed a consummate blackness, a hollow, cavernous blackness. The blackness of oblivion.

He was afraid to move, afraid that the blackness would somehow crush him. He listened to the spiraling ascent of his fears. Instinctively, he hugged himself and rocked back and forth. Then the terrifying reverie of the blackness was shattered; at the other end of the school, Molly Harvester called out his name and then the name of the boy.

The blackness pressed upon him, insulting him from the distant voice as if he had been placed in a jar and sealed. Like an insect.

My God, I can't breathe!

Amber dots flecked the blackness, floating toward him like slanted candle flames. Something within the deepest regions of his fear took flight. His thoughts plunged.

I am alone. There is no one else in all the blackness.

He waited.

A blast of warm air, like the wind from a burning bush, poured over him. The soundless void began to vibrate. Wings rustled. Shepherd felt his blood pound in his forehead.

Windkiller stood before him.

The creature's eyes bore down upon him. A faint, ghostly light began softly to illuminate the creature, but Shepherd noticed only a taloned hand reaching toward him.

It held Dale Taylor's small hatchet.

Unable to resist, Shepherd took it, and in his mind a voice darkly whispered, *Your nightmare awaits.*

The blackness receded. Wings lifted, spun out another gust of warm air. And the creature was gone.

Out into the hallway Jack Shepherd moved, one hand clutching the hatchet reluctantly. It was a somnambulist's walk. And when he raised his arms, they jerked like a marionette's; and he knew that Windkiller manipulated the dark strings that controlled him.

He turned to his right, went down the hallway to the far side of the building where another flight of stairs began its descent to the first floor of the school. And there a sound from the past slowed him.

The mechanical thrumming filtered down upon him.

Is that The Singer behind you, Jack?

There was a rattling of metal wheels; the shadows expanded, and Jack Shepherd began to bound down the stairs. The darkness ballooned in front of him.

Twice he slipped and fell on the wet landings. When he reached the bottom floor, he felt safe. The Singer hadn't followed, but by degrees he sensed the presence of another childhood nightmare.

Krk, krk, krk, krk.

The demon Muskie was waiting. This time Jack knew he couldn't run, couldn't hide. He would have to face his fears. Cautiously he sought the hallway connecting the main building with the gymnasium. He knew where he might find the demon. He remembered the way. Half-stumbling through the darkness, bumping against a few of the metal lockers, he drove himself to the door of the boys' locker room.

And suddenly past became present.

Hatchet hidden behind his back, Shepherd waited for the old demon Muskie, waited outside the door of what had transformed into his grandpa's chicken house. And it was no longer evening, no longer a dark-

226

ened hallway. Instead, it was a years-ago, white-hot scorch of a morning that forced the large man to shed his shirt and wipe his brow with the back of his wrist. Sweaty, nerve-tightening minutes passed.

The old bastard senses the trap. Laying low in the chicken house.

With a fresh transfusion of courage, he stepped into the dressing room and the illusion held sway, for he had entered the humid, dusty, smelly confines of the low, rectangular chicken house.

Wooden roosts constructed of long square rails lined one side of the single room in angled tiers that reached to the ceiling. Beneath the roosts were nesting boxes, piles of old feed sacks, rolls of chicken wire, wooden egg crates, and thick layers of chicken droppings, the latter of which Grandpa Shepherd would skim away as fertilizer for next spring's garden. The other half of the building was a straw-covered floor replete with watering and feeding troughs. Three dusty, insect-coated light bulbs about fifteen feet apart hung from cords down the center.

Wading into the chicken house, hatchet poised, Shepherd found the building empty and silent except for two sitting hens softly cooing on their nests. All of the other chickens and ducks must have surrendered to the morning's invitation to patter about the farmyard.

A dusty, humid somnolence gripped the scene. Sunlight poured through the only door at the far end, but barely passed through the two dingy sets of side windows.

Sweat trickled down Shepherd's sideburns into his beard as he searched each nook and cranny of the building, expecting at any moment to find Muskie hiding behind a crate or a heap of feed sacks.

"Come on out, Muskie, I'm ready for you," Shepherd whispered, but his tone was laced with uncertainty and fear.

He crept to the far corner, squeezing beneath the roosts, careful to avoid fresh droppings, careful also not to take his eyes off potential hiding places. Nothing. He breathed a sigh of relief and swiped away the sweat stinging his eyes with his forearm.

Krk, krk, krk, krk, krk.

Shepherd turned. At the door, some sixty feet from him, something white tumbled through. Sunlight danced. Motes of dust stirred, funneling upward.

Krk, krk, krk, krk, krk.

Shepherd blanched. He felt his ribs press against his lungs and grip as if they were hands.

Wings spread high above his head, Muskie clambered toward him like some mythical beast released by a wanton god.

Krk, krk, krk, krk, krk.

Too terrified to scream, Shepherd scrambled backward, tripping over crates and rolls of chicken wire. A moan, high-pitched like that of a small trapped animal, escaped from his lips.

And then Muskie's white fury closed in.

There was nowhere to run.

Muskie, his intent viciously precise, slammed under the bottom roost and tore at Shepherd's legs with his bill and wings. Shepherd shrieked as if he had been scalded, and then, desperate, he smashed through two of the roost rails, somersaulting onto his face out

228

away from Muskie's advance. The hatchet slipped from his grasp. He rolled onto his back, his arms crossed over his face in a giant X. He was at the mercy of the demon.

There was a rush of wings and a sequence of frantic squawks. Shepherd tensed and gritted his teeth, still not quite capable of calling for help. But no attack materialized. More frantic squawks, more desperate flapping of wings, but no attack.

Shepherd lowered his arms and sat up. And stared in disbelief.

One webbed foot lodged in a roll of chicken wire, Muskie thrashed about helplessly. His long, serpentine neck slapped against the top of a crate. The angle of the roosts pinched him in on one side, preventing him from tearing himself free.

Never letting his eyes leave the shackled bird, Shepherd started to call for his grandpa. *No*, he told himself. He staggered to his feet and retrieved the hatchet. *No, this is my killing. Not Grandpa's.*

Muskie continued to writhe and struggle. Shepherd watched, lost all track of time. Soon the duck ceased, its eyes glazed with exhaustion. Hatchet above his head, Shepherd approached.

Got to fight them. Got to do this. Got to do it now.

He closed his eyes and clutched the hatchet handle with both hands, towering over the duck; his body trembling, sweat pouring down his face, his teeth clenched so tightly that his jaw began to ache.

The moment seemed to swim beyond the boundaries of time. Suddenly Muskie screeched in one last, totally desperate cry. Shocked by the intensity of the cry,

Shepherd hammered down as hard as he could and fell to his knees.

Warm liquid sprayed upon him like water from a garden hose. It trailed across his naked chest, splattering onto his neck and chin. He opened his eyes. The blood from Muskie's severed neck fountained high into the air. Its putrid odor filled the building.

And then the horror began.

Muskie pulled free, and in his death throes spun in a tight circle, scattering straw and dust and blood. Certain that he was being attacked, Shepherd clutched the hatchet and ran. A scream ripped its way out of his throat in a high-pitched single note.

The hallucination faded.

He slowed, and then began to inch his way through the darkness out into the hallway. And he never looked back.

He staggered through the hallway, tearing at invisible nightwebs of fear and panic. Windkiller had sent the dark vision, had released those terrifying moments from the past in order to gain complete control of Malcolm Shepherd's nephew.

Jack Shepherd tried to fight back, tried to draw upon his store of Godliness to save himself and his three friends. But he was weak, and the influence of Windkiller was strong.

Suddenly, at the base of the stairwell, the creature emerged.

Shepherd cowered back and a whimper escaped his lips.

Be my avenger!

Windkiller speared him with the owl-gleam of his

eyes, and the three words echoed in Shepherd's mind.

"Marked," Shepherd whispered. "The mark of the beast is on me."

And the creature stepped aside as Shepherd, like a newly descended avatar of revenge, began slowly, yet resolutely, to climb the stairs.

CHAPTER 17

The boy walked into the plaster fog. It surrounded him, pressing in upon him, suffocating his thoughts. He imagined himself walking around inside a huge pillow filled with down that threatened to bury him.

Windkiller's voice broke into the fog.

There is a place for you.

"No," the boy whispered aloud.

The voice made the right side of his head ache. Dark images of the fallout shelter flooded his mind. Confusion and panic slowed his steps.

A soft pattering followed him. The darkened hallway of the third floor seemed alive with other tentative sounds. Creakings. Whining metal. Skitterings. Whispers. The muffled *whoosh* of sudden flight. An unearthly background cry, harsh yet somehow inviting.

Someone crashing through the hallway on the first floor? A man's scream?

The boy thought: *Reverend Shepherd is our only hope. He has God on his side. It won't have to be up to me. God's going to help us.*

But as he crept through the hallway, conscious of the low rattle of his breathing, he doubted that anyone could help him. Even Reverend Shepherd. Shepherd, after all, was no longer a preacher. Did that mean he had lost his connection with God? The boy hoped it hadn't.

So why can't I call out for him?

His conviction teeter-tottered: one moment Shepherd was the answer; the next moment he feared to meet that man in the darkened halls of the school.

Questions and doubts spiraled like a minuscule galaxy in his mind.

Her hands trembling, Molly painstakingly poured a cup of water from the Thermos and lifted it over Taylor's chest.

"Thanks, Molly," he responded weakly, raising his head and shoulders as much as he could. He drank as greedily as a man lost in a desert. "So thirsty," he muttered.

Molly leaned toward him. "Not too much water left. Does your leg . . . does it hurt you pretty bad?"

Taylor chuckled softly. "Hurts like hell, Molly. Don't think it's broken, though. And the knee . . . I don't know. No feeling at all. Just numb. Might as well be a fence post from the knee down."

"Did that salve help the burns on your back?" she continued, her voice weary and strained.

"Feels all right, yeah. Itches, though." He swallowed and blinked his eyes rapidly. His fingers caressed the revolver. "Molly, I'm worried about the boy."

The old woman dropped her eyes and cleared her throat. She reached for two of the terriers, and they flattened their ears and circled her hands eagerly.

"I'm worried, too. And, you know, I closed the door here," she began, "so none of the other lit-tul dogs would wander off. Freddie, that darn lit-tul scamp, must've followed the boy. I went to the door a minute ago and called for him, called for the boy, and Reverend Shepherd, too, don'cha know, but nobody answered, and Freddie didn't come."

"He'll be a good watchdog for the boy," Taylor interjected hopefully. "Maybe we shouldn't worry about either of them."

Molly patted her chin nervously. "I . . . I heard a lot of commotion at the other end of the school. Then it seemed like it stopped. Might could mean the boy's found Reverend Shepherd, don'cha think?"

Taylor closed his eyes and nodded.

Something within him was afraid she was right.

The boy stopped searching for Shepherd in the largest room on the third floor, the one that had once served as the high school study hall. The room, a rectangle the size of a tennis court, was empty except for two sizeable tables and a scattering of chairs. At the back of the room was a door that opened onto a fire escape, but it was sensibly shut. The boy had slipped into the study hall because he thought someone or something was following him.

Soft patterings.

Inside the door he crouched and waited. He switched off the flashlight. More pattering. Something clawed at

234

the door and it creaked open. The boy tensed.

Suddenly a small tongue licked the back of his hand.

"Oh, man," he squeaked. Jumping to one side, he switched on the flashlight. His chest prickled with anticipation. Then he relaxed.

"Freddie! Oh, man, I didn't know it was you." He hunkered down to pet the dog even as his heart continued to pound in his throat. "Miss Molly's going to wonder where you are, fella. You going to help me find the Reverend Shepherd? I can't find him nowhere. Been looking in every room. Maybe he went for help . . . but I don't think so. You know, he would have told us if he was."

The dog nosed himself close to the boy, licking at his hand and whimpering to signal appreciation for the boy's attention.

"Well, we better start looking for the Reverend Shepherd again." But exhaustion blanketed him, and so instead of getting to his feet, he sat down and leaned his back against the wall. Freddie sprang into his lap and curled up. The boy giggled at the dog's affection and the ease with which he gave his trust.

"Good little dog, aren't you? Miss Molly sure likes you three dogs, doesn't she? I've never had a dog of my own, but I have some pigeons . . . and a hawk and a crow . . . I followed them to this school, and I don't know where they are now. My friend, Bobby Lee Hollins, he lives in Soldier where my Grandma Cartwright lives . . . Well, he has a dog about exactly like you except he has longer hair. His name is Tiger. Doesn't look like a tiger. No stripes or nothing. Bobby Lee, he-he just liked that name. Once when I stayed all night at Bobby Lee's, we let Tiger sleep on the sofa sleeper with us. Oh man, that was fun. Bobby Lee, he-he knows I ran away from home. He's my friend. And so are you now."

The boy paused to listen to the night sounds of the school: the soughing of the wind under the eaves, creakings, faint skitterings, and even the distant jangle of bells. He stroked the dog's back absent-mindedly. He could smell the smoke that had wafted up into the building from the burned van.

"Mr. Taylor got hurt pretty bad when his van blew up. Got burned some, and his leg . . . one of his legs got broken, I think. I got a piece of glass in my shoulder, but it didn't hurt too much. Mr. Taylor needs a doctor. So that's why we need to find Reverend Shepherd to help us get help."

Tears began trickling down his cheeks, silent tears, for he wasn't crying, wasn't sobbing and snuffling. Fear-generated tears. A necessary release in the shadows cast by the flashlight beam where no one could see him.

"Freddie . . . I'm afraid, you know, something's wrong with Reverend Shepherd. He talked real strange to me about everything being up to me and about knowing what to do. And I saw that rainbow of fire . . . and my pigeons . . . I wish. . . ."

He cried quietly; his head and shoulders jerked back and forth. The tiny dog shifted his position and whined apprehensively.

The crying ran its course.

Like a whirlwind of feathers, the headless pigeons suddenly materialized, hovered, and, as before, seemed to beckon him. Freddie barked and growled low at them, but the boy felt relief. It felt good to see

236

something he loved.

He took a deep breath, wiped his nose with the back of his hand, smiled, and pushed himself up and toward the door. As he and his companion followed the birds out into the hallway, the study-hall door leading to the fire escape swung open silently, and moments later the room was no longer as empty.

On the stairway, at the far end of the building from the room where Molly and Taylor waited for the boy, Shepherd prowled along, his thoughts swirling with the image of those two mammoth tornadoes he had witnessed that spring day as they screamed toward Half Moon. Only this time they looked different: the velvety funnels, towers of twisting fury, overflowed with every dark entity Shepherd could imagine, every demon his subconscious had ever spawned. They spun in a many angled round, merging at last in the image of Windkiller.

Winds of darkness released a demon. Destroyed the town. And the demon stayed. And the demon stayed.

Shepherd inched his way across the first landing, thoughts beginning to surrender completely to the dark task at hand. Somewhere in the shadows Windkiller would be watching him.

Shepherd slowed, contemplated the suggested outline of the steps. He held the hatchet with two hands, extending it high above his head as if he were a Mayan priest set to perform the ancient ritual of human sacrifice.

Trapped in the subtle demonism of thought and action, he slipped through the delicate curtain separating dream and waking.

This is not me.

"I've been marked," he whispered. "This is not me."

He could hear someone walking on the third floor. He heard a dog bark.

Hell hounds. Hell hounds coming after Grandpa's chickens.

The boy shuffled reluctantly past rows of metal lockers, unaware that if he were to return to the study hall he would find it . . . inhabited. Freddie pranced happily along beside him, tiny claws clattering when he rose on his hind legs and pressed against the boy's pant leg.

Gloom muffling the sounds coming from the study hall, the boy nudged an open locker door and it screeched in protest. Scanning the inside of it with his flashlight, he saw only dust and cobwebs. No one tossed textbooks here any more. No one left furtive notes. No one hid tears of embarrassment or anger here anymore.

No real students . . . Only shadow students walk these halls now.

Shadow students.

The boy could imagine them jostling through the halls, passing close to him on either side like cold breezes. Shadow students. He had seen them on those yellow-and-black pedestrian-crossing signs, signs shaped like a home plate, their bottoms reading, "Slow School"; he and Bobby Lee Hollins used to laugh at that phrase, trying to imagine a school inching its way down the street.

238

Shadow students. All rectangles and circles. The boy could see them in his mind, and then see them in the hallway. Classes changing. His thoughts singsonged to their surrealistic movement.

Black shadows walking . . . They have no feet . . . They have no hands . . . Perfect circle for a head. No ears . . . No eyes . . . No nose . . . No mouth . . .

And what are they? Shadows left by all those students having spent all those long days at Half Moon High School. Perpetual shadows.

Night school, he thought to himself playfully. Shadow students coming to night school taught by shadow teachers at shadow desks reading from shadow books.

And what do they learn?

All about shadows, of course.

It's like a science, perhaps. Or another language.

Can you speak shadow?

And the shadows laugh and talk, but no one else can hear them.

At the end of the night, a shadow bell rings which only they can hear, and they all go . . . back into the rubble of Half Moon or Half Moon's past.

Shadow students. Shadowings.

The boy leaned against the railing of the landing and looked down, stabbing the darkness with his beam of light. Fear had activated his imagination. But that's all it was. There were no shadow students. And there was no comfort in walking through these halls. It was too much like . . . like walking into a massive black box.

Black box.

"Dad?" he exclaimed.

And behind him the echo: *Dad?*

And below: *Dad?*

Each echo a different voice. One like the rebounding sound of dropping something down a well . . . or a cistern. One like children, chorusing in wild, high-pitched notes. One like the cry of a wild bird.

Freddie barked once and the bark dissolved into a whine.

The boy sat down on the top step. He felt abandoned. Freddie whined as if to ask why they were stopping. Burdened by self-pity, the boy rose and walked down one flight of stairs, flashlight beam dancing through the shadows. Freddie followed close to his heels. Rain water lay on the landing in small puddles, reminding the boy of the incredible cloudburst earlier.

"Reverend Shepherd?" he called hesitantly.

And as before the echo played with his words. Freddie growled low. Somewhere below them the stairs creaked.

"Reverend Shepherd?"

The beam pooled onto the second-floor landing, and then, like an actor stepping into a spotlight, a man entered the oval of light.

The boy felt dry horror.

Shepherd held the hatchet over his head; his eyes were amber dots, and a vein pulsed in his thick neck. The muscles in his bare chest and arms rippled. He stood as still as a Greek statue.

At the boy's feet, Freddie growled.

"It's me," said the boy, and this time there was no echo. "Reverend Shepherd, it's me. Ronnie. Ronnie Cartwright. You know me. Mr. Taylor needs help. He—"

Shepherd's murder-blank stare shifted from the boy to the dog.

"Hellhound," he muttered, advancing a step. "Son of a demon's hellhound."

Instinctively, the boy turned and scrambled up the stairs, throwing the beam wildly like a searchlight gone haywire. Freddie barked and then charged.

"No, Freddie!" the boy screamed.

He heard the hatchet crash into a step.

The dog yelped once as if he had merely been kicked. The hatchet blade had missed, and Freddie stood his ground. The dog growled and snapped as Shepherd wrenched the hatchet from the wooden step. There was a clattering and a shuffling.

Then total silence.

"Stop it! Stop! It's me! It's me!" the boy yelled at the top of his voice.

When the yells died away, he heard Shepherd's slowly advancing footsteps. Struggling with the paralysis of fear, the boy clambered to the top of the stairs and half-ran, half-slid into the long dark hallway. He switched off the flashlight; his mind reeled blankly as if waiting for instinct to take over.

Hide. Got to hide.

As best he could he caught his breath and chose a hiding place. Squeezing into a dusty locker, he quietly pulled its door closed, praying that its metallic click was not heard by Shepherd.

No, not Shepherd. God wouldn't allow that to happen.

The boy closed his eyes and breathed through his mouth. Darkness tightened at his shoulders and he trembled, trembled so violently that, by degrees, the metal locker began to vibrate and to send a tiny swell of movement to the lockers next to it. By clenching his fists to his sides, one hand grasping the flashlight, he gradually controlled his trembling, but the dust and dead air permeating the locker space clawed at his nose and throat. He had to swallow hard to avoid coughing.

With hatchet in hand once again, Shepherd stalked across the third-floor landing, his steps cautious, quiet. He moved easily, as if the darkness of the hallway were no hindrance. The boy listened with all of his being to determine exactly where his pursuer was, but soon other noises, a rustle of clipped steps, filtered through the small louvered slits near the top of the locker.

The boy imagined hooves. Their movement suggested that they had poured out of the study hall. And now?

They were near. Shepherd, too?

A few feet in front of the row of lockers.

The boy's stomach growled and he pinched it hard. His head swam and most of his body was bathed in sweat. A claustrophobic feeling clutched at his chest.

Hiding in the locker had been a mistake. He knew that now. He should have run. And Freddie. Oh God, Miss Molly's little Freddie.

The boy waited, painful tension in his bladder, shoulders aching from scrunching them inward.

In the distance, he thought he could hear an imperious calling. The jangled voices of Molly and Taylor. But they drifted through the school as if disembodied, as if he had dreamed them.

More waiting.

The hallway fell silent.

Concentrating on the louvered slits, the boy relaxed somewhat. But he continued staring into those slits

242

until, his eyes piecing out the darkness, he realized that a visage stared back at him.

His back jolted against the rear of the locker.

There was a fumbling at the metal latch.

With a miniscule whine, the door swung open.

No one there.

But farther out in the hall a figure turned and approached, and the boy knew that it was Shepherd and that he was not alone. Shadows gathered behind the hulking man like a gang urging their leader to violence.

Something flared in the boy's mind: *Blind him! Blind him!*

Impulse took command, and the boy speared Shepherd's face with the flashlight beam; yet it seemed for an instant to be no face at all, but rather a mask, a pallid mask with only one eye, one terrifying Cyclopean eye.

The handle of the hatchet hid the other eye.

And then the boy followed the arc of the hatchet blade as it swung upward.

CHAPTER 18

In the blinding light, Shepherd's face collapsed upon itself, crushed by rage and fear. The boy saw the edge of the hatchet quiver and jerk. And for what seemed an eternity, it was a stand-off.

Then recognition.

Shepherd's lips moved.

The boy remained perfectly still and kept the beam of the flashlight thrust into Shepherd's face.

Incredulous, Shepherd stared at the boy. He loosened his grip on the hatchet and closed his eyes. His eyelids fluttered.

"Oh God," he whispered feebly.

The boy seized the opportunity.

Like a frantic crab, he scrambled past the statue of Shepherd, sliding toward the stairs to his right, pumping his arms, swinging the flashlight as if he were a track runner carrying the baton in a relay.

The race was to survive.

He slowed only to take the stairs in stumbling, awkward vaults of two or three steps. Twice he slipped on their wet surface. Behind and above him he imagined the darkness gathering to pursue, imagined the twisted mask on Shepherd's face reasserting itself, and the shadows at his shoulders fueling his maniacal rage.

He doesn't *want* to kill me. He doesn't *want* to kill me.

It's the *shadows*. It's the *meanness*. It's the *evil* of Half Moon.

On the next flight of stairs, the boy stopped to look back, but instead of the crazed figure of Shepherd, he saw a huge winged creature, its eyes locked upon him with predatory concentration.

Sour waves of fear rolled over the boy. His sensations looped in a free fall.

He raced on.

Nimbly, he skirted the spot where he had last seen Freddie. A horrid image rose in his thoughts, freeze-framed there, and he knew that it would be with him always, one in a series of grim reminders of the endless night.

As he neared the bottom of the last flight, he heard a pathetic howl drift down from the third floor, the howl of a man in total anguish.

For the boy it released a reservoir of dread and emotion; a scream tore from his throat, and he began to call out. "Help me! Somebody! Help me!"

He ran the length of the bottom-floor hallway, ran and ran, and it was the horror of running through a tunnel that seemed to have no exit.

Molly and two of the terriers met him in the hallway and helped him into the room where Dale Taylor lay injured. Shadows dwarfed the lantern light, but compared with the shadows elsewhere in the building, these seemed friendly to the boy. These shadows spoke of safety.

Minutes later, he felt weightless. He was hunched in space, tethered to a light that he recognized only after his breathing leveled out. It was the gas lantern.

He was safe, he reasoned. For the moment.

Molly and Taylor leaned toward him, their shadows, spawned by the lantern light, swaying jerkily as if they were dancing to a broken record. The boy's memory sketched out piecemeal what had occurred: driving himself through the hallway, finding Molly at the doorway of the principal's office, her body nimbused by the lantern light, and seeing Taylor, both hands gripped upon the revolver, riveted to his approach.

He had screamed at them to close the door, and the rest of what he relayed must have bordered on total incoherence. He had rushed into Molly's arms and cried and hugged her. But once the door was closed and locked, he began to feel the bright warm force that bonded the three of them together. Everything was reduced to a simple equation: the redoubt of the principal's office represented good; everything beyond the door represented evil.

Taylor had one hand on his shoulder trying to calm him.

"It's all right. All right now, Ronnie. It's all right. It's all right, son. You're safe here. It's all right."

Molly added her mutterings of comfort, and then they lapsed into silence and listened. It was an awesome silence broken only once when Taylor spoke.

"Everybody stay away from the door. Stay here against the wall. Everything will be all right." Somehow there was not enough conviction in his voice.

They braced themselves against the wall opposite the door, bunkered behind the lantern. Taylor and Molly huddled to either side of the boy; Molly sat with her knees tucked sideways beneath her and the two terriers against her lap. One of her hands fluttered nervously near her mouth.

To cut down on the pain in his left leg, Taylor kept both legs out flat in front of him. His right hand held the revolver, and his eyes never left the door.

After a long span of silence, Taylor searched the boy's tear-stained face and spoke gently. "Ronnie . . . are you all right now? Can we talk a minute?"

The boy nodded. Taylor's face, sallow and pasty, betrayed the man's attempt to block out the bolts of fiery pain shooting through his leg. And the boy caught the faintest whiff of the burned flesh on Taylor's back and wondered where he got the strength to keep from passing out.

"Ronnie . . . now, are you sure . . . are you sure it was the Reverend Shepherd?"

"Yes, sir. He was on the stairs and he came . . . he came after me. Only . . . only it really wasn't him, was it?" Tears strangled his words.

"No, Ronnie. You're right. It wasn't really Reverend Shepherd. Something's happened to him," Taylor replied, then shifted himself slightly and rubbed at the thigh of the injured leg. "Something happened . . . coming back to this town . . . the memories. Like ghosts, you know. And, you know, . . . you know, it's my fault. I should have taken him home this afternoon. This town—"

"Wasn't nobody's fault," Molly interrupted, her voice quavering. Not for us to understand, don'cha see.

Some kind of evil . . . oh, I've known for months it was in Half Moon . . . all the strange things happening. I knew all along. And now, don'cha see, it-it got that fine man—just like the storm got my Carl—it got Reverend Shepherd and filled him with evil. I had a vision . . . I should have stopped Ronnie from going . . . it's Wind-killer did this to Reverend Shepherd."

Taylor lowered his head as if embarrassed by her comments, or as if to hold onto some element of reason, something that could explain away or perhaps simply deny the darker mysteries of Half Moon down.

"He wasn't alone," the boy muttered.

Again, Taylor searched the boy's face, seeking nuances of revelation that words never quite offer. "What do you mean, Ronnie? What do you mean, 'he wasn't alone'?"

"I mean, it was like . . . like things, like shadows all around him . . . like what we saw out by the van."

Taylor nodded slowly and glanced across at Molly. She forced a smile as she placed her hand on the boy's wrist.

"Tiny and Fritzie here have been good lit-tul men," she began, and the change in the subject immediately comforted the boy. However, when he focused on the two small dogs jockeying for a share of Molly's lap, he remembered. He felt something jerk and twitch in his stomach.

Molly chuckled nervously. "But . . . Freddie," she exclaimed, "now I know that scamp followed you. Why he has to be such a, such a bold lit-tul adventurer . . . well, and so when you went looking for Reverend Shepherd, I stood at the door and called for that scamp, but I suppose he was tagging along with you. . . ."

Her expression tightened and her eyes seemed to bulge with a fearful expectation.

For an uncomfortable run of seconds, the boy said nothing. Could say nothing. There were no words—only the freeze-frame image of the dog attacking the hatchet-wielding man.

Then, with a voice that sounded as if it came from under a thimble, the boy said, "Little Freddie's gone."

He leaned against Molly's shoulder and the tears came, and again she comforted him, reining her own emotions.

"I'm sorry," the boy murmured through his tears.

Uncertain of what else needed to be said, Taylor added, "I'm sorry, too, Miss Molly."

Molly stared fixedly at the lantern. "I . . . I always knew," she said. "I always knew that someday, don'cha know, he would get into some . . . trouble that he couldn't . . . oh, I thought maybe a car or a truck . . . he was always running off, crossing streets without looking, wandering out to the county road. Mr. Carl, well, he knew, too. That lit-tul dog . . . he was just full of himself with adventure . . . just full of himself." She found her handkerchief and dabbed it around her mouth. She held back a flood of tears.

Still leaning against her shoulder, the boy whispered, "He tried to protect me. He barked and ran at the—at the Reverend Shepherd . . . to protect me. He was . . . he was brave . . . brave little dog. And God just let him get killed. Why? Why did He?"

Molly patted the back of his head. "Oh, my land's,

we . . . we can't know that, don'cha see. Same as when . . . as when Mr. Carl got lost . . . and the people of our town . . . there's some kind of purpose, don'cha know. We all gone have to believe that or, or life would be like being kept in some big ole dark dungeon never knowing why we were there or if we were ever getting out. There's some kind of purpose, Ronnie. There just has to be."

He pulled away from Molly's shoulder and straightened his back against the wall. His next words were directed primarily at Taylor, but through a residue of tears, they sounded rhetorical.

"What's going to happen, now?"

Taylor shifted again, pondering the question carefully. "We've got two choices as I see it: We can either stay here and wait till morning and hope that somebody comes looking for us or stumbles upon us accidentally, or . . . or we can try to find some help yet tonight." He glanced at his watch, its crystal starred with several cracks. It was ten minutes until midnight.

The boy's eyes darted to the door. "What about . . . what about the Reverend Shepherd? Will he . . . is he going to try to kill us? And what about . . . whatever else is out there?"

Reflexively, Taylor's fingers toyed with the handle of the revolver. "We'll be safe here. We'll be OK if we stay here."

An uneventful half hour passed.

Exhausted, the boy slumped against Molly and drowsed, but never fully lapsed into sleep. The old woman remained alert, stroking her terriers, and crying very softly to herself.

Alive to every sound, Taylor fought the pain in his leg and back, and listened, listened with as much concentration as he could muster. He sensed the darkness about to stir.

Someone walking. He heard someone walking through the halls on one of the upper floors.

"Miss Molly," he whispered. "Do you hear something?"

Before she could speak, it began.

A tortured animal sound, pitched to a pathetic wail, echoed downward. Bouncing discordantly, it created the illusion of a dozen or more amplified voices.

"Good God," Taylor murmured.

The boy snapped awake, and the terriers began to bark so excitedly that even after Molly shushed them, they wouldn't cease whining. But the tormented howls from above continued unabated.

"Is it the Reverend Shepherd?" the boy asked in a hushed tone.

"I'm afraid it is. Oh, good God . . . I'm afraid it is," said Taylor.

The wails became screams, and the screams trailed a shuffling rush of steps as someone descended the stairs, falling occasionally, crashing into the walls. The anguished cries maintained a heightened pitch.

It was the terrifying rabble of someone being pursued.

Collectively, the boy, Taylor, and Molly tensed and watched the locked door. No more than fifteen feet from them, it caught the spray of lantern light up to just above the doorknob. Shadows covered the top half of the door, a door that offered a tenuous security at best.

Clasping both hands on the revolver, Taylor held it firmly in front of him and aimed it directly at the door. The boy saw muscles flex in Taylor's neck and forearms; as the clamour neared, he felt a sinking in his stomach.

A breathless scrambling . . . a stifled shriek . . . and suddenly the thud of fists upon the door.

"Save me! Help me! *Save me-e-e-e!* Demons! Save me! God, please save me."

Shepherd's voice hammered through the door and the boy scrunched himself against Taylor.

"Let me in! *Save me! Dear God! Oh, dear God!*"

"No," Taylor whispered to himself. "No, I can't." He stayed frozen in position.

There was a clatter of hooves, a muffled roar of movement like a stampede or like the drumfire of the cloudburst earlier. Something smashed against the door, and it nearly gave way. One seemingly endless scream punctuated all other sounds, and Taylor, his hands now shaking uncontrollably, tried desperately to squeeze the trigger, but couldn't.

The long scream passed; the clatter of hooves dissipated.

And then the silence was total.

Beneath the door, a rivulet of blood inched its way toward them.

CHAPTER 19

Transfixed by the satiny ribbon of blood, the boy jerked in surprise when Taylor lowered the revolver and shouted, "Shep! Shep! Oh, good God!"

At first the boy and Molly stayed back as Taylor, straining against pain and exhaustion, crawled past the lantern, pulling the shattered leg along to one side.

"Shep, I'm comin'. I'm comin'," Taylor hissed through his teeth, and then hesitated as he turned to the boy.

"Ronnie, bring your flashlight here."

And that was enough to snap the boy out of his dark reverie. He and Molly slowly, tentatively, followed Taylor to the door, dreading the hollow silence of the moment, anticipating the worst. A faint hope flickered through the boy's mind that they wouldn't open the door, that they would leave it shut forever.

The terriers cowered back, fearful of the fresh smell of blood.

Taylor edged another foot closer to the door, and the boy noticed that the rivulet of blood—*Shepherd's*

253

blood; it was Shepherd's blood; each of them knew that—soaked into the knee of Taylor's pants.

"OK, now listen, Ronnie," said Taylor. He studied the door; pain was etched at the corners of his eyes and mouth. He wiped beads of sweat from his forehead with the back of his hand.

"Here's what I want you to do: Switch on your flashlight and then reach over and run that bolt lock back . . . and just push, just push the door open and get back out of the way. You and Miss Molly just stay back. Keep the little dogs back, too."

The boy nodded and Molly gathered the two dogs up and cradled them against her stomach. Taylor braced himself behind the revolver, which he pointed directly at the door.

"OK, do it," he whispered.

When the boy touched the bolt, his fingers numbed. For an instant his breathing seemed to catch, and he lowered his hand and made a fist to stop it from trembling.

"Go ahead," said Taylor gently.

The bolt slid free and the knob turned easily.

The boy gave the door a moderate push and stepped back. A collage of orange and black lights poured in, an eerie, preternatural light, dust-filled, spliced with rays from the lantern and from the angle of the flashlight beam.

The swing of the door caught at Shepherd's shoulder. The blood-soaked figure lay across the light so that the area from his chest to his thighs was all that was visible. For a blinding, maniacal instant, the boy thought there was no head attached to the shoulders.

Blood trickled and pooled on and around the body.

"Shep. Oh, my God," Taylor winced.

"I'll . . . I'll get the first-aid kit," Molly stammered, and set the curious and frightened terriers on the floor.

Because Shepherd was lying on his back, the severe chest wounds became apparent immediately. In an ever-widening circle, blood stained Shepherd's chest and spread to his waist. The mottled light revealed mangled flesh and pulsing spurts of blood.

"Oh God, I'm sorry, Shep. I'm sorry," Taylor whimpered.

The boy, his head swimming in a gray sea of revulsion, watched as Taylor dropped the revolver, grabbed sterile gauze patches from Molly's outstretched hand and pressed them onto Shepherd's chest.

Molly leaned closer and directed the boy to shine the light on the wound so that Taylor could see what he was doing.

"What on earth . . . ?" she began, and left the obvious question hanging in limbo.

Taylor worked feverishly and spoke in a tone that sounded disembodied. "It's a real bad cut . . . maybe . . . maybe stab wounds. Pretty deep. Oh, good God, he's gonna lose a lot of blood. Damn it. These cuts . . . looks like something . . ."

Trampled. The word caught in his throat. *Something trampled on him.*

"Give me all the gauze. Damn, we've got to slow down this bleeding."

Taylor's hands and wrists were covered with deep red gloves of blood.

Suddenly the boy heard his own voice overlay Taylor's.

"He must have dropped the hatchet. But he had it

. . . he did . . . and he—"

Molly clawed his arm with her sharp, thin fingers. She looked into his eyes and shook her head to discourage him from saying more.

Taylor seemed oblivious to the boy's observation about the hatchet. Both hands pressed firmly on Shepherd's chest, he gazed into the darkness of the foyer and hallway.

"Jesus, what did this? Will somebody tell me that? What did this?"

Having succeeded in slowing the flow of blood, Taylor supervised Molly and the boy in dragging Shepherd's body a few feet into the principal's office. Shepherd, barely conscious, rolled his head slightly; his eyelids twitched and, once, he opened his eyes, but could not, it appeared, focus them.

Taylor hovered over the man's face, then surveyed the shocked, stunned expressions of Molly and the boy.

"He's got to have a doctor right away. He's just lost too much blood," Taylor explained. Talking helped suppress a crowd of amassing emotions. "So . . . so, Ronnie . . . son, now, you're gonna need to go for help. It's Shep's . . . it's Reverend Shepherd's only chance, do you see?"

The boy raised his eyebrows and swallowed, but said nothing.

Taylor, his attention drawn to the shadowy hallway, outlined a plan of sorts. "Take your flashlight and make your way out to the county road. OK? You know how to get to the county road from here?"

"Yes, sir," the boy heard himself respond.

"OK, then, get to the road and go west on it toward Soldier. Turn left on it down beyond Miss Molly's place and go toward Soldier. Try to flag somebody down, but don't get right out on the road. Might be a trucker out this time a night. I don't know. Try to flag somebody down and tell them we need an ambulance. It's an emergency." Taylor paused.

"Is there anyone living at the Richfield's place now I wonder?" he asked rhetorically.

"I think the Richfield's youngest boy lives there," Molly offered.

"That's about a mile and a half from town. If you don't see a car or a truck, run on to the Richfield's place. Collis Richfield—have Collis phone for an ambulance. OK?"

Before the boy could nod, Taylor added, "You need to hurry, son."

Flashlight in hand, the boy stepped around Taylor and Shepherd's body.

"Be careful, Ronnie," Molly whispered.

In a few seconds, he was through the foyer, moving quickly out the front doors. The broken chain rattled and lingering smoke filled the night air, suddenly cooler than it was earlier. A yellow partial moon, perched high in the eastern sky, offered a sickly, malignant spray of light.

There was a portentous silence. No wind. No background sounds of night insects.

As the boy started across the schoolyard, flashlight creating a path, his knees buckled. Shepherd's bloody wound shuttled through his thoughts; he fell to his knees and dry retched.

257

Reverend Shepherd's only chance, do you see?

Juxtaposed against the image of the bloodied man were other images: one of a stalking figure, hatchet raised, face a mask of twisted rage; and one of his beloved pigeons, a hovering cloud of protection.

They saved me! They want to help me!

The boy got to his feet slowly, and he stopped long enough to relieve himself. As the urine poured from him, he shivered violently. And then he thought of Taylor and Molly—they were depending upon him. He made up his mind that he wouldn't disappoint them; exhaustion and fear clawed at him, but he was resolute.

You will know what will make it stop.

The words bolted through him like electricity.

There is a place for you. Here, in my darkness.

The auditory hallucinations warred.

"No, I'm going for help," he blurted. And he began to run.

CHAPTER 20

Nothing's familiar, the boy thought to himself as he ran.

Streets, the rubble of houses and other buildings—everything seemed different. It was like running through an alien landscape, a moonscape of someplace that had slipped completely from memory.

He couldn't find his tree house. He couldn't find the burned shell of Molly's antique shop. And worse, he had the uneasy feeling that he was beginning to circle back on his route.

Tiny fires sprouted here and there in the darkness, blocking his way, channeling his movement. He thought of Taylor's twisted, swollen leg and of Molly's fear-worn face. And he wanted out. Out of the responsibility.

He wanted to run away.

But I can't! I've got to find help!

He thought of Shepherd's mangled, bloodied chest. What could have done that? And then he thought of the winged creature which had loomed at the top of the stairs. The creature had looked like . . . now he remembered . . . it had looked like Zephra Firethorn's painting at the sesquicentennial, the painting that depicted the legendary Windkiller.

It's real. The creature's real and it hurt the Reverend Shepherd and it's going to—

The fear dazed him: it hit him like an icy wind on naked skin.

Tears of frustration and desperation threatened, but then suddenly, in the distance, he saw his pigeons, ghostly white suggestions swirling through the night.

Flashlight piercing the darkness, he ran in their direction and kept running until he realized that he was on the road heading out of town. He passed the sawhorses and nearly yelled for joy, because it was like entering a magic gate into a realm of certain help, a realm apart from the nightmare of Half Moon down.

He slowed as he reached the county road—*head west toward Soldier*—Dale Taylor's advice flooded home. The asphalt felt good beneath his feet. It felt solid and substantial. It promised that someone would come along shortly, and then the nightmare would be over.

Breathless, he looked both ways into the shadowy vanishing points of the road. No traffic. A soft warm breeze rustled the weeds at the road's shoulder. He fought back a wave of disappointment and forced himself to concentrate on the task at hand.

"Got to get to the Richfield place. Got to find Collis Richfield," he muttered, gritting his teeth, tightening his grip on the flashlight.

Ahead, the pigeons dived, sweeping ghostly curves through the darkness, and encouraged him to follow the path of the road. The boy walked on, but his grasp on the reality of the situation was tenuous at best. It was all too much like fantasy. Like a "Solo Adventure" in Dungeons & Dragons.

He smiled at the pleasant memory of playing that elaborate tabletop game with his friend, Bobby Lee Hollins. The fantasy adventure context of the game was so easy to surrender to—so easy to imagine yourself questing for treasure armed with daggers and magic, prepared for lurking monsters. As hero, your character possessed strength, dexterity, intelligence and a half-dozen other traits that protected him from harm. And with one roll of the dice, "hit points" could score, or a "saving throw" could be attempted.

But not here. This wasn't fantasy.

A few minutes later, he glanced over his shoulder, sensing that he was being followed. There was no one, but behind his eyes a voice was stirring, the familiar intrusion that he knew now must be the voice of Windkiller. This time it spoke no words. Instead, only deep, rich laughter emerged, a dizzying laughter.

The boy stared directly above him into the cloudless night sky. There, circling like a predatory bird tracking a mouse, the huge winged creature spun shadows into threads of airy blackness.

Run! Run for help! the boy's own voice of survival insisted.

And he did, but Windkiller, gliding on ebony wings, kept him always in view.

"This has got to be it."

Weary, hounded by a persistent dread that he would never find help, the boy stopped at the rusting mailbox and studied the shadowy outline of a house fifty yards or so from the road.

"This has got to be the Richfield's place," he muttered.

He felt alone. The pigeons had disappeared; the winged demon above him had slipped into some pocket of the night.

The boy bit on his lip nervously and with his flashlight scanned the wet clay driveway. For thirty yards it cut a straight path, then angled gently to the left so that it fronted the distant house.

The house, a two-story graying clapboard, was dark except for a faint light in a first-floor window. Taking a deep breath, the boy started walking up the driveway, concentrating on the feeble light, straining to recall anything at all about the Richfields—and Collis Richfield in particular.

He knew that Collis, only son of Thad and Millie Richfield, had been regarded as a derelict, a no-account bum, by most folks in the area. In his late twenties or early thirties, Collis had shunned education, barely learning to read. It was said that it took Collis the entire week to read the Sunday comics. He shunned work with equal fervor. In fact, the boy could remember only one positive trait that anyone ever attributed to the young man—turkey calling.

Collis Richfield, they said, was one of the best wild turkey callers in the state of Alabama, maybe in the entire South. His odd talent had won him numerous calling contests, not to mention a wealth of admiration among area turkey hunters, all of whom wanted Collis to share his trade secrets.

He'll help me. I'll wake him up and he'll help me.

The boy quickened his pace.

The light in the first-floor window seemed to grow brighter.

Soon he was close enough to view the house in some detail. But his heart sank at its signs of disrepair. Last spring's storms had torn away shingles, broken windows, and loosened siding. A large oak branch had gashed a hole in the roof. Most of the windows were now covered with plywood or cardboard. One of the front-porch supports had split and was threatening to give way.

Who could live here?

He swallowed back his doubts and took a few steps toward the front door. Suddenly, his pigeons materialized behind him, hovering, beating the darkness with their wings, but creating no sound. He smiled at them and lifted one hand to show them that he welcomed their presence. They lingered, treading the air and pulling away from the house as if they wanted him not to enter it.

"Hey, there's help here," he whispered. "I'm going to get help."

He waved them off and hurried up the steps. For a score of seconds he knocked on the door and called out, "Is anybody home?"

And then he tried opening the door and found that it was unlocked.

He stumbled into a shadow-strewn front room, his eye drawn immediately to a lantern resting on a table in the far corner of an adjacent room. He started to call out once again, but a sudden movement choked off his words—from out of the shadows behind the lantern a hand lifted free and settled atop the table.

A voice, high-pitched and strained, an old man's voice, followed the movement.

"That be you, Papa?"

Surprise and fear anchored the boy in his steps. A foul, musty air coiled around him. There was another movement near the lantern. Instinctively, the boy drew in his breath and watched.

Half of his face bathed in the white glare of the lantern, Collis Richfield patiently rested his clawlike hands, spurs for thumbs, on the table. His emaciated frame trembled slightly as if buffeted by an inner wind; his long sun-wrinkled neck craned as he cleared his throat. And his lips quivered, anticipating words; his head twisted to one side so that the boy saw only one eye, large and liquid, which didn't blink. The other eye withdrew into the shadows, preoccupied with something. The illuminated side of his face was lapped and folded with age.

"Took your own sweet time comin' back, Papa," Richfield exclaimed. "You brang Mama, too?"

With all the strength of his will, the boy pushed himself forward.

Collis Richfield's hairless, misshapen head retreated into darkness.

"Who's there? Who you be?" he stammered.

The boy inched ahead until he broke through the circumference of light. "Ronnie. Ronnie Cartwright," the boy mumbled softly. "I'm Ronnie Cartwright and . . . and I need help." His voice took on volume as the urgency of his task overcame his fear.

"I need help. You see, Mr. Taylor and Miss Molly . . . Mr. Taylor is back at the school and he's hurt bad and so's the Reverend Shepherd. Something . . . something hurt him real bad and if I don't . . . they sent me here to get help. You got to call an ambulance. Mr. Taylor said for me to find you, Mr. Richfield, and get help. Please, you got to help. There's something evil in the school. Please help."

Collis Richfield's head dipped into the light. He listened to the boy's heavy, excited breathing.

"Fools," Richfield whispered. "Man got to be a pure fool to be in that town." He paused, seemed to study the boy, then let his glance wander toward the door.

"There be something out there," Richfield continued. "Something more powerful and mysterious than anything I know. That's for damn sure. Something mighty strange and a damned sight more dangerous than anything I ever seen. Turned me old, don't you see?"

"Mr. Richfield, sir, . . . could you help? Can you call an ambulance? Mr. Taylor and Reverend Shepherd need help real bad. Honest, they do. I'm not making this up. Please."

Richfield stared at the floor, and then, even as one eye appeared to remain angled downward, it seemed to meet the boy's in the same glance, like a trick portrait or an optical illusion. There was anger and distance and misery in the man's voice when he spoke again.

"They say my folks is dead. Life and death. Ain't much difference, is there?"

Nervously the boy stood his ground and looked around the room for signs of a telephone.

"Ain't got no phone, boy. No use for one."

"Can you help me? Could you drive me somewhere to get help? Could you drive Mr. Taylor and Reverend Shepherd to a hospital?"

Richfield stiffly reached off to one side, retrieved

something white, and placed it on the table. To the boy it appeared to be a pile of chalk pieces.

Richfield fondled the sticks lovingly. "I can call somebody for you, boy," he said. "I can call and maybe get you some help."

The boy relaxed his shoulders and breathed a sigh of relief. But as he watched Richfield handle the sticks, he frowned.

"What are those?" he asked, gesturing toward the sticks.

"These is what I call with, boy. These is bones."

"You mean, these are what you call turkeys with? You're talking about calling wild turkeys?" Disappointment swept through the boy. He tried to grasp his thoughts, but they slipped away like small fish.

Richfield glared. "Boy, I can call anything with these. Anything. You hear me?"

The boy nodded and then watched and listened as Richfield stroked one bone across the surface of another.

The shadows seemed to amplify the sound: *ke-ouk, ke-ouk, ke-ouk*.

It was hypnotic—so much so that when Richfield rose from the table, grasped the lantern, and motioned for Ronnie to follow, he did so without hesitation.

Like Richfield's shadow, the boy clung to the man's heels as he led the way out the back door and beyond a dilapidated shed, a pickup truck, and an assortment of abandoned furniture and appliances. The boy shot a glance at the pickup, but turned his eyes away when he saw that two of its tires were flat.

"Right up here it be," Richfield exclaimed. "This is where I call when I need help, don't you see?"

But the boy saw nothing promising—only a clearing beyond the trash and two small mounds of red clay.

"I don't see anyone. Where is anyone to help?" the boy pleaded.

"Hush now. Jist hush and listen," Richfield snapped.

Standing at the foot of the two mounds, Richfield began to stroke one of the bones across the surface of another. The boy lingered a few feet behind.

Ke-ouk, ke-ouk, ke-ouk.

The sound seemed to pitch everywhere at once, as if calling into the night forever.

Richfield repeated the pattern a number of times, then paused. The darkness drew down around the lantern, the man, and the boy. Even before the new sound fully emerged, the boy began to back away.

From within the mounds of clay—the normally silent graves of Thad and Millie Richfield—the pattern of bone scrapings lifted free.

Ke-ouk, ke-ouk, ke-ouk.

By the time the pattern completed itself, the boy was running hard toward the road.

He walked west.

Tired, disappointed, nearing hopelessness, he had trudged on for over half a mile when unblinking head-lamps and the dull roar of an engine slid out of the darkness behind him. He turned to watch the lights and the unmistakable sound approach.

His heart began to beat in his throat.

Oh, please be help! Please!

From the grind and heavy roll of the vehicle, the boy anticipated that it was a truck. And his spirits rose, for he had always heard that truckers were quick to help someone in a jam.

Spearing the night sky with his flashlight, the boy edged into the middle of the road and waved his arms. The vehicle, then less than a quarter-mile away, had begun to slow. Down-shifted gears groaned and air brakes whooshed and hissed.

The boy stared into its headlights and noticed a set of red lights winking off and on several feet above the powerful white beams.

It's a bus! It's a school bus!

And then he felt even more assured of help.

Moments later, the bus wheezed and clanged to a stop beside him. It appeared to be a school bus that had been painted solid black, though the paint was visibly peeling and chipped. There seemed to be no letters of identification on its side, suggesting to the boy that the bus might be the kind traveling rock groups used between engagements.

Gray, shadowy faces peered down at him. Adult faces.

This is help! his mind shouted with joy.

The doors of the bus sucked open, and for a terrifying instant, the boy saw no driver.

"Hey little pilgrim! Whatchoo doin' in the road?"

The shadows filling the area around the steering wheel parted and a very tall, very thin black man leaned toward him and smiled. White teeth mirrored forth. The voice was warm and friendly and sincere.

"Hey, you headin' our way, little pilgrim? We gots room. We shore do."

Relief danced in the boy's chest as he stepped up into the bus. The driver's large strong hand grasped his arm and pulled him into the darkness.

"Lookie dis, little pilgrim. We gots you a seat right behind me. Sit yourself down an' tell me where yer fixin' to go."

Dust and the smell of disuse rose in puffs around the boy when he sank into the seat. But he didn't mind because here was help. He could sense it.

The bus roared to life, and the boy, leaning forward so that he could virtually speak into the driver's ear, hurriedly recounted his need for help, splicing in rushed details about the conditions of Dale Taylor and the Reverend Shepherd. The driver listened, nodding his concern from moment to moment.

On the verge of tears, the boy concluded his plea.

The driver squeezed the boy's arm. "Don'choo worry none 'bout it, little pilgrim. I know jus' what ta do. Hey, it's gone be fine. You say yer name is Claude? Is dat right?"

The boy giggled and shook his head. "No, not Claude. My name is Ronnie. Ronnie Cartwright."

"Well, hey Ronnie Cartwright. My name is Brown. L.C. Brown. And them initials, why they stands for 'Lucky Charm.'"

"Oh, I bet they don't either," said the boy, suppressing another giggle.

"Shore nuff does. But most folks, they jus' call me 'Fetch.'"

"Fetch? Why they call you that?"

"Umm, I 'spect it's cuz I fetch peoples from one place to another."

And the black man's laughter surrounded the boy like a security blanket.

His anxiety softened, the boy glanced over his shoulder at the other passengers. There were men and women, mostly white; some were chatting; some sleeping; and some were staring out the window in that blank reverie common to passengers everywhere.

A few seats back, an elderly woman who seemed vaguely familiar smiled at him. Directly across the aisle, a boy about his own age rested the side of his face against the window.

Ronnie tapped the driver on the shoulder. "Where all these folks going?" he asked, for it suddenly occurred to him that it was a curious hour for so many people to be riding somewhere in a dilapidated bus.

"Umm, well, friend Ronnie, these here souls be on a pilgrimage. Yes sir, a pilgrimage. They's all had the callin'."

"Oh, is this like a church group?" the boy asked.

The driver nodded. "Yes sir, you might could say dat's true. Kinda like a church group." Suddenly the driver reached one hand down to the side of his seat and shuffled a paper sack.

"Say, pilgrim Ronnie, bet a month's pay yer hungry. How 'bout it? Gots a mess a shelled peanuts here. Need a soul to share 'em with."

The boy brightened.

"Oh man, yeah, I am sorta hungry," he said, taking the sack from the driver.

"Gots a big cold Thermos a sweet ice tea by me, too."

And so the boy relaxed, munched on the salty peanuts, and drank a Thermos lid of cold tea. The gray-black asphalt widened before him; tensions drained away, and he thought of his companions back at the school. Help would come for them. The nightmare of Half Moon down would be over. No more shadows.

No more demons. No more voices calling him toward the fallout shelter. Tomorrow he would return to Soldier, to Grandma Cartwright's, and never run away again. Never. He would go back to school to be with his friends—special friends like Megan Whitlock and Bobby Lee Hollins.

The rhythm of the road lulled him. He slumped into the musty seat and curled his flashlight into the crook of his elbow. Soon he was asleep, unaware that the bus was making a series of turns, that it was no longer headed toward Soldier.

The boy was awakened by the chanting. And when the bus rumbled to a stop, the chanting grew louder.

> And who will you send to fetch him away,
>   Fetch him away, fetch him away;
> Who will you send to fetch him away
>   On a dark and starless morning?

He wheeled around to face the chanting passengers and their ghostly monotone voices. His eyes met those of the elderly woman who had smiled at him earlier. And he shuddered.

It was the Reverend Shepherd's mother . . . only it couldn't be . . . the storm, the storm . . . and there were others. The boy began to recognize the good citizens of Half Moon, the ones whose lives had been snuffed out by the winds of darkness.

Frantically the boy turned to the driver. "Where are we? What's happening? Where are we?"

The driver chuckled softly and shoved open the tall,

narrow doors of the bus. "We're home."

But those words had not been spoken by the driver.

The boy across the aisle from Ronnie slid toward him and repeated the words. For the first time, Ronnie saw the boy's face. Recognition flooded through him. He was looking at his own ghostly double.

The passengers began to rise and file out. Ronnie watched, too amazed, too frightened to speak or move, and he knew now where the bus had stopped. It was the area behind the school's gymnasium. The bus had returned to Half Moon.

When the other passengers had stepped from the bus and through the gymnasium's back door, Ronnie's double gestured for him to follow. And he did, for there seemed no point in running. There seemed no escape.

At the gymnasium door, Ronnie hesitated, glancing back at the bus driver, a silent plea for an explanation.

"So long little pilgrim," the driver called, and the bus rattled away.

Hidden from view until that moment, the dark creature, the Windkiller, the one that had sent the ghostly legions to retrieve the boy, gently flapped its huge wings as if in triumph.

CHAPTER 21

Taylor leaned back from Shepherd's body and looked into Molly's pinched face.

"I've used up all my Boy Scout training," he half-chuckled, but the false mirth drained rapidly from his voice. "I don't know what else to do for him, Molly."

"The bleeding's stopped mostly. At least, there's that," she murmured hopefully.

He glanced away and rubbed his eyes. Because the swelling in his left leg had increased, he had ripped his pants up the seam to make the leg more comfortable.

"So much blood," he intoned. "I did this to him. I could have helped him somehow."

"Don't you be thinking that. Don't you be blaming yourself," said Molly.

Taylor shook his head and touched Shepherd's elbow. "I don't think . . . he's going to make it. Never get help in time." He sighed and swallowed back tears.

Molly scanned his fear-blanched face. "We've done what we can for Reverend Shepherd. Now it's the boy I'm worrying about. Out there. I pray he won't run into no trouble."

"I do too, Molly. God knows I do." He picked up the revolver at his side and stared at it.

"Should have had him take this along. Forgot about it. The boy . . . Ronnie, he's been through a lot tonight. My God, he's tougher than I was at his age."

Molly closed her eyes and seemed to be mumbling something to herself very softly. Then she dabbed at the sweat on Shepherd's face and tucked a blanket higher on his chest.

"I'll sit up with the Reverend," she said. "You lie on back and rest your eyes. Try to sleep if you can. The littul men and I, why, we'll watch to see if he starts bleeding again."

Taylor, noticeably in pain, pushed himself away from Shepherd's body.

"OK, . . . yeah, thanks Molly . . . that's a good idea. My head's feeling a little strange. Maybe if I rested a second . . . we'll be all right, Molly. This'll all be over soon."

Memory touched Dale Taylor like warm loving hands, spinning him back in time to a gorgeous autumn day when his future magically fell into place. And magically seemed the right word.

That day, the Saturday after Thanksgiving, he was behind the counter at Knox's Grocery in Half Moon talking with Jack Shepherd, who was toying with the idea of going into the ministry.

As they talked, Carol Mae Matthews, a senior at Goldsmith College, walked in. Taylor hadn't seen her since high school and had never really considered her to be attractive. But a few years of maturation had wrought a marvelous change. Everything about her seemed more womanly; she was no longer a thinnish, self-effacing girl.

The three of them had launched into the obligatory discussion of the past. High school nostalgia. Whatever happened to so and so? That kind of thing. It was pleasant beyond the memories, for Taylor found himself drawn to Carol's confident sense of herself. But it all might have ended right there—so much might have ended right there—if Shepherd hadn't offered a suggestion.

"Let's go to Sherman's and have some lunch."

So they did. Stanley Knox, who often hinted to Taylor that he wanted him to buy him out and take over the store, told him to take a long lunch break. "You won't get to take 'em when you run this place yourself," he added.

The Half Moon Cafe, a dingy, meagerly frequented establishment with red vinyl-covered booths split and torn from age and vandalism, gladly took them in. Sherman Sparks, an emaciated man who shook violently from the onset of Parkinson's disease, registered shock and pleasant surprise on his face to see three lunch-hour customers.

They ordered Sherman's special: hamburger steak wrapped in slightly raw bacon strips anchored to the meat by toothpicks. The meal came with green beans, a roll, and sweetened iced tea (you couldn't get any other kind). Comic bravado dominated as they took turns pretending that Sherman's special was edible, facetiously tossing off witty little nothings like, "My bacon has a warm spot on it," and "How come your roll is not the same color as mine?"

Laughter. Good cleansing laughter. They were older, and looked back to more innocent years. And they looked out into the streets of Half Moon, and as inconsequential as the place was, they each knew somehow they would always call it home.

There was something else: the way a climber slowly, methodically, descends the massive face of a rock, Dale Taylor was falling in love with Carol Mae Matthews. Right there in the Half Moon Cafe. For the most part, Carol Mae knew it, or at least sensed it, probably because she was seeing Dale Taylor a bit differently than she had in the past. And maybe that was the start of love.

Later in the day Jack Shepherd began to see the whole picture, too.

"You know something?" said Carol Mae, forcing down a final bite of bland green beans. "I haven't been back in the high school since graduation."

Shepherd looked at Taylor and they exchanged smiles.

"Well, Miss Matthews, ma'am, that's our next stop," Taylor drawled exaggeratedly.

"It'll be locked up, won't it?" she countered.

Shepherd aimed a hand shaped like a pistol at Taylor, and clicked his thumb in a playful assassination. "This man knows how to get into Half Moon High," he said.

After Taylor successfully battled Shepherd to pay the tab, they were off. Stealth and cunning weren't necessary to break into the school; the fire escape at the second floor opened into the home-ec room, and the window closest to the fire escape had a broken lock.

Always had. Probably always would.

"I burned a lot of cherry pies in here." Carol Mae smiled as she surveyed the kitchen area where Mrs. Denson, the home-ec teacher, still walked the beat.

"So that's what we used to smell," Shepherd quipped. "I always thought it was coming from the chemistry lab."

More of that cleansing laughter.

And then a meandering tour of rooms, and at one point, Shepherd got separated from Taylor and Carol Mae.

Thanks, Shep.

They sat at one of the study-hall tables on the third floor, and Taylor tried hard not to allow his attraction to Carol Mae to become too obvious.

"Mary Hinton got me through advanced algebra in this room," Carol Mae mused. "Without those study-hall sessions, I would never have made it."

"Oh, I don't believe that. I remember that you always made good grades, and now here you are fixin' to graduate from college. You must have big plans for all those courses in psychology and—what else was it?—education?"

Carol Mae smiled and shook her head.

"No big plans. I thought I wanted to be a high-school counselor. You know, help kids through all those crises we all went through. But, right now at least, my future is kind of foggy."

"Why?"

She rolled her eyes and looked away. She was confused, and it embarrassed her.

"Well, it seems that most of my friends at school are getting married, and . . . well, I'm getting waves of Old

277

Maiditis, I guess." They both laughed, a spontaneous, nervous response.

"What's the problem? You can be married and have a career at the same time, can't you?"

She shrugged her shoulders. "That's what everyone says. But I'm skeptical. I really am. My older sister, Diane, tried it, and it ended in divorce. So . . . anyway, let's talk about you. Someone told me a couple of years ago that you were going to make a career out of the army."

Taylor made strangling gestures at his throat. "Heaven forbid!" he cried.

But it felt good to have an attractive young woman giving her attention to him. And despite her apparent confusion about her own future, she managed to retain a positive view of herself. She still liked herself, and that was appealing to Taylor in a magnetic way.

"No, I spent a couple of years in the army. Six months in Vietnam. The army's a place for losers as far as I'm concerned. I spent most of my tour as a clerk. No real combat duty, though—hey, I've got to show you this."

He fished through his wallet and pushed a photo toward her. "That's Grunt Taylor!"

"Oh my," she exclaimed, taking the photo and stifling a chuckle.

"It's a mock-up of me in full combat gear. All of us had one made to send back to the folks . . . so I just kept mine in my wallet. Still good for a laugh, isn't it?"

"Dale, you know, I've always admired the fact that you did so well in school and sports . . . and took care of yourself after your parents were killed. That took courage, I know. I know you're going to be successful

278

at whatever you do from this point on."

It all sounded like something you might write in a high-school yearbook. Yet there was something about the moment—an outsider would have labeled it corny or melodramatic—but nonetheless it was one of those decisive moments which do occur in people's lives—something that brought forth a declaration.

"You're the first to hear this, Carol Mae—I'm going to buy Knox's Grocery. By next Thanksgiving, when you drive through Half Moon, it'll be Taylor's Grocery."

What neither knew was that by next Thanksgiving Carol would be Mrs. Dale Taylor, and Half Moon the promised site of happily ever after.

The memory reeled on, capturing every scene from the afternoon in its minutest detail. Before he snapped to, however, new scenes, dark ones, spliced onto the familiar, the known.

Carol Mae was standing in the foyer of the school building holding a little girl by the hand.

"This will be our daughter. Her name will be Jennifer."

Taylor looked at her and began to smile until his eyes scanned the blackened caul, and he blinked back in fear.

"Don't be afraid," said Carol Mae. "Half Moon is dead. Everyone left behind is a ghost. And so will Jack Shepherd be. And so will you be."

Molly had fallen asleep.

Taylor smiled wistfully at the exhausted angle of her head against her shoulder. Her terriers nested close like

279

tiny guardians of the old woman's sanity.

The ole gal has spunk, he mused.

Then his thoughts turned again to Carol Mae, and as they did a chalky white fog began to seep under the door.

Carol Mae stepped through the door into the room.

Dale Taylor was a man on the leash of a starving heart, starving for affection, starving for the food of his soul's companions.

He surrendered eagerly to the Windkiller-begotten illusion.

Carol Mae's invisible hands, ghostly hands, caressed his face, his shoulders, his chest, and worked methodically toward his injured leg. Her touch aroused him, and he recalled how her fingers could set him on fire.

Then desire gave way to a new sensation—a release from pain. Ghostly fingertips tapped along his battered thigh and probed, with feather softness, the swollen knee.

Responding to the healing hands, he began to move the leg, bend and twist it with little pain. It felt strong enough to stand upon. But the ghostly healing hands lifted free, and he heard himself call out, "Wait. Please don't go."

The apparition failed to shroud the lantern light or to animate the line of shadow on the door, but Taylor knew that it was Carol Mae. He knew her touch and the smell of her body, its rich sensual warmth as on nights when she would come to bed naked.

Desire and fear and disbelief waged an inner war.

He saw that Molly was still asleep. Then he focused upon Shepherd's stony face and winced at an icy stab of apprehension.

He's going to die. My best friend is going to die. It's my fault.

He tried to force himself to think about the boy, but the apparition interfered with his concentration. Warm cottony feelings and memories of Carol Mae sleeved his consciousness. And the pain and stiffness and swelling in his leg continued to abate.

"Carol Mae, I need you," he whispered, but the apparition fled.

As if prompted by a draft of air, the door suddenly swung open. Reflexively, Taylor held his breath. He felt to one side for the revolver. Then the shadows beyond the doorway rained tinsel and ghostly silver. The image of Carol Mae materialized, naked, smiling, siren warmth in her voice.

"Jennifer's asleep. Let's be alone."

The all-too-familiar words reached into him, and the memory of innocent, wife-to-husband seductions rose to greet those words. And Taylor found that he was standing, virtually without pain, his eyes locked onto the soft curves of Carol Mae's body. He began to follow her into the darkness of the hallway, her ghostly image providing the only illumination necessary.

Tethered to her beckoning smiles and gestures, he struggled along at a distance from her, limping like some mythic hero on the verge of metamorphosis. Memories of desire emboldened him. Good desire. Good moments when the bond of husband and wife had been so strong that he ached whenever they weren't together.

She's not lost. Not lost. She can never be lost.

Deeper into the school he followed her, followed and let dark dread tear at his heart: the cold nauseating image of another man touching her.

Jesus, no . . . I couldn't stand that.

Suddenly, rounding a corner, he lost track of her at the opened door to the fallout shelter behind the stage. Ice coated his throat. The darkness beyond the narrow door seemed impenetrable.

No . . . I've lost her.

And then he heard her voice.

"Come, and I'll be real again, and so will Jennifer."

He entered the shelter and saw them, diaphanous outlines twenty feet away. Carol Mae and Jennifer. Like a family portrait.

"One step more, and we'll be whole," said Carol Mae.

Warmth slowly reclaimed his senses.

One step more.

The ghostly outlines rippled, began to fill.

Shadow into flesh. Shadow into flesh.

"Oh, God," Taylor muttered. "I've missed you. I've missed you so."

Then Carol Mae gestured for him to stop. "No," she exclaimed. "Go. We'll follow . . . but don't look back."

Puzzled, Taylor drank them in with his eyes, smiled, and turned for the door, the image of their wholeness intact in his mind.

Shadow into flesh.

The surge of warmth staggered him. *It's real*, he shouted inwardly.

And the only thing in the world he wanted to do was turn and let them run to him so that he could surround them with his arms, with his love, and forget about

Jack Shepherd and Molly and the boy and Half Moon down.

Not lost.

And so he turned to welcome them back into his love.

He never saw the darkness stir deeper within the shelter.

CHAPTER 22

The boy closed the gymnasium door behind him, but for a minute or two he braced his back against it while his heart trip-hammered. His breathing sounded like window panes cracking.

Slowly, very slowly, he recovered.

What will I tell Mr. Taylor and Miss Molly?

He had failed. It was as simple as that, and now he would have to go back and explain. Windkiller's shadows, his ghostly legions, wouldn't let him get help.

Reverend Shepherd is going to die.

I can tell them that I tried. That I ran to the county-line road, but no cars came along. That I ran to two farmhouses, but there was no one at home. Lic. Lie to neutralize their disappointment.

The boy flashed his light through the empty, darkness-laden gymnasium.

If only I could pray, he thought, his eyes tearing, blurring his vision. Maybe Jesus could help in a time like this. Maybe Jesus knew how to fight what controlled Half Moon. Maybe Jesus could save the

Reverend Shepherd.

"Dear Lord Jesus," the boy whispered.

And he thought of Bobby Lee Hollins. He was trying to pray and all he could think of was Bobby Lee. His crushed face. He recalled that Bobby Lee, who had never attended church, did not know who Jesus was. The boy found that hard to believe, and yet Bobby Lee knew a little song about Jesus and would sing it often to the delight of the older boys at school. Then one day Ronnie had told Bobby Lee that it wasn't a nice song, that he would go to Hell for singing it. Bobby Lee stopped only after he had received a vivid account of the horrors of that most infamous of all dark places.

Hell must be like tonight, the boy reasoned soberly.

"Dear Lord Jesus," he whispered again.

But all he could think of was Bobby Lee's song, and no amount of concentration could keep it from reeling through his mind.

> *I don't care if it rains*
> *   or freezes,*
> *I'll be safe in the arms*
> *   of Jesus.*
> *I can lose my shirt*
> *   and britches,*
> *He'll still love us sons*
> *   of bitches.*
> *Am I Jesus'*
> *   little lamb?*
> *Yes, you goddam*
> *   right I am.*

So much for prayer. And that made him sad.

Would they blame him if Reverend Shepherd died?
Is it my fault?

His desperate thoughts whisked through him like another gust of cold wind. He felt numb all over. He just wanted to hide, hide in the gym until morning. By then surely someone would have come to find them, to save them.

Again, he scanned the empty gym with his light. To his left spread wooden bleachers which covered one entire side of the gym and angled up to meet the girded roof. Total capacity of the seating arrangement was about three hundred, and the boy could recall basketball games in which nearly every seat was occupied and cheerleaders were chanting and the noise level was deafening.

Now, ironically, the silence seemed deafening.

To his immediate right, tucked behind a partition, was a small room that served as the kitchen area for the school's lunch program. Armed with trays, students would file by the long rectangular window and watch as hefty cooks, hair-netted and alive with chatter, would ladle portions of state-regulated food and encourage pickier eaters not to frown at their helping of creamed spinach.

At basketball games this area was magically transformed into a concession stand where members of the Pep Club, amid clouds of giggles, dispensed Hershey bars, Baby Ruths, watery Cokes and Pepsis, bags of peanuts in the shell, and overflowing sacks of popcorn, all at prices absurdly beyond what they should have been. All proceeds, of course, went toward band uniforms or some such school enterprise.

But the right side of the gym was dominated by the

286

stage with its massive, traditionally wine-colored curtain vaulting down seemingly from the heavens. Now the curtain was closed, but as the boy touched it with his light, he recalled special times like the annual "Talent Night," a largely comical effort by the high schoolers to perform for the community. There were parodies and piano solos and skits.

His favorite Talent Night performance was a skit entitled "The Magic Helper," about a pixie-being who helped a poor student into realizing that he could do the work fine on his own.

Magic Helper.

If only. . . .

The hardwood floor, once varnished to a high glossy sheen, was now dull and opaque. In the months to come, dry rot would attack it and honeycomb it until it would not be safe to stand on. Time would also deface the logo in the center-jump circle. There, one of the more creative Half Moon students had, some years ago, painted the snarling face of a black panther—Half Moon Panther, that is. A convincingly frightening depiction, the panther had piercing yellow eyes, eyes that, according to stories the boy had heard, could mesmerize you, make you blind and deaf, or turn you into a hopeless cripple. The boy didn't really believe such nonsense, yet, he had always been careful never to allow himself more than a fleeting glance at the panther's face.

From where he stood, he could shine his light to the far end and catch the shimmer of the fiberglass backboard and the rim of the basketball goal. The familiar white net had apparently rotted and fallen away; the same was true for the goal directly in front of him.

Among his projections into the future, the boy had pictured himself one day filling those nets with jumpshot after jumpshot or with game-winning free throws. Victories in overtime.

Last spring's winds of darkness had changed all that. Forever.

Still contemplating what he should do, the boy walked out onto the basketball court and stopped in front of the stage. The cooler night air, occasionally filtered through by a breeze, met with little success against the humidity locked in the gym. He could feel his back and face begin to bead with sweat. He was tired and thirsty, and he thought about the bus driver's Thermos of iced tea. But getting relief would mean returning to face Miss Molly and Mr. Taylor and Reverend Shepherd . . . *if* Reverend Shepherd were still alive.

Confused, the boy shifted his weight from one foot to the other. And he listened. A whisper? Soft rustlings? The darkness in front of him seemed to part and a faint gray light dawned. The rustle heightened as the stage curtain opened and the gray light brightened enough to reveal a living-room set, and as he watched, figures materialized. Six people. Six people in Victorian attire. It was a play, and by degrees the boy could hear the players' lines. Rapt in amazement, he became an audience of one.

"Yes, I remember the General was called Ernest. I knew I had some particular reason for disliking the name."

"Ernest! My own Ernest! I felt from the first that you could have no other name!"

288

"Gwendolen, it is a terrible thing for a man to find out suddenly that all his life he has been speaking nothing but the truth. Can you forgive me?"

"I can. For I feel sure that you are sure to change."

"My own one!"

"Laetitia!"

"Frederick! At last!"

"Cecily! At last!"

"At last!"

"My nephew, you seem to be displaying signs of triviality."

"On the contrary, Aunt Augusta, I've now realized for the first time in my life the vital Importance of Being Earnest."

All the embracing and the exaggerated stage action brought a smile to the boy's lips despite the weirdness of what was occurring. And one of the actresses—yes, he was almost certain—was Miss Molly . . . Miss Molly Harvester, the high-school drama student.

The boy brightened even more, now totally caught up in the fantastic hallucination. The ghostly players bowed, rose, and turned toward a backdrop screen depicting a fireplace and a mantel. The screen rattled in a slow ascent, and, as it did, a block of shadow descended at center stage.

The hanged man seemed to dangle by an invisible thread.

The scene stabbed the breath out of the boy; he backed away a few steps and the curtains shuffled together.

Behind him, eerie applause.

He wheeled around. The same gray light that had illuminated the stage now speared in a half-dozen narrow shafts across the bleacher area. The hollow applause dwindled, and the audience, numbering perhaps in the dozens, stared at the boy.

Despite the masklike opaqueness of their faces, the boy, his eyesight fear-sharpened, began to recognize a scattering of individuals—his companions on the bus ride: the Reverend Shepherd's mother, Harold Masterson and his family, Carl Harvester . . . and even the boy's father and mother.

It was a ghostly legion: the restless spirits of Half Moon down made to walk again by the dark powers of Windkiller.

Seated in their midst, seemingly occupying a position of leadership, was the boy's double, a nebulous, gray-white outline.

Too frightened to scream or move, Ronnie stood, trancelike, subdued by the blood-freezing sight, its weirdness magnified by the play of phantom light.

Above the crowd, perched high on one of the girders, was the death-watch figure of Windkiller. Then it took flight, seeming to shrink in size as it flew toward the stage. The curtains opened to allow it entrance before closing with an ominous whisper.

Suddenly the boy's attention was drawn away from the flight of the creature to the area of the court directly in front of him. Shafts of light danced across the center-jump circle, revealing not the Half Moon Panther, but a new logo: the menacing icy expression of Windkiller.

The familiar birdlike cry, high-pitched and shrill, distant and yet somehow close, filled the haunted gym and freed the boy to run, to run away from the pursuit of his own screams.

They met him in the hallway.

The ghostly players and the suicidal janitor beckoned him toward the open door of the fallout shelter. Mesmerized, he choked back his screams. Beyond the ghosts, in the palpable darkness of the fallout shelter, he could hear voices.

The strong death smell of the ghosts poured over him, seemed to weaken him. He felt trapped, felt like an automaton being mechanically directed into the shelter to meet the ultimate source of all the horror.

"No-o-o!" he shouted.

And as the shout filled the hallway, a milky flurry of wings streamed from the shelter. The headless pigeons broke the mesmeric hold of the ghosts, and the boy raced away, pulled by the saving appearance of his beloved birds.

You will know what will make it stop.

Reverend Shepherd's darkly prophetic words returned with even greater force than before. Seated near the lantern, the boy glanced at Miss Molly, only vaguely aware of what she might be thinking.

Driven from the macabre encounters in the gym, he had found his way back to the small redoubt and the protective company of the old woman and her dogs. She had met him with anxious questions about help, though she assumed that since he had returned alone, none was on the way.

The pigeons had disappeared.

When the boy looked into Molly's face, he knew that

he must tell her the truth. She listened to his story: the account of meeting Collis Richfield, the strange bus ride, and the gymnasium ghosts. She shouldered his tears.

"It's all right, Ronnie," she consoled. "Reverend Shepherd . . . we might could be able to help yet. We've done what we could, and you tried your best. He's resting . . . his bleeding's stopped. Has lost so much blood . . . is weak and I'm supposing he's in shock. I'm just plenty sorry we asked you to go for help. It was dangerous for you to be out there. Mr. Taylor's gone off somewheres while I was asleep. From here on we'll stay together. I'm plenty sorry you had to go through what you did." She stared blankly at a wall, unconsciously stroking one of the terriers.

"Our man of God is dying," she continued. "Windkiller. It was Windkiller . . . Windkiller drove him mad and trampled on him."

Confused, the boy brushed at his tears. "Is it going to drive Mr. Taylor mad, too?"

Molly kept her eyes on the wall. "Mr. Taylor's already mad with grief. He lost his wife and his lit-tul girl. Maybe he has to find them even if it means losing all his senses."

And despite a certain defiant resolve to stick it out, to win over what held the school and the town in its grip, there was an unmistakable tension in the air, a fear-activated tension directed toward the central question: would they survive?

Against the wall next to the door, Shepherd's badly wounded body, covered by a woolen blanket, was mute testimony that they might not.

*   *   *

A tenuous, evanescent cry rose from afar. The boy recognized it and knew that it controlled Half Moon. He also knew this and so did Molly: the dark force was tightening its hold.

There was so little time to decide what to do—and how to do it.

CHAPTER 23

In the gray muted wash of light, Taylor hunkered down and extended his arms. He smiled and choked back a surge of heart-pounding anticipation.

"Never leave you behind again," he exclaimed.

Jennifer smiled shyly, tentatively reaching toward him with one arm. Her eyes twinkled with little girl coyness.

"Listen, Daddy," she murmured. "Listen to what I can do."

Taylor's smile broadened as he cocked his head to one side, expecting his daughter to recite something or to break into some song she had just learned.

But she didn't recite or sing. Instead, she wiggled her fingers. She made tiny winging motions with her hand. She giggled softly.

And then the ghostly buzzing began.

"No, Jennifer, don't do that. Please don't do that, sugar."

Taylor rocked back on his heels, and the stream of bees flowed freely from what had been his daughter's hand, and arm, and face. They poured toward him and through him like a driving, icy, moistureless rain.

His tortuous cry was torn from him by the rush of the ghostly bees. And he shuddered as a pocket of cold air seeped into his flesh. Stunned, he lowered his face into his hands.

"Why did you look back? Why did you look back?" The bitter-edged voice brought him momentarily out of his despair.

"Carol Mae?" Through the diaphanous gloom, he could see her outline, recognized the sharp tone of voice she used when angered with him.

"Why did you look back? Why did you look back? We were whole. We were whole."

The condemnation dissolved into a screech, more the sound of a frightened bird than a woman.

"Carol Mae, I'm sorry. Give me another chance. I don't want to lose you."

And now he could see her. Her eyes flash points of anger, her lips tilted in an unnatural crooked smile, her naked body now a merging—half bird, half woman.

The darkness beyond her parted.

Blue light nimbused the departing ghost of Carol Mae.

I've lost her.

Taylor stood and reached out, his lips quivering. The ever-dimming outline of his wife merged with a block of shadow. Wings lifted, then enfolded the apparition.

I've lost her.

The odor of musk and decay filled Taylor's nostrils. And as he stared at the looming figure of Windkiller, a hellish silhouette against the matrix of blue light, anger rose within him. He clenched his fists at his sides.

Carol Mae and Jenny. They're gone forever.

He couldn't see the creature's face. But he understood that it was real. Jack Shepherd's ravings—the legend of Christmas Oak—all of the impossible stories of Half Moon down—they were all impossibly true.

Desperate thoughts entwined him as if with heavy chains so that he could not move, could only listen and gaze at the brooding, implacable figure of Windkiller. Such a creature could easily destroy him; it could have destroyed Molly, the boy, Shepherd and himself whenever it would have pleased.

That's its way.

The fires, the storms, the ghosts, the shadows—Taylor, the sudden revelation fueling his anger, recognized Windkiller's ultimate weapon—its cruelty. Not death, but suffering. It sent ghosts, and the most haunting of all the ghosts it sent was loneliness.

Lost. My God, I'm lost.

But his anger held sway, his hatred of the elemental cruelty, and with a blind-rage summoning of his will, he charged at the figure, bare hands as his only weapons.

Windkiller's cry pitched high, rivening the darkness.

Taylor stumbled once, then crashed to his knees. For an eternity of moments, he closed his eyes and cupped his hands over his ears. As the cry slowly dissipated, he rocked back and forth.

He felt alone. He felt like a coward.

He pulled within himself, a prisoner of darkness.

Part Four

THE BIRDS OF DAWNING

CHAPTER 24

The hooting of an owl speared through the silence like a beam of light. The boy, asleep in one of the sleeping bags that Molly had spread out near the lantern, stirred, mumbled something, and curled tighter into a fetal position. Molly blinked half awake. She heard the call of the owl, imagining, until she snapped more fully awake, that it was calling her name.

Reality suddenly asserted itself. Leaning against a wall with her legs out flat on the floor, the old woman looked around. Taylor had not returned. The confusion of the moment was like a dull ache. But the ache sharpened to a heart-stabbing pain when her eyes pieced out Shepherd's covered body. And she felt her heart would cleave down its center when she glanced away from Shepherd to the small mound in the sleeping bag.

Dear Lord, he's suffered too!

Then she heard his dream-evoked mumbling, and her heart felt whole again.

Oh, Molly, what you gone do?

The two terriers, having been drawn to the door by some sound or smell, began scratching at it with their tiny claws.

Warming to the sight, the old woman shakily pressed herself to her feet and stepped around the lantern.

"Here, what's this, lit-tul men? Y'all need to go out and do your business? Oh, well, I see. I haven't forgotten y'all completely."

She unbolted the door as quietly as possible, swung it open and smiled at the terriers. But with legs stiff and ears pricked at attention, they sniffed the air and whined.

The click of small paws tunneled up the hallway out of sight, then passed near them, and headed for the stairs. A faint white outline materialized. Whatever it was stirred puffs of plaster dust as it clattered by and began to negotiate the steps.

"Freddie?" Molly exclaimed, and took a few stutter steps toward the nebulous movement.

"Oh, Freddie, we thought—"

The small dog reached the top of the first flight, and a shadowy figure stooped and picked it up.

"How do, babe," said the figure, in a tone at once cold and yet lined with mirth.

Molly spider-pressed her fingertips over her heart. Her knees trembled. The boundary of the oval lantern light fell far too short to help her see. The darkness seemed distant and unreal. And unreachable.

"Carl? Oh, is it . . . ? And, oh, I did wait, don'cha know. But the shop . . . and then we had to come here . . . and now. Oh, please help us, Carl. The shop . . . and my owls, all my owls, . . . and, oh, Freddie . . . is that really Freddie?"

The shadowy figure stroked the dog's head. "Wind-killer burned the shop, Molly. An' Freddie, he's been with us. Soon he'll be with us for good. An' I can't help you, Molly."

"Oh, yes, Carl. Please, yes, you can help us. Of course you can."

But the shadowy voice chilled her.

"Town's been wrong. Cut down Christmas Oak. Windkiller's come for revenge. Got this here school, got Reverend Shepherd. Y'all er next. Half Moon's down so far it'll never get back up, don'cha see that?"

"No. No, Carl. No one can take our town . . . can take us."

"It all belongs to Windkiller, Molly babe. We've always belonged to Windkiller. The creature knows what we fear."

Hearing those words, Molly stiffened. Anger, charged by a moment of recognition, welled up into her throat, hot and bitter. "You're not Carl. Go away. Go back to your darkness."

"Soon enough, Molly. Soon enough. Windkiller wants the boy. It's the boy."

"You're not Carl . . . not my Carl."

"Not *yours*," responded the figure. "Not *yours* . . . never again."

A high-pitched cry drifted through the stairwell windows, and on the heels of the cry a sudden gust of wind lifted the shadowy figure; like a dark kite, it spun through a window and rose into the night.

The dog raced down the steps and tossed himself at Molly's waiting hands.

"Oh, Freddie," she cried. "It's really you, lit-tul man." She hugged him to her breasts and he squirmed excitedly before she set him to the floor.

Then silence. Then a purling rustle of wings filled the void. Something fluttered, braced itself, landed, and anchored its talons to the newel post at the foot of the stairs.

Tiny, yellow-rimmed circles of fire flashed at the old woman. The owl was staring directly at her, its body a crystalline glimmer through the shadows. And she was drawn to it, puzzled, fascinated, lost in a pleasant memory.

The owl hooted softly, and the old woman smiled.

"I am your friend," she whispered as she approached it. "Make me wise, sacred bird. Share your wisdom."

Behind her, the terriers, joined by their missing companion, pranced in place, muffling barks and forcing whines. The owl settled into stony permanence. It did not stir even as the old woman's trembling fingers groped nearer.

She closed her eyes and touched, and the feathers of the owl were glass and ice. They claimed her fingertips with the fiery grip of extreme cold.

She opened her eyes and an intense spotlight dropped around her with magical precision. And the vision flooded the dark cave of her thoughts.

She saw a door leading into a deep darkness, and within that darkness Dale Taylor cowered against a wall. Then a suggestion of light neared the frightened man. It was the boy, Ronnie; an aura of amber light circumferenced him as he helped Taylor from the darkness. The shadowy tapestry of the vision blurred, then cleared, revealing that the boy, accompanied by a shower of hovering white birds, waded further into the throat of blackness. Beyond him, blue flames bordered a curtained box. Some malign presence—Molly could feel it—watched him, coaxed him, seduced him. The boy drew near, and Molly felt a tidal wave of panic roar toward her. Suddenly the curtains parted, but the vision faded to gray. There was a moment of release. Then an explosion of light.

The owl spread its wings, lifted free of the old woman's grip, cut a spiral path through the stairwell windows, and disappeared.

Shaken and confused, Molly returned to the lanterned room to find the boy awake petting Freddie. She composed herself, repressing a desire to share her vision, for she knew that she must search out the right way to express her newfound convictions.

But only the bravest warrior . . . can defeat the creature.

"It's Freddie," the boy suddenly exclaimed. "Miss Molly, look. It's Freddie. He's okay. He's come back."

"My stars, isn't he a scamp? Didn't care a thang if we was worried about him," she chortled. "Ronnie, if you'll let me see the top of that Thermos, I'll give the lit-tul men a sip of water," she continued, masking what dominated her thoughts.

"Oh, sure. Just a cup or so left," the boy mumbled.

"Here we go, gentlemen," Molly cooed. "Nice water for thirsty lit-tul men."

The three dogs jostled one another for position around the flat container of water. Their pink tongues touched the liquid tentatively at first, but eagerly once they knew what it was.

"So thirsty!" Molly exclaimed, flashing a smile at the boy.

He returned the smile and continued watching the dogs lap at the water. "I bet Tiny and Fritzie are really glad to see Freddie, aren't they? I thought the Reverend Shepherd had—"

When he saw Molly's eyes brighten with fear, he regretted the unnecessary reminder.

"Yes," said Molly. "I know they'll welcome him back, don'cha know. They . . . they've been a three-some for so long . . . they would be lonely as the wind and the rain without him." Her eyes drifted to Shepherd and her words, tear-choked, seemed to dissolve on her lips. The boy felt hot needles of sorrow for her.

"I do wish," she continued, her voice strained, "I do wish . . . and pray that help will come for Reverend Shepherd. He's holding on, but . . . well, I don't know for how much longer."

She lifted the blanket to examine Shepherd's chest and the bandages. Then she poured some water onto her handkerchief and pressed it tenderly onto his forehead.

"Can't imagine where Mr. Taylor has gone off to, except maybe to get help."

"I can go find him," the boy offered. "He couldn't get far on that bad leg. I can go find him."

Molly turned away from Shepherd.

"No, you best be staying here. And we . . . I'm supposin' we need to talk."

Nonplussed, the boy hesitated as if poised on the

edge of a confession. Something trivial perhaps, and yet it was something he had to say. "Miss Molly?"

"Yes, Ronnie?"

"Well, ma'am, you see . . . last night when I was in my tree house I got real hungry."

Pressing his fingertips together, he paused, searching the old woman's face as if the proper words were stamped there.

"I didn't have any food," he went on. "I had eaten all of it and I was real hungry . . . and so, . . . and so, I'm sorry I took that box of crackers from you. I stole it, and I'll pay for it, but I'll have to get money from Grandma Cartwright before I can."

"Oh-h-h, Ronnie," Molly smiled, "you scared me sneaking into my kitchen like that, but, oh, let's not call it stealing. Let's say you *borrowed* those crackers. Same as, you know, I might borrow a cup of sugar from one of my neighbors. Besides, the real thief is not you."

"It's not? Who is it, then?"

"Well, I'm thinking the real thief is those winds of darkness that took our town. Stole it from us. Stole our loved ones and left . . . a lot of demons and ghosts . . . and they tried to steal Reverend Shepherd, too. Tried to steal all his goodness."

The boy shook his head. "Those shadows out there did it. That's what did it," he exclaimed. "Reverend Shepherd tried to be good. He tried to warn me about what was happening. Maybe now the shadows got Mr. Taylor, too. Then they'll come after us, won't they? What are they, Miss Molly? What's out there?"

Molly sighed audibly, sadly.

305

"I've had another vision," she confessed. The words seemed painful to voice. "I know where Mr. Taylor is, I believe. I know what's out there . . . and what must be done." Her voice tore like rotten cloth.

"Ronnie, I don't remember now whether you told us this or not," she said, shifting the subject momentarily, "but would anyone else know where you are? Did you tell anyone where you were going?"

The boy frowned. "Just one. I just told one person. Another boy. But he won't tell. He promised he wouldn't tell anybody where I was going."

"Well," Molly replied, "perhaps he'll break that promise." She clasped her hands and smiled weakly. Again, it seemed to the boy that she was harboring some secret, some foreknowledge that gave her reason to maintain hope.

"I'm one to believe that our dark night will be over soon," she murmured.

She described her vision in detail. The boy listened, rapt in wonder and fear. "It's the fallout shelter," he whispered when she had finished. "That's the dark room . . . I know it is. But what does your vision mean?"

As if hypnotized, Molly stared into the lantern. "Long ago, the Indians of this area thought there was a dark force in Nature they called Windkiller, a—"

"Did Windkiller attack Reverend Shepherd?" the boy interrupted.

Molly touched her fingers to her lips. "Don'cha see, Ronnie, it's a legend. Windkiller is the name given to that dark force. Windkiller is a dark force, don'cha know, that keeps on being reborn in all sorts

306

of strange ways."

The boy motioned vaguely toward her with one hand. "Is Windkiller the voice I've been hearing?"

Arching her eyebrows, Molly peered down at one of the terriers that had curled up in her lap. "Legend has it that the voice of Windkiller can be heard by some. The creature can send nightmares and dark visions to frighten us. It can take the wind and the night air and turn them into all kinds of ghostly shapes. It loves lonely, haunted places like . . . well, like this school. It remembers Christmas Oak once stood here. Its home. A place of its own. It has come back to claim its home, don'cha see . . . and we're in its way. It has so many powers. It can control all the shadows in lonely places. Windkiller has Half Moon in its power. And we . . . well, we're just Half Moon's shadows."

The boy leaned closer to her. "It can make you die, I bet. Isn't that right? It can make you die."

Molly's eyes bulged slightly. "The legend . . . well, it's told that if you look into the eyes of Windkiller, you go mad. If it chooses, you die. Inside. Inside, you die," she explained, touching her chest with an extended finger. "But you go on living as a ghost."

"Oh, not really," murmured the boy, incredulous.

Molly nodded, a telling gesture of her conviction.

"Can we fight it? Can we fight Windkiller?" the boy asked.

The old woman scowled, and memory transported her to that day long ago when she'd listened to the words of Momma Nanwha in her hovel near Moon Lake.

"A wise old woman told me something once . . .

maybe it's our only hope. Oh, her words went something like this: 'Courage and love will blind Windkiller. But only the bravest warrior, aided by friendly spirits, can defeat the creature.'"

Then she looked directly into the boy's eyes. "Windkiller . . . he wants you, Ronnie. You must be our bravest warrior."

The boy squirmed; something icy roiled in the pit of his stomach. "No . . . no, why me?"

She gently clasped the back of his hand. "The birds, Ronnie . . . Windkiller knows you love birds. He can draw strength from your love of birds . . . your love of nature. That strength will keep his darkness alive."

"But it's . . . it's not fair," the boy stuttered, and Molly looked away.

Not fair.

This is not fair, the boy reasoned.

You will know what will make it stop.

And for the first time, the boy thought perhaps he did know. And knowing was the most frightening part of all.

Not fair. Like parents dying. Or like the world of Bobby Lee Hollins.

It was not fair that God gave Bobby Lee a turkey's face.

"Turkey face": that's what the meaner kids at school called him; some of them said it right to his face. And it did—that was the worst part—his face did look like a turkey gobbler: narrow head, nose splayed, mouth like a cardboard box of cereal that's been torn open. Some

308

of the teachers couldn't understand his little bleating voice, and that would frustrate Bobby Lee, and the bleating would grow more frantic, more pathetic.

Not fair. That's what it was.

And girls. Some of them felt sorry for Bobby Lee. Some were just as cruel as the boys. And while a few of them might be nice to him on occasion, they certainly didn't flock to be his girlfriend.

Yeah, not fair.

Every day.

Valentine's Day was the worst day of all.

When Ronnie had purchased an extra-fancy card for Megan Whitlock—one of those big, padded red-heart numbers that cost a whole dollar—he was surprised to see Bobby Lee buy one just like it.

"Gone give it to somebody in our class," Bobby Lee explained, flushing with embarrassment. "Shoot, this card's took a whole month's allowance. More, really. Been savin' up since Christmas, seems like." A crooked smile jagged across his face.

"Didn't know you liked anybody special," Ronnie had replied.

"Oh, well, . . . yeah, I kinda do. Never bought no card like this'un before, though. I'm bettin' yours there is for Megan, ain't it?"

Ronnie hesitated. "Yeah . . . yeah, it is. Was goin' to leave it in her locker over the noon hour."

"Hey, I'm gone do that, too." Bobby Lee's expression exploded with pathetic joy. "Let's do it together, OK?"

"Maybe . . . yeah, but who's yours for?"

Bobby Lee reddened. "Hey, no . . . I can't tell ya 'cuz

309

y'all'd laugh at me, I know."

"No. I'm your friend, Bobby Lee. I won't laugh. Honest."

Bobby Lee fingered the extravagant valentine; his good eye seemed to spin all the way around in its socket. "Leslie Ashmore."

Ronnie couldn't have been more surprised, his expression more incredulous, than if Bobby Lee had suddenly disappeared in a cosmic cloud of stardust.

"Whatsa matter?"

Ronnie had trouble finding the "on" switch for his voice. "Oh, man," he finally muttered. "Nothin', I mean, nothin's the matter. Leslie's super lookin'. I guess, well I mean, I guess you'd call her beautiful."

And she was. While Ronnie thought that Megan was the prettiest girl in his class, he had to admit that Leslie Ashmore was spectacular—a miniature Olivia Newton-John. Only better.

He looked into Bobby Lee's grotesque little face and his heart sank. There was a better chance that Bobby Lee would flap his arms and fly away like a bird than that Leslie Ashmore would ever be Bobby Lee's girlfriend.

Not fair. That's what it was.

Despite Ronnie's attempts to dissuade Bobby Lee (maybe the whole idea was crazy, he maintained), they ended up going ahead with the locker plan. But the gods smiled down on their efforts in one respect: fortunately, Bobby Lee never got to see Leslie Ashmore's response to the valentine.

Ronnie did, however.

He happened to be on his way to the rest room that

afternoon when Leslie Ashmore and Sharon Sims were bouncing to their dancing class. They stopped at their lockers, spun along in a cloud of throaty giggles. Ronnie held his breath as Leslie swung open her locker, tossing some catty, flippant remark Sharon's way.

A moment of silence. Then Leslie exclaimed, "Hey, Share, someone left a letter in my locker."

Sharon pounced on her shoulder, peering over, giggling. "Oh, wow, really! Read it to me. Who's it from?"

Leslie laughed and pulled the envelope out of her friend's view. "Hey, girl, . . . this might be *personal*," she flounced.

And Ronnie was thankful to hear that, for he feared she would reveal who it was from.

His fears were quickly realized.

"Oh, a secret admirer," Sharon cooed sarcastically— perhaps a bit jealously, too.

"Well, I suppose I have no secrets," said Leslie, feigning a starlet's false sense of privacy, and tore open the envelope.

Ronnie felt an urge to sprint by them, snatch the card, and sprint away, saving his friend from unseen humiliation.

"Oh, yuk," Leslie smirked. "Look at this *card! Look* at this card! Gawd, isn't it just awful?"

Sharon began to laugh uncontrollably.

The wall Ronnie was leaning against suddenly felt like the inside of an oven.

"I can't even read who it's signed by, can you? Oh, this is just a joke, isn't it? Larry Gilmore, right?" her blue eyes swam with delight.

311

Sharon grabbed the card. "No, wait. It isn't Larry." And then she clasped one hand over her mouth and lapsed into the histrionics of mock horror.

"What? Whose name is it? I can't make out the letters," a puzzled Leslie whined.

Sharon braced her shoulders, looked straight into Leslie's eyes, and whispered harshly, "Bobby . . . Lee . . . Hollins!"

"No!" Leslie screeched, whirling the card to the other side of the hall as if it were a lizard or a dead mouse someone had planted in her locker to gross her out.

Anger welled into Ronnie's throat.

"Turkey face," Sharon intoned, incredulous. "Oh, Leslie, if you touched that card you're gonna catch the uglies." Then she laughed until a teacher stuck her head out a nearby door and frowned.

"I think I'm going to be sick," said Leslie, clutching her stomach. "Let's get to class. Come on."

They swished away trailing groans and laughter.

Bobby Lee's card lay on the floor, hardly discernible from other stray paper and trash littering the hall. Ronnie lifted it and tucked it into his shirt. And he wondered whether Bobby Lee, wherever he was that second, felt the stab of humiliation. He prayed he didn't.

One of the beauties of existence is that some moments pass unseen by the very people they would destroy. And one of the great travesties of existence is that the Leslie Ashmores phantom their way unscathed through their school years . . . vampires sucking the blood out of the hearts of innocent boys.

Not fair.

The memory of Bobby Lee's valentine released the

boy, and he thought of his mother.

There's just a kind of meanness in the world.

And then he glanced at the corpselike figure of Shepherd.

Not fair.

"I know what will make it stop," the boy whispered to himself.

CHAPTER 25

The cry of Windkiller came again; only this time it ghosted through the walls into the room with deeper, more resonant notes. The captives listened, tensing themselves in expectation of some dark intrusion, some new threat lurking in the haunted school. But nothing came. Nothing except a numbing sleep into which they fell as if the cry had sedated them.

They slept, and that morning dawn never reached Half Moon.

As they slept, Bobby Lee Hollins, miles away, dreamed. In the dream, he and his friend, Ronnie Cartwright, were walking at the edge of a deserted asphalt road with uncommonly barren terrain to either side. It was a white-haze spring morning, warm, promising to be hot before noon. Fogged by humidity, the sky spread above them, a gray-blue dome broken by the intense white balloon of light that was the sun.

No cars passed them. Bobby Lee chattered at Ronnie about something he wanted him to see: a dead mother opossum with babies still in her womb had been smashed by a car during the night.

"You oughta see it, Ronnie. No kiddin', you oughta see it," he declared, his feet kicking up murky orange clay dust.

Ronnie's face was blank, his mouth rigid, his eyes steely. He walked stiffly as if his muscles were locked.

"Why you want me to see something that's dead? When you going to grow up, Bobby Lee? I've seen enough dead stuff."

Bobby Lee slowed, allowing Ronnie to put two or three dusty yards between them before he scrambled back even with him.

"Well, we're walkin' right toward it. It's just ahead," Bobby Lee jammered. "You oughtta see it. Little pink possums comin' out her side. You oughtta see it."

"Those babies are dead!" Ronnie snapped. "Don't want to see no dead babies or no dead mother, I'm telling you. Go on and let me walk by myself."

"But Ronnie . . . man, you oughtta see it." Bobby Lee stopped, shuffled in his tracks.

Ronnie trudged on, his shoulders slumping as if they were weighted down with heavy sandbags.

The low-hanging white haze began to lift in the distance, and Bobby Lee stumbled ahead a few feet for a closer look at what the rising sheet-haze was about to reveal.

It was a curtain.

Looming against the gray-blue sky, the solid black curtain stood the height and width of a drive-in movie screen. At the bottom of the curtain there was a small door, and it was clear that Ronnie's steps would take him right to it.

Something told Bobby Lee that he had to warn his friend: something evil lurked behind that door. Dust swirling up into his face, Bobby Lee ran, but even as he increased his speed, Ronnie outdistanced him with his walking, and grew smaller, dwarfed by the enormous curtain into which he was headed.

The door became a dark speck, a vanishing point in the landscape of black surrounding it.

"Don't go in there!" Bobby Lee yelled.

Ronnie kept walking.

"Please, Ronnie, no! No-o-o!"

Bobby Lee ran harder, gulping the dusty air, his sides stitched with exhaustion, his face hardened with fear.

Ronnie reached the door.

"Don't! Please, don't!" Bobby Lee screamed at the top of his voice.

The door opened and drew Ronnie in; it seemed to suck him in with a blast of air. And suddenly Bobby Lee was only a few feet from the door. Hot sun, Alabama magic at work, surreal, fantastic. He could see that Ronnie's path led him into a black fog, tricked out with shimmering blue flames.

Then the door closed.

Bobby Lee, feeling more alone than ever before in his life, watched as the huge black curtain slowly dissolved, melted like a tremendous block of ebony ice. The chill of it poured over him, and he strained his good eye to find Ronnie.

An instant later, an open-oven-door rush of heat

swept away the momentary chill. The curtain was gone. The dusty shoulder of the road reemerged, and so did Ronnie. But there was something different about him. Resolutely, he walked ahead of Bobby Lee, his outline gray and opaque.

"Wait up, Ronnie. Man, where'd you go? What'd you do behind that door?"

Ronnie started to cross the asphalt road, not pausing to look both ways or to alter his zombielike gait.

"Well, hey, wait up!"

The warm humid air thickened around Bobby Lee like syrup. His cries sounded like metallic garglings.

A foreign sports car zoomed toward Ronnie out of a mirage pool.

"Watch out, man, there's a car! There's a car, Ronnie!" Bobby Lee's throat burned; he struggled to get out onto the road and push Ronnie from the path of the car, but something shackled his legs. The car wasn't slowing.

It doesn't see him.

"Ronnie!"

Bobby Lee tripped; the dusty shoulder slammed into his chest. He looked up . . . and the car . . . the car roared through the ghostly outline of his friend and sped into the distance. "Goddarn," Bobby Lee whispered. With a single push-up he scrambled to his feet.

"Ronnie! Goddarn, man! That car! Man!" he yelled excitedly, but he was trembling with fear. "Man, it looked like that car went right—"

Ronnie angled onto the opposite shoulder of the road, and there the world, the domain of the dream, exploded with intensely bright white lights. Bobby Lee shielded his eye.

"God almighty darn," he muttered. "Ronnie?"

The walking figure of his friend cast a long, pyramid-shaped shadow and kept walking, moving deeper into the expanse of light until the shadow, stretched thin, seemed to snap back upon itself and disappear.

And so did Ronnie.

Bobby Lee jerked awake as if an invisible string were attached to him from the ceiling, and an invisible manipulator had brought him suddenly to life.

Only a dream.

The ragged army cot, his bed, beaded moist with sweat, creaked under his spasmodic movement.

Only a dream. But Ronnie's in trouble.

The gray light of morning speared through the front room curtains of the cracker-box mobile home he shared with his mother.

"Momma?" he whispered, still reeling in the aftermath of the nightmare.

His mother, curled into a fetal position, her pink nightie hitched around her waist, lay dead to the world on the sofa-sleeper. She had kicked off the sheet covering her, and now, to Bobby Lee, she looked terribly small and incapable of offering help.

Besides, he knew she was tired and would sleep until late morning because she worked as a barmaid at a place called The Oasis and normally didn't get home most nights before two or three. She depended upon him to put himself to bed and to rustle up his own breakfast.

He got off his cot and drifted toward her. A dust mop of brown hair, tousled, individual strands graying here and there, covered much of her face and fell in shaggy clumps onto her pale shoulder.

"Momma?" Whisper softer this time. He shivered and cupped his elbows. I wish my pop was here, he thought to himself. Momma doesn't ever know what to do when something comes up.

"You're gonna have to take care of it your own self, Bobby Lee. Honey, with no daddy around, you're gone have to be a man a lot sooner than most kids. I'm sorry about that, but that's the way it is."

How many times had he heard that speech? It was permanently catalogued in his memory.

He lingered by the sofa-sleeper, hoping she would sense his presence and awaken, even if momentarily, to solace him.

I had a bad dream, Momma. About my friend, Ronnie. He runned away from home. I know where he went. He's in trouble, Momma, he's in trouble. I know he is.

But she didn't awaken, and so Bobby Lee reluctantly turned away to get dressed for school, or at least to get dressed, because going to school this morning was out of the question. He was facing a decision, a decision about a phone call.

After he had dressed, he meandered to the kitchen to scrounge up breakfast. His empty stomach growled and his glass eye itched. It always did when he was nervous or upset. For some reason all the moisture would dry around the edges of the eye, and it would burn as if someone were rubbing salt into it. His last eye doctor had given him a vial of something to keep the eye slightly wet, but as of yesterday the vial was empty.

Standing in the kitchen, he glanced back to the living room at the soft mounded form of his sleeping mother. He sensed that she had never come to grips with his mangled face and especially the glass eye. Often, at a meal or when she was talking to him, he would notice that she was staring at it, mesmerized by it as if it were the eye of a waking serpent. Since birth, he had had a new glass surrogate—*surrogate* was the eye doctor's term for it—every three years or so, including one last year. Knowing that his mother fretted over his getting a new surrogate, he had tried to joke about the whole matter to quell her unease. Driving home from the doctor's office, she had asked, "How does this one feel, Bobby Lee? Is it gone be all right?"

"Oh, yeah, Momma," he had responded, and then, having flattened his palm over his good eye, added, "This new one's so good I can see Christmas with it." And smiled, hoping his mother would stop being so serious.

To his surprise, she had started crying.

Bobby Lee sighed, pulled down a box of Fruity Pebbles from the cupboard, found yesterday's unwashed cereal bowl, and, as quietly as possible, brimmed it full. At the refrigerator he paused to rub his irritated eye. *Goddarn, it's gone be red all day now.*

The virtually empty shelves of the refrigerator released their chill air into his frowning face: No milk. *Goddarn!* He considered substituting a can of Mountain Dew, but decided against it. Decided against breakfast, in fact, after chewing a few dry flakes of Fruity Pebbles.

Goddarn, I'm hungry.

And scared. And confused. *Ronnie's out there in trouble.*

Bobby Lee thought he knew what had prompted the nightmare: guilt. Guilt, pure and simple. Last night while his mother was at work, Herman Jackson, the Catlin County deputy sheriff, had called. Ronnie's grandmother had contacted everyone imaginable and had recalled that Ronnie often spent time with Bobby Lee.

"Bobby Lee, have you seen your friend, Ronnie?" the sheriff had asked.

Your friend: Goddarn, he is.

"No, sir."

"Would you have any idea where he might be?"

My friend, Ronnie. The only friend I got in the world.

"Well, no sir . . . I can't . . . I don't know where he is."

"You let me know if you think of where he might be. Your friend could find himself in serious trouble. I think maybe you could help him out."

"Well . . . I promised. He just runned away. I don't know where he runned to."

"OK, son. But if you think of anything, you call the Sheriff's Department and ask for Sheriff Jackson. I'm just trying to help your friend, Bobby Lee. I want you to understand that."

"Yes, sir. I do."

Bobby Lee had gone to bed feeling hollow inside.

Goddarn it, I promised I wouldn't tell and I won't.

And then the dream.

Your friend could find himself in serious trouble.

Something told Bobby Lee that he already was.

At the kitchen table, he peered into his bowl of dry cereal, pushed it away, and looked again toward his sleeping mother. Decision time. Better hadn't use the phone here. he got up, cautiously walked back near the sofa-sleeper, unclasped his mother's pocketbook, and fished a quarter out of her coin purse.

I think maybe you could help him out.

Remembering where the closest pay phone was, Bobby Lee slipped out the door, his thoughts focused entirely on the only friend he had.

The pink-faced monkey screamed and shielded her baby, which had, seemingly, a death grip on one of her nipples.

"All you monkeys stink!" Bobby Lee bleated at the wire monkey cage, the centerpiece of Soldier's community park.

And he was right. Mingled odors of animal musk, mildew, and monkey droppings radiated out from the rectangular cage inhabited by a dozen mostly adult monkeys. The stench would intensify as the days grew warmer.

But, all in all, the park was one of Bobby Lee's favorite places; only three blocks from home, it was a good area to come to late at night while his mother was still at work and swing in the swings, skip rocks into the nameless muddy stream that flowed through the park, and pester the monkeys.

He liked the latter best of all.

On a field trip once, his science teacher had given the

class the name of this particular species of monkey, but he couldn't remember it. To Bobby Lee, they were just monkeys. Plain old monkeys. In a bizarre way they attracted him. He could spend hours watching them, studying their faces.

They were the only living things he knew of that seemed uglier than he was. He could look at them and feel superior; he could look at them and feel the same disgust that people felt when they looked at him. There was something oddly therapeutic about being able to come to that cage and shout obscenities at those creatures. Other kids did it to him, so it only seemed fair that the monkeys should exist for Bobby Lee to vent his anger and frustration. And fear.

"You're ugly and you stink!" Bobby Lee yelled. "Turkey face! Shit face!"

Yeah, it felt good. The park was empty, and no one was using the pay phone over by the bandstand. He had already made up his mind to skip school. Besides, he was nearly a half-hour late now. The phone call would be much more important, wouldn't it?

What's at school anyway? Mean and cruel kids who make fun of you. Girls who giggle at your voice because you sound like a sheep. Boys who screw their faces and press a marble into one eye, imitating you, until a teacher makes them stop.

"Goddarn ugly monkeys!" he shouted.

The mother monkey suddenly lunged into the wire and screamed at him. Bobby Lee jumped back, then gritted his teeth angrily.

"Ugly old bitch! Go screw yourself! Hear me! Go screw yourself!"

323

Trembling with rage, he picked up a rock and hurled it into the cage.

"Ugly! You're not my friends! Sons a bitches! Ugly old thing!"

The sound of the obscenities burned at his ears. He felt ashamed, deeply ashamed. He didn't talk that way normally. But it felt good.

"Goddarn it!" He began to cry and the tears stung around the glass eye, so he took it out, clenched a fist over it, and ran to the creek. He glanced down at his fist, feeling a new surge of anger. He uncurled his fingers and whispered at the hazel-colored eye staring placidly up at him.

"You ugly, ugly sucker. I hate you. You're no friend. Blind ugly sucker."

Then, as a final gesture, he tossed the eye into the stream and sat on the bank, gritting his teeth while he cried, and behind him the monkeys joined together in a chorus of screams and chatterings.

It took fifteen or twenty minutes for him to find his eye.

Carefully, he wiped the silt and moss from it with the bottom edge of his tee-shirt. He slipped it back in the socket and cringed with the burning sensation. Probably has a zillion germs on it now, he reasoned to himself, but I don't give a darn. I hate it anyway.

Last year he had tried to talk his mother into letting him wear a patch over it, like a pirate—which is what, when he was younger, he loved to dress as at Halloween—but she wouldn't hear of it.

Goddarn.

More tears threatening, he dawdled over to the monkey cage, where he was met by a new round of screams and cries. The monkeys stared at him, cautiously sizing up whether he was going to yell or throw a rock at them, and by degrees they fell silent, and lapsed into their climbing and swinging antics and their neurotic pacing, a pacing like that of his thought patterns, the internal debate on calling Sheriff Jackson about Ronnie.

Over near the pay phone, two young women, both pushing baby strollers, were entering the park. Time to do whatever I'm goin' to do, Bobby Lee admonished himself. The two women chatted happily; he could hear the pleasant lilt of their voices. They were friends, no doubt, sharing baby experiences, comparing developmental phases and that sort of thing. In the cage, two of the monkeys huddled upon one of the narrow platforms. One picked at the other's coat, grooming him.

My only friend in the world. I'd like to help him.

Suddenly his attention was drawn to the canopy of tall oaks behind him. There was a blur of white, fluttering, then the gentle sounds of wings thrumming. And a spray of blood.

Ronnie's pigeons! Goddarn! It's them!

But no sooner had they appeared than they seemed to burst like bubbles, leaving only the mysterious chill of illusion.

The illusion glowed in Bobby Lee's mind, dimming little as he started to run. He was breathless by the time he dropped his quarter in the coin slot and dialed the Sheriff's Department. Then confusion: Sheriff Jackson, the receptionist told him, was off duty that day but could be reached at home. Nothing about this was going to be easy, the boy realized.

"Sheriff Jackson?"

A sleepy voice replied, "Yeah . . . this is Jackson."

"Oh, . . . you see . . . I'm Bobby Lee Hollins. And . . . I think I've got something to say about Ronnie . . . you know, about Ronnie Cartwright."

"Yes, son. What is it?"

Bobby Lee felt his throat constricting. *Breaking your promise.*

"Well, . . . I'm not sure."

"Son, where are you now? Can I come and let's have us a talk?"

"Well, . . . OK, I guess."

Sheriff Herman Jackson, a tall, well-built black man with a neatly trimmed moustache and kindly eyes, picked up Bobby Lee at the park and they drove around in Jackson's patrol car. Bobby Lee, though impressed with his first ride in such a car and fascinated by the huge revolver on Jackson's hip, couldn't find the nerve to break his promise to Ronnie.

"Am I gone get in trouble for skippin' school?"

Jackson glanced at him, started to smile, but then quickly frowned and shifted his eyes back to the street.

"Oh, now it seems to me that what we're doin' here is official business. Official Sheriff's Department business. That's what I can tell your school so you won't get in trouble."

"Well, that's good, 'cause I don't want to get into

no trouble."

Jackson studied the street ahead. "I just hope your friend, Ronnie, is not in trouble. Don't you."

"Yes, sir." Bobby Lee swallowed the words.

"I reckon you're about the only person I know who can help your friend."

"Yes, sir."

"You about ready to tell me what you know?"

Bobby Lee rubbed at his glass eye.

"But . . . ya see . . . I promised I wouldn't tell."

His voice pitched high, tottered on the edge of tears.

Jackson shook his head. "Your friend, Ronnie, is lucky to have a friend like you. Not many people these days have a friend who'll keep a promise. No sir, not many."

Bobby Lee wiggled uncomfortably in the seat.

Suddenly Jackson looked at his watch. "Say, Bobby Lee, have you had any breakfast?"

"No, sir," he replied; an image of the bowl of dry Fruity Pebbles flickered through his thoughts.

"It's the middle of the morning and I haven't had any breakfast either. What say you and me go out to Boggs's Truck Stop for some breakfast. Can't expect a man to do important po-lice business on an empty stomach, now can we?"

"No, sir. But I . . . I don't got no money."

"Well . . . we'll just call this an official po-lice business breakfast."

A smile crept in at the corners of Bobby Lee's twisted mouth.

Three miles outside of Soldier, Broggs's Truck Stop perched on a high clay bank with a large sign on storklike legs announcing its presence. Every trucker in the South knew that it was a great place for breakfast. Bone-jarring ruts pocked the asphalt lot and dust claimed its outer edges where the hulking eighteen-wheelers waited for their drivers to eat or catch a quick nap. The smell of diesel fuel drifted beyond the restaurant and service station area into an abandoned and badly eroded field that was slowly yielding to the spread of kudzu vines.

Inside, the restaurant was reasonably clean and comfortable. No fancy decor, though the ledges bordering the booths sported philodendron plants and near the cash register a special beam supported a trio of hanging ferns. As the sheriff and Bobby Lee slid into a booth, the breakfast rush had largely exhausted itself. A few men, some in blue and some in tan uniforms, lingered over coffee, but the harder working contingent had departed several hours ago.

A heavyset waitress in a pink-and-white uniform greeted them. Bobby Lee experienced a certain pleasure in noting that a knotted string of small warts trailed down like a tear from the corner of her left eye.

"Who's your partner here, Sheriff?"

"Gilley Ray, this is Bobby Lee Hollins. He's helping me with a missing person's case."

"Whew, my!" she exclaimed, wheezing from the effort of balancing all her weight without swaying too much from side to side.

"What's y'all gone have to eat this mornin'?"

Sheriff Jackson ordered both of them a big breakfast, the most that Bobby Lee could ever recall eating. And he appreciated the fact that the sheriff skirted the issue of Ronnie Cartwright.

"What you plannin' to do this summer, son?"

"Well, uh, you see, my pop . . . well, he sorta don't live with me and my momma. And, well, he-he said I could work for him some this summer."

"What kinda work does he do?"

"Oh, you see, he-he tears down old buildings and keeps the wood and metal and stuff like that. And I can help him pick up old boards and nails and stuff. And maybe . . . I think this summer, well, you know, Momma and him gone get back together. I b'lieve they will."

Jackson smiled. "I hope they do. I sure do. They got 'em a mighty fine son. I know that."

"I don't mind it a lot stayin' by myself at night. I'm pretty depend-a-bull."

"Well, I can see that."

Later, eggs, biscuits, and grits having disappeared, Jackson stretched himself back in his seat.

"Sure hope Ronnie Cartwright, wherever he is, had him a good breakfast like this."

Bobby Lee stared at his empty plate and grew silent. A frown pinching his forehead, he soon broke his reverie.

"Does anybody live in Half Moon?" he asked.

Jackson studied the boy's face. "Half Moon? Lord, son, Half Moon, Alabama's a ghost town. There's one old woman who still runs an antique shop there, but that storm last spring . . . why you ask about Half Moon?"

"'Cause. 'Cause that's . . . that's where my friend, Ronnie, runned away to."

329

"Are you sure about this, Bobby Lee?"

"Yes, sir, I am. He used to live there. That's where he runned away to," he muttered, then cupped a hand over his good eye and started to weep.

"Hey . . . hey, Bobby Lee," Jackson whispered. "It's all right. You did the right thing. Now, let's you and me take us a ride to Half Moon and see what's there. I bet maybe your friend, Ronnie, he be glad to see you about now."

CHAPTER 26

A chilling laughter nudged them from a fitful sleep. Although it was well past dawn, darkness covered Half Moon.

More laughter. The terriers stirred and looked to Miss Molly for comfort. The laughter tumbled upon itself, cascading from the third floor down the stair-well, then echoing through the hallway. It was a woman's voice.

"Is it help? Has somebody come?" the boy asked hopefully, but when he caught the intensity in the old woman's eyes, the signs of confusion and fear there, he was embarrassed that he had asked. Help wouldn't come trailing demonic laughter.

Molly, bags under her eyes and wisps of unruly hair sprouting like horns, fussed softly with the terriers to quiet them and then peered up at the ceiling, her head twitching nervously.

The peals of laughter choked off into shrieks, anguished shrieks: the insane voice of the haunted school.

"Is it real?" the boy muttered. "All those things we've seen and heard . . . are they real?"

But his words were barely audible through the frenzied cries from above, and as the cries pitched sharply higher, the boy cupped his hands over his ears and rocked from side to side.

Although it seemed longer, the maniacal voice ceased its clamor before another five minutes had passed. A collective sense of relief permeated the small room.

"Who is it?" Shyly the boy looked at Molly. She forced a wry smile. It was as if she knew a secret she might not share. "Who is it? Is it nobody?" the boy persisted.

The old woman shook her head, pursed her lips, and arched her eyebrows. "Oh, it's somebody, don'cha see," she replied.

The boy's whisper came out like a tiny puff of wind. "Who?"

Molly paused. "It's Miss Cassandra Ayrans Whitby. And they've come to take her away."

Her comment seemed to thicken the shadows in the room. Calmly, the old woman heated the last of the water and tinkered with the lantern. It was apparent that it would run out of fuel before much longer.

Soon the mildly acrid smell of instant coffee filled the room. She handed the boy a cup of instant chocolate and then fixed herself a cup of the coffee. The boy drank, and the warmth of the liquid radiated through him magically.

"It's good," he intoned, allowing himself the comfort of a smile. And the smile tugged at the corners of his mouth until he glanced at Molly, who, in turn, was staring at the closed door.

"What is it, Miss Molly?"

Stiffly, she raised her arm and pointed a gnarled finger. The boy automatically followed the line of it; together they saw, through the dimming lantern light, the doorknob turning slowly.

"Scoot over this way toward me," Molly directed.

Suddenly fists began to pound upon the door.

The boy's mouth felt dry as if all the saliva had been sucked out of it. Then the pleas for help, muffled cries in a ghostly, toneless voice, penetrated the door.

"Save me! Help me! *Save me-e-e-e!* Demons! Save me! God, please save me!"

Something jerked in the boy's chest. He felt the hairs on his arm stiffen, his skin tingle.

"It's the Reverend Shepherd," the boy whispered.

"Let me in! *Save me! Dear God! Oh, dear God!*"

The cries split, then multiplied into disembodied echoes. There was a shuffling movement. Haunting groans.

For affirmation, the boy stole a glance at Shepherd's body near the wall. It stirred ever so slightly, then became as still as stone.

Beneath the door, blood found rivulets and streamed toward them, then abruptly slowed and pooled. A white mist began to writhe up from the pool, thin and indistinct like the plaster-dust fog that drifted through the halls.

The walls of the room began to vibrate.

"No, please, no," Molly pleaded softly.

The door suddenly exploded open, dangling by its top hinge. But there was nothing or no one beyond it.

The boy edged closer to Molly and held one of the

whining terriers against his stomach; the old woman tried to console the other two.

When the vibration petered out, the shrill cry, eerily distant, found its pattern. Harsh notes lilted through the hallways.

Shadow call.

It played on. Siren song. Wild, ominous prelude.

Then it abruptly stopped, and from somewhere beyond wafted a haunting applause.

The white mist thickened, animated by wings. The headless pigeons erupted from within it, birds of dawning seeking their old master. The boy knew that he must respond.

"I have to go now," he said. "I know what will make it stop."

And Molly understood.

Muscles aching, head dizzied with sleepless exhaustion, the boy winnowed his way through the halls, halls illuminated by the faint aura of the pigeons. The wounded hawk and the crow joined the pigeons, scrambling ahead in a flightless journey into the darkest part of the haunted school, the lair of Windkiller.

Come into my darkness. I have a place for you.

Windkiller's voice tore into his thoughts, but the boy felt no panic this time. Only resolve.

Only the bravest warrior. . . .

The words buoyed his confidence. Energy from an unknown source surged through him.

At his back, small fires erupted, and with the sight of them he raced ahead to where the pigeons and the wounded hawk and the crow had gathered: the fallout shelter—a cavity of blackness filled with a dark festival of shadows.

The pigeons flew into the shelter's narrow corridor, illuminating the pathetic figure of Dale Taylor slumped against a wall. And the boy began to feel the oppressive warmth of billowing flames.

The smell of smoke and the muffled roar of fire drove forward, spreading from the hallway leading to the gymnasium. Another round of demon fires, the boy reasoned. Like the ones that brought down Molly's antique shop and destroyed Mr. Taylor's van. He could imagine flames leaping out of the face of the Windkiller logo in the center of the gym floor, twisting, whirling like a tornado of fire. The path of the flaming funnel would slam it into the stage, and fingers of the raging fire would reach out and tug at the massive curtain, and soon the entire gym and all its memories . . . and all its ghosts . . . would be engulfed in a miniature Hell.

"We got to get outta here!" the boy cried, pulling at Taylor's limp body. "Fire! Come on!" he screamed.

Slowly, Taylor responded. Minutes later, they were out into the hallway heading to the front doors of the school. Molly, lantern in hand, met them.

"Ronnie, let Mr. Taylor put some of his weight on my shoulder. We got to help him out."

Molly's voice seemed to come at the boy out of a closet. In the dim lantern light, her panicked movement appeared almost comically absurd, for when she draped one of Taylor's arms over her she bent like a straw under his bulk.

"Help me, please, Ronnie!" she called.

"Get me to the doors and I can make it from there,"

said Taylor, wincing from the pain as he tried to put weight on his left leg.

Coughing from the smoke he had inhaled, the boy slid under Taylor's left arm and lifted with all his strength, but even with their efforts combined, he and the old woman could do no more than drag their companion toward the doors.

"Lit-tul men, get on out of the way!" Molly shouted as the three dogs jumped and skipped excitedly in front of them like wind-up toys.

In the next several anguished minutes, there was no talking, only struggle. Lungs and eyes filling with smoke, they struggled. With their bodies pressed closely together, the boy felt a bond of sorts, something magical binding them in their survival effort.

But it won't be enough, the boy thought to himself, his muscles throbbing, his breath rasping from exhaustion and smoke.

It won't be enough.

Beyond the front doors, they helped Taylor lower himself to the steps. From there he managed to crawl and drag his body far enough away from the school for at least temporary safety. Molly stood shakily, dazed, one hand clutched to her breasts. The terriers bounced into each other at her feet; seeing them there, the boy fleetingly wished that he shared their animal oblivion.

Then he forced himself to look back at the burning school, columns of black smoke pouring from the gym and the roof of the main building.

Reverend Shepherd! He won't survive!

With that dark thought, the boy paused to hunker down at Taylor's side. The man's face glistened with sweat and his eyes were indistinct in the morning air,

air that was veiled, that hid the sun. Half Moon seemed to be in the midst of a dust storm, with smoke from the conflagration darkening even further the grayish-brown light of day.

"What about the Reverend Shepherd?" the boy asked, his mouth tightened at the corners with tension.

Taylor shook his head and coughed harshly. "No . . . no, Ronnie. We can't go back in there now. I want you and Molly to go on down to the county road and wait for help. I'll be all right here. I can stay far enough clear of the fire."

The boy looked at Molly and she nodded, reluctantly agreeing with Taylor's plan. Then Taylor's head and shoulders dropped, and the boy sensed that the man was on the verge of passing out.

Molly, her amazing strength and fortitude more evident than ever, reached toward the boy.

"Come on. Maybe I can try to get the ole Pinto started. Let's go on now and do what's best to be done."

He rose to go with her, but in doing so he turned momentarily away from the school, feeling helpless, knowing somehow that their efforts were futile.

Come into my darkness. I have a place for you.

The voice spun the boy around. He glanced at Molly and then back at the school. He began to run.

"Stop, Ronnie! No, stop!" Taylor called weakly, watching with disbelief as the boy disappeared into the school.

"We have to let him go," Molly exclaimed. "It's something he's got to do . . . and he's our only hope."

CHAPTER 27

Having borrowed Sheriff Jackson's handkerchief, Bobby Lee slipped his surrogate eye out of its socket and tried to clear it of whatever was creating the burning sensation. As Jackson drove them toward Half Moon, he continued his easy, comforting monologue, punctuating it now and again with a question or a lead-in for Bobby Lee. Since leaving the truck stop, neither had mentioned Ronnie Cartwright. It had become a kind of game: see how long we can talk without bringing up Ronnie Cartwright. And Jackson was a master at the game; yet, concentrate as he might, Bobby Lee couldn't focus his thoughts long on any other topic.

"That eye givin' you some trouble?" Jackson asked, his attention flickering only an instant away from the road.

Bobby Lee shrugged his shoulders and wetted his lips. "Yeah, some. Darn thing. Wish my mom'd just let me wear a patch instead. Heck, I wouldn't mind a patch, you know. Better'n this darn thing anyways."

Jackson followed with some remark, but it failed to register in Bobby Lee's consciousness because just as Jackson spoke they passed a large billboard facing them on the right side of the road. A large billboard that seemed to be covered with a dark-colored curtain. Seeing it numbed Bobby Lee, paralyzed him if only for an instant. The dream returned. *Ronnie's in trouble . . . the curtain is goin' to swallow him. Goddarn.*

The billboard skated past.

Bobby Lee, fingers trembling, pressed the surrogate eye back into place. Once again, Jackson's reassuring voice held sway. A fatherly voice. Bobby Lee listened, a question forming on his lips. Then he spoke. "Do you . . . you know, do you got any kids?"

Jackson chuckled. "Good Lord, boy, I'm not even married."

"Well, you know . . . I bet you'd make a good father. I mean, someday when you find a wife and get married."

This time the chuckle escalated to a hearty laugh. "Hey, now that's a real nice, a real nice thing for you to say, Bobby Lee. And if I do ever have any kids, I think I'd like a boy just like you. You know that?"

It was Bobby Lee's turn to laugh, though it dwindled quickly to a nervous giggle. "You wouldn't really want a kid like me. I mean, I'm a white kid. You wouldn't want a white kid with only one eye and talks funny."

"Hey, son, you've got something that's more important than color or anything else."

"I do?"

"That's right. You've got character. Heart. I can tell that. You're goin' to be a fine man one of these days."

Warmth tickled in the pit of Bobby Lee's stomach. "I

bet a sheriff's got to keep secrets, don't he?"

Jackson smiled at the sudden topic shift.

"Oh, it depends. Depends on whether keepin' the secret's goin' to be more hurtful to the people involved than not keepin' it."

"You think I'm doin' the right thang? I mean, not keepin' Ronnie's secret. Goddarn, he's the only friend I have and—"

"Hey, trust me. It is. It's the best thing to do, and he won't stop bein' your friend. I just know he won't. It's the kind of thing a sheriff has to know." He winked at Bobby Lee and smiled.

"Just havin' one eye, you know what I can do?" the boy asked shyly, a grin spreading slowly across his face.

The sheriff shook his head.

"Well, don'cha see, I . . . I can wink at all the girls anytime I want to."

They both laughed: the sheriff, a deep, resonant laugh; Bobby Lee, a bleating cackle. And the laughter carried them another mile or two. They would reach their destination by noon.

"Sheriff, do you b'lieve in dreams?"

The boy's hollow little voice seemed to echo through Jackson's thoughts. "What you mean, *believe* in them?"

"Well, you know, thangs you dream about comin' true?"

"Everybody has dreams about what they'd like to have happen, but you still have to go out and work hard and try to make those dreams come true."

"No, that's not what I mean. I mean, bad dreams comin' true."

"You have a bad dream last night?"

"Yes, sir. I dreamed . . . ," his voice trailed off. "I dreamed about Ronnie. Somethin' real bad and weird, you know, happenin' to him. You think it could really happen?"

"Oh, I see. My ole grandma used to have 'visions' about things that were comin'. Course, she always told us kids about them *after* they happened. No, I guess I don't believe in it. It was probably just you worryin' about Ronnie that caused that dream."

"Yes, sir."

But that huge dark curtain kept looming in his mind's eye, kept gleaming even as they pulled into Half Moon and Jackson moved the sawhorses that blocked the entrance road.

The dark curtain horror blinded the boy. But it was the shroud of darkness hanging over the rubble of the town that sent a tingling down Jackson's spine. He removed his sunglasses and peered through the windshield at the murky air.

"My God, . . . what's goin' on here?"

CHAPTER 28

It's inside my head, Ronnie exclaimed to himself as he stood at the entrance to the fallout shelter. The mysterious birdlike cry dizzied him. He swayed slightly; somehow the cry had found an opening in his consciousness, a crack in his sanity, and had entered. A bit of the dark world.

The cry was an invitation to surrender.

Give yourself up and the darkness is yours. Forever.

Impulsively, he stepped into the shadowy opening, and what he felt was a coldness . . . the touch of his dead father's marble hands. He jerked, but he couldn't free himself, and ahead of him he could hear a gathering roar, a rush of wind that pitched to a demonic howl. Behind him, the fires spread inexorably through the school. Suddenly the suction from that mysterious wind pulled him deeper into the shelter. The wind died down, and what greeted his senses was a soft, dusty silence. An air of reverence.

The unexpected appearance of the hovering pigeons frightened him. He held his breath. Then he remembered and knew. They had switched allegiance. They were no longer controlled by Windkiller. Something, perhaps their homing instinct, had made them return to him, and now they were his again, friendly spirits, comrades into the unknown.

Wings beating furiously, the pigeons descended in a cloud of white, and their tiny clawed feet held fast to some object, something they had brought to the boy. Hesitantly, he reached for it, and as his fingers coiled around the handle of Taylor's hatchet, he experienced a wave of courage.

I can fight it! his heart shouted, but his joy dissipated slightly when he recalled that the Reverend Shepherd had stalked him with that same hatchet.

No, not the Reverend Shepherd. Windkiller made him do it.

The darkness was complete except for shafts of gray light spinning a few feet to either side of him. When his eyes adjusted to the mottled darkness, he concentrated on the gray areas. He knew that Windkiller would be stirring ghosts, ghosts of loneliness, ghosts of memory.

"Come on. Come on and do it," said the tender, feminine voice near him.

The gray, indistinct form of his mother materialized. She was leaning toward him, her hands extended. "You can do it. Come on. Come on, honey."

It was a familiar tone, tapping memories. She must have used that same tone when he took his first steps, and he could remember hearing it when he had learned to ride his first bicycle and she and his father had run along beside the wobbling bike.

"Use both hands, son. Do it like I showed you."

His father materialized out of the gray to his left.

Baseball practice in the backyard. More memories.

Don't want to disappoint them.

His steps, mechanical, bordering on torturous, took him further into the darkness, but always the forms of his parents stayed a few steps ahead, and their voices retained the warmth of encouragement.

The sight of them made him want to drop the hatchet. He worked his lips stiffly in an effort to speak to them. Then suddenly they disappeared . . . no, merely replaced by other ghostly figures: the drama students; the janitor; a wild-eyed woman, crazed, laughing her maniacal, Cassandra-laughter as she had years ago; and the boy's own double.

The darkness shifted, thickened smoothly like theater lights lowering for the beginning of a performance. He was standing in an aisle of sorts, the air around him cool and dank. At the far end of the aisle, there seemed to be an elevated table surrounded by blue flames. On the table rested a black box, two-feet square; the front of it was covered by a curtain.

Black box.

Beneath his feet, the aisle glimmered, catching light from an unknown source. In the mirror floor, he glimpsed a panoply of faces: demons, wraiths, one hideous mask after another. And a face filled with confusion and fear.

His own.

He stopped. Every fiber in his body wanted him to turn around and run. Run away. And keep running.

The familiar birdlike cry tore through the air. He knew, he sensed now that its source loomed beyond the black box. Intermixed with the cry was a jangle of bells.

Too late to run. Too late now.

You will know what will make it stop.

He tightened his grip on the hatchet.

Cautiously he neared the black box; the blue flames, one at a time, extinguished themselves. Waves of a cloying animal smell surrounded him. Closer he stepped until he was no more than two feet from the box, the top of which was aligned with his shoulders.

And he waited.

There was a whisper of wings behind his ear. The ghostly pigeons hovered, nimbusing him with a secret light, fueling his courage and resolve.

The rhythm of the predatory cry and the jangle of the bells quickened, and over his ragged breathing he strained to hear his heartbeat, for he imagined that it had stopped. He closed his eyes.

Windkiller rose; its huge wings swept upward.

The entire shelter quaked. The floor groaned, and behind the creature a fiery pit suddenly yawned wide; flames leaped around its edges.

The curtained black box disappeared; the boy stood in the looming shadow of the creature, hatchet poised above his head, eyes still closed. His courage wavered and his mind reeled out a dark litany.

Look at the creature.

Don't look . . . Don't look . . .

Look at the creature . . . and go mad. Look at the creature . . . and die . . . Inside . . .

Become a ghost.

The eyes of Windkiller, torches of hate, bore down upon the boy. He could feel the creature's stinging breath and could smell the pungent odor of death.

Then wings brushed past the boy's shoulder, and he opened his eyes in time to see the ghostfall of the headless pigeons, to see them drive with their claws into the eyes of the towering dark spirit. Again and again, the pigeons released their fury upon the face of Windkiller. And the rage of the soon-blinded beast threatened to bring down the walls of the shelter.

The creature cried out, jerked violently, and pitched forward; and as it did the boy seized the moment, seized his only chance, burying the hatchet deep within the creature's heart.

A shadow streamed toward the boy with brutal quickness and force. The bolt of pain, the fire in his chest staggered him. He screamed, and the scream redoubled itself until his ribs seemed to collapse as if crushed by the force of the scream and the iron-brand pressure in the center of his chest.

As he opened his eyes again in horror and shock, he saw the extended cloven hoof retract and disappear within the darkness.

The shelter began to vibrate. The creature clutched numbly at the hatchet handle, tottered, and then fell backward into the fiery pit. There was one final cry, long, agonized, destined to echo forever in the boy's mind.

The terrain below the shelter quaked and thundered and then the jaws of the flaming pit closed. And there was darkness and silence.

I'm dying.

The boy's thoughts drifted in his mind like an icy fog.

I'm dying. Inside.

For a moment, he imagined that his double smiled down at him, then faded. He felt disoriented, felt that he had dropped from reality into a land of cold, brilliant light.

This is dying. Inside.
Becoming a ghost.

He lay there, silent, motionless, unaware that his pet crow and the wounded hawk had gathered at either side of him. And above him, the ghostly pigeons spun tiny silken arcs. His body was growing cold.

Then, one by one, the ghostly birds, the birds of dawning, descended softly. One by one they threaded into his lifelessness, weaving webs of vital heat. One by one, again and again, webs of nature's healing fiber, ghostly, mysterious, a ghost-weave of love.

And the boy stirred.

He felt himself being lifted from the land of cold, brilliant light through realms of darkness up out of a bottomless pool of black water. Until he was awake. And alive.

The birds were gone.

Gone forever, he reasoned.

Half Moon is free.

On a note of finality, all the demon fires burning throughout the school ceased.

Minutes later, Ronnie stumbled out the front door of the school. Near the burned hulk of the county's van, Sheriff Jackson and Bobby Lee Hollins leaned over the reclining figure of the Reverend Shepherd, who appeared to be conscious. Miss Molly and Taylor and the three terriers huddled close by.

Bobby Lee was the first to notice Ronnie. He yipped with joy and sprinted toward his friend. "Ronnie! It's Ronnie! Goddarn, he's OK!"

The others turned to watch the scene.

Ronnie smiled weakly as Bobby Lee crashed into him, hugging him with all his strength.

"Goddarn," Bobby Lee muttered tearfully, happily into Ronnie's shoulder.

And the darkness over Half Moon began to lift.

EPILOGUE

Dale Taylor, still unaccustomed to his crutches, stiffly and awkwardly maneuvered himself over the freshly waxed floors. The psychiatric wing of the Catlin County Hospital seemed alien, almost frightening to him. Sheriff Jackson walked beside him until they reached the lounge area, then held back.

Discordant sounds—whines, cries, jumbled, anxiety-riddled talk—pressed around Taylor as he entered the sparsely furnished area. His eyes drank in the dull ivory of the concrete-block walls and the aimless movements of the patients, some attired in white hospital gowns, some in regular clothing.

He scanned the room, searching for Jack Shepherd. A nurse had told him he would find him here.

"You remember me?"

A gnarled hand clawed at his face from the side. Startled, Taylor nearly lost his balance, for the thigh-level cast on his left leg made even standing precarious business.

"You remember me?" The old man, horribly

349

hunched over, shook the gnarled hand as if it were a baby's rattle. He had gray-blue slits for eyes, and his hairless head was dotted with brown liver spots as large as dimes. He smelled of urine, body odor, and bleach.

Taylor brushed past him, discomfort gurgling in his throat.

"Everyone 'cept me is filthy," the old man called out as he drifted on. "Filthy and rotten filthy."

Holy God, Shep, where have they put you? Do you really belong here?

A tall black man hugging a bright-red fire truck to his chest stepped aside to let Taylor venture deeper into the room. Taylor nodded at him, and the man unleashed a loud, shrill imitation of a siren. And before an attendant could reach him and calm him down, the man fell to his knees and began to push the toy fire engine in a frenzied circle.

Taylor hesitated again, chiding himself for not asking a nurse or an attendant to direct him to his friend. There were twenty or thirty patients milling around and none appeared to be Jack Shepherd.

"You a detective?"

A young man with a shy grin and wild, partially dilated eyes jumped in front of him.

"You look like a detective," the young man continued, uncontrolled strings of saliva threading out the corners of his mouth. "I'd like to be a detective when I'm older."

Balancing himself, Taylor stared into the young man's pimply face. "I'm looking for Jack Shepherd . . . he's a big man with a beard."

"You get shot in the war? You a war hero?"

Taylor shook his head.

The young man frowned. "How'd you hurt yourself? Fall off the moon?" An elvish grin replaced the frown and widened to a smile which Taylor tried unsuccessfully to return.

"No, I . . . I had an accident. I—"

"Oh, sure. You ever see a ghost?"

Taylor flinched at the offhand question.

The young man suddenly gestured toward a far wall. "Nurse told me that dude over there did. That one. Hope I never do. I'd like to be a detective when I'm older. You a detective? I'd like to be a detective if my parents let me. I'd like to be a detective. Who wouldn't?" With a playful shrug of his shoulders, the young man flitted away.

Taylor swallowed hard and focused on a man seated in an overstuffed chair under a floor lamp. The man had propped an opened copy of *People* magazine in his lap. It was Jack Shepherd. Fire points of relief spread through Taylor's chest as he approached, but he found himself cringing at the sight of Shepherd's thinness, his drawn face, and the patches of white in his reddish-blond beard. He looked disensouled.

There was a calm, drug-induced placidity in Shepherd's expression; Taylor studied the expression, and then it all came rushing back like an involuntary retching: Shepherd in the darkness of the Half Moon school, a bell tolling, the hum of ghostly bees, the chilling, disembodied voices of Carol Mae and Jennifer, and the presence of something huge and dark and implacably evil.

No . . . lost. I'm lost.

The parade of images passed. Taylor cleared his throat.

"Hey, Shep. How doin', friend?"

A gray oblivion mirrored forth from Shepherd's eyes. He lowered the magazine; he showed no spark of recognition.

"Shep? How have you been?"

Jesus, what a stupid question. How's he been? He's been through Hell.

Shepherd looked smaller, looked as if layers of flesh and soul had been stripped away.

An uncomfortable silence held sway.

Taylor broke it with a burst of words. He talked of his knee operation, of Molly Harvester's move to Elderness, of Ronnie Cartwright's bravery, and of things at the Development Office. But it all seemed trivial somehow.

"Going back to Half Moon tomorrow, Shep," Taylor added.

Perhaps he wanted to see it, perhaps he only imagined it, but Taylor believed that something glinted, something sharpened in Shepherd's eyes.

"That's right, Shep. Sheriff Jackson and I gone pick up Miss Molly in the morning . . . we got a marker for Carl Harvester . . . a nice one . . . it'll put Molly's mind to ease."

Taylor fought what happened next. That prickly, embarrassed tone of a man on the verge of tears took over his voice. He reached down and placed his hand upon Shepherd's. Shepherd followed the movement but said nothing.

I'd give anything to hear his preacher ways, thought Taylor.

"Shep, someday it'll be OK . . . I wish you'd say something to me. Hell, anything. I know you want to . . . give me some sign you're gone keep fightin' to come back . . . like we all are. Shep, what happened to you . . . it's my fault . . . and, holy God, I feel . . . I just feel so damned bad . . . will you ever forgive me?"

A nurse tugged at his shoulder, reminding him that his visiting time was up. And later, as Taylor struggled to find sleep, he replayed the final moment, and in each replay he saw a certain brightening of Shepherd's eyes . . . some silent affirmation.

From her third-floor vantage point, Molly Harvester stood at the window and watched dawn steal across the grounds of the Elderness Retirement Center. The manicured lawn, green with a water-soaked brightness, gently sloped down to an artificial lake where three white ducks cut silky smooth paths from one side to the other. For the past week, Molly had arisen early to view that first pink light from the east and to watch the trio of ducks. And to recover her peace of mind.

She would fix herself a cup of tea, only one, and set it on the window ledge and think about the events at Half Moon, the people, her life there, her final night there, and, mostly, about Carl.

"Carl," she whispered. "If you can hear me, please be near. I get so lonely real early of a morning. Late at night, too. But, don'cha know, I miss you the most early of a morning. Miss gettin' up and havin' a cup of tea or coffee with you."

The trio of ducks began their return voyage across the lake. Molly hesitated, lost in the beauty of their silent gliding.

"It's nice here, Carl. Don't go thinking I'm suffering

353

here because I'm not. Elderness is a fine enough place. Lots of folks here my age and several nurses and a doctor come by regularly to check on all of us, don'cha see. Oh, and I'm feeling OK. Fine, you know, physically. I just get a lit-tul blue.

"This here apartment is what's called an efficiency apartment, you know. Just two rooms, but the lit-tul men and I—it's all the room we need."

She stopped, patted at the tears in the corner of one eye with her fingertips.

"Sheriff Jackson and Mr. Taylor, why, they've been so good to me. Mr. Taylor, he just got out of the hospital last week and has a cast on his leg and has to get around on crutches. It's a blessing to have such friends, and now, of course, crazy, wonderful ole Carmilla Carfax is living in the apartment next to mine. So much fun she is. Still so full of life. Why, she won't let me stay blue ever for long. Always planning something for us to do, or someplace to go. Land sakes, she's a dear."

Carefully she sat herself down in a chair that she kept next to the window.

"Carl, you know, there's something more I need to say. A lotta disturbing things went on while Mr. Taylor, poor Reverend Shepherd, and that boy, Ronnie Cartwright, and I were in the school. So many strange and awful things in Half Moon. I try to understand them. Carmilla, she tells me don't think about them, and I suppose she's right. That boy, I'm sure of this, saved us from all the darkness. Bravest thing I've ever known. Battled Windkiller. And he set all the spirits of Half Moon free. I believe that.

"But Carl, don'cha see, all the time I was in Half Moon, I kept athinkin' you'd come back. Now I know you won't and so I had to do something to make myself accept it, you know . . . so Sheriff Jackson and Mr. Taylor, well, they had a marker made for me. Today is Memorial Day, Carl, and it seems fitting . . . I'm gone go to Half Moon with them today and we're gone put down that marker."

Her tears came easily. "Please understand," she sobbed. "I'm not forgetting you."

In a corner of the room, the terriers pricked up their ears at the sound of Molly's sadness. As she cried, by degrees the air around her seemed to vibrate. There was a buzzing at her right ear, and then a soft yet clear voice.

"Molly, babe?"

And she listened.

"Molly, babe, it's me, Carl."

A barely audible, tear-choked noise escaped Molly's lips. Then the intruding voice continued.

"Molly, it be OK."

"Carl? Oh, Carl, am I hearing things?"

"Molly . . . Lady Molly . . . my lit-tul weird princess. I can't stay, but I'll never leave you."

The voice seemed to hover near her ear so that she jerked around to see its source.

"Carl, I don't see you. Is it really you?"

"Molly, I'll be waitin' out there for you."

"Where, Carl? Oh, where you gone be?"

"Jist out there. Jist out there somewheres beyond the night."

"Please understand, Carl. Please."

"I do, Molly. I understand."

And the voice was gone.

Two hours later, Carmilla Carfax, wearing a lavender dressing gown trimmed in yellow, whirled into Molly's apartment balancing a full cup of coffee on a tiny saucer. Her hair, dyed raven-black and coaxed into penny-sized ringlets, was bound in a bright red scarf that matched her lipstick and seemed to intensify the paleness of her complexion.

By this time, Molly was dressed and waiting for her company.

"Well, Moll, Lady Harvester, you sure are gussied up, and look at me, still in my wake-up garb. No wonder I's never able to catch a man. Hah! But then I never saw much sense in gettin' fixed up if I didn't have some place to go. You know what I mean?"

Molly smiled at her friend and her eyes twinkled. Carmilla cut off whatever Molly was about to say.

"Goodness now, lady, you seem in fine spirits today. Still goin' back to Half Moon today? Yesterday you weren't too sure."

Molly nodded. "Yes. Yes, I'm going. And, oh, Carmilla, I do think it's gone be all right."

She was tempted to tell her friend what had happened a few hours ago, but she decided she was not quite ready to share it. There would be a time later, perhaps, when she would.

"I'm gone be ready to live the rest of my life," Molly added, feeling only slight embarrassment from the melodramatic statement.

In exaggerated fashion, Carmilla arched her eye-

356

brows and winked at Molly over the rim of the coffee cup.

"Good! Oh, that's so good to hear, Molly!"

The loops of Carmilla's Queen-of-the-Night serpent bracelet clinked, and she flashed a hand sporting three cheap-looking gold rings.

"And Molly, I've got a surprise for you," she continued.

Molly chuckled. "Oh my, what is it?"

Carmilla put her coffee cup and saucer down and spoke with her hands.

"You and me, doll, are goin' to Chicago! We're goin' to visit my sister, Freda—you know, the spiritualist one. Now, don't go shakin' your head, 'no,' because we're goin'. Oh, Molly, it'll be fun!"

"But . . . but Carmilla, the expense! I can't afford it!"

"Yes! Yes, ma'am, you can! Besides, we'll stay with Freda, and we'll get a flight discount for bein' such old gals," she laughed. "We'll see the town and do crazy things. Oh, Molly, let's go!"

Molly smiled a tentative "yes," and suddenly there was a knock at the door.

"There's your company," Carmilla exclaimed as she gathered up her cup and saucer. "I better scat. Plan on Chicago, dearie, or I'll put a curse on you," she joked.

At the door, Carmilla greeted Sheriff Jackson and Dale Taylor, rapid-fired a self-introduction, and fluttered past them before they could do more than nod and smile.

"Do come in, Sheriff and Mr. Taylor," said Molly.

Taylor maneuvered himself on the crutches until he was a few feet inside the door. The sheriff, carrying his trooper hat in one hand and a brightly wrapped package in the other, smiled and asked Molly how she was doing.

"Oh, land's, I'm fine, and the lit-tul men are fine. Elderness treats us very kindly. And, oh, I sure do thank you two for seeing about Carl's marker. It's so important to me, don'cha see."

Then she drifted her tone. "Can I get you some coffee?"

Taylor rocked forward slightly on his crutches.

"No thanks, Miss Molly. Thing is, we probably ought to get on the road to Half Moon. I've been taking advantage of the sheriff here long enough, what with him taxiing me around lately."

"How is the leg?" Molly asked.

Taylor chuckled. "Won't be running any races right away. Just going to take some healing . . . like everything else. They . . . they turned down my grant requests for Half Moon. So, it's just gone take longer to get the town on its feet again, but I'm not gone to give up on it. Not for a minute. I'm gone to rebuild the store on my own. Can't get financial help on it, and I don't have a site for it exactly, but I'm gone back to Half Moon. I'll make it work out eventually."

Fidgeting with her hands, Molly nodded and smiled weakly. "I've thought some about moving back to Half Moon. I don't know. A lotta bad memories there I can't get out of my mind."

"Me, too. I've had some nightmares about that last night. Maybe nobody will ever really understand what went on. I've tried to deal with it in my mind, you know. But . . . there's no explanation, it seems," said Taylor.

"I know one thing," Molly began. "I sure don't wanna talk to that psychologist fella again. I thought he was gone haul me away to the funny farm when I tried to tell him what we saw in Half Moon."

Taylor and the sheriff laughed.

Looking nonplussed, Molly continued. "Sheriff, do you see the Hollins boy? You know, Ronnie's lit-tul friend?"

"Yes. As a matter of fact, he and Ronnie'll be in Half Moon today helping Bobby Lee's daddy at the school."

"Oh, are they gone try to fix up the school?"

"No, Miss Molly," Taylor chimed in. "No, it's been decided that the school be torn down. This Mr. Hollins and his crew specialize in tearing down old buildings. They've got a deadline, so they're working right on through the holiday."

"That school . . . it saw lotsa darkness," Molly muttered.

Silence crept forward; Taylor shifted uneasily on the tips of his crutches. "Saw Jack Shepherd last night, Molly. He's . . . in time things'll be better for him I believe. Well . . . we better be going. But, oh, before I forget, I brought you a gift. The sheriff's got it there."

Molly took the package and frowned. "My, I do wish you hadn't spent your money on an ole woman like me."

"It's . . . it's just something, sort of . . . to start over with."

Molly's expression registered puzzlement. With difficulty she clawed through the wrapping to reach a container the size of a shoebox. Taylor helped her pull open the flaps at the top, and, with both hands she lifted an object free. As she stared at it, her entire body trembled and a smile, as wide as she could possibly smile, brightened her face.

The large glass owl was the most beautiful she had ever seen.

Sweating from the late morning humidity, Bobby Lee Hollins pulled his tee-shirt over his head, yanked it off, and tossed it to one side. He looked down at his pale, spider-thin arms and pondered glumly whether he would ever be as big and strong as his father. But at least he was here, in the abandoned Half Moon school, helping his father salvage lumber, nails, bricks, and anything else that might be sold or used again.

His father and three other workers were in another part of the now nearly-demolished building maneuvering the big concrete wrecking ball that could flatten any structure. Bobby Lee's assigned task was to gather up any unbroken lattice boards and larger beams, jerk the good nails out of them, and stack the lumber in a neat pile.

It felt good to be working with his father, and, best of all, he hadn't been yelled at once.

Maybe Pop likes me better now. Maybe he'll come home to Mom and me.

Smiling to himself, he attacked the head of a nail with the claw of his hammer, struggling with it until he was breathing heavily. He paused to wipe the sweat from his forehead with the back of his hand and to glance at his friend, Ronnie, who seemed lost in a meditative reverie.

"Hey, Ronnie, what'cha lookin' at?"

Ronnie had wondered what it would be like to return

to the school, had anticipated fear and dread, but had been pleasantly surprised to find no lingering residue of the nightmarish experience six weeks ago.

"Not lookin' at nothin'. I'm just thinkin'."

Bobby Lee wrestled ten seconds more with the same nail, then stopped again.

"Ronnie, did you really . . . I mean, you really see the thangs you told me about?"

"I swear it, Bobby Lee. I saw them. And I didn't tell you about everything."

Bobby Lee's one good eye flitted nervously. "If I'd seen them thangs . . . man. Man, I'd a messed my pants, you know. Goddarn, I would've."

Dropping a lattice board that he had been holding, Ronnie began to brush dust from his hands. "Listen, Bobby Lee, there's some place I need to go. Just for a minute. OK? I'll be back. If your daddy asks about me, tell him I'll be back."

Bobby Lee straightened. "Sure. I'll do that. Some place you gotta go?"

"Yeah." And Ronnie started to walk away.

"Hey, Ronnie . . . you know, . . . Goddarn, I'm glad you're my friend."

Ronnie smiled over his shoulder. "I'm glad, too, Bobby Lee. I'm glad, too."

The glistening white marker read: IN MEMORY on the top line; then below it, CARL M. HARVESTER, 1913-1982. As if he were setting down a slab of fragile crystal, Sheriff Jackson lowered the marker into the shallow rectangle of dirt.

"Don't it look just as fine as you please?" Molly

361

exclaimed, her eyes snapping with pleasure. "I just can't thank . . . can't thank both of you enough for getting this marker. Eases my mind considerably."

"We wanted to do it, Molly. Half Moon is going to remember people like Carl Harvester," said Taylor.

The three of them stood in silence, meandering in private thought before they could loop back to the present.

Jackson turned in the direction of the school where they could hear the sounds of the wrecking crew. "I believe I'll go over for a minute and see Bobby Lee. Kind of a special little kid to me. I'll be back shortly."

Taylor and Molly watched him walk to the patrol car.

"The sheriff thinks Carl's body will be found eventually. Then we'll have a proper burial," said Molly doubtfully.

Taylor nodded before she spoke again.

"Just one of God's mysteries that his body's never been . . . recovered."

Shifting the tips of the crutches to rebalance himself, Taylor, conscious of the subject change, replied, "I still believe in this town. I'll rebuild my store, and someday it'll be a fine little town again."

"Would you like to build your store here?"

Molly's question took him by surprise.

"What do you mean?"

"Well . . . in other words, I own this property . . . and I might want to invest in the grocery business, don'cha see. This spot should be as good as any for starting Half Moon up again."

Taylor shook his head. "That'd be fantastic, Molly. I . . . I don't know what to say."

"Better just say 'yes.' Maybe our Half Moon can be like that ole mythical Phoenix bird."

He smiled and stared at the cottony-white clouds scudding low over the area.

"What I really need . . . I mean, what I really want is Ronnie's courage. That boy has courage."

Molly, her face thoughtful, glanced down again at the marker.

Taylor looked at her and swallowed back a wave of emotion.

"I know you miss Carl, Molly. Miss him like I miss Carol Mae and Jennifer. I'll never forget them."

"Some things . . . they're not meant to be forgot . . . ever," Molly replied.

Loneliness is the meanest ghost of all.

Ronnie climbed into his badly weathered tree house and slumped against one wall. He missed his parents, missed living in Half Moon, and missed his pet birds, especially the pigeons. He thought about being alone, about loneliness, about his battle with the creature, Windkiller.

And once, shuttled along upon the wind perhaps, the echo of the creature's final, anguished cry resounded. He cupped his hands over his ears, but the echo dissipated in a matter of seconds.

The sense of loss was more frightening, more threatening than any creature.

He pressed his fingers to his chest and felt the dull ache of the deep bruise there, the mark of Windkiller, and wondered how he had survived. Maybe there really is a God, he thought. Maybe I just gave up on Him t'oo soon.

The wind gently rocked the tree house. The massive oak held firm.

Then he scrambled to the porthole and reached out into the air. He let his hand dangle there, a flag of his disposition, a signal call for reassurance of some kind.

He was about to pull the hand back into the tree house when something happened.

Something he could feel: the cold, feathery touch of hovering wings.

TALES OF TERROR AND POSSESSION

MAMA (1247, $3.50)
by Ruby Jean Jensen
Once upon a time there lived a sweet little dolly, but her one
beaded glass eye gleamed with mischief and evil. If Dorrie could
have read her dolly's thoughts, she would have run for her life —
for her dear little dolly only had killing on her mind.

JACK-IN-THE-BOX (1892, $3.95)
by William W. Johnstone
Any other little girl would have cringed in horror at the sight of
the clown with the insane eyes. But as Nora's wide eyes mirrored
the grotesque wooden face her pink lips were curving into the
same malicious smile.

ROCKABYE BABY (1470, $3.50)
by Stephen Gresham
Mr. Macready — such a nice old man — knew all about the children
of Granite Heights: their names, houses, even the nights their
parents were away. And when he put on his white nurse's uniform
and smeared his lips with blood-red lipstick, they were happy to
let him through the door — although they always stared a bit at his
clear plastic gloves.

TWICE BLESSED (1766, $3.75)
by Patricia Wallace
Side by side, isolated from human contact, Kerri and Galen
thrived. Soon their innocent eyes became twin mirrors of evil.
And their souls became one — in their dark powers of destruction
and death . . .

HOME SWEET HOME (1571, $3.50)
by Ruby Jean Jensen
Two weeks in the mountains would be the perfect vacation for a
little boy. But Timmy didn't think so. The other children stared at
him with a terror all their own, until Timmy realized there was no
escaping the deadly welcome of . . . *Home Sweet Home*.

*Available wherever paperbacks are sold, or order direct from the
Publisher. Send cover price plus 50¢ per copy for mailing and
handling to Zebra Books, Dept. 1625, 475 Park Avenue South,
New York, N.Y. 10016. Residents of New York, New Jersey and
Pennsylvania must include sales tax. DO NOT SEND CASH.*

MYSTERIES TO KEEP YOU GUESSING
by John Dickson Carr

CASTLE SKULL   (1974, $3.50)
The hand may be quicker than the eye, but ghost stories
didn't hoodwink Henri Bencolin. A very real murderer was
afoot in Castle Skull—a murderer who must be found before he strikes again.

IT WALKS BY NIGHT   (1931, $3.50)
The police burst in and found the Duc's severed head staring at them from the center of the room. Both the doors
had been guarded, yet the murderer had gone in and out
without having been seen!

THE EIGHT OF SWORDS   (1881, $3.50)
The evidence showed that while waiting to kill Mr. Dep-
ping, the murderer had calmly eaten his victim's dinner.
But before famed crime-solver Dr. Gideon Fell could serve
up the killer to Scotland Yard, there would be another
course of murder.

THE MAN WHO COULD NOT SHUDDER (1703, $3.50)
Three guests at Martin Clarke's weekend party swore they
saw the pistol lifted from the wall, levelled, and shot. *Yet
no hand held it*. It couldn't have happened—but there was
a dead body on the floor to prove that it had.

THE PROBLEM OF THE WIRE CAGE   (1702, $3.50)
There was only one set of footsteps in the soft clay surface—and those footsteps belonged to the victim. It
seemed impossible to prove that anyone had killed Frank
Dorrance.

Zebra brings you the best in
CONTEMPORARY FICTION

PAY THE PRICE   (1234, $3.95)
by Igor Cassini

Even more than fortune and fame, Christina wanted revenge on the rich, ruthless scoundrel who destroyed her life. She'd use her flawless body to steal an empire that was hers for the taking—if she was willing to PAY THE PRICE.

SOMETIMES A HERO   (1765, $3.95)
by Les Whitten

Betrayed by passion, Strabico stood to lose all he had fought for to the global power of Big Oil. He would have to stake the woman he loved and his very life on a desperate gamble against the forces of wealth and power.

AUGUST PEOPLE   (1863, $3.95)
by Ralph Graves

For Ellen, the newest daughter-in-law in the Winderman clan, August's vacation with the family is a bitter time of feeling left out of the family circle. But soon Ellen reveals the flaws in their perfect family portrait, and secrets long hidden begin to surface.

TEXAS DREAMS   (1875, $3.95)
by Micah Leigh

For Fontayne, power is an aphrodisiac. She gambles in the playground of the world's oil empire as if it were a child's sandbox; but as she nears the pinnacle of her desires, a past scandal surfaces and threatens to destroy all her carefully planned TEXAS DREAMS.

THE LAST WALTZ   (1777, $4.50)
Nancy Zaroulis

This is the saga of Marian and Isabel. Each was destined for a marriage without love and a love without hope. Each was fated to play a role in a scandal that would rock the opulent society of Newport and shatter the rigid conventions of turn-of-the-century Boston.

Available wherever paperbacks are sold, or order direct from the Publisher. Send cover price plus 50¢ per copy for mailing and handling to Zebra Books, Dept. 1625), 475 Park Avenue South, New York, N.Y. 10016. Residents of New York, New Jersey and Pennsylvania must include sales tax. DO NOT SEND CASH.